CW01510622

THE

SHADOW

AND THE

STARDS

BOOK TWO OF THE FOUNDATION STONE SERIES

Date Due	WRC

16823

DEAN G E MATTHEWS

Copyright © 2021 by Dean G E Matthews.

ISBN	Paperback	978-1-952750-17-5
	Hardback	978-1-952750-18-2
	Ebook	978-1-952750-19-9

All rights reserved. No part of this book may be reproduced or transmitted in any form or by any means, electronic or mechanical, including photocopying, recording, or by any information storage and retrieval system without express written permission from the author, except in the case of brief quotations embodied in critical reviews and certain other non-commercial uses permitted by copyright law.

Printed in the United States of America.

CONTENTS

Introduction ix

Prologue xi

Chapter 1: Trover Born. 1

Chapter 2: Warning Signs. 6

Chapter 3: Duran and the Dragonlet. 18

Chapter 4: Karnack Moor. 31

Chapter 5: Trickery and Half Truths 36

Chapter 6: All Hail Gradine .45

Chapter 7: Troublesome Vermin 52

Chapter 8: Stone of Iniquity .63

Chapter 9: Greyswords and Ardent Wolves 69

Chapter 10: Spies Mind Reading and Truth. 82

Chapter 11: Devided, We Fall 88

Chapter 12: The Price of Power 99

Chapter 13: Consequences .113

Chapter 14: Dangerous Games 123

Chapter 15: Lascana's Gambit. 135

Chapter 16: Collard-Ray. 148

Chapter 17: Choices of the Head and Heart 155

Chapter 18: Dungeon's and Greyswords 162

Chapter 19: The Unrelenting Darkness 182

Chapter 20: The Grey and Black Wilderness 194

Chapter 21: Aridain, Magical Waters & Sapphire Sprites 200

Chapter 22: The Horns of a Dilemma. 211

Chapter 23: The Blacksmith and the Silver Coin. 220

Chapter 24: Psychic's Pawn. 226

Chapter 25: Renagades 239

Chapter 26: The Circulation of Events 257

Epilogue 261

Afterword 265

Glossary 267

Author Biography 281

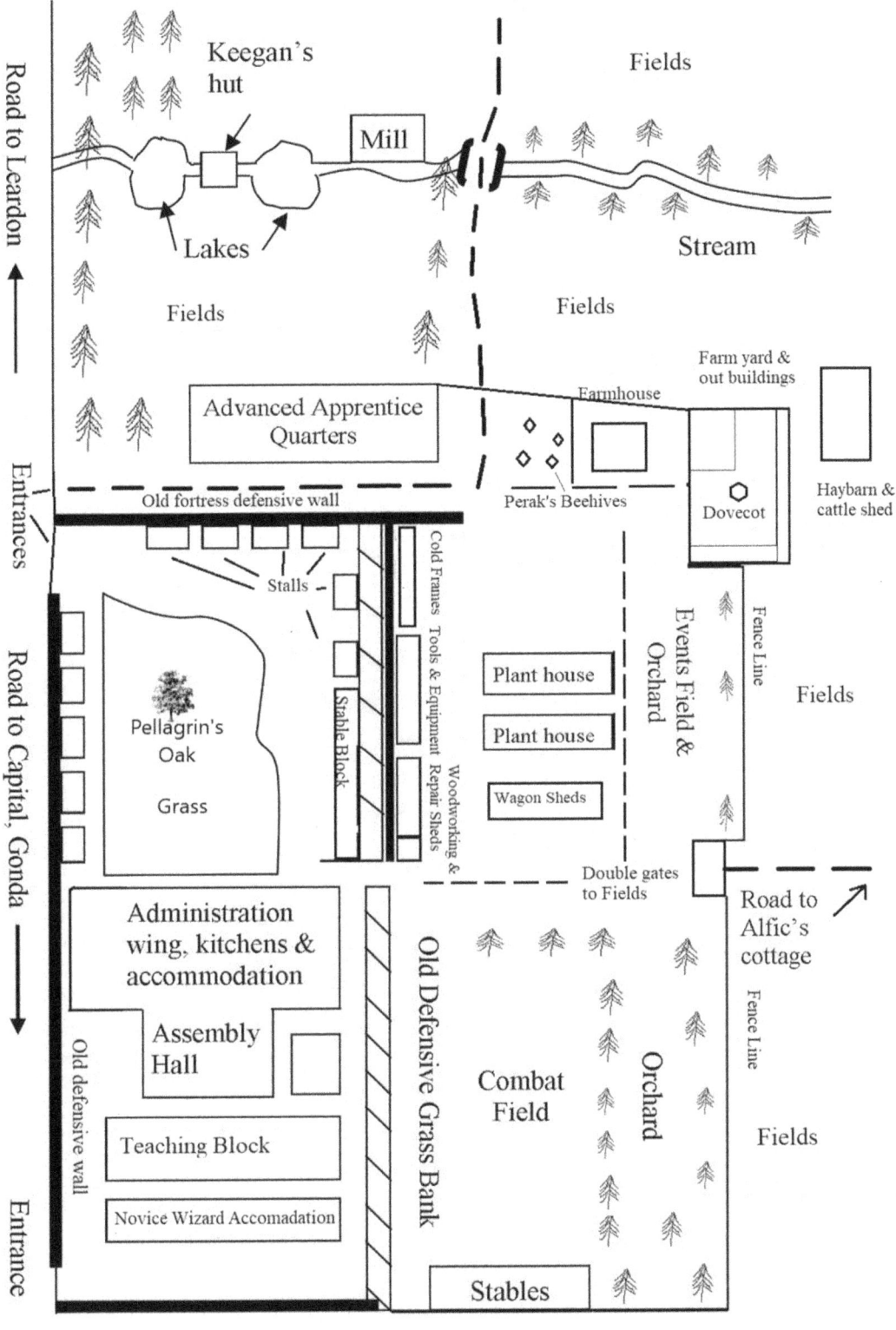

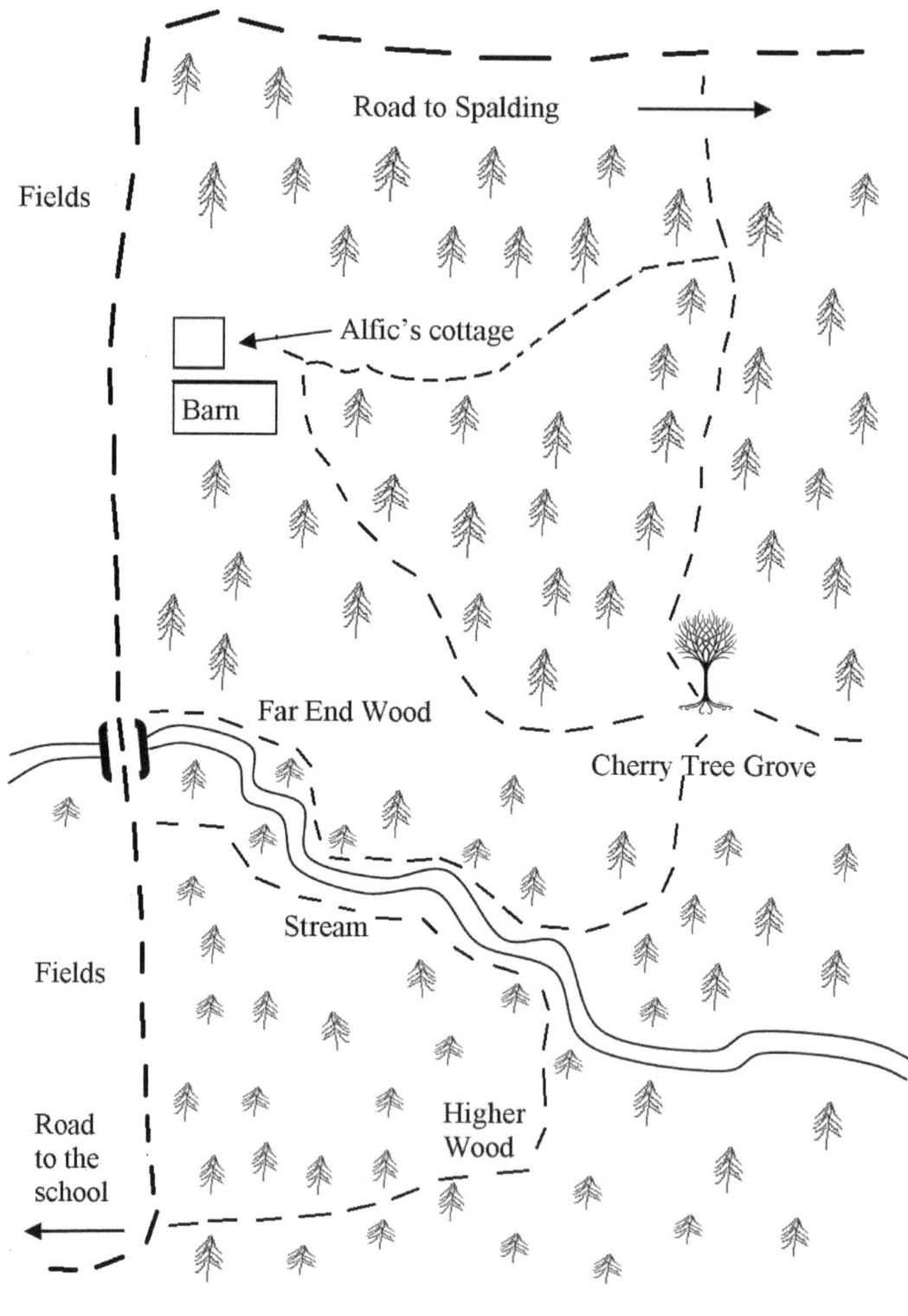

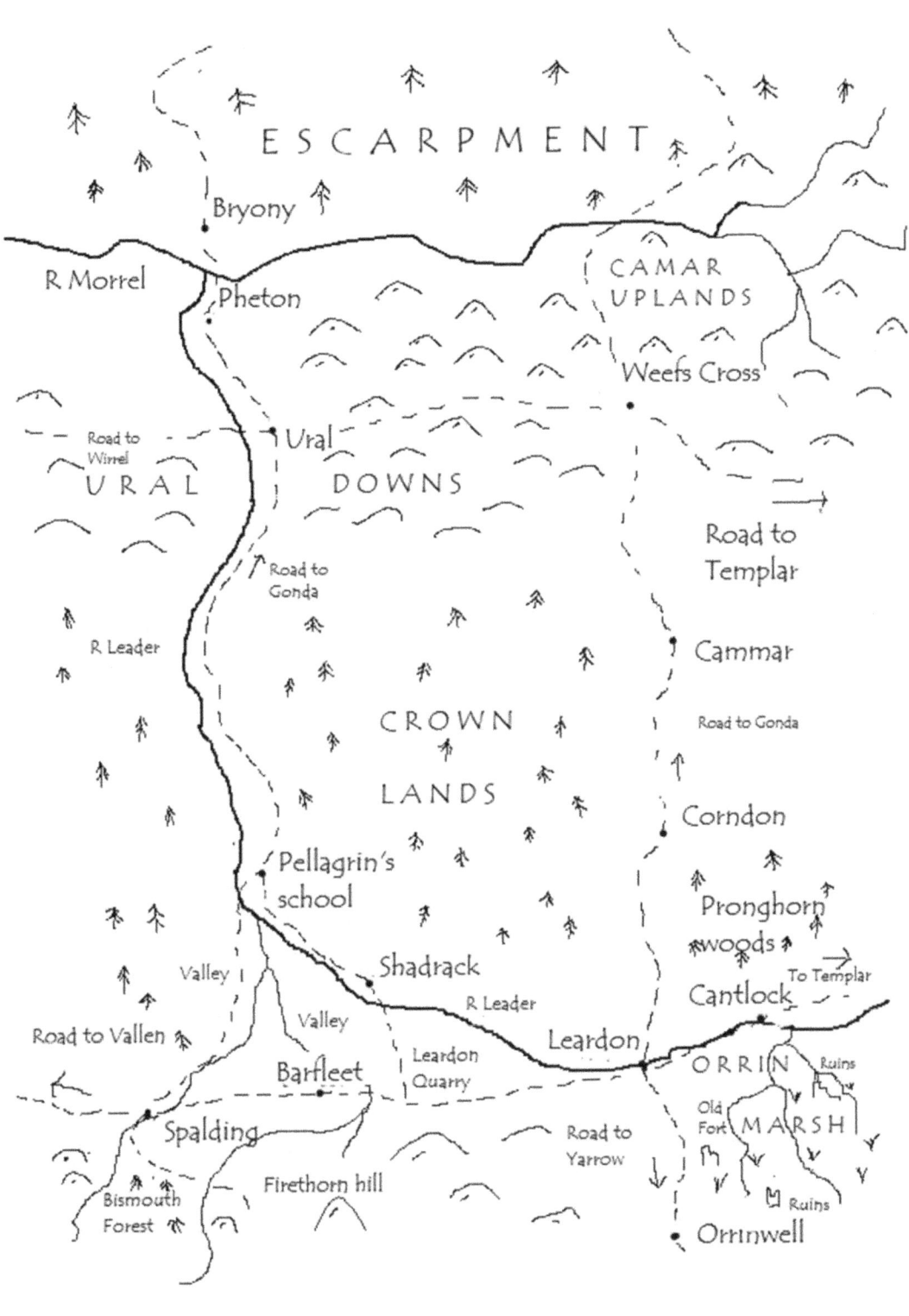

INTRODUCTION

Thousands of years ago, the gods, in order to bring balance and harmony to the many races of Aymara, made the Firebrand stone born of darkness, and the Chimera stone born of light. Created to bring balance and harmony to a war-torn world, their balancing influence worked for a time. However, as the races advanced and reason prevailed once more, the Chimera stone was forgotten and disappeared; leaving the Firebrand stone's evil unchecked, and the world is once more ravaged by unremitting war.

That was until a dragon lord from the north, together with his followers, stole the Firebrand stone and splitting it into four segments; hid them from the gaze of the power hungry.

Peace reigned for a time, but as war threatens the land of Durbah and the surrounding lands once more, the gods decide to act and Aridain Bruin is born, championed by the goddess Seline, his task, to destroy the stones. His magic, uncontrolled and unrestrained, attracts a dark opposite, championed by the dark god Fornax. This creature, the Dark Taal, is destined to kill Aridain, salvage the stones and usher forth a new reign of darkness; but having tried and failed to kill the inexperienced youth and his family, the Dark creature bides its time.

Now however, as the Bruin family attempt to come to terms with the events unfolding at the school, they also have to stop Aridain's evil uncle, a dark wizard called Kuelack, from attempting to subvert the school and its students, and stop him finding the stones and expand his growing empire.

PROLOGUE

His knuckles popping loudly, Kuelack curled his hands into tight-knotted fists as Alfic, his clothes and skin blackened and torn, materialised from the cloying smoke and scorching flames. With a snarl, Alfic picked up a needle-sharp spear lying at his feet.

'Now you will pay for your sins, Brother,' he sneered.

As the cavern shook and shuddered around them, Kuelack, focusing on Alfic's hate filled face, smiled and said, 'It's not I who will pay, it's you; no more will you defy my rule, you self-righteous oaf. I am the more powerful sibling now.'

'Your overconfidence was always your weakness,' Alfic taunted, as Perak, together with Vara, Mace and Keegan, emerged suddenly through the flames, oblivious to the debris falling all around.

'Fool, your family and friends cannot help you. I will simply sweep them aside.'

Wiping at his smoke-filled eyes, Kuelack stared in astonishment as Alfic appeared suddenly before him and thrust the spear into his chest. Gasping in shocked surprise, Kuelack seized the shaft and looked in disbelief at Alfic's gloating face. 'How…?'

'You are the younger brother and you will always be inferior,' Alfic hissed, twisting the spear violently.

Clawing frantically at the shaft in a desperate attempt to remove it, Kuelack wrapped his hands around Alfic's throat, determined that they should die together…

'Kuelack! Kuelack! let go, you're choking me! Kuelack wake up!'

Focusing on Gradine's red bloated face, Kuelack uncurled his fingers from his wife's throat and then sat bolt upright.

'What in Henna's beard is wrong with you?' croaked Gradine, throwing the sheets aside and massaging her throat.

'It's nothing!' he snapped, breathing heavily.

Then, wiping at the sweat that stung his eyes, he peered about the darkened bedchamber.

'Is this about your brother again?' Reaching for a glass of water, Gradine took a long swallow, then in a calmer voice said, 'I told you, you have nothing to prove to him or anyone else. Your success and your status are proof enough of your accomplishments.'

Staring at his hands uncomprehendingly, his eyes having adjusted to the darkness, Kuelack swung his legs out over the edge of the bed. Then, plucking Gradine's hand from his shoulder, he attempted to focus his chaotic thoughts. He peeled his sweat soaked nightshirt from his lithe, taut, muscular body and walked over to the marble-topped dressing table. Sitting upon it was a large ceramic blue and white bowl filled with water. Plunging his face into the cold water to clear his head and cleanse his thoughts, he swilled it over his slick black hair. Towelling his head dry, he turned angrily and said, 'Then why do I always feel inferior, incomplete? It's as if whenever our paths cross, there is always unfinished business, an unspoken challenge between us; he's like a dark cloud hanging over me, an itch I can never scratch.' Exhaling loudly, he rubbed at his eyes violently, letting out a frustrated growl. 'Despite my victory at the fair, I still feel as though he won. With Almagest's death, I thought it would break my cursed brother and his pack of rodent spirits; but Almagest's demise seems only to have galvanised them.' Then slamming his fist down hard on the bed, he spat, 'I swear that if I have to make the entire world pay for his refusal to acknowledge my supremacy and my many accomplishments, then I will.'

Gradine lit the night-light on the stand next to the bed and then sat down beside him, her intoxicating perfume infusing the surrounding air. 'You will always be his younger brother, that you can never change; if he intimidates you so much it can be "fixed", kill him and be done with it.'

'And risk him becoming a martyr? No, I have plans, plans that will ensure my brother and his family's obedience, but, before that, he must suffer as I have at his hands over the years.'

Gradine then smiled shrewdly, her eyes glinting from beneath thin, light brown eyebrows, her thin-lipped smile more like a grimace. 'You will prevail. I have no doubt of that. You have drive, and ambition, that's why I love you.'

'Love,' he scoffed, 'we both know we're not united by love.'

She then took up her blue, inlaid enamelled hairbrush and began pulling it through her golden, light brown hair.

'As you say, we have a mutually beneficial union. You get the benefit of my father's power and position and I...'

'... Married a very talented Wizard, who is destined to be Head of the School's Council and who will sire you gifted children to rule after we take the throne.'

'My point is, you mustn't let him stifle those qualities I see in you, and if you're worried that your actions at the fair have damaged your rise to power, it's nothing a rousing speech and a few good deeds won't fix. My father always says, take care of the details and everything will fall into place. Don't let this obsession with your brother cloud your judgement, Husband, or blind you to what must be done; if you do, he's already won.'

'You don't know these people like I do,' he growled. 'If my cursed brother rallies the teachers behind him, we would have a war here at Pellagrin's; a war would destroy the school and its students.'

'So, don't let it. Once the populace sees that you are here for them and that you are on their side, Alfic and his friend's annoyances will matter not. Here, take one of these,' she said, offering him a small lozenge-shaped capsule from a small inlaid box sat upon her night stand, 'it will help you relax; Father swears by them.'

Taking the proffered sweet, he washed it down with a glass of water.

'So, is everything going to plan?' smiled Gradine, changing the subject.

'Yes, thanks to my source,' he said irritably. 'Once I have the shards in my grasp, the loyalty of the dragons and the cult are assured.'

'The cult! The only thing those fanatics care about is appeasing Fornax, their manic blood god.'

'Exactly, blood and sacrifice,' confirmed Kuelack loudly, 'my own suicide troops, fanatics, prepared to do anything for favour in the afterlife.' Then, pointing down beneath his feet, he said arrogantly, 'although believing every suicidal cultist can sit beside one god is dim-witted in the extreme.'

Just then, a baby's cry issued from the bedroom.

'Gabion needs feeding. Think about what I said.'

Kuelack watched her keenly as she glided across the darkened room towards the nursery, the light from the oil lamps accentuating her fine lines and bestowing her figure with a silken sheen underneath her light green chiffon nightdress.

The birth of their son hadn't spoilt her figure, or her ivory skinned good looks. *Marrying the daughter of one of the most powerful men in Gonda brings its own rewards,* he thought amorously.

Walking across the room to his rosewood, gold inlaid chest, he searched through the many draws and changed into a fresh shirt and breeches. Donning his red, opulent reedmace moth silk slippers and confidently navigating the lounge's plush fittings in the gloom, he walked quietly through to his office. Falling into his sumptuous black and dark red leather studded armchair, he clicked his fingers and several glow globes on the walls burst into life. He then rested his chin morosely on his fists and gazed around the room, studying the locked glass cabinets filled with his collection of artefacts collected from around the world, some containing magic, others just aesthetically pleasing. He then considered the tapestries and his many paintings hanging from the walls, his eyes finally settling on the commissioned portrait of himself stood beside his luxurious chair in his finest robes, the candles flickering light portraying his façade in a hard-no-nonsense light. Unlike his prideful picture, he felt no sense of accomplishment, no sense of satisfaction in his trophies, despite being surrounded by everything he'd ever desired. His father had been right, he was his mother's son. Gradine had also hit the nail on the head -he could never back down. All he'd ever asked, all he'd ever needed, was an admission from Alfic that he was the superior brother. If the lives of Alfic's family and friends are the price to pay for his lack of servitude, then so be it. Taking a deep breath, he rubbed his neck and shoulders in an effort to calm his rising anger.

'Do you have to do that around me?' he said, shaking his head in disapproval.

'Don't be so prudish, Kuelack,' said Gradine, silently entering the office while carrying the suckling Gabion. 'I received a letter from my father yesterday.'

'How is Agrestal these days? I take it his manipulation of that imbecile of a King is proceeding to plan?'

'Yes, although he's resisting of late. Apparently, Queen Ennul still has some influence.'

'Not too much, I hope. Our plans depend on Pheronis being at our beck and call. What of the Balefire witches?'

'They too are proving difficult.'

'A man with an army of spies and he can't get one of them into a witch's coven?'

'Don't raise your voice, Kuelack,' she hissed, indicating the contented Gabion. 'Apparently, their recent increased activity has revealed hidden allies and power, power that they have somehow kept secret from my father's spies over the years, although he claims a solution may have presented itself.'

'Good, we need someone inside their headquarters as soon as possible.'

Gradine then said offhandedly, 'Oh, Father also reports that the Black Lotus harvest is the best he's ever seen, meaning your shares are rising steadily.'

After a lingering silence, Gradine said abruptly, 'You know she'll oppose you, don't you?'

'Eventually, yes, Mother will confront me as she always has. In fact, it wouldn't surprise me if she's listening in even now. You and Alfic will not stop me, do you hear me Mother, NOT STOP ME!' he shouted into the candle-lit stillness.

Standing and pressing his head against the wood-panelled wall, Kuelack spun around to look at Gradine.

'I will cleanse the world of the weak, sweep away the flotsam; wipe their poisonous seed from the world, ensuring a strong, vibrant and dominant race steeped in magic, for we are the superior beings.'

'Of that I have no doubt,' replied Gradine gravely. She then looked down at Gabion tenderly. 'I'm putting our son back in bed. Stop worrying and do the same. The problems will still be there for you to tackle in the morning.'

Cupping his head in his hands, he watched as Gradine faded into the darkness. He then closed his eyes and smiled. *In this world, you made your own luck and yours, Alfic, will soon run out. Then, my dear brother, when the time is right, your son will be mine.*

CHAPTER ONE

TROVER BORN

Rubbing the dirt from the road between his fingers in the sultry autumn air, the young blond-haired warrior squared his broad shoulders and looked out to the tree-lined horizon; the edge of the Blinks escarpment plummeting nearly two thousand feet to the fertile Gondarian plain beyond; named so because if you weren't vigilant, you could be killed by the aggressive wildlife in the blink of an eye. A remnant of the original wilds that had once dominated the Durbarian landscape, the Blinks, stretched for over twenty leagues in either direction, creating a barrier between the capital, Gonda, and its fertile plains to the north, from the villages and towns to the south and southeast.

Having started out on horseback from Pellagrin's two weeks previous, Vanir had travelled to the capital and the Wizards Provost Guild, Almagest's intended destination. Having established that the pre-eminent Wizard had failed to reach the capital, he had retraced his steps, stopping many a traveller and trader plying their wares on the main road between Pellagrin's and the capital city. However, no one had seen or heard anything of Almagest, his driver or carriage; that was, until he had reached the clay-mining village of Bryony, located close to the edge of the Blinks. While there, he'd established that an ornate carriage matching its description had stopped to change horses at The Wyvern Inn.

Standing up straight, Vanir grasped the reins, placed his foot in the stirrup, and swung his leg up and over his grey mare. Urging his mount forward beneath the dappled shade of the trees that lined the road, he trotted for half a league before it turned abruptly on the crest of the escarpment. It made perfect sense; if someone had assassinated Almagest, this was the perfect place to hide the evidence because the very nature of the terrain would deter a search.

He turned at a voice, his hand automatically reaching for the hilt of his sword. He then relaxed as two children emerged from the undergrowth, demanding and insistent, as they tried in vain to herd a group of unruly, squealing pigs.

With children and pigs milling around him in confusion, the mare skittered and pranced. 'Whoa Girl, it's all right,' he placated. Then, recognising an item of clothing that looked out-of-place, Vanir span around in the saddle, 'Hey, you there boy, hold on!' he commanded.

'Yes, Mister,' the boy squeaked, a concerned look on his face.

Dismounting, he approached the terrified boy. 'It's okay, Son, I mean you no harm,' he smiled, squatting and taking hold of his shoulders. 'You look extremely fetching in that pointy hat.' Vanir smiled. 'Tell me, where did you get it?'

'I found it, honest!'

'Can you show me?'

'No, I don't want to,' quailed the boy.

'Did you find it down there?' he said, pointing to the imposing, densely packed trees.

The boy nodded his head vigorously.

'I told you not to, Aran,' admonished the girl scathingly, 'but you never listen.'

'It's all right; he will not get into trouble. I'll tell you what, if you show me where you found it, I'll give you a Sontar; on one condition, mind you, you let me have a look at that hat.'

'Ok,' he smiled uncertainly, handing it over.

'And here's a Sontar for you, girl, if you look after my horse.'

'My name's Freya.'

'There you go, Freya.' And he handed her a shiny copper coin.

'Thanks, Mister.'

'Ok Aran, lead the way.'

Topping the rise, they pushed through the lush vegetation that became thicker the further in they ventured. Suddenly, the boy stopped and shook his head vigorously.

'Aran, we had a deal.'

'It's too scary down there. Even our pigs didn't like it; nasty things were watching me.'

'Ok Aran, I believe you, just tell me where you found the hat.'

'Just down there,' he said, pointing into the shadows, 'there's a wagon, all swanky like, lying against a large tree. It's not far.'

'Thank you, Aran. Here's your Sontar. You've been very helpful; spend it wisely now.'

'Thanks Mister.'

Listening to the boy as he clambered hastily uphill over the rocky terrain, he stuffed the hat into his crimson leather bodice, then stood and scrutinised the vegetation. Rumour had it that the vegetation of the escarpment and the surrounding land had become intolerant and aggressive with forethought, assaulting anyone who encroached into its domain; protecting what remained of its primeval ruins. Now, he was in no hurry to test the rumour, but if he was to be sure, he had to search for and find the carriage.

Resuming his search, he continued downhill, slipping and stumbling down the increasingly difficult incline, and over jagged rocks that broke the surface at regular intervals. Fresh earthy smells assailed his nostrils and sparkling pollen grains filled the air as he navigated the tangle of foliage. Here and there shafts of golden sunlight penetrated the thick canopy, the sun's rays illuminating small islands of wild flowers and golden grasses, and Sprites, imps and nymphs of all species buzzed around his face, chattering angrily at his unwanted presence. Things scurried and scampered from beneath his feet and strange unfamiliar noises resonated through the dense canopy together with more familiar sounds, and in the distance, something large lumbered through the brush. Surrounded by this intoxicating environment, he felt a very profound sense of self as he tried to imagine what the land must have been like when this magical forest covered the land. This wondrous feeling didn't last long, however. At odds with the beauty and tranquillity, intertwined and permeating the exotic atmosphere was a feeling of malice and spite, making him feel as though a thousand eyes were watching him. Crossing a sunlit clearing, he entered the darkened forest once again, and it wasn't until his eyes adjusted to the gloom that he saw the remains of the carriage. Almost unrecognisable, it lay sideways against the base of a large tree, that together with the forest vegetation, and spurred on by unearthly magic, endeavoured to overwhelm and eradicate the foreign object.

'A Cleaver tree,' he despaired. 'Why did the carriage have to settle against a Cleaver tree?' As quietly as he could, he approached, meticulous in his foot placement, wincing at every sound beneath his feet. As he crept closer through the shadows, the final resting place of the school's carriage became more apparent, as did the deep scars inflicted by the tree's lethal spikes which peppered its framework. Then, peering to his right, he saw the destruction the carriage had wrought as it had careered through the thick undergrowth. Peering cautiously into the interior, he turned at an unearthly sound, his hand instinctively going to his sword once more; this in turn stirred the red tinted and streaked branches above his head.

Remember where you are Trover Born, this place is no different to the Wilds where you grew up so don't provoke the Blinks' wildlife, he thought, and quickly snatched his hand away.

Opening the carriage door, he peered inside. Lying on the floor amongst the carnivorous plants, creeping inexorably over the ornate carvings and expensive trim, were the bloodstained remnants of clothing, ripped and torn as if some half-crazed beast had run amok. On further inspection, the rags turned out to be the dark green cloak, trimmed in white and gold worn by Almagest, but of the wizard, there was no sign.

Probably taken by a beast of some kind, he thought.

He turned his head at a low moaning sound, which was quickly followed by another. Spinning around, his nerves jangling, he peered into the shadows. Suddenly the water-soaked floor of the carriage, rotten with the escarpment's infestations, gave way, and he fell against the tree's trunk. Grasping one of the many invasive vines, he kept perfectly still as with a loud groaning sound a branch, tipped with jagged spikes, crashed through the carriage's side, splitting it in two. Suddenly, one end of the carriage broke away and he felt himself falling with it. As another thick branch spiralled in from the side, it dislodged one of the carriage's springs that boomeranged through the air, embedding itself into the trunk where he had been standing moments earlier. Hauling himself into what remained of the carriage, he then leapt to the forest floor as another branch ripped through its remains, smashing it like tinder wood and sending it spinning into the ravine below. Without a backward glance, he ran as fast as his legs would carry him, stumbling and tripping through the dense foliage, following the carriage's destructive path. To his relief, he emerged on to one of the many hairpin bends in the Gondarian highway that snaked its way down through the forest. Shaking his head and bending over to gain his breath, he heard the low moaning sound again, only this time it was much closer.

Drawing his sword from the holster upon his back, he held it out in front like a talisman, 'Show yourself, you cowardly creature,' he growled as much from fear as from rage, 'come sample my sword's edge!'

The trees parted, and he stepped back in disbelief. Part abomination and part sapient, the dark, skeletal creature, a deviation from the natural order, sported Almagest's face. It stared at him with eyes that had overseen countless negotiations and presided over many treaties; eyes that had seen over one hundred and fifty dawns. Bearing its sharp fangs from between thin, crusted lips, the creature shifted its attention to Vanir's sword. Hissing frustratedly, it disappeared back into the thick undergrowth, leaving Vanir alone in the silence on the Gondarian highway.

CHAPTER TWO

WARNING SIGNS

'**M**orning Munch kin,' said Lascana, as Aridain ran eagerly into the kitchen. When he stopped and looked around disappointedly, she said, 'He's not here, dear.'

'But I got up really early this morning.'

'I know,' she said, 'but your father's really busy with the harvest. You'll just have to be patient.'

Cradling Aridain's disappointed face in her hands; her mothering instincts couldn't help but feel sorry for him. Alfic's new schedule, implemented at Kuelack's bequest, working late nights and early mornings meant he returned home every night completely worn out and exhausted.

Lascana smiled sadly as she watched their son gobble up his breakfast, recalling the quizzing she and Alfic had given him the morning after their frightening encounter in the woods.

To her and Alfic's dismay, Aridain had disclosed quite nonchalantly that he was fated to die at the creatures' hands. Questioning their son as to why, Aridain had just shook his head. They had also enquired about the mysterious voice but Aridain would not, or could not, say whom it belonged to, but he had revealed that, as far as he was aware, it had been with him his entire life and that it posed no threat. Also, it had encouraged him to release the Sapphire Sprites into the woods for the sole purpose of restoring magic to the wilds. Having put him to bed later that night, Lascana had filled two glasses with her homemade sloe gin and had joined Alfic by the fire. They had sat quietly for a time contemplating the flames when Alfic had asked, 'So, the question remains, are these sprites causing the strange occurrences all over the school?'

'Strange occurrences?'

'Yes, people and farm animals acting strangely. Sorin says his bull, Jasper, won't let him near, now his heifers are coming into season, and he says his rams are now particularly aggressive, and look at your fellow stall holders, this has all happened since our son released the sprites into the woods, everything has gone haywire!'

'Why would the sprites be responsible?' Lascana had asked.

'Because they are the land's lifeblood; their magic affects everything.'

'You think our son is responsible, don't you?' Lascana had said with a scowl. 'Because you've turned your back on magic, our son must suffer for your stubbornness? He released the sprites with only good intentions. If you want someone to blame, blame your brother. It's his retribution. He's affecting the animals somehow, I know it, and it's keeping you and Perak so busy, so exhausted, that you can't even raise a smile, let alone any opposition.'

'We've been through this Lascana. Either I keep playing Kuelack's game or I give up under the pressure, which is exactly what he wants, and I won't give in, not to him. Besides, it's not so bad. I just imagine every Timber rat, every Scarrion lizard, every grey squirrel that I kill is Kuelack,' he had said, attempting a smile and failing miserably. 'Lascana, it's for Aridain's safety that I do this.'

'And in the meantime, you are a pawn who Kuelack manipulates as he sees fit.'

'For the time being, yes.'

'Not acceptable Alfic. When will it end? How long will you placate your brother?'

'Listen Lascana, no doubt Kuelack already knows our son has power, thanks to my treacherous sister, and by letting us know he knows, Kuelack thinks he's in control. This means we don't have to be as compliant as he would like.'

'Very well, but if I sense for one moment Magen's teachings are leading Aridain astray, or he's in any danger, I will pack our bags and leave.'

'Before you go off half-cocked Lascana, think of the people we'd be leaving behind. The workers under my care, like Elgin, Elimi and Micas, for instance. Then there are the stall holders, people and friends who, without our help, would be at Kuelack's mercy.'

'You would bargain our son's life for that of our friends and fellow workers?' But the instant she had spoken the words, she realised they're insincerity. 'You certainly know how to hit below the belt with your propensity to help the weak and defenceless Alfic Bruin.' Then, throwing him a frustrated look, she had said, 'You know it's not in my nature to be so callous. They're just the words of a protective mother who fears for her children's safety.'

'Lascana I... children's safety, what do you mean, children?'

'I'm pregnant again!' Lascana had smiled, as she watched Alfic's bewilderment, which quickly turned to a realisation that slowly turned to understanding. 'Close your mouth Dear, you look like a startled mud Guppy.'

'Well, Fornax's freckles, that was morning sickness! I wondered where you kept disappearing to.'

Shaking her head, Lascana exclaimed, 'Of course it was. For a man everyone turns to for advice, you can really be naïve sometimes.'

'You're pregnant, and you've been placing yourself in danger knowing this!' he had chastised, his voice rising by several octaves. 'What were you thinking? Oh no, Kuelack!'

'I swear you're the father,' she had smiled meekly.

'This is no joking matter, Lascana, when my brother finds out you're pregnant...'

It was for purely selfish reasons she had announced their good fortune at that particular moment. Perhaps it was an act of defiance on her part, a statement proclaiming that no matter what Kuelack did or said, their lives would carry on, regardless.

'... For this brief moment, just be happy,' she had smiled, 'rejoice in the new life we have created.'

But their joy had been short-lived as Alfic, in his no nonsense way, had pointed out, 'We knew this struggle wouldn't be easy Lascana, but this is one hell of a time to bring a child into the world.'

'If not now, then when Alfic?'

'Well, what's done is done and you know I would die rather than see our children raised as servants of Kuelack.'

'I know you would, as would I.'

Returning to the present, she decided on a course of action. Collecting Aridain's empty plate, she said in a steely voice, 'Don't be sad, munch kin, you'll see more of Daddy, I promise, now get your coat, it's time to go.'

Lascana opened the cottage door and gazed eagerly out into the early morning gloom. Barely able to discern a procession of heavily laden wagons, creaking and rattling as they passed the front door, she donned her cloak and, drawing the hood over her head, she set off towards the school.

With a thick coat in hand, together with his sword and shield, his tiny footfalls muted in the fog, Aridain ran past her excitedly to the end of the garden. He was in such a hurry that when he opened the gate; he ran straight into Harold, the school's long serving senior functionary.

'Whoa, steady there young un, I was nearly singing tenor then.'

'Sorry Mister,' said Aridain, attempting to don his coat while at the same time hold on to his sword and shield. Failing hopelessly at both, he tumbled into the mud.

'Hello Harold, sorry about our little whirlwind,' said a despairing Lascana as she rolled her eyes. 'He's off to fight Furies and Trolls.'

'Even Furies and Trolls don't go out in this weather,' smiled Harold, lifting Aridain onto his feet, 'although fighting evil would make a pleasant change from collecting extravagances for Madam Gradine.'

The kindly grey-haired servant then turned, and leaning close whispered sincerely, 'I know the past month has been difficult after certain information and revelations have come to light, but just remember Lascana, you and your family are not alone, there are those at the school who do not trust the word of Kuelack.'

She studied his grey melancholy eyes and grasping the elderly servant's head in her hands; kissed him on the cheek.

'Thank you for that Harold, you dear man, it means a lot,' she smiled. Then, thinking quickly, she said, 'If it's no disposition, any information you could furnish us with would help.'

'Hmmm.' Beckoning Lascana closer, Harold whispered, 'Well, what I've heard is that Kuelack and Ramus are about to embark on an extensive journey together and that during Kuelack's absence, Gradine will be handling his affairs. Then Harold pronounced loudly, 'Well, good day to you Mrs Bruin,' and raising his cap, he disappeared into the enshrouding murk.

Shivering, Lascana shut the gate and drew her cloak tight around her shoulders. 'Well, no surprises there,' she mused cynically. Kuelack always struggled to keep Gradine's obsessive lust for power in check. She recalled Kuelack's marriage to Gradine...

She, Alfic and Perak had stood in a remote corner of Senator Agrestal's manor house after the ceremony feeling like fish out of water, while Vara, dressed in her finery and in her element, had mingled with the cream of society.

'Seline, help us, look at them,' Perak had mused, 'the ruling classes, all corduroys and blow waves.'

Alfic had chuckled, 'with nothing else to do, they amble through life without a clue as to what's going on in the real world, they've more money than they know what to do with, I pity the realm, if any of them had to do any real work.'

Watching Vara flitting around the room, a large glass of wine in her hand, Lascana said, 'You know Vara confided in me that's if she had her own way, she would live on The King's Way in Gonda, whereas you would quite happily live in a tent in the middle of a field. It's a mystery to me what you saw in each other. You're so both totally different.'

'Well, perhaps there's some truth in the saying, opposites attract, Lascana.'

About to reply, Lascana was interrupted by the appearance of the bride and groom.

'Is something amusing, Lascana?' Gradine had enquired.

'Ahh Gradine, Kuelack, congratulations,' greeted Perak.

'Thank you, Father.' Kuelack had replied, smiling tentatively.

'We were just commenting on the surroundings, very nice,' Lascana had lied.

'It's ok Lascana, you can admit it. You're jealous; breeding always tells.'

'She's right there,' Perak had hissed under his breath.

Unable to contain herself, Lascana had replied in a brusque voice, 'There's more to life than money and chattels, Gradine.'

'One's status is nothing to be ashamed of. Success breeds power and position in life, Lascana; not honesty and certainly not humility!'

'It's just an opinion, Gradine,' emphasised Alfic. 'We mean nothing by it. Do we, Dear?'

Lascana remembered clear as day, Gradine looking them up and down disdainfully...

'Don't apologise Alfic; we get what we deserve in life.'

The challenge had been too tempting to ignore. She could feel it now, the anger overriding all caution, and she had embraced the challenge with gusto.

'Just because you're the daughter of a Senator and now married to a Wizard on Pellagrin's council, that doesn't give you the right to speak to people as if they were a speck of dirt on your shoe. It's time somebody taught you humility, reminded you of your place in the world.'

'And you're the person to do it, I suppose. My father was right; he said we'd get no thanks for introducing you and your family to culture and sophistication.'

'Gradine, that's enough.' Kuelack had chastised.

Gradine smiled innocently. 'Oh well, if you can't appreciate culture, at least you can do something more attuned to your status, like the dishes.'

'Gradine, that is ENOUGH,' growled Kuelack.

But Lascana had not finished and turned on Gradine like an enraged Virion cat.

'You just don't realise how lucky you are, compared to those less fortunate than you; do you? All of your possessions, all of your power, more-begets-more until nothing ever makes you happy: none of it, and you are the result,' she had sneered, looking at Gradine disdainfully.

'Why you... you... common scullion maid,' Gradine had spluttered, her pasty skin taking on the colour of beetroot.

'You're causing a scene, Gradine,' Kuelack had said testily.

Then, with a dangerous stare, Gradine warned, 'You will regret your words, Lascana. I'll have you thrown out of your cottage and living in a pigsty.' Then, turning to Kuelack, Gradine had raged, 'Get her out of my house! NOW!'

'It's ok, Kuelack, I'm leaving, and you're right Gradine, I can't lower the tone anymore, you've done that all by yourself,' and with that she had spun on her heels and stormed out leaving a stunned Alfic and Perak trailing in her wake...

'You don't like Auntie Gradine, do you Mummy?'

Brought back to the present, she said, looking down at him harshly, 'That's not your concern, young man!'

She looked around at the chilling, all-enshrouding autumnal fog that for days had blanketed the school and surrounding countryside and brought with it an unnerving silence. Even the Dark Creature had disappeared, swallowed it seemed like Harold's silhouette in the murk.

'It's okay, Mummy, it's not here,' Aridain replied confidently. 'It hasn't been here for a while.'

'Aridain; that enough.'

'But it's like you're talking.'

'No buts young man.'

'Oooh.'

Despite her annoyance, Aridain's confidence reassured her. She had come to rely on her son's uncanny insight regarding his evil twin, although her relationship with many of the school's residents had suffered because of her son's resemblance to the elusive creature. This included Celia, who had seized upon the opportunity to question Lascana's chastisement of Duran's recent behaviour. Sorin's spouse had argued that the likeness by association had somehow affected Duran, even going as far as to suggest that Aridain had enchanted Duran and also compelled Selva to help release the creatures from the fair. Falling out with Celia had been her biggest regret, as Aridain enjoyed visiting so much; she had been the aunt to Aridain that Gradine and Magen never were.

Hearing Perak and Sorin's familiar muted voices mingled with the occasional lowing of the cattle, Lascana called to Aridain, drawing him close and hugging him fiercely.

'Now, I've finally convinced Celia to let you play with Selva and Duran once more, and I want to keep Celia as a friend; so, do try to get on with Duran,' implored Lascana. 'Now, I have to talk to your grandfather, so hurry over to the farm. Off you go.'

'I'll try Mummy,' he smiled, 'and you mustn't blame yourself. It wasn't your fault.'

She shook her head despairingly and watched as Aridain disappeared into the mist, thrusting and parrying with his wooden sword, Mace's lessons plainly evident as he disappeared into the gloom. She then turned and called out to Perak across the mist-shrouded fields.

Huddled against the dampness that had seeped into every fold and crease of her clothing, Lascana ambled through the fog behind the herd of long-horned cattle together with Perak and Sorin.

'You must admit it was funny,' laughed Perak, wiping at the dampness dripping from his nose with the sleeve of his thick, tanned coat. 'The look on Keen's face when the hammer rebounded and hit him on the nose was hilarious; then, when he stumbled backwards into the drinking trough...'

Adjusting the rim of his wide brimmed weather-beaten hat, his weathered features creased against the damp fog, Sorin, the school's jovial farmer chuckled, 'Poor Keen, he looked like a drowned rat in his Sunday best, it was one of the highlights of the fair.'

'I didn't know chopping meat made you so morose,' stated Perak, and again, they fell into fits of laughter.

'I just wish he could see the funny side of life sometimes,' Lascana chuckled.

Smiling, she looked sideways at the grinning Perak, who wore a long leather raincoat and hat and carried a long hazel stick with which to encourage the cattle. Over the last thirty years, the two men, as well as teaching Alfic and Keegan the nuances of grounds keeping and farming, had helped guide every new member of staff, including the late Nailer Tadman and the Pike brothers. Sorin, a practical and logical man, rarely allowed his emotions to dictate common sense and, to Celia's annoyance, he had dismissed the recent revelations concerning Aridain as brainless superstition. He saw the world in black and white and always gave good, solid advice to that effect; so, to him, it was just nonsensical to tar Aridain and the creature with the same brush.

Now shrouded in the early morning gloom, she looked across the field pensively in an effort to locate their cottage, the one remaining guardhouse of four that had policed access to the school and its grounds in more dangerous times.

'We had to pull a few strings and Almagest helped a lot,' confirmed Perak, noticing Lascana staring whimsically in the cottage's direction.

'It was thanks to you, Father, that we moved into the old abandoned guardhouse,' Lascana mused.

Shaking his head, Perak murmured, 'I felt so sorry for you when you came to live with us. Do you know, Sorin, that for two years Lascana and Alfic had to endure Vara's rhetoric,' he continued, 'constantly reminding them of how lucky they were that we took them in? Then there were the lectures on how she could help them become "socially aware" and make influential friends; it's no wonder you were so eager to leave Lascana.'

'There was no reasoning with her; she even blamed me for poisoning Alfic's mind against her,' confirmed Lascana.

'So that's why Alfic was so desperate to work all that overtime.' Sorin chuckled.

'Vara's never satisfied, even after everything I've given her, including the grandest dwelling in Spalding,' mumbled Perak. 'There are many women who would be proud to call themselves my wife.'

'Thinking aloud?' smiled Sorin.

'What? Oh sorry, even when she's not here, Vara has a habit of spoiling the day,' groaned Perak.

'Vara will never change and neither will you,' continued Sorin with an assured certainty. 'The older the person, the more set in their ways they become.'

'I'll bet you never had this much trouble from Celia? She's a good wife and a good mother.'

'Oh, Celia has her moments, I can assure you, but I can't complain.' Sorin shook his head and chuckled, 'She's put up with my eccentricities and me for years; that woman deserves a medal.'

Seeking the school through the branches of the orchards' apple and pear trees, Lascana could just make out the numerous firefly lights shining from within Pellagrin's spires and vaulted roofs.

Fascinated by the citadel's past and its role in Durbah's formation, Lascana had discovered that the school's founder, the revered Wizard Pellagrin, established the school nearly six hundred years ago. The citadel was built as a beacon of light in an age of darkness and became a sanctuary from the chaos and barbarism of the age. Over the centuries, Pellagrin and his followers eventually brought peace and stability to the region, ushering in a new age of reasoning as common sense and understanding prevailed. Over the years, more structures and land were added to the school as races, young and old, weary of war, conflict and suffering, sought out the school in search of reason and wisdom.

Lascana shook her head morosely. Once Pellagrin's school had been the yardstick that every other school aspired to. However, since Head Wizard Almagest's disappearance, a dark melancholy had descended, as if the school itself mourned his passing. With Kuelack's initiation as Head of the School, his victory would be complete; and the friends' simple, carefree moments together would become a thing of the past.

One more reason to act before our way of life disappeared altogether, Lascana reasoned.

She thought of Mace, locked up in the school's dungeons after defending Alfic at the summer fair, yet another victim of Kuelack's insanity, and Kale, who had been forced from his position as Animistic teacher. Alfic had been right. Despite the danger, they couldn't just leave their friends to their fate without so much as a by-your-leave.

'What happened to the days when our only concerns were whether we had time for another ale before we went home?' mused Perak, as if reading her thoughts.

'Or how we could prevent the carrot root fly from decimating the crop?' Sorin added mournfully.

'Kuelack happened, that's what,' Lascana cursed. 'Thanks to that murderer, you're snowed under with work and a man short.'

In an attempt to sound upbeat, Sorin said, 'Not anymore. We've been given approval to take on more hands.'

'Finally come to his senses, has he?' queried Lascana.

'Even Kuelack appreciates he has to eat,' explained Sorin. 'He and Gradine won't do without their luxuries. Perak's already recruited a strong lad from Barfleet village, Simon Tubney. I think you said his name was. He seems nice enough.'

'Alfic gave him the third degree,' Perak chuckled. 'The poor lad didn't know what hit him.'

'Making sure he wasn't one of Kuelack's spies, I wager,' concluded Sorin. 'Poor lad.'

'It's Alfic's way,' explained Perak. 'We're 'interviewing' another candidate this afternoon, Amus Holt is his name. He's from Navar originally, but has recently been working in Shadrack village, across the cutting from Barfleet, as a handyman and rat catcher.'

They continued across the field in silence, each lost in their own thoughts, the only sounds, the occasional bellow of the cattle as they trudged across the grass.

Struggling to put her next thoughts into words, Lascana looked toward Perak and then said tentatively, 'Did you know that when he was born, Vara wove a spell over Aridain?'

'Spell, what kind of spell?' replied Perak.

'A deflection spell, apparently it…'

'I know what it does, Lascana. How did you find out?' demanded Perak impatiently.

'Kale, he said it could only have been Vara.'

Perak shook his head despairingly. 'You see Sorin; this is the measure of the woman.' Then, noticing his friend's nonplussed expression, he explained, 'It's a spell that deters any person asking about or detecting one's magic.'

'And did it work?' asked Sorin.

'Well, yes, but that's not the point.'

'She was reinforcing the spell with treats,' confirmed Lascana. 'How would you feel, suddenly finding out someone had bewitched your children without your permission?' Lascana growled.

'But he's safe and sound, not bewitched, yes?'

'That's not the point,' insisted Lascana petulantly. 'This is nothing to be laughed at, Sorin.'

Chuckling, Sorin said, 'It's a good job that Aridain's so active, otherwise he would have ended up fatter than Duran.'

'Sorin, this is serious,' but when she saw his grinning face, Lascana smiled. 'I'll still be having a word with my mother-in-law.'

'It must be serious, Lascana called Vara mother-in-law,' chuckled Perak, and before long they were all laughing raucously.

They ambled behind the herd, corralling them in the direction of the topmost field. Penning them in and securing the temporary gate, they then walked back towards the track as the sun endeavoured to break through the murkiness.

Making up her mind, Lascana pulled back her hood and said seriously. 'I think we should set up a meeting with the stallholders. With Keegan banned from the school and Mace in jail, our numbers are growing thin, so it falls to us to tackle the thorn in our side that is Kuelack and an increasingly belligerent council.'

'You're asking us to what… break Mace out of prison, kill Kuelack and become outlaws?' declared Sorin.

'All I know is, we can't sit idly by while Kuelack isolates us one by one, while he and his associates take over the school. If we don't do something, the days of simply wondering whether the carrot root fly is eating the crop will be a thing of the past.'

'I don't know; we're talking treason,' Sorin wavered, 'to act against the council… to act against the school…?'

'Sorin?' asked Perak, watching the farmer suddenly stand stock-still and stare into space. 'Are you all right?'

'Ssshhh, can you hear that noise?' Sorin mused, holding up his hand. 'It sounds like the fluttering of dragonfly wings.'

'I can't hear anything. Are you sure?' asked Perak quizzically.

'Yes, it was there for a moment, but it's gone now.'

CHAPTER THREE

DURAN AND THE DRAGONLET

Now on his own, his imagination running wild with the fun and adventures he, Selva and Duran could have, Aridain peered nervously into the dense fog, seeking the twin gates that separated the school grounds from the fields. Climbing each gate in turn, he clasped his sword and shield tightly and then walked cautiously across the playing field. All too soon, he heard the familiar sound of small leathery wings tracking him from above and, for once, he was glad of the dragonlet's company. Since its release, it had remained close by despite Aridain telling it to fly home, wherever that was.

'It's a good job I know where I'm going,' shouted Aridain into the gloom, in an effort to boost his own confidence, 'because, dragonlet, you could easily get lost in this fog.'

As he walked across the grassy field, he readied himself for battle, imagining trolls, hobgoblins and witches searching for him, their leering red eyes penetrating the greyness and their chunky, coarse, clawed hands reaching for him, intent on eating his innards for breakfast. Suddenly there was a noise to the left and two shadowy figures ghosted past in the mist. Unable to control his fear any longer, his feet slipping and sliding on the wet grass, he ran through the fog in alarm, heaving a thankful sigh of relief when the farm finally reared up out of the mist. Pausing briefly to look over his shoulder, he unlatched the front gate, ran up to the front door and knocked loudly.

When the door opened, Aridain bolted beneath Celia's outstretched arm as she peered into the miasma with the help of a candle.

'Aridain?' exclaimed Celia, wrapping her dressing gown tightly about herself against the all-enshrouding dampness. 'Are you all right?'

'Hello Aunt Celia,' squeaked Aridain, relieved to be out of the fog. 'Are Selva and Duran ready yet?'

'They're upstairs,' she said, looking at him cautiously. 'Go dry yourself by the fire. You're all wet.'

Aridain sniffed the air... Lavender biscuits? That's why Aridain loved Auntie Celia so much. She was always cooking something and her house always smelt of delicious food and cosiness. It made him feel secure, like his mother's cuddles, or like Chipper's familiar presence. Suddenly feeling sad, Aridain remembered when he and Chipper would visit and sit down in front of the fire with Selva and Duran. Then, with a glass of hot milk and a lavender biscuit, Celia would read them stories of giants and Dragons. Aridain suddenly began to cry.

'Hey, what's the matter?'

'I miss Chipper, Auntie Celia.'

'Yes, I do too, dear. He was a sweet, loyal friend. So, are you looking forward to school?' smiled Celia cheerily in an effort to change the subject.

'Mummy and Daddy are. They say it will do me good to focus my boundless energy,' said Aridain, cluelessly. He then looked up at Celia with intent. 'Because I look like the creature, Aunt Celia, it doesn't mean I'm bad.'

'Aridain dear, why do you say that?'

'Because that's what you thought.'

Celia crouched in front of him, and gathering him in her arms, cried, 'Oh, Aridain, I'm so sorry. I know it's no excuse, but unlike children who see the world through naïve benevolent eyes, grown-ups fear things they don't understand; we're not as adaptable or as accepting of the bizarre. For a while, rumour swept through the school and I guess I got swept up in it, too. I don't know how I could ever have thought of you as I did. I'm so sorry, Aridain.'

'It's okay, Aunt Celia, don't cry.' He smiled, patting her on the shoulder and then, remembering something he had read, Aridain said, 'The truth always outs in the end.'

Very profound Aridain!

Oh, hello voice, I haven't heard from you for a while.

The scholarly works of Maester Griffin, I believe, confirmed the voice.

Wiping at her tears, Celia kissed Aridain's forehead and, smiling, said, 'Here, have a lavender biscuit.' She then walked to the base of the stairs and, clearing her throat, shouted, 'Selva, Duran, Aridain's here.'

From overhead there came the familiar sounds of laughter and giggling, and like a distant rumbling of thunder, the portly, curly-haired Duran, followed by Selva with her long, fair-haired, curly locks streaming out behind her, ran down the stairs and burst into the kitchen.

'Aridain,' squealed Selva.

'Selva,' beamed Aridain.

'Where have you been?' cried Selva.

'Helping Mummy. My dad's been very busy.'

'Yes, so has mine. Spooky outside, isn't it?'

'Only to a girl,' teased Duran, who lunging suddenly, snatched the half-eaten biscuit from Aridain's hand and stuffed it into his mouth.

'I saw that, Duran Corvuss. There's plenty for everyone,' admonished Celia.

'You are such a baby,' scolded Selva.

Duran poked out his tongue, then smiled craftily.

'Come on Aridain, let's go outside,' ordered Selva, turning her back on Duran, who was struggling to eat another doughnut-sized biscuit without choking.

'Remember, don't stray too far, children, and come back and eat sometime. We don't want you wasting away,' shouted Celia.

'Come on, let's go and fight some darklings,' giggled Aridain, taking charge, confident once more now he was with his friends. Running excitedly out of the back door and into the fields, it wasn't long before the heavy mist had saturated their clothing and soaked through their footwear. Feeling as if they were the only souls in a world of grey abandon, the three friends slowed, then gazed about in the eerie silence. Suddenly, Duran pressed closer to Selva and Aridain.

'Did you hear that?'

'They say when it's quiet and grey, ghosts and foul beasts rule the day,' Aridain chuckled, winking at Selva.

Selva looked at Aridain questioningly.

Seeing Duran's worried face, Aridain laughed. 'I'm pulling your leg Duran. It's only the dragonlet; it won't hurt you.'

'How do you know?'

'Because it's my friend.'

'Are you sure?' said Duran, feeling a little braver.

'Of course.'

'Why's it following you around?' asked Selva.

'I don't know, perhaps because I freed it from that nasty man, but it never hurts me and it's hurt no one else.'

'It's a dangerous animal, you should kill it,' said Duran decisively.

'Why?' questioned Selva. 'Like Aridain said, it's never hurt anyone, but it needs to go back to the wild.'

'Well, I'm not stopping it!' insisted Aridain irritably.

They carried on across the field for a few minutes towards the line of large skeletal walnut trees that loomed above them out of the mist.

'Over there, I thought I saw something move,' hissed Duran apprehensively.

'You're imagining things. It's only the trees,' scoffed Selva.

'It was a black moving shape, I tell you. Maybe it's that monster that looks like Aridain?'

'Don't listen to him Aridain, he enjoys being nasty.'

'Do not!' replied Duran.

The twins, now terrified, suddenly stopped and huddled behind Aridain who, certain it wasn't the Dark Creature, held out his sword and shield protectively, as out of the thick miasma loomed a large black shape that issued a deep lowing sound. Duran yelped, and Selva issued a high-pitched squeal. Aridain, unable to contain himself any longer, laughed. 'You should have seen your faces.'

'Duran, it's Jasper the bull, you idiot,' cried Selva, slapping him around the arm. 'I was really scared.'

'Owww, that hurt,' shouted Duran, hitting Selva back.

Presenting his shield, Aridain, a dark look on his face, pushed Duran backwards. 'That wasn't nice, you don't hit girls,' warned Aridain as Selva started to cry.

'Why not?' shouted Duran. 'She hit me first.'

'You just don't. Boys are a lot stronger than girls and we can really hurt them.'

'Then Selva shouldn't hit me first.'

'Daddy says only cowards hit girls,' said Selva tearily. 'You're such a bully, Duran Corvuss.'

'Are you calling me a coward?' shouted Duran, advancing towards Selva; however, when he saw Aridain's determined look, he decided he didn't like what he saw.

'Don't worry Selva, it was a sissy hit anyway,' taunted Aridain, daring Duran to fight back. When Duran ignored him, Aridain turned and walked off into the fog. What Aridain didn't notice was the worshipful look in Selva's dark brown eyes.

During its years of captivity, the dragonlet learned that humans will exploit and subjugate anything for a price. It should have returned to its troupe in the Southern Wilds the moment the youngling freed it; after all, its proximity to humans was the reason it had been captured in the first place. However, the dragonlet had come to realise that it was arrogance of the first degree that had led to its capture. Conceited and egotistical, it thought its reputation combined with a fiery breath would keep it safe, disregarding the fact that wiser and more ferocious members of its kind had died at the hands of humans.

Cursed to obey the human with its ability to ensnare beast kind, the wagon owner had forced him to perform and entertain. The consequence if he resisted was pain and suffering. Unable to escape, it seemed he would be forever at the wagon owner's whim. That was until the day this youngling human had released it, a youngling possessing an archaic power that commanded attention. This power permitted the dragonlet an insight into the boy's psyche, and it had been pleasantly surprised. This young human seemed to empathise with his surroundings and all the things that lived in it.

Its proximity to the young mage had also brought other benefits; it had afforded him a modicum of resistance against the persistent callings of yet another powerful animistic. Despite the dragonlet's long years, it seemed life still had lessons to teach it.

Perched in the branches of a walnut tree, the dragonlet watched and listened in mute fascination as the youngling and the female argued with the little fat human. This behaviour baffled and confused it, as humans only ever united against his kind, big and small. Then, continuing its focus on the scene playing out below, the dragonlet watched as the youngling continued to defend the female against the little fat human, who displayed the typical behaviour it had come to know so well. This action, along with many other observed selfless acts, had earned the youngling a grudging respect from the dragonlet, not an easy thing to achieve. Perhaps the boy was different; perhaps they weren't all the same after all. In fact, he had demonstrated traits that any self-respecting dragonlet and its troupe would be proud of.

But are you worthy of my trust, youngling?

'You must have been very brave, Aridain,' enquired Selva. 'If that horrible ugly creature attacked me, I would have been scared with fright.'

Swinging back and forth over the stream on their favourite rope swing, Duran shouted sarcastically, 'If it looked like Aridain, then it must have been scary.'

'You're only jealous Duran because you would have run away,' said Selva scathingly, and then sweetly she said, 'Were you scared, Aridain?'

'Of course he was,' Duran claimed, poking out his tongue.

Aridain looked at Selva meekly. 'Don't tell Duran, but I was a bit scared,' he whispered. 'My Dad wasn't though; he was really brave.'

'Well, I think you're brave,' said Selva, kissing him on the cheek.

Startled, Aridain turned and looked at Selva bizarrely.

'Urgh, that's disgusting,' said Duran, and he launched himself out across the stream once more, swinging back and forth in happy abandon. Then suddenly Duran said, 'I think Keegan should kill the dragonlet, before it kills someone else.'

'Not so loud Duran, it'll hear you,' said Selva, sitting on the leaf litter next to Aridain between the impressive buttresses of a large oak tree.

'Don't be silly, it can't understand talk,' mocked Duran.

'I'm trying to make friends with it, so don't keep saying nasty things,' said Aridain passionately. 'You wouldn't be very happy if someone locked you away for years and made you do things you didn't want to.'

'Why would you want to make friends with it? It's not a human or a cat or a dog, it's an animal.'

'Cats and dogs are animals! Really Duran, I despair sometimes,' said Selva, placing hands on hips and shaking her head disapprovingly.

'Some animals are better than humans,' Aridain exclaimed. 'At least animals don't kill for fun.'

'I still think it should be killed,' said Duran.

'No one will kill it, I won't let them,' said Aridain purposefully. 'The dragonlet saved my life.'

'Well, you can always keep it as a pet, I suppose,' offered Selva.

'I told you, it's free; no one owns it.'

Stepping back on to the bank, Duran secured the rope and joined Aridain and Selva beneath the oak tree.

'Well, the teachers will want it killed,' Duran persevered.

'I won't let that happen either; I'll just have to talk to it.'

'Don't be silly, just shoo it away.'

'You know it's true that Aridain can talk to animals, Duran,' insisted Selva. 'You just won't admit it.'

'Can't,' Duran sneered. 'But he certainly looks like one. Mum said the reason we were not allowed to play with Aridain was that he looked like the creature and they had to be sure he wasn't dangerous.'

'Liar! Liar!' screamed Selva.

'It's true, I overheard Mum and Dad arguing about it,' stated Duran.

'It's not true. Tell him, Aridain.'

'It's true, Selva,' confirmed Aridain sadly.

'See, Aridain is a monster and will suck out your brains,' laughed Duran.

'Why are you such a horrible brother?' screamed Selva. 'Aridain is not a monster.'

Sat morosely with his chin on his knees, Aridain stated, 'My Mum said that grown-ups fear what they don't understand, that it's not their fault.'

I like the way your mind works, Aridain Bruin. I think it's time.

'Shut up, voice,' mumbled Aridain, moodily.

'Aridain is not a monster, so there. Now let's talk about something different,' smiled Selva. 'When I go to school, I'm going to be a healer,' she said proudly.

'Boring,' said Duran. 'I want to see Aridain eat a whole badger or a deer. That would be neat.'

'Well, at least I know what I want to do when I go to school, Duran,' snapped Selva. 'You don't!'

'I want to fight and have adventures.'

'You don't go to school for fun, you go to school to learn,' Selva lectured. 'What about you, Aridain?'

'I don't really know what I'd be good at, but I enjoy fighting with my sword and shield, and I like animals and I like being outdoors.'

'I'll be better than you,' said Duran. 'Daddy says when I grow up, I'll be a great swordsman.'

'Why do you always have to lie?' said Selva crossly. 'You know that Mummy and Daddy worry about you.'

'It's not a lie. When I grow up, I want to be a great conqueror, and if people don't do as they're told, I'll put them to the sword,' announced Duran in a gallant voice.

'My dad said you don't become a soldier just to kill people; you only kill as a last resort, when all other means have failed,' educated Aridain. 'In the army, you follow orders; it teaches you discipline and respect for other people.'

'Well, that doesn't sound much fun,' said Duran dejectedly. 'You have to kill people if they invade your country.'

'That's different,' said Aridain.

'How would you know, anyway?'

'Because my dad and grandpop were both in the army.'

'Well, it sounds fun to me.'

'It's not funny killing people. It's not like one of our games with pretend killing, Duran; in real life there's blood and gore and everything,' shivered Selva.

Duran stood up and grabbed Aridain's sword. 'I don't care; I will kill all who stand in my way,' he said, poking Aridain in the chest.

Shocked from his reverie, Aridain jumped to his feet and, giggling, picked up a long stick. He then turned to Selva, 'Don't worry Princess, I will save you from Dacron, the evil Wizard,' and he leapt to the attack.

25

As the mock fight progressed, Aridain, being more practised with a sword, became aware of Duran's increased agitation and anger as he pressed the attack. Remembering his mother's plea concerning Duran, Aridain, determined not to cause another fight, left an opening and Duran, with a furious look on his flushed, plump face, thrust the sword into Aridain's middle.

'Hey! That hurt,' hissed Aridain, rubbing at his stomach.

However, Duran wasn't listening, and he ran around as if he'd won the swordsman's gold brocade. 'Ha ha, I won, I won. I killed Pellagrin the Brave.' High on his success; Duran threw away the sword and once more grabbed for the rope.

Forgetting the incident, Aridain leapt to his feet and, giggling, launched himself from the bank towards the spinning rope with Duran, as Selva pushed the two boys back and forth, the branch groaning and creaking. Releasing the rope, the pair leapt onto the bank.

'I'll bet you can't do this,' said Duran, launching himself in a clockwise direction over and around the stream.

'Look out!' shouted Selva, as Duran headed straight for the trunk of the oak tree.

Impacting the tree with a thud, Duran let out a painful yelp as he spun around on the end of the rope.

'Jump Duran,' giggled Aridain, 'before you fall in the stream.'

'It's not funny. Stop laughing and help me,' said Duran seriously.

Realising Duran was terrified, Aridain reached out and grabbed his leg in an effort to pull him in.

'Selva, grab my shirt.'

Selva grabbed for Aridain but wasn't strong enough, as the boys' combined weight threatened to drag her into the stream, and from fear of falling in, she let go. With Aridain clinging to Duran's leg, their combined weight was too much. Unable to hold on any longer, the rope slipped from Duran's grasp and the two fell into the stream with a splash. Selva screamed as the two boys floundered around in the water, coughing and spluttering. Aridain found the bottom and scrambled from the water while Duran stumbled and floundered his way to the bank.

Selva ran to help her brother up the bank. 'Are you all right Duran?'

'Leave me alone. I saw you two laughing at me. You did that on purpose because I beat you at sword fighting,' screamed Duran petulantly.

'Stop acting like a big baby, Duran!' yelled Selva.

'I'm not a baby, you are. You're always sticking up for him.'

'Well, if you weren't so horrible all the time!' shouted Selva.

Duran, his anger taking over, pushed Selva to the floor, then picking up the wooden sword, threw it. It hit Aridain squarely in the chest.

'Owww!' shouted Aridain, clutching his chest.

'Duran, you're a horrible brother,' screamed Selva, stamping her feet. 'I hate you.'

His patience exhausted, Aridain was thoroughly fed up with Duran's nastiness. However, before he could react, Selva screamed as the dragonlet, in a blaze of blue and green, appeared from the trees with an angry hiss, darting between himself and Selva, heading straight towards Duran. Landing squarely on Duran's chest with its sharp claws drawn, it forced the startled youth to the leafy floor.

'Help me? Tell it to leave me alone,' whimpered Duran.

'I can't talk to animals, remember?' Aridain said angrily.

The dragonlet turned towards Aridain with a green-eyed stare that conveyed thousands of years of Dragon-honed logic; its membranous, turquoise, leathery wings quivering in anticipation and its long, sinuous, forked tongue flicking over the tip of Duran's nose.

Don't worry, I won't hurt this one. He just needs a lesson in humility.

Confident that Duran wasn't in any danger, Aridain turned away in order to hide a furtive grin.

'Aridain, what are you doing? Help Duran, it's going to kill him!' cried Selva.

'Be quiet, Selva, or you'll just make things worse. The dragonlet will only release him if he says he's sorry to you, for pushing you over,' said Aridain gravely.

'I'm sorry,' whimpered Duran.

'Duran, the dragonlet is protecting Selva. If you don't mean it, it will get angry,' said Aridain, rubbing at the painful bruise on his chest.

In response, the dragonlet bared its needle-sharp teeth and hissed menacingly.

Duran's face turned white with fear and he snivelled, 'Ok, ok, I didn't mean it. I'm very sorry, I don't want to die.'

'Okay, apology accepted.'

With a flap of its leathery wings, the dragonlet took to the air, but instead of disappearing back into the trees, it alighted on Aridain's shoulder.

Introductions over, I think you've earned my company.

It is done, echoed the voice in his mind, conveying the feeling that something momentous had taken place.

'What do you mean, voice?' asked Aridain.

Encountering only silence, Aridain peered sideways hesitantly, eyeing the dragonlet with trepidation, the unmistakable odour of ash, cinders and damp earth filling his nostrils.

I think it's time you and I had a talk, thought the dragonlet.

'Aridain, what are you doing?' questioned Selva. 'When Duran asked for help, I think he wanted you to get rid of it. Now he'll think you're to blame.'

'Selva, I don't care. No matter what I do, I'll never please him,' replied Aridain, peering at Duran contemptibly as the plump youth climbed tearfully to his feet. 'I don't think we will ever be real friends.'

'I'm going home,' said Duran unhappily as he stomped through the sodden field. 'And I'm telling my dad about you and that... that thing.'

Approaching meekly, Selva quickly replied, 'Don't worry Aridain, I won't let him tell any lies about you. Will you be all right?'

'I'll be fine; besides, I've got a new friend to talk to,' replied Aridain cheerfully.

Smiling coyly up at him, Selva suddenly leant forward and kissed Aridain on the cheek. She then ran after Duran.

Aridain watched the twins disappear through the trees as the fog at last started to thin, brushed aside by a strengthening breeze, allowing the morning sunshine to shine through after what seemed like an eternity of gloom. The dragonlet, alighting on the ground, watched him curiously while perched upright on its hind legs.

Sat cross-legged on the ground, Aridain stared back. 'Duran deserved that,' said Aridain, unrepentant. 'He's a bully.'

He is your typical human, full of confidence when things are going their way, but full of anger when they don't.

'I thought he was my friend, but he's not. Chipper was my only real friend.'

Chipper?

'Yes, he was our dog.'

So, you owned him like the carnival vendor thought he owned me, hissed the dragonlet intensely. *I thought you believed animals should be free.*

Aridain thought for a moment. 'Chipper was different. He was a member of our family and people accepted him. It's very unusual for a person to have a dragonlet as a pet or even as a companion.'

A pet!

'Pet is a word we use for an animal that wants to be with us; it's normal. If Chipper really wanted to, he could have run away any time.' Aridain paused for a moment, then asked, 'Why are you protecting me, dragonlet?'

Who said anything about protecting you? The dragonlet remained silent for a moment, then looked up at Aridain, wisdom and cognitive thought evident in its bejewelled eyes. *You saved me from that animal entertainer; I wish to return the favour.*

'I hope it's a decision you don't regret. My dad says grown-ups don't trust you because you're dangerous and people fear what they can't control. But I know you better than that.'

The dragonlet looked at him quizzically. *It's not my fault humans can't control their fears. If men try to hurt me, I will defend myself; it's all Dragon kind has ever done.*

'But killing is against the law. If you want to stay here, you will have to gain people's trust.'

I am not concerned with the ways of men.

'How that horrible man treated you was wrong, but if you go around hurting people, they will never trust you.' Aridain stared at the dragonlet oddly before asking suddenly, 'Why didn't you just burn through your cage?'

It was reinforced with magic.

'So why didn't you just fly away, or escape when he let you out?'

He was a controller, spat the dragonlet, as if that explained everything.

Aridain looked at him blankly.

The dragonlet hissed menacingly, *He was what you humans call an Animistic.*

Picking up a stick and listlessly scraping at the soil, Aridain looked across at the dragonlet that returned his stare with shrewd, calculating eyes.

I will stay and gain people's trust, but I'll never be a pet, and don't think for one moment I will get to like you.

'Good, I'm glad that's settled,' smiled Aridain, feeling a lot better. 'Have you got a name? Friends always use names.'

Yes, I have a name, said the dragonlet.

After several seconds of silence, Aridain said irritably, 'So, what is it?'

I am a dragonlet, not your friend.

'I know that, silly, but Dragonlet sounds boring.'

There is no need to call me anything; I can communicate with you very easily, said the dragonlet decisively.

Making up his mind, Aridain said, 'If you want to follow me around, you must have a name. I know I'll call you Sabra.'

CHAPTER FOUR

KARNACK MOOR

Having ridden for a day and a half, Karnack reined in his mount beside the old ruined Fort of Orrinwell that stood just off of the main road between the area capital, Leardon, and the mining town of Yarrow to the southeast. Sat on the edge of the Orrin Depression, a large area of marshland southeast of Leardon, the old round fort once a bastion of power now stood abandoned and forgotten, covered in trees and scrub and shrouded in a continuous mist.

Sat listening to the wailing of the mysterious and little-known inhabitants of the marshes, Karnack fingered the malignant strands that now firmly secured his eye patch to his skin and thought back to his fatal meeting with Kuelack after the debacle at the school's summer fair.

Ushered into Kuelack's quarters by one of the many students who supported the dark mage, Karnack, with no wife or children to threaten, had faced Kuelack confidently. How wrong he had been...

'So, what have you to say for yourself?' Kuelack had demanded, looking up at him with an ominous scowl from behind his desk.

Stood resolutely in front of Kuelack, he had replied confidently. 'I take it you are referring to your childish sibling fight?'

'You defied me,' he had raged, 'in front of the whole school!'

'I hardly think...'

'Hold your tongue!'

'I am charged with keeping order. Our agreement made no mention of how.'

'If you wish to keep your position here when I take over, I suggest that for your own sake you adjust your outdated moral compass and do as you're told!'

'Are you threatening one of the four?'

Karnack physically winced then, as he recalled the hot lancing pain that had pierced his empty eye socket together with the left side of his face, sending him to his knees in agony. The pain had left him gasping for air and almost spent.

He had climbed unsteadily to his feet. 'What have you done?' He looked up at Kuelack then in shocked surprise when he realised what was happening. 'You had Arhass enchant my eye patch. Are there no depths to which you will sink, no dirty deception you won't undertake?'

Kuelack had peered at him from grey piercing eyes under dark foreboding brows and hissed, 'I took a chance recruiting you to our cause, and it seems my concerns were justified. This is just a guarantee, should your resolve falter, something to ensure your loyalty.'

'But this is nonsense; I simply have to remove...'

But when he had tried to remove it, malignant strands pierced the skin around his empty eye socket, grafting the patch to his face.

'Now perhaps you'll think twice about defying me. In the future, I suggest you show me the respect that is due, because any attempt to remove that filthy piece of leather will result in your death.'

'That's really what this is all about, isn't it, Kuelack? Acknowledgement and praise, you seek approval for your crimes; you want the people to endorse what you are doing.'

Kuelack had raged, 'I need no approval from the people I intend to rule. They will bow to my will or I will destroy them.'

He now realised there was no sitting on the fence, no balancing of friendship and duty. He couldn't leave Kuelack's employment, even if he desired it...

'Greysword!'

His mind focusing on the present, he turned towards the voice of a greasy-haired man dressed in thick threadbare black and tan leather armour who had appeared from the brush.

'Black Brow will see you now.'

Urging his mount forwards, Karnack followed the brigand, who led him through the trees to the fortress's old iron portcullis, buried in the depths of the abandoned forest. Tasked with contacting the local smugglers' ring, his mission was to entice the gang leader Black Brow to anarchy, with the promise of a share of power once Kuelack ruled.

Studying the spacious, dark, dank tunnel, Karnack recalled that the fort was the remnant of a stronghold held by the Wizard Zakan. It had been destroyed from the inside by soldiers loyal to Wizard Sakar, Principal of Pellagrin's at the time, who, pursuing the Mage to this fortress, defeated Zakan after the malicious mage had laid siege to the school.

He urged his horse past heavily armed guards into a vast courtyard, bathed in the marshes' dull, insipid light. Many fires burned around the courtyard, highlighting groups of men sat chatting and gambling, and in backlit rooms in run down towers he glimpsed men fornicating with women in various stages of undress. In another corner, piled against the foul, moss-stained walls, were crates of what he presumed was contraband, but the crucial thing he noticed was that Black Brow's gang were well armed.

'You can leave your horse over there,' ordered the man.

Taking note of the renewed confidence in the brigand's voice, no doubt bolstered by the presence of his fellow gang members, Karnack dismounted and walked his horse over to an old rotten wooden roof beam. Doubting he could make it to the entrance on foot if there was trouble, he loosely tethered his horse, just in case.

Searching the gloomy interior while his mount munched contentedly on hay strewn across the floor, Karnack studied the dirty, morose faces of the men peering back at him.

'Your sword, give it to me,' ordered the man.

'If you know about the Greysword Brotherhood, then you know we do not surrender our swords to anyone,' stated Karnack resolutely.

Abruptly the atmosphere changed and, sensing that the situation could turn ugly, Karnack, planting his feet, reached over his shoulder and slowly untied the straps to his sword's holster. He then wrapped his fingers around Ferocity's hilt.

'I didn't ride all this way to converse with one of Black Brow's lackeys,' Karnack demanded assertively. 'I came here to speak with your leader?'

'So, Kuelack sends Sword Master Karnack Moor to negotiate. He must be desperate!'

From out of the shadows, a large heavily built man appeared, dressed in thick, dark brown leather armour. He had an acne-scarred face and a large black swirling tattoo covering his entire forehead.

Relaxing but still alert should the need arise to escape quickly, Karnack said, 'This is not a negotiation, the deal is that Kuelack will let you stay here in your own place, and keep your territory and all you have to do in return is what you always have... ransack, pillage and cause havoc... be an inconvenience and a distraction... keep the local militia occupied.'

Looking around at his men, Black Brow stretched out his arms, and announced, 'What sort of deal is that. We're already here, we have weapons and with those weapons we rape and pillage. What's in it for me and my men?'

'A share of the spoils once Kuelack has what he wants, also he will allocate you weapons built at the school's forges, in return for certain illegitimate items.

'That's it?'

'That's it.'

Turning to his men, Black Brow chuckled, 'Finally, acknowledgement of our contribution to society.'

Black Brow's announcement was met with cheers and drunken laughter. Then, his face like thunder, the bandit chief let out a raucous bellow, 'Does Kuelack think I'm stupid? That's no deal at all.'

Then, turning and eyeing Karnack, the bandit leader said curiously, 'I may be a bandit, but even I know of the famed honour of Greyswords. What has he got over you that would make you his lackey?'

Drawing his sword in one swift movement, Karnack pointed it towards Black Brow and said angrily, 'You're not dealing with the local militia, or local watch. This is Kuelack, and when he comes to power, and he will, anyone not allied to him will be counted as an enemy.'

Unhitching and mounting his horse, his eyes narrowing, Karnack said, 'If you do as he asks, you will be rewarded. If not, you and your petty organisation will be destroyed, root and stem, the choice is yours.'

Spurring his horse into a trot and feeling as though he couldn't sink any lower, Karnack, a taste of ashes in his mouth, rode out into the grey misty world of the marshes.

CHAPTER FIVE

TRICKERY AND HALF TRUTHS

Attired in her most imposing purple opalescent dress, matching hair and headscarf, Vara strode across the churchyard, the sun's light trying desperately to force its way through the mist.

Feeling relatively pleased with herself, Vara turned her thoughts to the landlord, Mr Gould, who, with the confidence of a politician, having promised he would treat his tenants more leniently, had begun charging extortionate rent yet again. Many years ago, she had carried out a one-person crusade against the devious landlord who, unknown to Alfic and Lascana, had re-let their rooms while they had stayed with her during Aridain's birth, so, she had invented a potion to cure him, supposedly, of a fabricated infection, and had instructed him to drink the special potion down-in-one. She smiled unashamedly as she pictured him trying to get out of bed, only to find he couldn't move until he urinated the concoction from his body. His false sincerity strengthening Vara's resolve and bringing the child in her to the for once more. She grinned like a Virion cat as she pictured Edwin Gould, suddenly developing bad breath; preventing anyone from venturing near, lest they are rendered insensible. It was one of the many perks of her profession.

As the sun's rays burst through the gaps in the mist, Vara counted the gravestones and thought of all the past villagers that lay here, some family names going back nearly four hundred years; people that were part of the village's history lying beneath her feet, as was her mother. The Minster itself had records going back even further, to nearly five centuries ago, when the first people to resettle the area built the original wattle and daub house of worship.

Stopping in front of her mother's resting place, she replaced the withered daffodils with her mother's favourite flowers – carnations. Then, resting her hand upon the gravestone, she closed her eyes and sat for a moment in the stillness.

'Mother, I hope you are at peace beneath Mother Seline's all protecting embrace. It's no more than you deserve. Perhaps if you'd had an easier life, you would still be here today and for that I can never forgive our father. In the end, you had no choice but to save my sister and me and endure as you did, so do not feel guilty or fret over our upbringing, for you did the best you could under the circumstances. It was Father's weakness and lack of devotion that led him to succumb to the evils of this world, and for that I hope he rots in the furnaces of Fornax's fires. I cannot put into words how much I miss you, your warm, tender smile and reassuring presence.'

Her visits to her mother's grave always left her feeling sad and angry, but she attended to it regularly nonetheless. It was the least she could do after all her mother had sacrificed and endured for her and her sister.

After sitting quietly for half an hour, Vara, wiping away a tear, looked around at the Rumble trees, quivering their soothing messages through the soil and the long grass now going to seed. Then, steeling herself and squaring her shoulders, she grasped her bag and slowly got to her feet, scattering rooks and jackdaws that cropped, pecked and scratched unafraid at the grass-covered graves. She then strode determinedly past her home, towards the Corner House Tavern. Approaching the coach and the team of horses, now eager to run, she held up her trusty bag to the assistant driver and then climbed aboard. An hour later, the coach reached the school and Vara, securing her bag from the driver, untied her headscarf and shook the damp from her coat. As the coach resumed its journey and disappeared from the main gates, Vara, picking up her bag, approached the large oak timbered doors that marked the keep's entrance.

Confronting the stern-faced guards stood by the twin granite pillars that held up the grand ornate plinth above, she announced, 'Vara Bruin, I'm here to see my son Kuelack.'

'Are you expected?' one of them enquired.

She smiled astutely. 'Of course.'

Pushing open one of the imposing doors, she entered the warm, log-fired atmosphere and then looked around at the hustle and bustle.

'Nothing changes,' she murmured.

It had been an age since she last visited Pellagrin's old walled fortress; it still held that solid, reliable quality, giving the impression that this bastion of reason would remain unyielding and unbreakable even if the entire world went to rack and ruin. Looking across the Great Hall, she saw her friend, Merle, leading a group of youngsters. Merle pointed at an interesting feature here and a fascinating aspect there while conducting a tour of the old fortress.

Small and chubby, the Colour Magic teacher walked with purpose aided by her trusty walking stick, her podgy grey-haired head bobbing around on her concertinaed neck and her wrinkled face sprouting a single hair from a prominent mole. Vara listened as Merle lectured to the class.

'Nearly six hundred years ago, during darker times, Pellagrin built this fortress to repel enemies and attacking tribes. Later, they added a roof with the aid of sturdy oak supports and roof beams placed at regular intervals along the battlements. The old fortress is still the school's beating heart and houses the senior staff as well as dealing with all financial and administrative matters pertaining to the school. However, your new quarters, common rooms and sleeping wing now form the largest building on the grounds; located three hundred metres away in that direction,' signalled Merle. 'The construction of the latest student building started nearly three hundred years ago, in response to the steady year on year increase of students…'

Peering above her thick glass monocle, her pudding face lit up in a beaming smile, Merle exclaimed, 'Vara, how are you?'

Kissing and hugging the portly woman, Vara said, 'It's good to see you too, Merle.'

'You haven't visited in ages. Where have you been?'

'You know how it is.'

'Still at odds with your children, huh?'

'They're the reason for my visit.'

'I wish you luck. Old sins make long shadows.'

'I am greatly saddened to hear about Almagest. I know you two were close?'

Shaking her head Merle hissed, 'He was a great man, I see dire consequences for the school now he's gone, Vara.'

When Vara said nothing, Merle, smiling bravely, said, 'Still, we cannot let our fears influence the new recruits now, can we? Well, I must get on... students to educate. Nice to see you Vara, take care.' Then, squaring her narrow shoulders, the Colour Magic teacher smiled and re-joined her students.

Leaving the tour and organised confusion of the atrium behind, Vara stood and looked up at the steps that suddenly appeared more like a rock face than a gently ascending set of stairs. Her breathing becoming laboured and feeling light-headed, she tried to ignore her growing trepidation. Struggling for control, she chastised herself. *What is the matter with you, witch? You've faced bigger issues than this.* Unable to move, she stood transfixed, her hand grasping the intricately detailed oak wood panelling tightly as the fortress walls gyrated and leapt around her.

'Excuse me?'

'What? Yes, of course,' she apologised, the world suddenly snapping into focus as an apprentice dressed in the robes of Pellagrin's school pushed past. A sealed envelope clasped in his hand; the student wore robes the colour of eggshell, with grey colouring on his lapels, collar and cuffs, signifying he was a student of Earthen magic, under the tuition of Teacher Palmer.

Wiping the beads of sweat from her forehead, she took a deep breath, then squared her shoulders. Ascending the stairway to the third-floor, deliberately placing one foot in front of the other, she arrived at the lavender and Lily-of-the-Valley infused corridor on the top floor. Steeling herself, she marched to the end of the hallway and stood resolute before the thick oak door of Kuelack's apartment. However, she didn't have time to plan her actions as the door swung silently inwards.

'Come in, Mother!'

Assuming an imperious pose, Vara took a deep breath. Then, in her most aloof and superior manner, strode into Kuelack's reception room. Sat at his lavish dark wood desk while scribbling on a roll of parchment and looking immaculate as always, Kuelack, dressed in his deep burgundy red robes, instructed, 'Do sit down.'

'I'd rather stand.'

Looking up from his paperwork, Kuelack sat back, his confident smile changing to a dark squall of foreboding. Folding his arms across his chest, he instructed forcefully, 'Sit down, Mother!'

Vara felt the terrible force of Kuelack's words upon her person and the two glared at each other across the table until finally, under the force of his gaze, Vara felt her legs buckling and she crumpled into the chair that slid into place behind her.

He smiled smugly. 'That's better.' Then, after a very uncomfortable pause, he said, 'So, how are you, Mother?'

Ignoring his enquiry, she countered, 'I see you're still dabbling. Look at you, you're thirty-two Kuelack, but we look the same age.'

'It is the art I have chosen,' smiled Kuelack, 'and a powerful art it is. Although I'm not the only one dabbling, am I Mother?' His smile then turned sinister. 'Eavesdropping is a nasty and unwelcome habit, don't you agree?' he said bluntly.

'If you say so, nevertheless, I know of your plans regarding my grandson,' replied Vara, equally blunt.

'So what, you're here to try to dissuade me, kill me even? In that case, I'm afraid your journey was for nought.'

'And now I suppose you'll threaten me to silence with his life, just as you did Magen with her children. Legend says the stone influences the power crazy until there's nothing left but possession of it,' eulogised Vara.

'But I am no ordinary Mage,' he bellowed. 'My power is too great.'

'Like many before you, you're meddling with forces you don't understand, forces that have already compromised your ability to think straight, forces that may well have compelled you to kill Almagest, Torsk and Cardia.'

'Eloquently put Mother, as always, but please don't treat me like a fool. I've researched the legends.'

'If you have, then why would you even contemplate reuniting the Firebrand shards?'

'For control and for power, and a desire to rule, to dominate; to bring order to an order-less world, lessons you taught me as a child.'

Vara exclaimed, 'Lesson's I taught you?'

She sat in stunned silence, her mind returning to a time when she was forever visiting Head Master Almagest's office to explain Kuelack's behaviour. Regardless of her warnings and despite his slight frame, he repeatedly goaded boys bigger than him into fights, in an effort to prove he was their equal, but always losing despite his best efforts. Regularly, he returned home from Pellagrin's crying tears of anger, his clothes torn and ripped, his body covered in cuts and bruises despite the constant reprimands. Realising he would never win, Kuelack, instead of learning humility, did what all bullies do; he assembled a gang to back up his posturing and then continued challenging anyone that stood against him. Backed by his gang and his confidence growing, Kuelack then challenged Alfic. The previous defeats he suffered at his older brother's hands only making him more determined, more resolute. Never knowing when to back down, he became increasingly frustrated, accusing Alfic of being a coward when he turned his back. Kuelack could not marry compassion and understanding with strength and determination; nevertheless, he advanced through the ranks and by sheer force of will became the youngest Wizard ever to be voted onto the Sivan Council. Now it seemed that determination to dominate was all-consuming and fuelled his search for the Firebrand shards.

Her voice almost pleading, she blurted, 'Your art, Kuelack, is a trifling thing compared to the Firebrand shards. Having read the legends, you must know that you cannot control them through sheer force of will.'

She watched him intently as he straightened up and walked indignantly towards the window. When he said nothing, Vara shook her head despairingly; her son's silence told her everything she needed to know.

'The stone, even split into four, subjugates the possessor!' shouted Vara. 'Pellagrin himself knew this. That's why one of the greatest mages of our age hid them.'

'I will master the shards,' he proclaimed proudly. Then, in a voice filled with conviction, he announced, 'It was you who taught me that strength and power are everything, as is the money to finance that power. I'm the embodiment of you. I'm the son you always wanted; can't you see?'

Refusing to be side-tracked, Vara stated clearly, 'The stone is elemental and chaotic in nature, and you cannot control it. Your lust for it will become like a drug until it takes over completely. If you reunite the shards, civilization's petty concerns will matter for nought as it doesn't choose sides, neither does it have favourites. Through you, it will destroy us all.' She heaved a big sigh and, in a voice tinged with remorse, said, 'All I ever wanted was for you to be successful, but it seems I've spawned a tyrant. My greatest fear now is seeing you become Head Wizard here, allied to the shards. There is still time, Kuelack, to change before it's too late. It's about doing the right thing now; renounce this path you have chosen. Let me help you, because once on this path, there will be no turning back.'

'It's too late for that. Once people see mine is a better way, what I have done for the school...'

'Every tyrant in history has claimed his way is best.'

'A tyrant! You have me all wrong. People like you can't see beyond the ends of their noses, they just need someone to raise their expectations, to make them see...'

'Kuelack, enough!'

Hating what she knew she must do, she slowly reached into her ingredients bag hanging from her shoulder. Throwing a handful of club moss mixed with phosphorous at a candle on the desk, the mixture exploded in a cascade of blinding purple and orange light, however, as Vara produced and threw another concoction towards Kuelack an intense wind hurled her and the mixture across the room. She landed with a thud against the far wall. Through a haze of pain, Vara watched as Kuelack, hunched over and rubbing at his eyes, collapsed slowly towards the floor. Thinking she'd succeeded, she crawled painfully towards her bag, sorting through its contents now spilled across the floor. Even though she'd inhaled only a small dose of the powder, she could feel the mixture infusing her body, paralysing and controlling. Finding the small bottle containing the antidote, she drank it down.

'Ha,' spat Kuelack, 'very clever Mother,' and tasting his finger he said, 'A hint of Lily-of-the-Valley, Hops, Yarrow and a hint of the highly toxic, Spotted-Feverfew daisy. Bolstered by witchery, a mixture designed to paralyse me.'

She watched helplessly from her position laid prone on the floor as, with a series of pops and clicks, Kuelack stretched his neck. Straightening up, he spun around with menace.

'Did you really think your potions and powders would be a match for a Master of the Dark Arts?' Bending over her, his face looming large, he grasped her hair. Then, hauling Vara to her feet, he sat her back in the chair. He then squeezed her aching body with a fist of power.

'Very good Mother, I knew you would try something, but I never guessed you would attack me in my own chambers.'

'My intention was to paralyse you…!' she wheezed.

'And that's the only reason you're still alive. You must have known that I wouldn't allow you to oppose me in any way,' he sneered. 'Don't look so shocked. After all, I was taught deception and dishonesty from the master of trickery and half-truths, by the woman who specialised in pitting people against each other, especially her own children.' He then slammed his fists onto the tabletop, making her start. 'Well, congratulations Mother, I am the result of your efforts. Are you not impressed?' he hissed.

Feeling the antidote taking effect, she sat rigidly; looking up at him with her hands clasped together in her lap and, for the very first time in many years, she felt tears stinging her eyes. It was then that Pellagrin's words came back to haunt her.

Do not fret Vara Bruin; with our protection, your grandson stands more than an even chance.

She closed her eyes in trepidation and despaired as her fears about Aridain's future started to bear fruit.

'You cannot be serious enough to think a six-year-old boy is any threat to you?'

'In the future, a boy that powerful could become a very great threat indeed if not guided appropriately, I would much rather he grew up as an ally.'

'I don't understand.'

'Oh, I think you do. There's also his resemblance to this Dark Creature.'

Vara looked around the room in desperation, the hopelessness of her situation all too apparent. She had driven Kuelack to this, but not all was lost. Apart from their similar appearance, Kuelack had not made the connection, but if nothing was done, it would be only a matter of time.

'If you value his life and I know you do, you will keep this discussion here today private and cease any contact with the boy. Do I make myself clear?'

Vara looked at Kuelack defiantly.

'DO I MAKE MYSELF CLEAR?'

She nodded miserably. Despairingly, she studied his stony face and shook her head sadly.

'Kuelack, my youngest and most cherished, I'm now only just beginning to understand the monster to which I have given birth.'

Releasing her with an easy wave of his hand, Kuelack smiled. 'Now go, and remember, I'll be watching.'

Vara climbed painfully to her feet, putting on a performance as she always did. Collecting up the contents of her bag from the floor, she walked from the room with as much dignity as she could muster.

CHAPTER SIX

ALL HAIL GRADINE

Mass Martin stepped out into the gusty afternoon wind, wrapping his thick cloak about him as he set off towards the main building to attend yet another insufferable meeting with Kuelack. The Dark Lord was a man with ambition, like himself, who believed that the superior should preside over the inferior; however, their partnership was an uneasy one. They had become like two equally matched combatants circling each other warily in the ring; neither trusting the other; waiting for the slightest sign of weakness, but neither willing to make the first move.

Walking upon the cobbled path between the neatly tended borders, planted with nodding rows of autumn crocuses and cyclamen growing beneath small neatly cut bay trees, he came upon the Goddess Seline's statue and watched, captivated as the gusts of wind swirled water into the air from her bowl of plenty. It was said that if the water stops flowing from Seline's statue, that a great disaster will befall the school. *It was only a prophecy, and long may it remain so,* he thought.

Sat besides Seline's statue was Areca, teacher of magic and herb lore, and he returned her greeting with an insincere smile as she endeavoured to educate her class from the flapping pages of her formulae book. But as he passed, the students' conversations diminished, then stopped, as if at a premeditated signal. Psychic ability, as it always had, aroused mistrust and resentment. It was a response he had had a lifetime to get used to, even in these so-called enlightened times.

'It's a gut reaction, Student Martin,' his tutors had explained. 'No matter what a psychic's intent, ordinary people will never trust someone who, if they choose, could pilfer their every secret. The only course is to be the better person.'

While growing up, he had tried to heed their words, lead a normal life, but mistrust and resentment were rife, leading him to think there was more to their distrusting attitude. As he grew up, he started to question the meaning of normality and why he should conform at all until finally, he came to recognise 'normals' behaviour for what it was, envy and jealousy; they were covetous of his abilities, his kinds superiority; they just didn't like the fact that he was the next step in human evolution, a superior being. There is no dark or light magic, he mused, only me, and the strength and ruthless determination to use the tools I've been given.

And then one day, while searching through long-forgotten manuscripts, he came across a document, and within that document, he found hints of an uprising by mind walkers led by a psychic called Caberartus; an uprising that had ultimately failed. Delving further, with only clues and snippets to work with, he'd concluded that normals had attempted to erase this episode from history in order to discourage a repeat of the past. He had also found evidence of headgear, worn by warriors opposed to Caberartus, made of a rare metal called Indium, designed to keep mind walkers from your mind.

This time, he thought vehemently, *if the helmets are destroyed and we control the source, me together with my fellow Psychics can succeed where Caberartus failed.*

Shutting out the students' primordial thoughts, cast about by their primitive minds, he approached the single oak door set into the wall of the keep, guarded by a single warrior.

The lonely vigil harked back nearly a hundred and twenty years, to when this particular oak wood door nearly cost Pellagrin and its defenders the school. A Dark Mage called Zakan had, with a word, gained entrance along with a small band of followers after a month-long siege, having been aided by a traitor here at the school. He failed, however, because of a particularly vigilant young student wizard called Almagest who rallied the defences.

Returning his acknowledgement, the guard placed his hand against the twisted ivy-leaved scrollwork embossed with arcane symbols and muttered a single word. Grasping the ancient handle, Mass pushed and with a groan the door swung slowly inwards. Entering the keep, he returned the students' and staff's respectful deference and then started up the grand stone stairway. Upon reaching Kuelack's apartment, however, the door remained shut.

Knocking, it surprised him when Gradine opened the door, looking nothing like the spoilt, pampered socialite he'd become accustomed to seeing. She wore a utilitarian light blue blouse and tan breaches, with her light golden braided hair tied up over her head.

'What's going on here?' he demanded in his high, shrill voice. 'Where's Kuelack?'

'He's away and until he returns, I'm conducting my husband's affairs.'

He stared into her hazel eyes, trying to gauge her mood and fathom her intent.

'Had I summoned you to this meeting, would you have attended?'

'Certainly not!'

'But you're here now, are you not?' said Gradine, her ivory skinned face taking on a raptor like quality. 'What's the matter Mass, cat got your tongue, scared of a meagre woman?'

'We both know you are no meagre woman, Gradine.'

Staring at her astutely for several moments, he then peered into the apartment and inquired, 'And where is Ramus?'

'He is also away.'

'Strange, don't you think that I wasn't informed?'

It was a shrewd move, appointing Gradine to oversee his affairs. She was dangerous in an entirely different way: unpredictable and possessing of an underlying cruelty.

Knowing full well that the pair was on a mission to retrieve the Firebrand shards, he demanded, 'So, where have they gone?'

'I don't know. He only said he was on a mission to retrieve the shards.'

'Don't lie to me, Gradine.'

Pointing to her head, she said, 'You can take a look in here if you like; it's not as if I can keep any secrets from the great Mass Martin.'

It was true, even though she knew the purpose of the mission, she knew not where. His eyes narrowing, he said, 'Very well, I will attend your meeting and hear if you have anything meaningful to contribute.'

Entering the apartment, Mass glanced at Tallus, dressed in the brown-edged white robes of an Animistic teacher, who sat looking out from the bay window seat. Acknowledging Tallus's respectful nod, Mass watched Gradine warily as she sat down at Kuelack's desk, where she unfolded a small pile of papers.

'May I congratulate you Gradine on you and your husband's plan to incriminate Keegan and Mace,' said Tallus suddenly. Mass knew it was an attempt by the animistic to diffuse the tense atmosphere.

'It wasn't difficult,' said Gradine immodestly. 'The gamekeeper had been following Hogan doggedly; it was just a matter of getting all the elements in the right place at the right time. It's only failing is that the gamekeeper and the Greysword are still alive. If I had my way, they'd be dead and their heads adorning the school gates.'

'Yes, very accomplished, I'm sure. Nevertheless, thanks to Kuelack's lack of persuasion, Ramus and I had to endure an enquiry.'

'And had your control of Exedra been more complete, an enquiry wouldn't have been necessary,' Gradine sneered. 'We assumed that Exedra was ripe for control and manipulation. It should have been an easy matter for my husband to persuade Exedra to our way of thinking; but obviously she still retains some sensibility.'

Unperturbed by Gradin's accusations, Mass replied calmly, 'If the plan is to succeed, she must be seen to be backing us of her own free will. If the school's residents discover she is being coerced, Alfic's suspicions would be validated and the people would rally to his side, undoing everything we've strived for, she is simply not ready for that yet.'

Gradine turned, and with savage intent said, 'That is not your decision.'

'The mind is 'my' speciality. I'll decide when she's ripe for exploitation,' said Mass slickly.

Gradine's eyes narrowed and with a piercing stare she said, 'I have my husband's complete trust and, like him, I will not tolerate your excuses or innate blunderings.'

'Don't get notions above your station Gradine, Kuelack knows that without me he can kiss his plans goodbye.'

'I don't understand why we have to skulk around; it would be an easy matter for us to grind these people beneath our feet.'

'Your enthusiasm is appreciated, Tallus.' Then, almost inaudibly, Gradine growled, 'However, Mass is right, we must proceed with caution or else everything will be undone.'

Mass studied Tallus's gaunt-looking face, feeling an affinity with this young man who, like him, ran away from home to Pellagrin's; only instead of Gonda, he ran away from the capital of Srinigar, Allanal; a rigid, religious nation ruled by zealots, where magic is outlawed. As he understood it, Tallus's parents chastised and isolated him to purge him of his gift. When that failed, they informed the Sringarian priesthood, an order of fanatical extremists, to condemn his magic and sentenced him to death.

Just then, there was a knock on the door.

'Good, she's here,' announced Gradine. 'Tallus, if you would?'

'Gradine, gentleman,' greeted Magen, inclining her head. Then, with a look of indifference, Magen walked serenely into the room, followed reverently by Tallus and eased herself into a chair.

Turning away, she gazed out through the window across the combat field, watching as students dressed in the school's familiar deep crimson leather tunics, guided by the school's archery teachers, loosed their arrows at targets positioned beneath the stately chestnut trees.

Then she caught sight of her reflection in the glass, at the dark shadows and gaunt appearance caused by Kuelack's alien calling. Gazing from clear bright blue eyes, she studied a face scored with worry lines that had appeared around her full lips and upon her silky skinned brow.

She had come to realise that if she was to survive this ordeal, she would have to match her colleague's disdainful demeanours; even exceed them. Taking a deep breath, knowing the comments her appearance would draw, she turned, withdrew her hood, and stared at them boldly.

'I am pleased to see you are recovering from your 'family squabbles', Magen,' stated Mass boldly, 'although I'm thinking it was much more than that.'

'And may I congratulate you, Mass, on your bold move to coerce Exedra into placing you instead of Savarin on the council, especially in my brother's absence.'

'Thank you, Magen, although I don't know what you're implying. My only thought was of a more efficient way to carry out the tasks your brother has set for me.'

'We both know that efficiency has nothing to do with it, or loyalty to my husband,' spat Gradine.

Feeling the bruises now nearly healed, Magen rubbed absently at her forehead and her thoughts turned to the events following Alfic and Kuelack's altercation at the fair...

'You would interfere with my authority,' Kuelack had raged, 'defy me in front of the whole school!'

'Punish me,' she had pleaded, kneeling, head bowed in front of him, 'but please don't hurt my children. I'll do anything.'

'Dear Sister,' he had said almost kindly, 'you must understand my position; if I treat my subordinates mercifully, our enemies will think me weak.' She had watched in trepidation as he had taken a calming breath. 'However, any useful information you can provide me with could determine how merciful I will be.'

Like a drowning person grasping at straws, she had blurted, 'Yes, yes, I have. A few weeks back, when Ramus confronted me, he asked if I would join him. He said together we could defeat you. I refused. That's when Ramus tried to kill me, I swear it on my children's lives.'

The mental and physical beating had been as savage as it had been heartless and consoling herself that her punishment could have been a lot worse; she had picked herself up off the floor.

'I hope a lesson has been learnt today?'

'Yes, it has, thank you Brother,' she had said submissively.

'Good, I'm glad that we understand each other, and for you and your children's sake, I pray we never have to do this again.'

As if nothing out of the ordinary had happened, Kuelack had turned and walked towards his desk. 'Oh, one more thing, while I'm away, I want you to keep an eye on Mass. I don't trust him.'

She had replied with as much dignity as she could muster, 'As you wish.'

'Good, now run along.'

Appalled at her brother's callousness, she had hastily left his chambers…

If only Vanir had returned sooner with the news that he'd found Almagest's carriage; now everything had changed and whether she liked it or not, this was her world now, a world where only the strong would survive. She still cared for Alfic and her father, less so for her mother, but on the other hand, she still felt, despite his cruelty and his threats, a profound loyalty to Kuelack. It was wrong, she knew; it shouldn't be, but it was.

'Right to business,' announced Gradine. 'Thanks to Tallus's insect spies, it seems the Bruins aren't as compliant as we thought, so something must be done. I cannot risk Alfic and his family uniting the shop keepers against us, so I have decided that he is to die,' announced Gradine, looking meaningfully in her direction. 'Tallus, I'm assigning this task to you.'

'To me, what of the school, the teachers?' questioned Tallus sceptically. 'If I kill Alfic, surely there will be a reaction.'

'Don't worry, the older teachers have become apathetic, wallowing in the peaceful, stress-free life that Almagest has created here. They'll do nothing. With Alfic dead, the school will come around to our way of thinking,' declared Gradine.

'And what of the students?' asked Mass.

'That particular problem is in hand,' stated Gradine triumphantly.

'And what role am I to play in your grand schemes?' asked Mass.

'The task I have for you, Mass, is very special indeed. Ok, let's get down to business, shall we?' announced Gradine. 'We have a lot to get through.'

There was to be no more beating around the bush. Alfic was to be killed. His death, she reasoned, was just a consequence of the events taking place at the school. Gazing out the window upon the combat field once more, Magen reasoned that if she were to survive this ordeal, she must close off her sentimentality and compassion and put her family from her mind.

CHAPTER SEVEN

TROUBLESOME VERMIN

'You two look like a couple of drowned rats,' chuckled Keegan, helping Elgin climb out from the large, square, tin rainwater-collecting tank; located in between the school's two plant houses. 'I taught you that hornet flies are dangerous.'

'Hey, it's not funny, those things are bloody painful,' gasped Elgin grumpily, massaging the back of his neck.

'So, where did they come from?' Keegan asked.

'The timber sheds.' Looking at his brother accusingly, Elimi shook the water from his mop of thick, ginger hair and said, 'I don't understand it. When we entered the timber shed, Elgin just started waving his arms around.'

'Hey, don't blame this on me. I told you not to go in there!'

Decreed by the council, Keegan had gladly stayed away from the school and taken only a passing interest in its affairs; that was until Sorin had informed him Mace was under lock and key as punishment for defending Alfic at the fair. It was a situation that he could not, would not tolerate. So, risking the school's wrath, Keegan had once more taken to covertly tailing Kuelack and his lackeys and, in particular, Mass Martin and Tallus, his intent to find a way to help Mace and prevent any more of his friends disappearing.

'So, what are you doing here, Keegan, apart from laughing at us?' enquired Elgin wryly. 'We thought you were, you know, banned?'

'I was in there,' he said, quickly pointing to one of the plant houses, 'sheltering from the hornets.'

In fact, that was a lie. Earlier that day, he had spotted Mass Martin walking across the fields away from the farm. His curiosity aroused and using the walnut trees for cover, he had followed Mass along the cobbled path, watching as he disappeared through the tree line beyond the mill. It was then that he heard the excited shrieks and shouts of Aridain, Selva and Duran, who were playing by the stream. Concluding the psychic had been spying on the children, he had watched and followed the diminutive Mind Master as he had emerged from the brush and returned to the school.

'So, what were you doing in the woodworking sheds?' retorted Keegan.

'Mass Martin insisted we destroy the nest. We said it wasn't our job, but he insisted,' said Elgin.

Why would Mass Martin be so insistent about removing a hornet flies' nest? thought Keegan, looking oddly at Elgin and Elimi. *For that matter, how would he know there was a nest in the woodworking shed in the first place?* Then it struck him: the brothers' appearance was no accident. His thoughts returning to the present, Keegan said sternly, 'Go to the apothecary and get something to rub on those stings. I'll deal with this.'

'Keegan, please don't do anything stupid,' pleaded Elgin.

'Hey, it's me!'

Making his way to the timber shed, he opened the door carefully. Immediately, his senses were assailed by the aroma of sawn and chiselled wood; but it was also accompanied by the faint tang of vinegar. Together with this smell, he heard an all too familiar droning sound. Upon searching the roof timbers, he located an undulating pumpkin-sized mass clustered around one of the timber beams. Deeming his pursuit of the Mind Master of more importance, he pulled the door shut.

Running as fast as he could, he reached the corner of the old perimeter wall where, quickly scanning the open courtyard, he glimpsed Mass Martin shuffling towards the food hall. Hurrying across the courtyard, he noted the Mind Master disappear down the storage alley behind the kitchens; suspecting a trap, he looked around cautiously. Peering into the early evening mist, he tiptoed stealthily between the slop barrels and empty wooden crates, listening for any signs of the psychic. Suddenly, there was a thud as the doors to the rear of the kitchens were flung open. Then two figures emerged dressed in leather aprons, each clasping a vicious-looking meat cleaver. Retreating behind the slop barrels, he watched, his keen eyes studying their uneasy behaviour as they searched the alleyway in front of them. Instinctively placing his hand firmly on his knife handle, he stood up.

'Label, Jarrow, what's going on?'

'There it is, GET IT!'

Keegan stared dumbfounded as the two cook's assistants, men he had known for years, charged with their meat cleavers held high.

'Hey guys, don't be stupid,' Keegan shouted, drawing his knife. 'What the hell are you playing at? It's me, Keegan.' Realising they had not understood a word, he rolled a barrel full of slops down the narrow alleyway in an effort to halt their progress.

Watching the two young men floundering around in a rotting mess of leftover food, he again tried to reason with them.

'Come on guys, I don't want to hurt you. What's going on?'

'Hiss all you like Goshen, we will kill you before you can feed off anyone here,' and climbing to their feet they advanced, slipping and sliding their way through the rotting food.

'Goshen! Are you crazy? I'm not a ghoul, it's me K...'

Avoiding their wild swings, he timed his rush to perfection as Jarrow swung his cleaver; he ducked and dived, driving his elbow up into Jarrow's midriff. With a loud gasp, Jarrow doubled over and when Label regained his balance, he was far too slow as Keegan pushed the pair sideways across the narrow yard. Ignoring their groans and gasps, he ran down the alley until he reached the kitchen door, knowing that the only way to end this was to confront the psychic teacher. Cautiously entering the hot steamy kitchen, he spun around to see Amy Dickson, the portly Head Chef, clasping a freshly plucked chicken in her hand and staring at him with a puzzled expression.

She exclaimed, 'Keegan, are you mad? What are you doing in here? Put that knife away, you'll scare the good-paying folk.'

'No-can-do Amy, I'm trying to catch a pest. I thought I saw one come in here.'

'You didn't see Label and Jarrow, did you?' asked Amy, scratching her head. 'They suddenly dropped what they were doing and disappeared out the back.'

'Yes, I passed them a moment ago; the pest has tricked them good and proper.'

Just then, the two men in question burst into the kitchen, brandishing their cleavers.

'There it is! Amy, move before it sucks your soul out through your eyeballs.'

Walking purposefully up to Label, Amy exclaimed, 'What are you babbling about? Get back to work. The customers need feeding.' Then screwing up her face and holding her nose, she said, 'Phew, you two smell like an Ardent wolf's scenting post.'

'Just step away, Amy. We'll deal with this creature.'

'Creature, have you gone mad? You haven't been on the snuff again, have you?' she asked, studying his face. 'I always said it would turn you crazy.'

But the men weren't listening and bundled the portly cook aside, advancing on Keegan, convinced he was a half-dead spirit.

Keegan, poised on the balls of his feet, made ready to pounce. Then, without warning, the legs of the two enchanted cook's assistants suddenly gave way and they collapsed to the floor. Spinning around, his knife poised to strike, Keegan cautiously entered the dining area through the thick oak doors; pushing past travellers and astonished students alike. Sensing Mass was close, Keegan located the weaselly man sat serenely at one of the sturdy round oak-built tables, a glass of steaming liquid in his hand.

'Careful, you might hurt somebody with that thing,' said Mass, a sly grin on his gaunt face. 'Please Keegan, sit down. You're causing a scene.'

In silence, and without taking his eyes from the grinning psychic, Keegan approached slowly. Grasping one of the wooden chairs; he spun the seat around, then sat astride it to enable him to get to his feet quickly should the need arise. Then, burying the knife in the tabletop, he stared boldly into the psychic's eyes.

'In light of the fact that you have been banished from the school, you're either very naïve or very stupid.'

'This is my job, to eradicate troublesome vermin, especially when that vermin imprisons my friends.'

55

Keegan watched as a serious scowl replaced Mass's smug, self-satisfied smile.

'Then you and your friends shouldn't challenge their betters. Do you think you can just follow me around and think I'll not notice?' said Mass sharply.

Feeling a childish sense of achievement, Keegan said, 'I only follow people who spy on children while they play in the fields or on fairground rides.'

'Since when is it a crime to enjoy a walk in the countryside or enjoy the delights of the fair?' countered Mass offhandedly.

'Don't make me laugh, since when have you enjoyed a walk in the countryside? If you're so innocent, why did you try to delay me?'

'Because I don't like being followed!'

Keegan decided to change tack.

'You know, there's a decree, forbidding teachers abusing their powers on the school grounds, especially regarding students.'

'I'm surprised you care,' said Mass offhandedly. 'It's well known you want nothing to do with people. Why is that?'

'What I do, in my own time, is my business.'

'And so is mine,' replied Mass irritably. Then more considered, he said, 'For the record, Mace's imprisonment had nothing to do with me, and my alliance with Kuelack is purely self-seeking. We are on the same side, you and me. We fight against the same things.'

Keegan watched as the small, arrogant, bald-headed man sat calmly dressed in his opulent blue and green trimmed robes, knowing his thoughts were as clear as an open book.

'I doubt that.'

Mass regarded Keegan haughtily.

'We both want what's best for the school and we both fight for what's right.' Mass Martin then smiled and shook his head. 'But I can see it in your eyes, read it in your thoughts; just like everyone else, you can't or won't trust my kind.'

'Maybe it's because "your kind" tried to turn us humans into puppets,' cursed Keegan.

He watched as Mass Martin smiled knowingly, then closed his eyes briefly. 'You humans will never learn that opposing a mind master is futile, let me demonstrate.' Keegan turned and looked up at Amy

Dickson, who had suddenly appeared with a pot full of stew in her hands.

Stood before a wary Keegan and staring straight ahead, Amy Dickson dropped the scolding liquid down Keegan's tunic front and into his lap.

Cursing, Keegan leapt to his feet to prevent the stew burning his skin. Amy suddenly looked down in bewilderment at the empty pot in her hand and Keegan's stew- stained tunic.

'Keegan, oh, I'm terribly sorry, I... I don't know what happened..., uh..., I must have been daydreaming, I'm sorry I ...'

'It's all right Amy, it wasn't your fault, it was mine,' said Keegan impassively.

Keegan waited until Amy had cleaned the mess from the floor and then moved his face closer to the Mind Master's.

'Now heed MY warning, Mass. Stay away from those children and my friends!'

'Why? Is there something particular about them you wish to conceal?' Mass said knowingly. 'I could wipe your memory of the past twenty-four hours, or turn you into a mindless idiot, but you already are. But I think instead, I'll have you arrested and put in prison for disobeying the Sivan's decree.'

Keegan tried to stand but found he couldn't move. He stared at Mass with intent, 'Remember you have to sleep sometime, so before you close your eyes at night, think of me drawing my knife across your throat.'

'Threats are difficult to carry out from inside a locked cell,' smirked Mass, as two of the school's guard, swords drawn, hurried towards them.

'Keegan Fold, you're under arrest for disobeying Sivan decree.'

His knife still embedded firmly in the tables top, Keegan's arms raised above his head of their own accord, they were then twisted behind his back. The guardsmen then roughly placed restraints about his wrists and Keegan, now free of Mass's manipulations, was marched compliantly from the kitchens.

Sat upon one of the ornate wrought-iron benches in the centre of the courtyard, shaded by Pellagrin's giant oak, Gradine shrugged indifferently as she read the report of Keegan's arrest. Not as permanent as death, but she would attend to that later. Her mood now suitably raised, she unfolded the latest letter from her father and read...

"I have sent two entire legions north to Zapata's border with King Pheronis's approval, to curb the incursion of the so-called barbarians ranging south across our northern border. Zapata's remaining dragon riders, still loyal to the throne, continue to endure despite our best efforts. Also, according to my network, Srinagar's religious leaders have placed their forces on high alert; responding to sightings of Navarian warriors crossing their eastern borders."

Gradine smirked. 'While that weak-minded fool Pheronis sits on the throne, powerless to intervene, the plan proceeds apace. Soon it will be all out war, and once the populous sees how apathetic the king has become, they will transfer power to her father and her husband. Then, having served his purpose, the king would be disposed of, quietly and discreetly.

King Pheronis, she had no sympathy for him, who, like all men, was so easily swayed by an alluring smile and the promise of a 'no strings attached' night of passion. It had been so easy for her father, having discovered the king's illicit forays as a younger man, to gain the king's confidence as chief advisor and spymaster. Desperate to keep this information from Queen Annul and hold on to his throne, Pheronis was now an unwilling pawn.

Conversely, their plan to control the school and quell its occupants was progressing slowly; thanks to the fly in the ointment that was Alfic and his interfering friends, so her strategy was simple, deny Alfic's family support and isolate them.

Standing and straightening the folds in her clothes, she folded the letter. Placing it inside her embroidered cloak, she hissed determinedly, 'Time to bolster the ranks'.

Reaching the entrance to the fishmongers, Gradine stood beneath the blue and white sign in the shape of a leaping salmon, swaying noisily in the breeze. She produced a vinaigrette, full of herbs, and held it beneath her nose to counter the smell, then opened the door. The inside of the shop was a very simple affair, with the walls and floor needing a repaint with lime wash. Fish were displayed on simple wooden display cases, together with freshwater mussels and crayfish caught in the school's two lakes. As well as local produce, there were oysters and prawns in barrels of brine, together with smoked mackerel and sea bass which were shipped upriver from the port of Tsana in Navar, and then by road to the school. At the back of the shop, behind the counter, was a door that led to the rear of the small shack where she presumed Irvine ate and slept.

Gradine rang the bell on the counter and Irvine suddenly appeared from the rear of the property, smiling warmly, 'Gradine, for what do I owe this pleasure? Not here to purchase fish, I wager,' he said, smiling impishly.

'Do not confuse me for my empty-headed sister-in-law,' she said, looking in disdain at his apron covered in blood and fish guts.

Frowning, Irvine said, 'What can I do for you, Gradine?'

Reaching inside the pocket of her cloak and throwing him a silver coin, she pointed at his display.

'Two of those,' she said, her face looking as though she'd discovered something horrendous on the bottom of her shoe.

'Carp, excellent choice. They're in their prime at the moment.'

Gazing in wonder at the coin and running his fish-stained hands through his short-cropped, russet brown hair Irvine, his emerald green eyes drinking in the coin's lustre exclaimed, 'Whoa, I can't accept this, this is more than I make in six months!'

Waiting for Irvine to appreciate fully the coin's value, Gradine continued, 'The greengrocer and the winemaker accepted my generosity gladly, as did the blacksmith.'

'Meaning no disrespect, Madam Gradine.'

'Then it's settled. You will accept the payment. There's no shame in craving beautiful things. You will find, Irvine, that my husband's rule is not such a bad proposition.'

'And the price for this... generosity?'

'Vigilance is all I ask and the odd snippet of information. If you prove your worth, there's plenty more where that came from.'

Gazing longingly at the coin's silvery lustre, Irvine considered, 'I'll have to think about it.'

'Of course, but I'm sure you'll come to the right decision in the end; I really want you to become part of our... the school's new order.'

'Well... if my friends have changed their minds...?'

'I'm glad you're beginning to see things my way.'

Absent minded, Irvine said, 'Oh, don't forget your fish.'

Gradine smiled. *Compared to Gable and Bern, that was easy.*

Exiting Irvine's store, she threw the fish disdainfully into the cobbled alleyway between his cabin and the stables, as if the fish had suddenly come to life.

This act was noticed by two cats and a Scarrion lizard. Sniffing the air eagerly, they appeared from beneath Irvine's fish shop and the stables next door. After a brief moment of posturing and hissing over the spoils, the cats and the Scarrion lizard, each with a prize, disappeared behind the free-standing shack.

In autumn's early morning heat, Vara peered out between the kitchen curtains towards the branches of a nearby oak tree and, sure enough, there it was, the Harvestman; sat in the upper branches, its emerald green carapace glinting in the dappled sunlight. Vara knew it had been sent by Tallus, under Kuelack's orders, to keep an eye on her. Unnoticed by others in the village, it had sat its lonely vigil ever since she had returned from her fateful encounter with Kuelack, never wavering, never deviating; leaving its post, she assumed, only to feed.

Her face set in a dark scowl while studying ancient scrolls; held down by multi-faceted glass paperweights, she knew her anger was not just the result of her forced separation from her grandson, or her self-inflicted incarceration; it resulted from her experimentation with dragon's blood. Peering about the kitchen, she stared at the grizzly contents of a bizarre ritual; relinquished by her kind centuries past. Half-emptied vials of dragon's blood stood in a wooden rack upon the kitchen workbench. Next to the stained and blooded instruments and above the smouldering fire stood a tripod bearing a pewter dish still filled with the thick dark liquid.

Knowing the risks associated with the exotic substance, she had taken just enough to help retain her youth and prowess. Now the only course available; if she were to defend her grandson successfully, was to play Kuelack at his own game, so she had slowly increased the dose. The curse of her kind, the ancient practice of blood magic could send her temper, her anger, spiralling out of control, if she was not careful, and she would slowly and inexorably turn into a debased yellow hag.

She only hoped that when the reckoning was upon her, she was strong enough to retain some sense of her humanity, some sense of right and wrong.

She looked up then. Sensing Lascana was on her way, Vara marched out of the kitchen, along the hallway and then peered out from the small window beside the front door; watching as Lascana marched resolutely up the cobbled road towards the rose-covered, wrought iron archway. Lascana was angry, as she knew she would be, so straightening her light olive skirt and simple, white blouse, Vara arranged her mop of striped dark green and white hair and watched Lascana as she slammed the garden gate behind her. Readying herself as Lascana strode up the path, Vara opened the front door, as Lascana raised her fist to strike.

Then, with as much dignity as she could muster, she said, 'Hello Lascana, I wondered how long it would take before you appeared.'

Lascana, lifting her chin and pulling her hood back from her face, said irately, 'Hello Vara, can I come in?'

Standing her ground, Vara announced firmly, 'No!'

'Very well, there's no need for me to come inside to tell you what I have to say.'

'Get to it then?' Vara stated seriously.

'Mace is in prison and now Keegan's been arrested.'

'Yes, I know.'

'So, what are you going to do about it? We're dropping like flies, Vara, and you just sit here like lady-muck, unmoved and apathetic...'

'I do not expect you to understand my reasoning in these matters, Lascana...'

'I'm not intelligent enough, is that it?'

Vara let out a long, steadying breath. 'That's not what I said...'

'Vara, this is bigger than your ego and bigger than my pride. There must be something you can do, a spell maybe?' Visibly calming herself with an effort, Lascana said, 'Hate me if you will. I don't care, but don't deny my son. He needs his family; he needs you!'

Vara then shook her head sadly. 'Me doing nothing is for my grandson's safety. Kuelack has fingers in many pies; ears and eyes not just around the school but all over the realm. He's just too powerful. It's useless resisting. If I interfere, Kuelack will react. He will kill Aridain rather than see him turned into an enemy. Magen is my grandson's teacher now...'

Lascana looked up at her in shocked surprise. 'You're scared of your own children?'

'Not of them, but what they're capable of.'

Lascana stared at her. 'It all makes sense now. You knew about the voice in his head, didn't you? It told you what might happen, so you cast a spell and filled him full of sweets.'

Vara felt her anger rising once more and gritted her teeth. She then looked towards the heavens and held her hands together as if in prayer.

'I am guilty of nothing more than ensuring my grandson's future.'

Being watched and listened to made it hard to get the message across without being heard. Then it came to her.

'Remember the landlord who evicted you and Alfic?'

Lascana regarded Vara with a puzzled stare. 'Of course I do. He deserved what he got; but what has that to do with ...'

Vara then grasped Lascana's arm in a vice like grip and, staring intently into her eyes, hissed, 'Then remember that, but if you've truly lost faith in me, or doubt my words, then trust your son's guardian.'

Lascana smiled, understanding crossing her face, 'As strange as it seems, I can sympathise with your dilemma.'

Relaxing slightly, Vara suddenly looked up and said ruthlessly, 'I think you've been drinking too much of that dandelion and burdock wine you're so famous for. Now good day Lascana, I have things to attend to,' and with that Vara slammed the door.

CHAPTER EIGHT

STONE OF INIQUITY

Skirting the southern border of Aymara along the Chondite coast, Kuelack held on tightly to the spines running along the back of the lithe, silver-scaled dragon that glided noiselessly on light night-time winds. Flying over the coastline, they came upon an outcrop of land that jutted out into the waters of the Navas Straight. Urged on by Kuelack, the dragon flew over a man-made walkway connecting the granite edifice to the mainland. Then, on Kuelack's command, the dragon banked sharply with an adjustment of its leathery, fibrous wings and thick sinuous tail. Diving silently between two steep cliff faces towards a fortress and its attendant buildings, perched precariously upon the stark rocky outcrop, the Dragon, in a burst of dust and straw, alighted in the darkened courtyard, scattering terrified horses, stable boys and attendants. Leaping from the dragon's back before the guards could call the fortress to arms, Kuelack strode towards the great hall, and gesturing, burst the large throne room doors from their hinges. Striding commandingly into the main hall, the magnificent dragon at his back, Kuelack stood imperiously with hands on hips, glaring around the sumptuously hung walls and ornately tiled floors. In the deafening silence, he studied the castle's nobles and dignitaries; their faces now set in various expressions of shock and bewilderment.

'Don't get up,' he sneered. 'Judging by this castle's luxury and opulence, and by your full tables and even fuller bellies, I'd say the seas have recovered from the centuries long devastation.'

'What is the meaning of this outrage? Where are my guards?' interrogated a rotund man dressed in sumptuous, kingly clothing, his bulbous face flushed with rage.

'Cowering in fright, I don't doubt, Bharest.'

Standing from a large, cushioned and gilded, ornate throne at the far end of the banqueting table, the portly ruler demanded, 'You have me at a disadvantage Sir, who are…? Wait a minute, I remember you, you're from Pellagrin's school; you were here during last year's trade negotiations. You accompanied Exedra Mane.'

Kuelack demanded, 'Sit down, you overstuffed fool. My reason for accompanying her had nothing to do with trade negotiations!' Then, with a look, he forced the King back down into his throne. 'This matter does not concern kings or their like, your wizard, Torkval, on the other hand…'

Kuelack watched expectantly as a slim, middle-aged man sporting thick, dark eyebrows and a thin, dark beard stood slowly from his chair seated next to the King. He was dressed in extravagant green and brown armour and carried an ornately decorated spear.

'I have feared the day you would return, Kuelack Bruin.'

'Return; what do you mean, Torkval?' Bharest boomed.

'Be silent!' snarled Torkval. 'This does not concern you.'

'You dare…!'

'Where is it, Torkval? Where is it hidden?' Kuelack roared in a voice that made the astonished throng recoil in fear. 'You know of what I speak.'

Stepping forward, Torkval said, 'You've had a wasted journey Kuelack, the shard is not here.'

'Shard, what nonsense is this, Torkval? I demand you tell me what is going on!' bellowed Bharest.

'Silence Bharest, if you want to survive this day, sit down and be quiet,' ordered Torkval. 'I know of this mage and his lust for power. He will not be satisfied until he has torn this fortress apart.'

Walking purposefully towards Torkval and Bharest, sat at the far end of the food-laden table, past the banqueters muttering nervously, Kuelack sneered, 'And I know you Torkval, the ambitionless Mage and his king who rules over the apathetic. I am not a frightened child, nor am I as gullible as these fat, indulgent dignitaries. One of the Firebrand shards resides here in this very hall, hidden in plain sight, so I will ask you one last time, WHERE IS IT?'

'Firebrand shard?' exclaimed Bharest. 'This is nonsense. We cannot give you what we do not have.'

'Liar!' accused Kuelack aggressively.

'Please Kuelack, we know not of what you speak.' placated King Bharest, throwing Torkval a meaningful stare, 'As we all know, the Firebrand stone is but a myth and even if it was real, we would be foolish indeed to hide such an object here. I assure you, apart from a few marble busts, one of which is a very good likeness of my lady wife, we are hiding nothing sinister here. Let us break bread and drink together so you and your mighty beast may leave this place in friendship.'

'Do you take me for a mindless Oscan bird with its head in the sand, Torkval? Offers of hospitality from this fool will not placate me!'

Accompanying Kuelack up the smooth granite steps, a look of confusion upon his portly face, King Bharest said, 'No, we take you as a man of reason who only believes what his senses tell him. Look around, if you must, take your time,' he offered.

Examining the fragile sculptures one-at-a-time, Kuelack grasped one of the stone columns in a fierce grip, studying its surface. It showed no additional discolouration and nothing out of the ordinary, only the bust. Then, feeling its texture, he turned to Torkval.

'This fortress and peninsula were left unscarred by Dacron's bid for power, it is made of granite and ironstone, is it not? The very same substance as the rock on which it stands, the remnants of an ancient volcano, if I'm not mistaken. The other plinths are made of the same rock, all except this one, which is made of a mineral called malachite, also known as the transforming stone,' said Kuelack.

Bharest said simply, 'It's been here for hundreds of years, a gift from Pellagrin the Brave, if my history serves me.'

'Ironic that part of the very same stone that caused so much harm should reside here. Bharest, you and the rulers before you have been deceived by the very man you trusted, with a delusion of exquisite complexity.' He turned and addressed the throng. 'All of you have been deceived. Haven't they Torkval?' boomed Kuelack. 'Observe; the object I seek is here.'

Kneeling, Kuelack pressed his hands against the cold malachite pedestal. At first nothing happened, but then slowly the plinth began to dissolve and decay until alone on the topmost step sat a small Malachite stone casket.

Suddenly, Torkval thrust his spear into the air, and a strange blue light flooded the chamber. 'Kill the defiler!' he bellowed.

The dragon roared as guards, together with the feasting guests, so meek and compliant only moments before, jumped to their feet. Brandishing any object that they could lay their hands on, their faces twisted in unrestrained bestiality, they ran shrieking towards Kuelack and the dragon.

Kuelack spun around at the sound of rasping steel as Bharest drew his ceremonial sword and ran towards him. The sword flashed, the king's speed undiminished with age, but Kuelack was quicker, parrying the sword's dulled edge as it arched towards him. He then twisted, tearing the weapon from the king's grip, and thrust it into his chest.

'You may kill this ruler, but you will not prevail... would-be destroyer of worlds,' gasped a voice that was not Bharest's. 'The people of this fortress... will defend the shard... to the last.'

'So be it, Torkval,' Kuelack declared.

Scattering the nearest attackers with a sweep of his arm, Kuelack opened the casket and grasped the small silken bag inside and held it up for Torkval to see. 'No one will prevent me from fulfilling my destiny, Torkval,' said Kuelack, pulling the sword free of the king's dead body, which flopped jellyfish like onto the stone steps. 'Not even this fortress's bewitched occupants.'

Stepping over the king's lifeless body, Kuelack thrust the small silken bag into the folds of his cloak. He then peered about the hall, now filled with enraged cries and the serpentine hissing of flames.

'Generations of mages before me have been charged with the shard's protection, to watch over and guard against corrupt, selfish people such as you, obsessed with domination.'

'You chastise me for my malice and yet you use these people to your own ends. We are not so different, Torkval.'

'Yes, and I do it willingly,' Torkval bellowed angrily. 'The shards are evil incarnate and the world will be a better place once the Elemental destroys them for good.'

At that point, archers appeared from the balconies around the hall's periphery and soldiers filed into the hall through the shattered entranceway.

'Kill Kuelack and that abominable dragon!' commanded Torkval.

With a gesture, Kuelack deflected the volley of arrows that lanced into the remaining banqueters, then with another gesture the archers' longbows burst into flames; causing the archers to release the flaming weapons. Screaming like enraged griffons, the packed ranks of archers then vacated their lofty positions and drew their swords. Below, the silver dragon scattered the surviving banqueters with a sweep of its scaly tail and blankets of fire, as the castle's suicidal residents clawed and tore at its armoured body.

'It's time you realised, Torkval, that I am not a man to be trifled with,' boomed Kuelack, gesturing once more. On his command, several stone blocks from the shattered doorway rose and then soared through the air. Torkval stood at the base of the steps and held his spear aloft, deflecting the rain of masonry.

'I wondered when you would show your hand, Torkval, now that your puppets are all but gone. I wonder; if they knew of your betrayal, would they still be so willing to serve you?'

'Don't waste your breath attempting to try and sway them to dreams of power and greed, Kuelack!' shouted Torkval. 'They are tied to me and subject to my power, oblivious to everything except defending the shard. Now return it to me.'

'I have not travelled all this way to be denied by the likes of a second-rate magician. I am the youngest ever to attain the rank of Wizard Master and for good reason.'

'And it's for the sake of the lands of Aymara and the fate of millions that I must deny you this shard or die trying,' shouted Torkval, placing the spear across his chest and chanting rapidly.

As the dragon set about the remaining soldiers with a roar of indignity; slashing them with its leathery tail and razor-sharp claws, it blasted a hole in the soldiers' ranks with red-hot flames just as Kuelack's power blazed. The resulting combination of power proved too much for Torkval, and the titanic forces scythed through his defences; blasting his body into bloody bits.

From his lofty position next to the throne, Kuelack scanned the hall. The fortress's remaining inhabitants, some injured and others dazed, looked around in bewilderment at the seared and shattered bodies of their companions and the fiercely burning hall.

With a look of pure want and wonderment, Kuelack took up the silk bag and, emptying its contents, looked down at the shard in his hand. Then, closing his hand around it, he felt its power surge through his veins. An all-encompassing crimson glow flooded the ruins, mesmerising the remaining defenders before they could flee.

'Listen to me, Torkval brought you to this; and because of his challenge, your friends and comrades are dead. They paid the ultimate price for his defiance. You will rebuild this ruined hall and fallen castle as a testament to me and my victory here.'

Kuelack then leapt upon the dragon's back and said resolutely, 'Now that we have the first piece, it will lead us to the next.'

Striding purposefully through the wreckage, the dragon soared into the night sky with a thrust of its leathery wings.

CHAPTER NINE

GREYSWORDS AND ARDENT WOLVES

Approaching the farmyard amidst a downpour, Alfic hurried across the soaking grass, a pickaxe in his hand. After closing the gate behind him, he made his way past the stone-built pigpens, chicken run and the imperial looking wood constructed dovecote sat in the middle of the farm's yard. Splashing through the puddles and mud, he heard the bellowing of distressed cattle intermingled with the sounds of cursing and swearing coming from the field beyond. Shutting the furthest gate behind him, he turned the corner into the field and came across a scene of chaos and confusion. The Pike brothers, covered from head to foot in dung and muck, were running around like a pair of headless chickens; struggling ineffectively to control the panicked cattle, that with eyes rolling around in their heads, bucked and kicked in fear.

Scanning the skies for a predator, his injured hand moving involuntarily to draw the sword that he no longer wore, Alfic demanded loudly, 'What's wrong with them?'

Elgin, his mop of curly, ginger hair plastered to his forehead, his face a picture of bewilderment, looked at him with desperate brown eyes and puffed, 'Alfic, thank Seline, we've never seen them like this before.'

'Predators?'

Shaking his head, Elimi squeaked, 'Haven't seen any.'

'Where's Sorin?' demanded Alfic.

'He's around the corner, behind the barn.' Elimi then looked at Alfic grimly, 'I'll tell you now; it's not a pretty sight.'

Running around the outside of the farm buildings and fearing for Sorin's safety, Alfic stopped in his tracks as he stared at the large heifer impaled on the metal railings separating the field from the orchard.

'What happened?' Alfic asked mournfully.

Examining the long horn with a mystified look on his weathered features, Sorin, his old tattered hat in his left hand, scratched his head of thinning shoulder-length grey hair with his right.

'I don't understand it. It looks like she tried to jump the railings.'

'The only way that would happen was if something really spooked her,' Alfic stated, brushing his wet hair back from his eyes and scanning the fields once more.

'Well, she hasn't been here long. The body's still warm,' said Sorin sadly, chin in hand. 'If we're going to lift her off, we'll need to rig an A-frame; any other way and we'll tear the carcass to pieces,' said Sorin.

'Come on, let's help the blunder boys herd these cattle in under cover.'

'Never was a name more apt,' Sorin chuckled, the effort creasing his weathered skin like a piece of old parchment. 'When it comes to brains, they didn't receive their fair share, did they?'

Mused Alfic, 'I often wonder what possessed my father to employ those two.'

A shout caused them to stop and turn to each other.

Running back around the side of the building towards the large barn, they skidded to a halt. Pointing to the midden heap and the half-eaten remains of a second member of the herd was Elgin, and he had a shocked look on his face.

'Oh no, not Jasper!' exclaimed Sorin.

Alfic knelt next to the chewed and shredded carcass, examining it closely. 'Probably defending the heifers.'

'Jasper's a big fella. To kill him would take something powerful,' said Sorin. 'This puts a whole new slant on things.'

'Ardent wolf,' confirmed Alfic. 'Look here, you can already see the wounds turning black where its teeth have ripped the flesh. I've faced one of these creatures before. If the wounds don't kill its prey, the decaying mucus that the teeth exude will. When I was posted to a garrison in the Mycean Mountains, a nearby farmer had his sheep attacked, and it looked just like this. The problem is, they don't only attack for food, they do it to hone their skills, they're semi-intelligent, you see, like a Gorgan.

With a look of revulsion on his freckled face, Elgin confessed, 'earlier today I found the remains of two dead sheep in the furthermost field.'

'Two sheep! How did they die?' asked Alfic, scanning the fields through the downpour.

'Something ate them,' replied Elgin dryly. 'Is it alone?'

'No, there are always two, a male and a female,' confirmed Alfic, shaking his head. 'They pair for life.'

Suddenly, there was a shout of surprise and a snarling, followed by a shriek. The three men ran around the side of the barn. Skidding to a halt, they saw a wolf, the size of a Brean Lion, stood astride Elimi on the muddy ground, his arms awash with blood, while all around stampeding cattle ran in all directions.

'Heelp meee, help!' Elimi screamed.

'Don't panic, Elimi, stay still.'

Then, in an attempt to distract the wolf, Alfic handed his pickaxe to Sorin and, with bellows and jeers, he began throwing conker-sized stones at the beast.

The Ardent wolf looked up menacingly and when Alfic stared into those large black in orange eyes, he saw recognition and a purpose.

'Alfic, we have to do something,' hollered Elgin.

'We will, as long as we keep our heads. Run to the barn, Elgin, and find something we can fight with; we'll keep it distracted.'

'That's all right for you to say,' declared Sorin sarcastically.

Forgetting about Elimi, bleeding on the ground, the wolf growled and started towards them; the rain cascading from the deep purple, iridescent fur along its back. Alfic noticed it followed his every move with intelligent forethought.

'Circle to the left, Sorin; we'll come at it from different angles,' shouted Alfic commandingly.

'Over here,' bellowed Sorin, hefting the pickaxe determinedly. 'Hey, I think your plan's working.'

Dodging left and then right, they threw more stones; the wolf tracking their every movement.

'Don't just lie there, Elimi. Get to safety. Elgin, we need those weapons NOW,' bellowed Alfic desperately.

'Keep your hair on,' shouted Elgin, throwing Alfic a twin-pronged hayfork while hefting a vicious-looking billhook.

'Now get your brother to safety, go to Alsike's, fetch help,' Alfic bellowed.

Alfic, yelling and screaming, ran towards the beast, the wolf snapping and dancing sideways as Sorin, wielding his pick axe, raked the beast's side. Howling in pain, the wolf turned its anger upon the struggling twins as they laboured towards the farmyard gate. Elgin struck out with the billhook as the jaws bit down, the razor-sharp teeth opening up a bloody gash in his calf. His leg gave way and he and his brother collapsed to the floor. Alfic, leaping to their aid, with Sorin hot on his heels, forced the wolf backwards. Then, turning to the fraught farmer, his breath coming in short gasps, Alfic yelled, 'Try for the eyes, Sorin. What it can't see, it can't attack.'

Sorin slashed at the elusive creature's face but slipped in the thick mud, landing with a wet thump. The wolf seizing upon the opportunity pounced, its bloody salivating jaws snapping in frustration as it reached for Sorin's throat. As the farmer held the pickaxe out in front of him in an attempt to stop the wolf ripping at his throat and face, Alfic came to Sorin's aid, driving the pitchfork into the beast's side, impaling the wolf's heavy muscular body with the sharp points. His nerves jangling, Alfic released the implement and, along with Sorin, watched as the creature, squirming and thrashing, emitted one last desolate howl. Loath to see any creature suffer, Alfic prized the pitchfork from the beast's side and raised it overhead. Suddenly, with a shout of defiance, Sorin ran forward and buried the pickaxe into the wolf's skull.

'Yeh, that's what you get for attacking my animals, you mangy mutt,' then seeing Alfic's bemused glance, Sorin added, 'and my friends.'

'We're not out of the woods yet,' stated Alfic.

'I know, the male won't be far away and they're bigger,' stated Sorin.

As in response to Sorin's statement, a second deeper baleful howl reverberated across the fields.

'That came from the trees by the stream,' announced Sorin, now clearly worried.

Turning to the farmer whose face and clothes, like his, were now soaked and covered in mud, Alfic, nodding his head slowly and breathing rapidly, came to a decision, 'We have to engage it here Sorin, otherwise people at the school will be at risk. Keep an eye out. I'll be back in a sec.'

Sorin, accepting the pitchfork and gripping it like a dying man clinging to a crumbling ledge, waited nervously.

Alfic re-appeared beside Sorin, making him jump, with another long-handled pitchfork clasped tightly in his hand. 'We'll both stand a better chance with these than a pickaxe,' Alfic smiled weakly.

The two men stood side by side in the rain, and watched as another wolf, a third bigger than the first, emerged from the stream's leafy margin. Sniffing at the air, it then loped towards them across the rain lashed field. Skidding to a halt next to the smaller female, it watched them wearily as it sniffed at the carcass.

'Cronin's eyes, that's a big animal, Alfic.'

'Steady Sorin, as long as we stay together, we can keep it at bay.'

'Keeping it at bay's one thing, but how do we stop it?'

'I'm working on that,' said Alfic, looking around desperately.

The male wolf snarled forebodingly as it sniffed and nudged at the corpse. Then baring its five-inch-long incisors, it turned towards them. As well as being larger, the male had longer, darker purple streaked fur that melded into spines along its ridged back that now stood up like porcupine quills.

Standing steadfast, Alfic and Sorin stabbed and feinted, lunging with their improvised weapons.

'Come on, come on! Is that all you've got? Come on, GET ON WITH IT!' shouted Alfic.

Snarling and pawing at the ground, its jaws snapping dangerously, the beast suddenly launched its sizable bulk towards them. The two men, bracing for the attack, brought their pitchforks to bear, but in attempting to prop his handle into the floor, the aging farmer was too slow and the wolf ripped the pitchfork from Sorin's hand, snapping the shaft in its powerful jaws. Then, turning on the rain-soaked farmer, it smashed him against the farm-building wall where he lay unmoving among a swathe of stinging nettles and brambles. Alfic wiped purposefully at the rain and sweat running into his eyes, fearing that this was to be his last day in the land of the living. Then, calming his fear, he climbed to his feet from the muddy floor. With a steely determination, he placed himself between the wolf and Sorin's inert form. It was then that he heard a voice urgently calling his name.

'HERE, I'm here,' he shouted thankfully as the wolf suddenly pounced.

Attempting to brace the pitchfork in the muddy ground once more, his previously injured hand erupted in pain and, unable to grip the shaft of the pitchfork, it slipped into the mud. Sailing overhead, the creature turned before Alfic could bring the pitchfork to bear and the enraged animal leapt, pinning him to the ground. As the snarling jaws reached for his throat, the enraged wolf lurched sideways, accompanied by a guttural bellow that split the air. Looking up, Alfic saw a large blond-haired soldier wrestling with the beast on the ground. Fuelled by battle madness, Alfic climbed to his feet and, picking up the pitchfork, ran to the aid of the armoured warrior. With adrenalin fuelled strength, he drove the pitchfork into the beast's side again and again. Then, the blond warrior, having gained his feet, drew his sword and severed the wolf's head from its body.

His nerves still jangling and with his hands on his knees, Alfic said, 'Thank you.' Then, recognising the armour of a Greysword, he gasped, 'Vanir. Right?'

Wiping the wolf's blood from his sword, the tall, blond, thick-built warrior nodded, 'Are you all right?' he enquired.

Relieved, Alfic smiled, 'Fine, thanks to you. I'm not ungrateful, you understand, but what are you doing here?'

Returning his imposing grey sword to its scabbard nestled between his shoulder blades, Vanir said, 'I came across your two men, Elimi and Elgin, while looking for you, and they told me what was happening here.'

Alfic looked up at the imposing warrior, having only ever exchanged pleasantries with the man before. However, he trusted Mace, who spoke highly of Vanir; having befriended him while in the army, having recommended him to replace Greysword Drabast, who had fallen in battle. According to Mace, despite being a hothead, Vanir was honest and plain-talking with a just sense of right and wrong. Also, according to Mace, Vanir's chat-up lines were legendry; combined with his blond-haired good looks, this almost guaranteed he could bed women wherever he was posted.

'So, what can I do for you, Vanir?'

'Mace warned me what was going on here at the school, but I chose to ignore him, alas, he was right. We became Greyswords to defend the school from all threats,' he stated resolutely, 'from within as well as without; now it seems I can't trust the very people I'm sworn to protect. Then I remembered Mace telling me of his old army compatriots and how they could be trusted.'

Alfic chuckled, more from relief than humour. 'This situation is just one of many we've encountered since Almagest's disappearance,' he said, indicating the dead Ardent wolves.

'Which brings me to the reason why I'm here,' said Vanir. 'Your sister commissioned me covertly to discover Almagest's whereabouts. I discovered his fate, but when I returned, Magen wasn't the same person. She'd changed.'

'Yes, courtesy of my brother, no doubt,' spat Alfic. 'I take it you heard...'

'About your disagreement at the fair, yes, I heard,' Vanir nodded.

Alfic then looked up at the handsome-looking warrior with his piercing blue eyes.

'Almagest's dead, isn't he?'

'Yes Alfic, and I'm sorry,' said Vanir sadly. 'I found his destroyed and decaying carriage in bits on the Blinks escarpment. But I don't subscribe to the conclusion that he was killed by monsters.' His gaze far away, Vanir said, 'I saw something that day, on the Blinks. At first, I thought it was Almagest, that he'd somehow survived. It had Almagest's face, but it wasn't him.'

Vanir then pulled two pieces of clothing from inside his armour; one was a thick white cloth and the other finer and a deeper shade of red; both were bloodied.

Alfic took the pieces of cloth from Vanir and felt at the fabric, a range of emotions clouding his face. 'Could it be you saw what you wanted to?'

'I'm from the Southern Wilds, Alfic, and believe me, I've seen some strange things. This was no figment of my imagination.'

'When you've quite finished exchanging pleasantries, a little help wouldn't go amiss.'

They both turned to see Sorin floundering as he attempted to extract himself from the sea of nettles and brambles.

'Hold on, old man, I'm coming.' Looking at Vanir, he teased, 'Crankiness, it's a sign of old age!'

Holding his side, his face a mask of pain, Sorin protested, 'I heard that!'

Wading into the forest of stinging nettles, Alfic smiled and helped the farmer to his feet. 'You look like a warty old toad.'

'Very funny, I don't think!' replied Sorin irritably.

Then more seriously, Alfic said, 'We need to get you to the infirmary; the way you're holding your side, I'd guess you've a couple of broken ribs.' Alfic then stopped in his tracks, prodding at the wolf's carcass lain amidst an expanding pool of bloody water.

'You're going to think me mad, but these wolves were targeting me. It was in their eyes, I saw recognition.'

Vanir exclaimed, 'Well, that's not normal, is it?'

'No, it isn't,' confirmed Alfic, shaking his head. 'This is the work of an Animistic.' Seeing their sceptical faces Alfic continued, 'These creatures may be semi-intelligent and can be aggressive, but they do not deliberately travel tens of leagues to the heart of civilisation to feed on livestock.'

'Tallus,' concluded Sorin painfully, 'but why would your brother task him to set these wolves upon you?'

'I'm not entirely sure it was my brother. Consider this - at first, he attempted to remove anyone he knew who was against him, Mace for one, Keegan and me. Managing to jail only Mace, his plans changed, and now, with my brother absent, the attempts on our lives have resumed.'

'So, whoever it is, feels threatened and thinks we're getting too close to the truth,' assumed Sorin.

'You could be right,' said Alfic sceptically.

'If not Kuelack, then who, Alfic?' queried Sorin.

'I'm not sure what's going on, but I'm sure it's someone closely associated with Kuelack.'

'A rival?' offered Vanir.

'That remains to be seen?' Alfic then slapped his forehead. 'Karnack!'

'What about him?'

'He allowed me to talk to Mace at the fair, despite my brother's orders.'

'So?' queried Vanir. 'Karnack can take care of himself.'

'With all that's happened at the school recently, do you honestly think that anyone is safe? He needs to be warned.'

'I can see why Mace holds your family in such high regard,' Vanir chuckled, a knowing grin on his face. 'If you're willing, I'd like to hear more of what has gone on in my absence.'

'Vanir, it would be our pleasure,' agreed Sorin, 'but first, I'd like someone to tend to my ribs?'

Vanir's eyes snapped open on hearing the sound of raised voices. Sitting up in the early morning gloom, he held his pounding head with a painful grimace. Through blurry vision, he looked about him uncertainly and realised he was lying on the floor. To no one in particular, he said, 'Where am I? Ah, now I remember.'

Having spent the afternoon at the farmhouse in the company of Alfic and Sorin, he had then wandered to the kitchens. With the day's events still playing on his mind, he met up with his two friends, Albain and Tance Melos, members of Pellagrin's guard. The three were enjoying a quiet, friendly drink when the Sergeant of the Guard, the burly Morgan Ormstrode, had appeared. Drinking games ensued, as they often did, and the three of them ended up in the barracks after their attempts to out-consume the seasoned campaigner had once more ended in failure.

Looking through blurry eyes, Vanir poked his head out into the corridor and watched as the Sergeant, carrying a flaming torch, bellowed into each of the six bunkrooms that housed the school's twenty-four elite armed guards.

'Sergeant? How do you do it? How can you drink that much and not..., what's going on?' he croaked from a throat that felt like sandpaper, 'and can you keep your voice down to a gentle whisper please.'

Gesticulating wildly and hurrying soldiers along the corridor, his eyes wild in the candles' flickering firefly light, Sergeant Ormstrode yelled, 'The barracks are on fire, you numbskull, can't you smell it? Help me evacuate the building.'

Movement to the left caught his attention and, peering into the gloom at the newly painted whitewashed walls in the darkness, he heard a man cough and say, 'Vanir, you are still here?'

Searching the darkness, Vanir replied harshly, 'There's not a drill scheduled for today, is there, Albain?'

'Do you think we'd get this drunk if there was?' exclaimed Albain, who, with a full head of long blond hair, was often mistaken for Vanir's younger brother.

Swinging his legs over the edge of the bottom bunk and peering into the corridor, Tance Melos, a bearded, dark-haired and moustached warrior from the ruined land of Turkana, and now attached to the school guard, said in a voice filled with Turkanian pronunciations, said harshly, 'Is the sergeant sure there's a fire, I can't smell anything.'

Struggling from his bunk bed, Albain Woodruff, rubbing aggressively at his eyes, leapt from the top bunk and stretched. Reaching for his clothes, he moaned, 'No, I get it. This is payback for those slugs we put in the Sergeant's beer last night!'

Vanir smiled and declared, 'Well, let's face it; cheating was the only way we were going to be the Sarg at cards.'

Vanir had known the pair while in the army. Albain, having grown up in the slums of Gonda, was young, outgoing and brash. He was the complete opposite of the reserved Tance, who originated from the ruined province of Turkana to the east; yet together they made the perfect fighting duo. Tance's weapon of choice was the Kultarr, a wickedly curved Turkanian sword; while Albain always argued that you shouldn't have to rely on just one weapon if you were to be an accomplished fighter.

'This is no time for hilarity. OUTSIDE NOW, THAT'S AN ORDER!' shouted Sergeant Ormstrode, poking his head around the doorframe.

'Ok Sarg, not so loud, how does he stay so sober?' said Albain, shaking his head.

Hastily strapping his sword to his back and following the Sergeant from the room, Vanir sniffed heavily at the air. Then, grasping Ormstrode's shoulders and roughly spinning him around, Vanir stared at him intently.

'I can't smell anything. Are you sure there's a fire, Sergeant?'

It was then that he looked towards the ceiling and, like sinuous grey snakes, wisps of smoke appeared, undulating over and between the ceiling joists.

'All right, so there's smoke,' confirmed Albain.

'Where's it coming from?' Vanir demanded seriously.

'The weapons lock up!'

'Ok. Vanir and I will tackle the fire. You two continue evacuating the men. We'll meet you outside. Vanir let's go.'

Vanir hurried along the passageway, following the Sergeant. As they neared the weapons lock up, they saw smoke billowing from the entrance. Crouching low and covering his nose and mouth with his arm, Vanir entered the lockup and, sure enough, a small fire was blazing fiercely in the middle of the hard-packed floor. Realising it had been deliberately set, he began stamping out the blaze. He spun around at the sound of the door being closed and then locked.

'Sergeant, what's going on?'

Morgan Ormstrode, hefting a long steel blade, said in a voice devoid of emotion, 'it's simple, you've shown your hand, Vanir, so now I must eliminate you.'

'Eliminate... what are you...?'

'It's nothing personal, you understand.'

Suddenly closing the gap, Ormstrode struck downwards with his blade. In one quick movement, Vanir drew his sword and parried the deadly blow.

'Why are you doing this? You may be able to beat me at drinking games, but not with a sword.'

He soon realised that the Sergeant wasn't listening as with wild abandon Ormstrode slashed back and forth with his weapon, backing Vanir against the wall. But as good a swordsman as the Sergeant was, Greysword Vanir, was better; having been specifically chosen for his prowess with a blade.

'Speak. What's wrong with you? Tell me, why are you doing this?' demanded Vanir.

Unfortunately, the Sergeant continued to attack, blindly hacking and slashing as if he was possessed of some otherworldly strength.

'I'm ordering you Sergeant, stop, I don't want to kill you,' implored Vanir grimly.

Adeptly, Vanir twisted the sword from Ormstrode's grip and then, quickly advancing, forced the point of his blade against his throat, 'Sergeant, that's enough! What is wrong with you?'

The Sergeant rolled backwards and, seemingly immune to the searing pain, picked up a handful of hot embers from the fire; throwing them towards Vanir. Then, his face set in an odious grimace, Ormstrode grasped a flail hanging from the weapons' rack and, swinging the weapon around his head, advanced once more.

Rubbing desperately at his eyes and face in an attempt to clear the burning soot, Vanir ducked beneath the deadly, spiked ball which, whistling overhead, dislodged chunks of masonry and plaster from the wall where his head had been. Seeing his chance, Vanir tackled the Sergeant, forcing him against the weapons rack. There was a sickening impact of many sharp weapons, but again, the Sergeant seemed oblivious to his pain. Vanir stepped backwards as Ormstrode looked up with bloodshot eyes from a face the colour of chalk. Then, as if nothing extraordinary had occurred, the Sergeant, without a sound, eased himself from the sharp points. Poised on the balls of his feet, Vanir, now all calmness and precision, avoided the ball and chain. Then, stepping across, he presented his sword and the chain wrapped around the blade. Vanir then stepped forward and hooked his arm beneath the Sergeant's armpit. He then spun around and, with prodigious strength, threw the crazed Sergeant to the floor. He then stamped down hard on Ormstrode's wrist, wrenching the flail from his grasp.

His blade at the Sergeant's throat once more he stated, 'Clearly you are not yourself so I will not kill you; too many people have died of late.'

As if waking from a nightmare, Ormstrode looked around with a bewildered stare and inquired, 'Vanir, what happened? What are you doing? What happened to me? Why am I on the floor with your blade at my throat?'

Then abruptly, with a look of horror, the Sergeant brushed at his arms. Screaming now and despite his injuries, Ormstrode leapt to his feet and ran towards a large barrel of drinking water. Immersing his arms up to the shoulders, he screamed, 'The flames - they won't go out. Vanir, why won't they go out?'

'Sergeant, calm down!' shouted Vanir, grasping Ormstrode's face and staring into his eyes. 'There are no flames.'

Oblivious to Vanir's reassurances, the Sergeant of the guard ran out into the night and the pouring rain still shrieking, 'The flames - I can't put them out. They won't go out!'

Vanir followed and tackled the now incoherent Sergeant, pinning him to the floor.

'Tance, Albain help me, here!'

'What's wrong with him?' hissed Albain, looking down at the Sergeant's frenzied features in bewilderment.

'He thinks he's on fire.'

'Sergeant Ormstrode believe me, you're not on fire,' said Albain, bewildered.

'You men help me. Tance, go and find Alsike, now!' Vanir ordered gravely.

But the Sergeant, his face a mask of pain, continued to squirm, rolling around in abject terror on the grass.

'My skin, it's burning, it's peeling away, help me,' he gasped.

Grasping the Sergeant by his collar and shaking him vigorously, Vanir slapped him hard. 'Snap out of it! There's nothing wrong with you, you're not on fire.'

Clutching at Vanir's shirt like a drowning man, his face contorted in pain, Sergeant Ormstrode gasped one last time and then slumped lifeless to the sodden turf.

'What just happened?' Albain enquired, confused.

Scanning the old darkened fortress opposite, Vanir said grimly, 'There's only one man at the school who is capable of this.'

CHAPTER TEN

SPIES MIND READING AND TRUTH

K ale woke from another fraught night's dreams of failure and regret. Yawning, his head fuzzy from lack of sleep, he climbed out of the camp bed, stood, and pooling water in his hands from the small barrel, threw the water over his face and through his hair. Rubbing at his red-rimmed eyes, he pulled on his clothes, then selected two pieces of rabbit meat and walked over to the cage containing Keegan's ferrets, Molly and Mo. Implanting thoughts of food upon the surreptitious creatures, he waited, and sure enough they appeared, sniffing at the air eagerly. Kale smiled as he looked upon the two unruly animals affectionately, as they enthusiastically devoured the rabbit portions squeezed through the wooden bars of the cage. Having proved invaluable in procuring a steady supply of food during their night-time forays, the ferrets reminded him of Torsk's creatures used for study, staring dolefully out from their cages, hanging from the walls and ceiling of the classroom. Although it had been necessary, he'd always felt sad for those creatures. They always looked so forlorn and powerless; so much better to study them in the wild.

I'm sorry, Torsk, he thought sadly. *Now I'll never teach the students as you tutored me; now I'll never make you proud.*

He also owed Keegan's apprentice, Drench, a dept of gratitude for allowing him to stay here at enormous risk to his own life. When asked why, the tall sinuous youth, only a few months his senior, had replied, "It was what Keegan would have wanted."

Wiping away tears of guilt and gratitude, Kale dressed. He then prepared a breakfast of eggs, bacon and fried potato. Washing the ingredients down with dark beer, he then rinsed his wooden bowl, glass beaker and iron frying pan with hot water heated on the wood burner. Staring unseeingly out through the shuttered window, at the sun's radiance now filtering through the lingering autumn mist, he thought, *Everything was falling apart, and where have you been Kale- wallowing in self-pity, cowering here in Keegan's shack, hiding away from the world like a cowering Mole-rat.*

If the roles were reversed, he knew neither Keegan nor Mace would have sat here cowering, waiting for the danger to pass. They would see justice done. However, the truth, instead of bolstering his confidence, only made him feel worse. Once more, he thought back to the strange circumstances of his dismissal and as hard as he tried, could establish no reason why. His reasoning spiralled back once more to the actuality that he was just a pawn in Kuelack's grand plan, that Tallus was always destined to take his place. He shuddered at the thought of what Tallus was teaching his students. The twisted animistic must now be revelling in his victory, having vigorously opposed his appointment as an instructor.

Opening the door onto a new day, he looked out from the porch and then back at Keegan's cot, empty now for two weeks. At first, he thought Keegan was doing what he did best, skulking and sneaking about, or perhaps he was just lying low. But as the nights came and went, he became worried as the gamekeeper would never leave his beloved ferrets for so long or, for that matter, his much-loved nephew. Then Drench appeared with news that Keegan had been arrested.

He kicked out then, in frustration. *I shouldn't be surprised,* he thought. *After all, Keegan was an action first, asks questions later man, unexpectedly outspoken for someone versed in the art of inconspicuousness.*

One thing, however, was certain; because of his apathy and his reluctance to help, two of his friends were now in prison. He then considered how long it would take before the school realised he was residing here.

He smiled then as his thoughts turned to the ray of sunshine that was Aridain, and the elusive presence he'd discovered residing in his head. What was it doing there? Was it there to protect him, or were its motives more sinister? Perhaps it was the school's psychic, Mass Martin.

He looked out across the fields towards Pellagrin's spires and domes, the peaceful, serene haven that had grown from millennia of warfare and strife. An outcast now, he was no longer subject to the school rules. He could quite easily leave and start a new life elsewhere and even find peace for a time, but he would be living a lie. Eventually, he knew the cancer, that was Kuelack, would catch up with him. *If Kuelack or Tallus thought the Harvestmen's attack had deterred me, that I have given up, they were sorely mistaken,* he thought vehemently. *As far as I'm aware, I am the only teacher willing to act against Kuelack, and I will not see the school destroyed; besides, I made Lascana a promise to protect the boy.*

Determined not to wallow in self-pity anymore, he took a deep calming breath, strapped his knife and holster to his forearm as he had seen Keegan do many times before. Then, fastening his cloak across his chest, he squared his shoulders resolutely.

Suddenly, a voice sounding surprisingly like his mentor, Torsk, echoed in his mind.

The guilt is not yours, Kale Sim. You did what you thought was right, your conscience is clear, besides, you still have allies and a purpose.

A knock on the door made him start and, hiding, he slowly drew the knife.

'Kale, are you there?'

Recognising the voice, he got to his feet and cautiously opened the door.

'Perak?'

Grasping Perak's hand, he shook it vigorously. Then, looking around suspiciously, he pulled him inside.

'Hello Kale. Ye gods, you look as if you've been pulled through a hedge backwards.'

'Perak, it's good to see you; it's good to see anyone. I thought I'd been forgotten.'

'What about Drench?'

'You know what I mean. So, what are you doing here?'

'I remembered Keegan's ferrets needed feeding,' smiled Perak conspiratorially.

'Thanks a bunch.'

'Don't look so crestfallen Kale, we knew where to find you, but recently things have been intense.'

'We?'

'Lascana and me.'

'Well, you took your time about it.'

'You heard about Keegan; I presume.'

'Yes, any word?'

'He's not dead if that's what you're worried about, although these days the truth is a subjective concept!'

'Well, harbinger of good-tidings you're not; a spell in the dungeons is as good as a death sentence.'

'Your presence here has also been noticed. If you're found here on the grounds, you know it's the death penalty for you.'

Kale smiled grimly. 'That's a chance I will have to take.'

'And what of Drench? All he's guilty of is standing in for Keegan.'

'I will not abandon my friends or my students, not now.'

'I had a feeling you'd say that.' Perak turned to Kale seriously. 'Listen to me, Kuelack's not stupid. I say Kuelack, it's Tallus really; he knows that if he keeps us busy, we'll be too tired, too occupied for anything else.'

'And with me hiding in a hole of my own making, Tallus can carry on unopposed,' spat Kale.

'I know what you're thinking Kale, but Tallus, fuelled by dark magic, is now a powerful Animistic.'

'Don't worry on my account, old man,' smiled Kale. 'This is something you'd know nothing about. Leave the nuances of animal calling to me.'

'Leave the nuances of animal calling to you, you say.'

'Don't take offence, I meant nothing by it.' Kale then stared perplexed at Perak, who now stood with eyes closed.

'Perak...?'

Squeaking and chittering filled the cabin, and when Kale looked down at the cage, the ferrets had poked their paws through the bars and were purposefully pawing at the small wooden stake holding the securing bracket in place. The stake removed, they diligently opened the cage door, and running over to Perak, climbed up his leg and onto his outstretched hands. The ferrets, now perched on hind legs, stared transfixed at Perak, who was muttering under his breath.

Opening and closing his mouth several times, Kale couldn't find the words. When he did manage to speak, all he could say was, 'You're an Animistic?'

'Very observant. Oh, by the way, Molly and Mo thank you for your efforts, but they say their bedding needs changing.'

Throwing the ferrets, a meaningful look, Kale said, 'Is that so.' He then asked, 'Since when have you been an Animistic?'

'Since I was a child.'

'But you've told nobody?'

'People knowing everything about you isn't always a good thing.'

'But your gift could help us enormously... with the creature, for instance.'

'Can you imagine what my son would do if he knew of my 'gift', what society... what Vara would think should she discover I'm more than good old reliable Perak Bruin, the groundsman. No, better it's kept secret.'

'Then why show me?'

'Because I'm tired of seeing you stumble around, peering cluelessly about in an effort to find the right combination. It's time you saw the light, time for you to become the Animistic you were meant to be.'

'Now that I'm beyond the law...'

'Let's just say you can benefit more from my magic than I can. Off you go,' he encouraged, smiling as Molly and Mo trotted back to their cage. 'So, now that serving of awkwardness is out of the way; I'd love a cup of tea.'

Taken aback by the barrage of information, a bewildered Kale ambled zombie-like over to the range, and filling the copper kettle with water, placed it on the small range. 'We've become acquainted, the creature and me,' he said abruptly.

'So, it's still here?' mused Perak. 'Many thought it had gone for good.'

'Oh no, far from it. I've developed a theory to explain why it hasn't been seen. I think that in its natural form the creature doesn't like sunlight, so to avoid that problem it takes on the form of the thing it consumes, a person or an animal say, so it can move around during daylight hours. During our investigations, Mace told me that the stewards, over on the king's land opposite, saw the creature's first human victim, a man called Celias Erkit. They blamed him for murdering two of the men working there and said it was revenge for his sacking; not realising that his corpse had already been identified.'

'So, why has it come back in these guises? What's its purpose? It could easily approach any one of us, kill us even, but it hasn't.'

'I think the creature's biding its time, waiting for something.'

'But what?'

'I wish I knew, but whatever it is, I think it involves your grandson.'

Kale poured them both a cup of tea and sat opposite Perak, waiting for him to say the words he knew were coming.

'Kale, these times are critical if we're to survive. You are now the only one with the freedom to act.'

'I will, of course, do what I can.'

'You will do more than that with my help and tuition.' Swallowing his tea, Perak then stood and announced, 'Now, prepare yourself, Kale Sim.'

CHAPTER ELEVEN

DEVIDED, WE FALL

The urgency of her appeal had had the desired effect. Lascana glanced around as the stall holders talked in hushed voices, their uncertainty and suspicions permeating the farmhouse's usually inviting, warm atmosphere like a dark miasma. To her right stood Alfic, who, like an angry sheep dog overlooking a nervous flock, perused the assembled stallholders with a foreboding look on his face. Next to him stood Sorin. The unassuming farmer, having had his doubts regarding the meeting, looked dourly towards the floor while pulling fiercely on a long, thin clay pipe. However, his sympathetic and forgiving wife, Celia, always ready to entertain, scurried around tending to their visitors like an industrious ant, trying her hardest to placate the disconcerted stallholders with tea and slices of fruit cake.

Lascana smiled. She imagined the current situation sat hard with the friendly, practical, down-to-earth couple, but they were good friends and if you were ever in need, regardless of the circumstances, they were always ready to help in any way they could. Rolling her eyes to the ceiling, Lascana observed as Lawna, the school's apothecary, now in her element, scuttled from person to person interrogating each in turn, her freshly applied perfume suffusing the room with roses and Lily-of-the-Valley. Sporting light brown, curly locks that reached down to her shoulders, Lawna was short and stout with sharp defined features like an inquisitive owl. It was also rumoured she'd had many illicit relationships about the school and fingers in many pies.

Dressed up as though it were a garden party, Lawna now tried her hardest to extract information about the latest fatalities from the undertaker, Milvus Bloch, a shy man with a passion for collecting insects, especially butterflies. Lascana could understand Bloch's interest in their exquisite splendour; being the perfect tonic to dealing with the dead. Stood to attention and dressed in his best tailored suit, Milvus was trying his hardest to ignore the intrusive know-it-all, looking at Lawna as though she were a bad smell, acknowledging her enquiries in short, clipped grunts.

Lascana, startled from her reverie by a sudden noise, glanced towards the ceiling as a burst of giggles and laughter issued from the three children who were playing happily together upstairs.

At least that relationship was one less thing to worry about, she thought.

'What can you see Aridain doing in the future, Lascana?' asked Sorin, following her gaze.

'Oh, I don't know, his mind is so flighty.'

'He must be interested in something?' Sorin persisted.

'Well, he loves reading, and he loves the countryside together with the creatures in it,' said Lascana sceptically, 'but I can see him taking after his father and joining the army.' She chuckled at a memory. 'Only a month ago, despite explicit orders to the contrary, I found him practicing with the students on the combat field again. Apparently, he crept through the orchard and just joined in!'

'And of course, Karnack didn't stop him,' smiled Sorin.

'Karnack may have the heart of a Brean Lion,' chuckled Lascana ironically, 'but with the younger students, he's as soft as a kitten. Anyway, Aridain was so upset when Karnack tried to take back the sword that he ran away with it, so Karnack insisted he could keep it as long as he promised to practise with it. Yes, I'm afraid he's far too adventurous for the farming life; his mind flits from one thing to another like a honeybee, trying to drink as much nectar as it can before it dies. What about your two, Sorin? Can you see either of them becoming farmers?'

'Sadly no, Selva has a very strong sense of justice and is very caring, while Duran is a handful right now, as you know. When we ask him what he wants to do, he just shrugs his shoulders. He can be very determined when we give him work to do, but if you try to correct him, he can become an angry young man.'

'Lascana, Sorin, Alfic, have you heard? Areca supplied the poisons that killed Tad Grearson and his nurse, and now she's cursed,' Lawna hissed gleefully.

'Ahh, Lawna; nice to see you too,' said Sorin sardonically.

Smiling forcibly, Lascana glanced quickly at Alfic, as Sorin rolled his eyes despairingly.

'Lawna, we're not interested in hearsay,' Alfic growled ominously.

'It's not hearsay, Alfic. I heard it first-hand.'

'From who, from who did you hear it?' despaired Alfic.

'Oh, I can't tell you that. I promised I wouldn't tell.'

Lascana laid her hand on her husband's arm as Lawna hurried over to her next victim, Janus Loker, the wine merchant. With a calming smile, she said, 'I know she can be trying, Alfic, but don't let Lawna's proclivity for gossip rile you, dear.'

Alfic huffed, 'How many times has her so-called gossip impacted upon people's lives, caused arguments?'

'Talking of trying,' interceded Sorin.

His white shirt and britches sporting their customary wayward flecks of blood, Keen the school's morose, superstitious butcher entered the room, staring furtively from beneath thick jet-black eyebrows. Individual and secretive, he was stubborn to the eighth degree; a man who was very hard to turn once he had made up his mind. Lascana then turned to watch Elias Tan, the baker, who had suddenly appeared at the school one day, two years ago. He had fled from the harsh regime of Calabash, the repressive authoritarian land, to the northeast. Reminding her of a debonair pirate wearing a bandanna tied around the back of his head plus ear and nose studs, and sporting a large black moustache, Elias conversed confidently with Irvine, the fishmonger; the pair's muted laughter unbefitting the fraught atmosphere. Ever the joker, the weasely faced slightly overweight Irvine, with his short-cropped hair, commented that the creature stalking the school wouldn't want to come near his shop, as the smell would repel it long before it reached his door. The wool merchant Casey Defray was also here. The normally shy and soft-spoken seamstress looked anything but the timid, introverted widow hiding behind layers of dark black hair. Now, like a self-assured huntress assessing its prey, the enigmatic clothier, her hair tied back with string and dressed in a long dark green hooded cloak, studied the room and its occupants studiously. Casey had also fled Calabash and had arrived only a week after Elias, also, she assumed, to escape the oppressive regime. Since then, Lascana had few opportunities to speak with her, and when she did, the conversation had always turned to politics and Durbah's disputes with Casey's homeland. Secretly, she'd hoped that living at the school, free from Calabash's harsh regime, would change Casey's critical nature and bring her out of her shell; as it had their friend Keegan, himself a former inhabitant of Calabash. But Lascana suspected her views had been drummed into her by the harsh administration, based on control and brutality. She often wondered what Casey was doing here if she missed her homeland so much.

As if possessed with a sixth sense, Casey slowly turned her hawk like gaze upon Lascana; she then smiled and turned toward the grocer Bern, who was maintaining a hard-fought conversation with the school's hulking blacksmith, Gable. An old school friend of Lascana's, the man mountain, his weight crushing the arm of Celia's flowery patterned couch, had taken a fancy to her at school, and she had reciprocated for a time, the blacksmith impressing her with his maturity, sensibility and gentleness.

She chuckled as she remembered the school's bully, Davos Strom, forcing his intentions upon her, and how he and the rest of the pupils had soon learnt not to upset the gentle giant or his intended.

'Something funny?' asked Alfic.

'Nothing in particular,' she sighed, 'just recalling past memories.'

'… You're not listening to me,' said Bern, his arms gesticulating wildly. 'Populations that breed out of control like Calabash, become frustrated and angry with sparse meagre rations; the result… King Bovid "the Just" uses it as an excuse to encourage the populace to go to war, to seize more land.'

'Calabash is the most powerful regime in the land. It has the greatest army,' interceded Casey proudly. 'If our leader demands obedience; my countrymen will obey.'

'Biggest army maybe, but numbers aren't everything. Discipline's the key,' pronounced Bern aggressively.

'And what if Bovid ordered your armed forces to go to war?' Gable stated seriously.

'Your people have become decadent, as have your armies; it would be no contest,' smiled Casey confidently.

'I put it to you, Casey, that when civilisation breaks down, regardless of orders, populations either hold out their hands and plead for aid, or go on the rampage and fight to get what they need. Bovid craves war; famine and discontent are all it takes,' lectured Gable.

'And my visits over the last few years to our northern borders, proves that your country is running out of recourses. I've seen the damage caused by those so-called blue painted barbarians,' growled Bern, standing with his hands curled into tight-knotted fists.

'What are you implying, Bern? Are you saying my countrymen have already invaded?' suggested Casey. 'That's the most ridiculous theory I've ever heard.'

'Bern please! Gable, Casey, what is wrong with you? Sit down!' ordered Lascana vehemently. 'You're making a scene.'

'And what if I am Lascana? Things need to be said!' challenged Bern.

Stepping in front of Bern, Alfic said impatiently. 'That's enough Bern, calm down, we're in this together, remember?'

Bern shook his head and then rubbed at his eyes. 'Alfic, Lascana I..., I'm sorry.'

Throwing Bern and Gable an exasperated look, Alfic turned to Casey and apologised, 'You'll have to forgive my friends, they're obviously not themselves.'

'No, they're not,' mused Casey. 'Strange indeed.'

'What was all that about?' questioned Lascana when Alfic returned to her side.

'I don't know. I've never seen those two act like that before. Something's not quite right.'

'Well, I'm not surprised. It's a miracle to me that the status quo has lasted this long,' concluded Lascana.

'You're right, this stalemate won't last; it's just a matter of choice now. The sooner the residents realise what my weasel of a brother is trying to do, the better.'

'Few people deal with chaos logically Alfic,' conciliated Lascana.

'Can you see these people believing your theory?' speculated Sorin apprehensively. 'Even if they do, they won't fight.'

'Then we'll just have to persuade them,' stated Lascana determinedly.

Pushing their doubts to the back of her mind, Lascana stepped forward and held up her hands for order, and the room went quiet.

'Thank you all for coming. Some of you will have guessed the reason for this meeting, some of you may not. We thought,' said Lascana, indicating Alfic and Sorin, 'that it was time to tell you, our friends, the truth about what is happening at the school and answer any questions you have to the best of our knowledge. Unfortunately, Perak and Keegan are unable to attend.'

'So, it's true!' exclaimed Keen.

'I told you!' said Lawna arrogantly, as murmurs and mutterings spread throughout the room. 'Keegan is in the dungeons because he attacked Teacher Martin.'

'That is what Kuelack would have you believe,' growled Sorin.

'It's also rumoured that Keegan, together with Mace, killed two students,' added Janus.

'He and Mace defended Tad from two students sent to kill him,' Lascana said angrily. 'Tad was killed to stop him corroborating Keegan's and Mace's testimonies.'

'Don't bother Lascana. Gradine explained everything clearly. She said there is no conspiracy and that you're fabricating a story to cover up your family's involvement with this creature,' said Keen confidently.

'You told her of this meeting?' queried Lascana.

'Yes, she told us you would try to discredit her and her husband. Her account made more sense than your conspiracy theories,' declared Irvine. 'And listening to this hogwash, I'm glad she did.'

'Husband,' joked Alfic, 'more like partner-in-crime.'

'She said, "Mace attacked Kuelack." I know it's true because I was there,' said Milvus.

'If you were there, Milvus, then you'd know I had my back turned and my brother was about to kill me,' disputed Alfic.

'You and Mace attacked Kuelack!' said Milvus angrily.

'I don't deny it, but it should be me that's punished, not Mace or Magen; but rest assured my brother will make them pay.'

Gable insisted, 'Mace had a sword; he shouldn't have been there at all. Keegan and Mace broke the law.'

'Gable, you know Mace. You know my sister.' Alfic then turned to the room in general. 'If it weren't for them, I wouldn't be standing here now.'

'We've enjoyed many peaceful years under Almagest's guidance, it's true. But Kuelack has turned the school into a thriving centre of business, student applications are up and trade is booming,' Irvine insisted.

'And rumour, distrust and treachery are rife,' countered Alfic.

Throwing her husband a thunderous look, Lascana continued unperturbed.

'Thank you for those words of wisdom, oh husband-of-mine.' Lascana then turned and addressed the room in general. 'It's curious though, don't you think, that three of the most physically capable people opposed to Kuelack are either under lock and key or dead? Take poor Sergeant Ormstrode, for instance.'

'Alsike said, Sergeant Ormstrode died of a stress induced heart attack,' stated Elias.

'A military-trained soldier killed by stress, don't make me laugh,' scoffed Alfic.

'So, you're also a healer now, are you?' insinuated Milvus.

'Ormstrode was my Sergeant when I was serving, a more professional soldier I've never met. His death was due to psychic meddling,' stated Alfic, jabbing at his head.

'And I'll wager Gradine didn't mention that under Kuelack's orders, Alfic and myself were set upon by a pair of Ardent wolves, summoned by Tallus,' insisted Sorin, 'Or the attack on Kale and Keegan by Harvestman, they also barely escaped with their lives.'

'Harvestman, Ardent wolves?' scoffed Milvus. 'You're living in a fantasy world; their kind haven't been seen around here for centuries. If Mass was meddling with people's minds, Exedra would have him expelled.'

'Listen people,' boomed Alfic, smashing one fist into the other. 'Kuelack knows if we're divided, we're weak. He'll then eliminate us one by one, a classic divide-and-conquer tactic.'

Stepping forward, Lascana held up her hands. 'So far, Kuelack's been very clever with his use of lackeys to eliminate and control all those who oppose him. Keegan and Mace imprisoned, for instance; associating my son with this creature; all attempts to frame us, and all the while he's absent, giving himself a watertight alibi.'

'If we join your fight, we put our own lives in danger. Surely, if we just do our jobs and keep our noses clean, Kuelack will leave us alone, perceive us as no threat,' Janus insisted.

'Sure, if you're happy being a fly in Kuelack's web; happy to live life under a dictatorship,' countered Alfic. 'If you think Kuelack will leave you alone, you're sorely mistaken. He craves power and dominion over everything and demands recognition for that power. Under his rule, this school will become more like an army barracks than a centre of learning.'

Everyone shook their heads and looked around in disbelief, and instead of a barrage of questions, the room remained silent.

'Lascana,' interrupted Milvus Bloch calmly, 'I think I speak for everyone here when I say we live in an enlightened society. The days of power-hungry mages are a thing of the past.'

Lascana knew that if she didn't salvage the situation right now, they could lose more of their friends to Kuelack's twisted ambitions.

'You're wrong, Milvus, you're all wrong. He already has control of the council.'

'Control of the council. Fantasy and poppycock,' huffed Keen.

'You can't be serious, Lascana!' exclaimed Lawna, her face reflecting a well-practiced look of shock. 'Almagest and Exedra would never allow it.'

Lawna's statement was met with a loud 'here, here'.

Shaking his head, Alfic growled, 'Sometimes people, your naivety knows no bounds. Exedra has been compromised. She is under Mass's control. She is no longer herself.'

'You can't be serious; you're honestly expecting us to believe that Exedra is under some kind of spell,' exclaimed Lawna.

'If Exedra was herself, my friends would never have been jailed,' roared Alfic.

'Then why not just eliminate her, like Tad or Ormstrode,' insisted Irvine irritably.

As one, the stallholders all nodded along in agreement.

'What do you think would happen if they killed Exedra?' Alfic growled.

'More serious questions would be asked.'

'Exactly, thank you Elias. There would be chaos at the school and they can't risk that, not yet. They need her to maintain the illusion that nothing is amiss, that everything's in order until they're confident they have the numbers to take the school; better to take the school covertly, one piece at a time, arousing no suspicion.'

'It's the boiling frog analogy,' stated Lascana.

'The boiling frog… What?' rumbled Gable.

'If you place a frog in cold water and then heat it up, the frog will slowly boil to death, but if you throw it into a pot of boiling water, it will jump straight out. We've lived with these troubles for months, probably years now; we've got used to them. If we arrived from somewhere else, and experienced what's happening here now, we'd all be up in arms,' explained Lascana.

His frustration boiling over, Alfic exclaimed, 'People, wake up! What possible reason would we have to lie? What have we to gain? My brother's ambitions are boundless, and he will not tolerate any interference. He's already proved that by beating my sister, Magen, to within an inch of her life for her defiance. He's a murderer and if anyone stands in his way, they will suffer the same fate as Ormstrode, Tad, Cardia and Torsk. He also sanctioned Almagest's murder!'

Once more, the room erupted into a cacophony of noise.

'Vanir found his carriage, Keen. He confirmed it; he's been murdered.'

'Poppycock!' spat Keen. 'This just gets better and better. Next, you're going to tell us is that Kuelack's after the throne. Why are we even discussing this?'

Throwing Lascana a searching look, Alfic spat, 'So, now you're questioning the word of a Greysword?'

'Thank you Alfic,' hissed Lascana, throwing him an evil stare.

When the noise subsided, Casey, who'd sat silently until now, asked, 'So how come you're in the know Lascana?'

Throwing her hands in the air in exasperation, Lascana said frustratedly, 'Because, for the past year, while all of you have carried out your daily lives, we have been waging a war of attrition.'

'Confusion and deception,' boomed Alfic, 'they are Kuelack's weapons of choice; it's what allows him to triumph.'

'Well, personally, I think you're just jealous of your brother's success, now that he's Head of the School,' said Keen.

Milvus stated, 'I agree; your scare tactics are not going to work here.'

'Gradine has already explained that Almagest's wagon careered off of the road when his horses were attacked by creatures from the Blinks,' said Lawna confidently.

'Wytchlem, I think Gradine said,' added Irvine.

'Oh, so you don't believe us when we claim we were attacked by Harvestmen and Ardent wolves, but because Gradine suggests mythical Wytchlem, that's fine!' shouted Alfic. 'Are you deliberately trying to goad me?'

'We all know how dangerous that road is,' said Milvus.

'Cardia and Torsk, however, they were killed by two stray Killdeers that escaped from their pens,' stated Keen aggressively. 'That makes much more sense than suggesting the Killdeer were deliberately persuaded to murder.'

'Then, in the dead of night, once the deed was done, the creatures trotted peacefully back into their pens and closed the gates behind them?' scoffed Sorin. 'Do you hear yourselves? Do you hear what you're saying?'

Lascana looked around at their faces and despaired. She could see that even their most staunch allies sported looks of disbelief and scepticism. Something was wrong, but for the life of her, Lascana couldn't fathom what it was.

'So, I'm assuming Kuelack has allies?' enquired Elias.

'As well as Gradine, Mass, Ramus, Tallus and Hogan are on the payroll, so to speak; and they are only the people we're certain of,' stated Lascana.

Once again, the room exploded into a disharmony of sound.

'Well, I for one am not going to sit and listen to this poppycock for one more second,' yelled Keen.

'I agree, I will have nothing more to do with this,' scoffed Lawna, turning on her heels.

'Nor I,' agreed Milvus.

Following Lawna and Bloch, Keen said, 'Your so-called truths are based on nothing more than rumour and hearsay.'

'Keen, I wish we were wrong,' said Lascana sadly.

Thanking Celia for her hospitality, Bern, anxious and looking very uneasy, said, 'Alfic, normally I'd be on your side, but I'm afraid this time you've gone too far.'

'I agree,' said Gable sadly. 'The hatred you have for your brother is warping your judgement.'

Watching them as they filed from the farmhouse, Alfic shouted, 'You came to hear the truth and now that you have, you won't believe it. Question Kuelack's motives, you'll see...'

'Fools, they are like a flock of wild Oscan's; when one bird runs, they all run regardless of the direction,' accused Casey.

Shaking his head despairingly and embracing Lascana, Alfic said, 'Don't fret, they'll see the error of their ways.'

'Henna's beard, what a fool I am, thinking this peace and tranquillity could last,' cursed Elias. Then, standing and pacing irritably about the room, he exclaimed, 'If what you're suggesting is true, we're going to have to choose sides, aren't we?'

'They will learn the truth,' said Lascana frustratedly, 'but by then it'll be too late.'

'Don't be too hard on them. They're scared. We all are,' said Sorin.

'No, that's not it. Something's amiss, Sorin. This isn't like them,' pondered Lascana.

'Did anyone else notice their hands fidgeting in their pockets?' postulated Alfic.

'Yes, the more irritable they became,' agreed Elias.

'I saw this also,' nodded Casey.

'Alfic, Lascana, I think it's time you told us everything,' demanded Elias.

'Yes,' nodded Casey impatiently. 'Tell us what you know.'

'Before we begin, I think we could all do with another cup of tea,' said Celia, exhaling loudly and shaking her head, 'I know I could.'

CHAPTER TWELVE

THE PRICE OF POWER

Sat astride the dragon's thick, scaly skinned back, Kuelack stared out across the Cealeon Desert, a vast sea of sand devoid of life that stretched from the coast, and from horizon to horizon.

Following the shard's ever-increasing glow, Kuelack urged the dragon north and skirted the ancient land of Parang; its once rich, fertile lands now a maze of treacherous, shifting swamps and marshlands. Stretching fan-like out across the lowlands, the marsh was fed by the majestic River Storna that spilled out over the mighty Abadon Falls. From there, the river flowed into a tangle of shifting mangrove islands where its sediments bled sluggishly into the Westreach Sea. Turning north, towards the devastated land of Turkana, the mismatched pair crossed into the Chondite Badlands; the landscape changing from the cloying reed and mosquito infested mangrove beds to bleached, tortured rock and barren scrubland.

Flying further north, and following clues from the diary, they entered Turkana, a land of moisture-starved vegetation, dried-up river valleys and wind-seared iron-red cliffs located on Durbah's eastern border. Turkana, once the most fertile and most powerful land in Aymara, was home to a proud and noble people who fought valiantly but in vain against the despot Dacron. Allied to the Firebrand stone and leading an army of evil, Dacron swept the proud armies of Turkana before him and raped the land. Now the survivors of this once noble nation eked out a living in what is now a blasted wasteland of bleached deserts and dried-up lake and river beds.

Kuelack steered the silver dragon across the once mighty kingdom for two days; responding to the shard's weakening or strengthening glow. Around and around in ever decreasing circles they soared; over sun-baked salt flats, dry snow driven deserts, mountain valleys and the skeletal remains of towns and cities. On the third day in the sun's waning light, they came across the remnants of a stone and mud-rendered village, abandoned long ago. Tired and irritable, the silvery white dragon alighted on the parched earth in a profusion of dust and sand. It watched guardedly as the dark mage leapt from its back.

Throwing the dragon a stuffed rucksack, Kuelack, searching the buildings and the surrounding desert terrain, commanded, 'Don't just stand there, help me search!'

The dragon hissed angrily, then closed its eyes, the serpentine form shimmering, shivering and shrinking until in its place stood the Dragon Lord Ramus.

Exhausted and ill-tempered, Ramus donned his clothes and took a deep gulp of air. Unsure of what he was searching for and muttering under his breath, he shuffled between the collection of ramshackle mud huts. An hour later, having found nothing but broken pottery and dry sand blasted stone, Ramus seriously contemplated leaving Kuelack stranded in the middle of the desert. Gazing out across the barren land, Ramus noticed a structure nestled in a deep gully, its tattered, wind-scorched cover flapping unfettered in the unremitting wind.

Oh well, in for a penny…

Walking beyond the ruins out into the parched landscape, with only the late afternoon sun for company, he recognised the small structure as a well. Its disintegrating bucket suspended from the winch by a perished rope. Leaning over the edge, he looked down into a dark shaft and quickly recognised the familiar sound of running water.

Appearing suddenly out of the bright sunlight setting over the dunes, Kuelack marched up to Ramus. While studying him fiercely with his piercing grey eyes, he enquired, 'How did you know that my sister had eavesdropped on our conversation? And I did not?'

'Didn't Magen tell you?'

'Deceit doesn't become you, Ramus. Remember who you're talking to.'

'Deceit! I didn't think details concerned you. Besides, you have far greater concerns.'

'I want to hear your version of events,' persisted Kuelack, 'she said you intercepted her on the way to see me. She claims while in your apartment you attacked her,' said Kuelack in a clipped tone. 'Why?'

Regaining his composure, Ramus replied confidently, 'I was concerned. Magen threatened to expose the plan to kill Almagest. I couldn't take that chance.'

'She said "your plan". She was quite explicit!'

'A slip of the tongue, I assure you.' His eyes suddenly lighting up, and pointing at the intensely glowing shard in Kuelack's hand, Ramus exclaimed, 'Look!'

Glancing into the well, Kuelack said, 'It seems we have a climb ahead of us.'

'This structure couldn't support a Hawknath Lizardwing, let alone a person,' said Ramus, testing the mechanism's strength. 'The segment has sat here for hundreds of years. It's not going anywhere. Better to start again in the morning when we're both fed and rested and can think more clearly.'

'If you want my help to avenge your family, you will do as I say!' ordered Kuelack.

When Ramus said nothing, Kuelack added, 'I thought so: now, there must be another entrance.'

Gesturing with his hand, Kuelack conjured a small glowing ball of light. At his command, the light glided downwards to illuminate smooth walls and a river of clear, cool water flowing far below. The glowing globe then appeared a few moments later, illuminating the crisp, cold desert evening a few hundred yards from the village.

'It seems you were right. Another entrance, one of many I'd wager,' said Ramus as they stared into a hole dug at a right angle to the shaft. 'Over there must be the access shaft, then from underground they dug these bore holes to access the water.'

'Very interesting Ramus, I'm sure,' said Kuelack apathetically, 'but it doesn't help us in the here and now!'

Lit by the brightly glowing globe and the shard's ghostly green light, the pair followed the shaft until it met the underground river.

Ramus, dangling his feet into the tunnel, stepped into the cool, fast flowing water.

'Judging by the smoothness of the walls, this waterway has been here for centuries,' said Ramus, basking in the cool, refreshing spray as it washed away the accumulated dust and sweat from days of searching the desert land. 'It's the perfect place to conceal one of the shards.'

As they navigated a bend in the narrow river, the sound of flowing water suddenly increased.

'See, look up ahead. The second shard is glowing in response to the first.'

Revealed in the shard's light, the water disappeared into a dark cavern. Above this shadowy maw, on a moss-covered shelf, lay the second shard.

Approaching the ledge, Ramus said, 'I think I can reach it.'

'Wait!' warned Kuelack, holding up his hand. 'Something's not right. This is too easy.'

Ramus waited impatiently while Kuelack closed his eyes.

'Anything?' asked Ramus.

Kuelack shook his head, but he did not look happy.

'Well, standing here and looking at it will achieve nothing. I think it's a case of try it and see what happens,' said Ramus, frustratedly.

'Your habit of rushing headlong into the unknown will be the death of you, Dragon Lord!' said Kuelack angrily.

Cautiously approaching the shelf, Ramus then stood on tiptoes and tentatively reached for the stone with his shovel-like hand. Hissing in pain, Ramus pulled his hand back involuntarily; dropping the stone into the water at Kuelack's feet.

'Curses, I've been stung,' hissed Ramus.

Before it could be swept into the dark emptiness beyond, Kuelack leapt and grasped the shard that, like a bar of soap, refused to be held. Carried along helplessly by the torrent, Kuelack plummeted over the waterfall's edge into the darkness, the glow globe lighting his fall like a depraved spectator. Ramus watched in anguish as Kuelack disappeared into the abyss.

Diving through the dark opening, his dragon eyes scanning the darkness; Ramus soon realised he was in danger. Huge deadly stalactites and stalagmites, protruding from the ceiling and the floor, materialised and then just as quickly vanished from the globe's light. With one last effort, he spread his leathery wings and sprouted clawed appendages. As the gigantic protruding rock structures threatened to tear at his membranous wings, Ramus, grasping the Dark Mage unceremoniously in his talons, plucked him out of the air mere moments before impacting the rocky floor. Ramus then landed heavily on the damp cavern floor, and the pair tumbled and slid to a halt.

'You fool,' he thundered, his dragon voice rumbling around the cavern, 'what do you think you're doing, you nearly got us killed?'

'Remember who you're talking to, Dragon Lord,' Kuelack bellowed above the roar of the cascading waters.

'I'm talking to a man who I've just saved from certain death, a man who needs me to fly him out of here,' said Ramus imperiously.

'This is the reason we came here,' snarled Kuelack, holding the softly glowing second shard in his hand. 'This is all that matters.'

'Not if you're dead, it's not.'

'You're alive, aren't you? Stop complaining and get us out of here.'

Mumbling under his breath, Ramus took to the air once more with Kuelack on his back and the glow globe lighting the way, twisting and turning through the stalactite-strewn cavern until they arrived at the waterfall's entrance once more. To their astonishment, bathed in the orb's light, a mass of black writhing tentacles reached for them from the tunnel's entrance.

'It's the moss that stung my hand when I reached for the stone,' boomed Ramus, 'but now it's changed; it's grown into something else.'

'It's only moss, burn it!'

Spewing dragon fire, Ramus blasted the entrance free of the unnatural sphagnum. He then banked around for another pass, only to find that the moss had choked the entrance once more. Twice more he tried before returning and alighting on the cavern's slick, water-drenched floor.

'So, the stone was trapped, after all,' barked Kuelack above the waterfall's thunder.

Back in human form, lying on the floor, Ramus huffed, 'It seems Pellagrin chose this location well, that moss reacts to stimulus of any sort.'

'Curse Pellagrin and his flair for the theatrical,' spat Kuelack.

'I told you we needed to rest, but, oh no, the mighty Kuelack wouldn't listen.'

'If I had known, I recruited a coward to help me claim what is rightfully mine; I'd have made the journey on foot,' said Kuelack deliberately. 'Now stop complaining and help me find another way out.'

Then, with a snort of derision, Kuelack sent the globe high into the cavern, its probing light scouring the cavern roof over four hundred feet above. However, all it revealed were slick cavern walls and spectacular frozen limestone columns. Then, manoeuvring the globe across the cavern floor, the light revealed a swirling watery vortex.

It seems there is no other way out except up there!' Kuelack proclaimed loudly.

'I knew it!' Ramus despaired, 'So, now what?'

'I'm working on it,' said Kuelack impatiently.

Stood naked in the darkness at the bottom of the immense cavern, warmed solely by the beating of his dragon-like heart, the torn remnants of his clothes hanging from him in tatters, Ramus watched as Kuelack, returned the globe of light to the cavern entrance and then allowed it to fade too almost nothing.

'What are you doing?' questioned Ramus, staring at Kuelack uncomprehendingly.

'Be silent and watch,' said Kuelack irritably.

Ramus watched as the faint light from the globe illuminated the tunnel's entrance and the bizarre undulating moss high above.

'That root is a plant, albeit a strange one, fuelled by magic, but like all plants, it responds to light. Notice that the root has stopped moving. It's attracted to movement and especially light, but without either, it cannot move or grow. If left long enough, I believe it would fade and die. But time isn't on our side, so I want you to burn the root around the entrance.'

'It's a waste of time. We've already proved that.'

'Stop quibbling and listen. Once you've burned the moss, I want you to get me into the entrance. It will give me enough time to do what I must.'

'As you wish, but this had better be the last time. I've only one more change in me,' hissed Ramus. 'Now lay face down.'

'What?'

'It's time to put your trust in me.'

Clasping Kuelack in his talons, the magnificent silver-scaled dragon flew up through the darkness towards the waterfall's edge. With a blast of flame, Ramus incinerated the black root now clogging the entrance of the tunnel. Simultaneously, he cast Kuelack head first into the passage before the root had sufficient time to grow back.

'Be quick, Kuelack. We dragons are not renowned for our hovering ability.'

His strength waning, Ramus watched as suddenly the entrance to the tunnel turned inky black.

'Come Ramus, before the spell is spent.'

Following the sound of Kuelack's voice, Ramus, reverting to a man once again, dived headlong into the cool waters. Coughing and spluttering as the waters cascaded over him, Ramus grumbled, 'This is so undignified.'

'Your dignity will be the least of your worries if you don't hurry up!' hissed Kuelack.

'I'm crawling as fast as I can!'

Already the inky blackness was dissipating, and Ramus could see Kuelack's silhouette walking slowly up ahead with arms outstretched. The root, drawn by their movement, started to expand and fill the tunnel once more.

'I suggest you duck,' said Ramus. 'The time for subtlety is over.'

With their route of escape disappearing rapidly and his strength waning, Ramus gestured. Flames filled the tunnel, its roar followed by the hiss of boiling water, and blistering steam filled the air.

Munching on a wedge of cheese, having recovered his sense of humour somewhat after a good night's sleep, Ramus allowed himself a self-satisfied smile as he recalled the previous night's battle with the bizarre black moss.

Having hauled the singed and dishevelled Dark Lord out into the desert night air and across the dunes, he had placed Kuelack in one of the battered stone buildings to recover; the mage still clinging to the shards, like a dying man clings to life. Sat in the silent darkness he had then watched, spellbound, as the unearthly black moss, resembling a tormented many fingered starfish, searched for them with writhing tentacles until finally it had withered and lay rotting on the desert floor.

'Ahh, the Master of Moss is awake at last. Perhaps next time when I tell you to rest, you'll heed my words.'

'I have no interest in your counsel; my only concern is securing the shards. How long have I been laid here?'

With a flourish, Ramus smiled, then, bowing extravagantly, announced, 'Nearly a day.'

'A day! Why didn't you wake me?'

'Why so grumpy, Dark Lord, is it because you know I was right? Or is it that you feel indebted to me? After all, I have saved your life twice now?' smiled Ramus mischievously.

'Understand this, Dragon Lord, your actions change nothing.'

'But the fact that you mention me specifically indicates that my actions rankle.'

Handing Kuelack the water-skin, Ramus enquired, 'So where to now, oh Master of Moss?'

'West,' snapped Kuelack irritably. 'To a temple called the Shrine of Thane.'

'Founded by a Balefire witch of that name, if I'm not mistaken,' said Ramus.

'There are no records of the temple's location, except that it's somewhere in the Monad Mountains, but the shards will show us the way.' Then, climbing to his feet, Kuelack grumbled, 'We've rested enough. It's time to go. I'll eat once we're in the air.'

Packing away their rations, Ramus transformed once more into a majestic dragon and allowed the Dark Mage, yet again, upon his back. Leaving the sun-parched wilderness of Turkana behind, Ramus climbed into the cloudless sky. They reached the border by midday, then flew west over Durbah's green verdant lands towards the land of Srinigar, located further to the west. Resting at the border for the night, they rose early the next day and flew noiselessly above Srinigar's precipitous hills, wide valleys, regimented cities and mighty temples with their spires pointing like accusing fingers out of the primeval forest-dominated landscape. Through the low-lying, rain saturated clouds they soared until, late on the second day, the towering edifice of the awe-inspiring Monad Mountains appeared, rising out of the forests on Srinigar's western borders like a dark, undulating sea monster. After resting overnight, they awoke early and guided by the glow of the shards, flew a spiral path until, in the heat of the mid-morning sun, they came across a crumbling moss and vine-covered structure that, unlike the previous two locations, seemed to hold no menace. The ruin, built into the sheer mountainside on the eastern flanks of a sharp-pointed peak, seemed abandoned. It stared aimlessly out across a tree-choked gorge, like an old warrior that had seen too many atrocities and wished for nothing more than to be left in peace.

Alighting on a wide-open stone platform, Ramus, standing as a man once more and donning clothes made hastily from old canvass found in the Turkanian sand blasted settlement, said, 'This place reminds me of the fortresses of my homeland. This isn't the first time a dragon has landed here.'

'Very interesting, I'm sure. Come on,' ordered Kuelack irritably.

The outer chambers were cold and damp, and thick saturated moss dripped water from the moisture-laden walls, but, as they penetrated the ruins further, the humid atmosphere disappeared, replaced by unbefitting, unnatural warmth. However, the unnatural warmth was accompanied by another less appealing smell that saturated the air of the corridors.

'Is that...?'

'Yes. That, Ramus, is the unmistakable stench of death and decay.'

'Something you are no doubt used to,' replied Ramus sardonically.

Distracted from his examination of the ancient structure, Ramus watched anxiously as Kuelack forged ahead.

'Take care, Kuelack. Have you not learnt anything from our previous encounters?'

His voice echoing down the darkened corridor, Kuelack snapped, 'Silence Ramus. When I need the opinion of a coward, I'll ask for it!'

Then, using the stone's guiding light, Kuelack led them to one of the inner chambers where they found, to their surprise, several fiercely burning torches set into the walls. Stepping quietly into the chamber, they heard the flutter of leathery wings overhead in the stillness, accompanied by strange clicks, taps and bizarre echoing murmurs. Venturing further into the large chamber, the soft flickering light revealed a tall needle-shaped monolith inscribed with symbols and strange writings, stood upon a stone dais, at least three times as tall as a person. Around these were four large flat stones forming a henge adorned with grotesque offerings; beside them, prostrate at regular intervals on the dusty floor and seemingly at peace, lay the crumbling skeletons of lavishly dressed women.

However, at the base of the needle-shaped monolith was a dark stone container stained with blood and below that the half-gnawed bones of a discarded body.

'There it is, Kuelack,' urged Ramus, 'pointing to a small hollow within the needle-shaped stone.'

'I can see that, you fool!' said Kuelack irritably. 'Search the chamber. We are not alone.'

Then from the inky shadows, their teeth gnashing and their bony hands clawing the air, several women dressed in bloodstained rags shuffled into the light from the chamber's periphery. Sniffing the air, the sickly skinned, hunch-backed creatures shuffled forwards; their cadaverous eyes and sharp, wrinkled, pockmarked faces, leaving the pair in no doubt as to what they were.

'Remember, they are not for eating sisters,' said one.

'But it's been an age since fresh meat walked so willingly into our midst,' replied another.

'Yellow hags,' hissed Ramus. 'The dehumanised forbearers of Balefire witches.'

'So some describe us,' intoned a haggard voice.

'We like to think we are the true essence of our ancestry, unlike those,' said another, pointing to the lavishly dressed skeletons.

Their elected spokesperson stepped forward and inclined her head.

'My name is Leercher, and we have been expecting you, Child of Nightmare. You are here to release our kind from centuries of internment. We are also humbled to be in the presence of the mighty Dragon Lord who will serve the "Elemental".'

Looking down at the witches disdainfully, Kuelack, turning his nose up at their nauseating stench, commanded, 'Be gone wretches, I have not travelled all this way to bandy words with depraved ogres who feast on sacrificial blood for their power.'

'But that is the Balefire way, the Balefire design,' cackled another, matter-of-factly.

'Do not even try to enchant me with your inane babble, I know of your trickery,' sneered Kuelack, 'and what you covet. Pellagrin approached your sisterhood. He entrusted your ancestors with protecting one of the shards.'

'You are correct, the Balefires' only reward being rejection,' hissed one. 'The stone's magic rewards only the devoted and the advocates now.'

'Why didn't you tell me this, Kuelack?'

Ignoring Ramus's inquiry, Kuelack sneered, 'I know that your ancestors tried to take the shard for themselves and that Pellagrin and his followers foresaw the cult's betrayal, its failed attempts leaving the stone unassailable to all Balefire kind.'

'For the Dragon Lord's purpose, the arrangement was ideal. Although we are now immune to its persuasions, that same curse prevents us from using it. It was an arrangement that had proved so successful that the shard has remained untouched and neglected for centuries. However, it was also a gamble. He realised the risk and that it would be only a matter of time before the champions of light and dark would again come into being and the stones discovered; all our fates are inexorably linked.'

'Champions of light and dark,' snorted Kuelack. 'Utter nonsense, yellow hag trickery. I have read of this prophecy. It's the ravings of a madman sprinkled with Balefire propaganda and hogwash.'

'The clues led you here, did they not?'

'Yes, and it has nothing to do with myth and faerie tales. I am the one destined to control the stone's power; so, stand aside.'

'Think what you will, only Balefires can hold the shards, for all others it is madness, a lingering death.'

'Kuelack, do not be so quick to dismiss this. Torkval mentioned the "Elemental"; I think the hags are talking about the same thing.'

'Be quiet, Ramus.' Turning to the hags and eyeing them threateningly, Kuelack said deliberately, 'I won't warn you again. Stand aside.'

'Why would we stop you? We welcome your arrival. The shard is yours because Balefire prophecy decrees that the Nightmare Child, in the company of a Dragon Lord, would herald a new age and release us from the stone's custody.'

To Ramus's surprise, the yellow hags parted, allowing Kuelack free passage to the monolith at the centre of the henge.

'Take the stone Kuelack, they cannot use it. Their very nature forbids it,' urged Ramus impatiently.

'We have told you the truth. We cannot wield the stone. It's yours for the taking,' repeated the leader.

Warily, Kuelack walked forwards and emptied the glowing shard into his palm. 'It is the third shard!' marvelled Kuelack avidly.

The hag dropped silently to its knees then, and in a tortured, pain-wracked voice chanted, *You are the fated herald. One Balefire cannot harm another.*

The rest dropped to their knees and followed suit, screeching, *One Balefire cannot harm another.*

'Forget dreams of power and debauchery under the banner of the stone. For when I finally unite it, I will wipe your kind from the earth,' proclaimed Kuelack.

'Know this Dark Lord, we have nothing to fear from you, you have touched the stone imbued with Balefire enchantment. Your lust for power and glory has sealed your fate. Now that you have acquired the third shard, are you both prepared for the challenge ahead? Would you like to know of the fourth shard's location?'

Kuelack turned his lustful gaze upon the witches. 'You would tell me this, knowing I will destroy you?' said Kuelack.

The chant resumed. *One Balefire cannot harm another. One Balefire cannot harm another. You are the fated herald.*

'The last shard is in danger of being consumed by the very forces that created it and must be secured. You haven't much time. But before we give you the location, we need the Dragon Lord's assurance that he won't harm us!'

'It is not him that you should be pleading to for your lives.'

The yellow hags began chanting once more. *One Balefire cannot harm another.*

'I am tired of your pathetic droning and your innate riddles, wretch,' snapped Kuelack. 'Now give me the location. I will not ask again.'

Ramus, sensing Kuelack's subtle manipulations, smiled and, turning toward him, said light-heartedly, 'You should be thankful I'm here. Now don't be a fool; they haven't told us of the shard's location.' He turned to the witches. 'I swear I will not harm you.'

'Good, your word is a binding promise. It is hidden in the fortress of Collard Ray on the flanks of Arrowhead Mountain in Northern Zapata; but is in danger of being consumed. Go now, quickly, before the final shard is lost.'

'Thank you, you've been very helpful.' Gesturing, Kuelack called upon his magic. When nothing happened, he gazed in shocked surprised at his hands and then furiously at the Hasp who returned his blistering gaze, serenely.

'One Balefire cannot harm another,' said Leercher resolutely.

Suddenly understanding what the Hags chanting implied, Kuelack said, 'Very clever witch, but what you seem to have forgotten is that this stone is also called the Siamang. Possessing the shards ensures me the loyalty of the dragons.'

'I gave my word,' said Ramus in sudden understanding. 'I will not forsake my honour. Too many people have died because of your lust for power.'

Staring at him with intent, Kuelack brought forth the shards and boomed, 'Your word is nothing compared to the power of the stone; I command you Ramus, destroy them, incinerate them now!'

As Kuelack's words resonated around the chamber, he felt his willpower crumble, together with his resolution and self-control; slowly replaced by a dark and primordial calling. As if from a faraway place, he watched as flames engulfed the chamber, leaving no corner, no crook, no bend untouched. The stones command now fulfilled, he looked around the chamber at the Hasp's blackened remains. Turning to Kuelack, he raged, 'Monster! Fiend! What have you done? They aided you, but you had me kill them, anyway?'

'They are Hasp, they are cannibals, the scum of the earth, they are wretches who deserve no place in the civilised world.' Kuelack then looked at him with abhorrence. 'Did you think acquiring the shards would be a child's adventure? If so, you are a bigger fool than I imagined. To achieve greatness, strength and a ruthless determination is what's needed, not squeamishness and weak stomachs.'

'This is not strength or ruthless determination; this is the stone's will, the stone's design; it is utter cruelty.'

'We have lingered here for too long,' said Kuelack impassively. 'Take me to Collard Ray and the final shard.'

Turning angrily, Kuelack's last command ringing in his ears, Ramus strode from the chamber towards an uncertain future. His thirst for revenge had led him to this end. Had he known the extent of the shards' influence and Kuelack's lethal determination; he would never have agreed to this undertaking. Now it was too late. His fate and the shards were now irrevocably linked.

CHAPTER THIRTEEN

CONSEQUENCES

Not an easy decision to make, Lascana had decided on a lethal tonic, subtle and untraceable, administered via Mass Martin's drinking water. Having never planned to kill anyone before, she had lain awake for several nights, tossing and turning, at odds with her conscience. It's not that she regretted her decision, she just wasn't a violent person; but neither was she a doormat that people could just wipe their feet on. Traumatic events demanded traumatic actions; if they caught her, the penalty would be equally traumatic, but she had to do something. Her family and friends, indeed their very way of life, were disappearing rapidly. So, with Kuelack and Ramus away, she had made the decision that if she were cunning enough; she stood a good chance of killing Mass and Tallus, and with the pair of them out of the picture, she could make Perak and Alfic's lives more bearable and make Kuelack take heed.

Her thoughts turned to the day, over a month ago, when she sat with Alfic, Keegan and Perak in the cottage after they had returned, hot and sweaty, from pulling poisonous ragwort from the pastures...

'How do you cope as a parent, knowing...?'
'Keegan, you haven't?' exclaimed Lascana.
'Haven't what?' Keegan had replied nonplussed.
'Got a girl pregnant?'
'Whoa Lascana, don't get overexcited, I'm talking about Magen teaching Aridain!'

Throwing Lascana an exasperated look, Perak said, 'It's not all about the teaching; with Magen here, Kuelack has the perfect informant.'

'Not the teaching! It becomes a problem if she starts teaching him dark magic!' Lascana had countered.

'I think you have no worries on that score,' said Keegan confidently. 'Aridain's an intelligent little mite, and besides, as long as one of us is here....'

'The infuriating thing is that even if we wanted to, we couldn't stop her.'

'It's at times like this that you hope you've brought your children up to recognise good from bad,' mused Perak sadly.

Looking at Perak sympathetically, she had said, 'First Kuelack and now Magen, is this a consequence of being brought up to value money and power over love and family? How can greed generate so much jealousy and mistrust?'

'Vara always questioned why you couldn't be more like his brother and sister, Alfic. I'm just so glad you're not,' smiled Perak.

'Your son and Aridain are the two good things to emerge from your marriage; be proud of that, Father,' said Lascana.

Alfic, his face the colour of beetroot, turned, and looking at them intently had announced seriously, 'Talking of our son, he will be attending school next season. Should I fall, I want you, Father, and you, Keegan, to promise me you'll take Lascana and Aridain as far away from Kuelack and the school as possible.'

'I always knew you thought highly of me,' Keegan said, smiling.

'What are you saying?' Lascana had exclaimed angrily.

'He's saying that should he die...'

'I know what he's saying, Keegan. It was a rhetorical question,' growled Lascana irately.

'Lascana. I need to know you will be taken care of, should I not make it,' continued Alfic.

'I've never had to explain to a six-year-old before that his father's dead,' postulated Keegan.

'And you never will. Why are we even talking about this?' said Lascana angrily. 'You're not going to die and that's an end to it...'

It was one more reason why she must be the one to do it. She was the one their enemies least expected to act decisively.

Lascana looked up towards the sky and the sun that, like the uncertainties she felt, tentatively explored the occasional breaks in the clouds; its rays exploring Pellagrin's while surveying the courtyard's grassy gravelled pathways, then vanishing just as quickly.

Marching towards the object of her quest, Lawna's apothecary, she turned her thoughts once more to the problem at hand.

She had contemplated approaching Vara with her dilemma, but knew she wouldn't help, and would no doubt attempt to stop her. She had thought to approach the school's Passive Herb Mistress, Areca, for the ingredients she needed, but had dismissed that idea straight away, leaving Lascana with only one option, shopping for and mixing the potion herself, and that had meant visiting Lawna's apothecary.

With a tendency to eat when she was nervous, Lascana, chewing on a Navarian sweet meat, peered into the brightly coloured shop-front window, displaying soaps, salves, perfumes and dried herbal remedies. Then, with the saying about 'never burning your bridges' prevalent in her thoughts and with the fragrant concoction of herbal aromas filling her senses, she entered, the tinkle of a bell above the door announcing her arrival. She spied Lawna standing behind her counter. The short, ample-breasted busy-body, while talking profusely to her customers, mixed, infused, boiled and blended several concoctions in tin-ware pans sitting on a small range, her headscarf barely containing her fawn curly locks that threatened to smother her elfin like face.

To her right on the wall were rows of shelves on which sat bottles of varying shapes and sizes containing coloured powders, liquids and concentrates. Directly behind the counter, stretching from floor to ceiling, stood Lawna's cherished sandalwood cupboard with labelled drawers containing rare herbs, spices and substances from across the length and breadth of Aymara. The rest of the shop was also laid out and presented in an enticing display of scented petals, fragrant soaps, candles and dried flowers, the tantalising displays reflecting Lawna's fairy-tale and flighty imagination, together with ideas on how to decorate your home.

The goose-like gaggle that filled the shop dying to a whisper, Lawna glanced up at her approach.

'Lascana,' Lawna squeaked, hastily returning to the task in front of her, proving to Lascana that once again Lawna had betrayed their confidence. 'This is a surprise.'

'I'll bet it is! This is a list of ingredients. Could you wrap them for me please, and quickly? It will save us both... unnecessary awkwardness,' said Lascana frostily, peering around at the hostile looks cast in her direction.

'So, how's the family?' Lawna asked nervously.

'Fine,' snapped Lascana grimly, deciding that discretion was the better part of valour.

'Are Aridain and Duran getting along all right?'

'Fine, they're just fine,' replied Lascana, irritably.

'Because you know that friendship can only endure so many bruises and scars.'

'You just can't help yourself, can you?' murmured Lascana.

'All I'm saying is that the status quo won't last.'

'My son has assured me that he will not antagonise Duran.'

'But what about Duran? I'm just saying. Take Catherine Gonfalon's son, for instance?'

Lascana looked absently at Lawna.

'You know, Catherine Gonfalon's son, who has a talent for herbs,' alleged Lawna confidently, indicating that she should know who Catherine Gonfalon was.

'What has this got to do with Aridain and Duran?' Lascana said testily.

'Well, he and a friend of his, a boy named Talvo, were found experimenting with Navarian orchid powder in their dormitory. Apparently, this Talvo confessed that it was Catherine's son that led him astray, blamed the whole thing on him.'

'I still don't follow?'

'All I'm saying is, don't let Duran lead your son astray!'

'I can assure you my son has more about him than Catherine Gonfalon's son, and would never let himself be led astray by Duran.'

'No, you don't understand Lascana; it turns out that on further investigation they found Areca's been concocting enhancing brews.'

'No, she hasn't, Lawna.'

'How do you know?'

'Because I just do,' said Lascana innocently.

Returning Lascana's perplexed stare, the short buxom gossip said in exasperation, 'Come on, think about it Lascana, if Gradine's concerned, then it must be serious.'

'Of course, Gradine told you,' said Lascana, now totally confused.

'Yeeeess, how did you know? Have you and Gradine been talking?'

Having regained her composure, Lascana, now confronted with Lawna's warped logic, felt her anger rising once more.

'Tell me, Lawna, why would Areca, at her time of life, start peddling illegal narcotics to students, especially with her excellent record? It just doesn't add up.'

'Well, I'm not surprised you're defending her. After all, it's a well-known fact that many years ago, Perak and Areca were an item.'

Then losing her temper completely, Lascana raged, 'That's rare coming from the mistress of illicit affairs. Who Perak saw and when is not the issue here, the unenlightened gossipers of this world are. Rarely do they realise the damage their idle tittle-tattle causes. When are you going to realise that there are bigger problems in this world than what goes on in back alleys and bedrooms of people's minds?' she hissed.

'So why is Areca in hiding? Why not explain herself?' said Lawna fiercely.

'Because gossips like you and your little cabal here have already tried, condemned, and sentenced her, regardless of the truth. Honestly Lawna, I think it's you who's been drinking too much of Catherine Gonfalon's son's herbal mixtures.'

Offended, Lawna said. 'Don't patronise me Lascana, I'm only the messenger, besides I know what herbs and spices can do in the wrong hands.'

'Can you please just assemble these ingredients?' she insisted angrily, stabbing at her list irritably.

Kuelack had no need to turn the school against them, Lascana fumed while drumming her fingers on the counter irritably. *Lawna and her friends would do that all on their own without him having to lift a finger.*

'Gradine's not so bad if you find the time to get to know her. She only wants what's best for us shop owners.'

Now we're getting to it.

'I asked about Kuelack, where he's gone. Gradine cleared it all up. She assured me he's at the capital on school business.'

Lascana threw her hands in the air and shook her head. 'Unbelievable, if Gradine said jump off of the fortress roof you would, wouldn't you? I'm not interested in what she has to say; she's a self-centred egotist, who's only looking out for her own interests.'

'Really,' observed Lawna, 'it seems to me that with your husband and Perak busy, the school and its problems have faded away.'

From all around, she heard the collective murmurings of agreement.

'And you are untrustworthy. Friendship and loyalty mean nothing to you,' barked Lascana. She then turned to the shop in general. 'Think what you will. I have more important things to do than stand here and waste my breath trying to justify my family's action to a flock of clucking mother hens that have nothing better to do than talk people down.'

With her blood boiling, Perak's wise words rang in her ears. "Only trust good loyal friends, Lascana, and never open your heart or go telling acquaintances your secrets, because when things turn sour, they inevitably use them against you."

Paying Lawna for her ingredients, she snatched them up, turned and pushed passed the knot of customers, and not one of them met her inferno fuelled gaze.

Opening the stout oak door set into the boundary wall behind the dormitory wing, Alfic stepped out into the darkened lane. Despite his insisting that everything was all right, he had come to the realisation that Kuelack's campaign was working. For weeks now he had been alienated from his family, the constant workload weighing heavily, keeping him, his father and the workforce so busy that they had no time for anything else; they were exhausted and needed help. In those rare moments when they weren't working, he and his father had approached various members of staff with little success. Some were just too scared while the majority had adopted the, 'if we ignore the situation, Kuelack will leave us alone,' route.

So, in desperation, he'd approached the weather wizard Savarin, a good friend of Almagest's, and his family, and asked if he could arrange a meeting with Rasbora.

From the barren lands of Zapata far to the north, the mistress of transformation had a fearsome reputation. Questionably the most powerful individual in the school, if not the whole of Aymara, Alfic knew that if they could pave a way to some kind of understanding with the Sorceress of the elements, they could change the balance of power at the school.

As he quietly pulled the door shut to avoid any unnecessary noise, however, the sound of harsh whispering could be heard in the gloom. Pressing his body into the door's recess, he listened.

'... you're leaving? Rasbora, you can't be serious.'

'It has become politically impossible for me to stay as long as your government insists on sending troops across Zapata's border.'

Savarin declared forcefully, 'Our government has made it perfectly clear this is not an invasion. We're only responding to incursions by painted devils from across the border?'

'You do not need an army to quell a few unruly tribesmen?'

'What about your students, Rasbora? Have you thought about them? They'll be at Kuelack's mercy. The games at the fair... the new draft...; with Almagest dead and you gone, he can recruit at his leisure.'

Alfic watched, intrigued, as Rasbora turned towards Savarin with a look of dismay. To see Rasbora with her guard down was rare indeed. But that look quickly vanished, to be replaced by a look of fortitude.

Fixing Savarin with clear blue eyes, from beneath long straight silver blond hair that shimmered beneath the starlit sky, she growled resolutely, 'He would be wise to tread carefully when it comes to exploiting the children at this school.'

'Would be? Rasbora, it's already happening!'

Dressed in a light blue and white wide-sleeved gown, bodice and stark white shroud, the enigmatic sorceress's attire was in complete contrast to Savarin, dressed in his dark hooded cloak and grim attire. So taken aback was he by her stark, cold beauty that Alfic didn't notice when Rasbora suddenly looked in his direction.

Her steely gaze rooting him to the spot, she said in a deep lyrical voice, 'Don't you know it's rude to listen in on people's conversations, Alfic?'

Emerging from the shadows, Alfic approached from across the lane.

'Forgive me Rasbora, it was not my intention to eavesdrop,' he apologised. 'You're looking well,' he said, smiling, the effort giving his gaunt features the appearance of a cadaverous vulture.

'I can't say the same of you, Alfic. You look as if you're about to drop from exhaustion.'

'It's nothing a good night's sleep won't cure,' he replied nonchalantly. 'Almagest told my father once that if pitted against the Mistress of the Elements, he feared the outcome; you are, after all, the last word in the art of transformation.'

'Compliments, Alfic, from you?' she replied in her deep, echoing voice. 'Now I know you're desperate! Tell me, why does the famed master of resourcefulness need my help?'

Deciding not to beat around the bush, Alfic said angrily, 'If it came to a fight Rasbora, who would you support, us or Kuelack?'

'Fight! Who said anything about a fight?' declared Rasbora.

Savarin interceded. 'It will come to that. It's just a matter of when.'

'He fears you, both of you, but if either one of you leaves, it's only a matter of time before his ambition engulfs the school,' stated Alfic desperately.

'I sacrificed my childhood, painstakingly studied my art from the age of five and endured a strict upbringing to attain this position at Pellagrin's; I will not engage Kuelack on a whim.'

'A whim, Rasbora. Kuelack has already killed four times on his way to power, and these are the deaths we know about.'

'So proud, so austere. Tell me Alfic, why do 'you' need my help?'

'Because you are wise, as well as powerful.'

'Not good enough! If you want my help, tell me why.'

'Why are you being so stubborn, Rasbora? I can vouch for Alfic; his father is a fierce friend, and he is his father's son,' announced Savarin. 'A more rational and astute man I've never known.'

'It's all right, Savarin,' said Alfic guardedly, taking a deep breath, 'We believe that the reason for Kuelack's prolonged absence is that at this moment, with Ramus's help, he is seeking the Firebrand Shards.'

Looking up at Alfic with clear, blue piercing eyes, Rasbora exclaimed, 'Firebrand shards!'

'Yes, it seems the stone was not destroyed,' said Savarin darkly.

'Rasbora, Ramus has thrown in his lot with Kuelack,' insisted Alfic, 'on the one hand he claims his innocence, while on the other he colludes with Kuelack.'

Her cold, calm demeanour turning decidedly frosty, Rasbora growled, 'Has he now?'

'So, Ramus deceives you as well.'

'Yes, Savarin, it would seem so,' she growled ominously.

'In his ongoing attempt to gain control, Kuelack's accusing anyone apposing him of subversive acts,' Alfic continued. 'This upheaval is undermining everything that is good at the school. We are fighting a losing battle.'

'So, the former captain of the school guard is in charge once more,' said Rasbora knowingly.

'We know Kuelack has approached you,' insisted Alfic. 'We also know he left disappointed.'

'As will you, my country and yours are on the brink of war.'

'Alfic, if there's a time to speak, it is now,' Savarin said severely.

Standing to his full height of six feet, Alfic puffing out his chest, looked with intent towards Savarin, then back to Rasbora.

'Forget countries and boundaries, Rasbora, for when Kuelack's plans come to fruition, borders will count for nothing.'

'My countrymen need me. Better to die for something than live knowing I did not act.'

Alfic stared across at the two oddly paired friends. 'Running away to your homeland is exactly what Kuelack wants, Rasbora. It will not change the outcome; only here at the school can you make a difference,' said Alfic gruffly.

In the blink of an eye, Rasbora closed the gap and grasped Alfic's face firmly in her hands. Lifting him from the ground with ease, she studied him intently without a flicker of emotion from severe, blue razor-sharp eyes.

'There is something else, isn't there? What aren't you telling us, Alfic Bruin?' demanded Rasbora.

His legs kicking in the air, Alfic mumbled, 'Now that would be telling, wouldn't it?'

'Alfic, what are you doing?' cautioned Savarin.

'Be careful of your tone, groundsman. Others have tested me to their regret,' warned Rasbora. 'Now what is it you're not telling us?'

'I will not share with turncoats.'

'Alfic, don't be foolish. Rasbora, that's enough!' warned Savarin, 'You're killing him.'

After a period of uncomfortable silence, Rasbora lowered Alfic to the ground.

Collapsing to his knees and rubbing at his throat and jaw Alfic croaked, 'It seems we are both destined to leave here disappointed, Rasbora.'

CHAPTER FOURTEEN

DANGEROUS GAMES

'ARIDAIN! We're not skimming pebbles over a pond; these are rocks. Concentrate, that's it, focus, picture your hands wrapping around it, now guide it, steer it, and place it on top of the second one. That's it, very good.'

'That was easy. I can do more, Auntie Magen, let me show you!'

With exuberance Aridain picked up the rocks that, spinning and whirling, suddenly hurtled through the air, one of them ricocheting from a large tree trunk, the other splintering against the cottage wall just below one of the windows.

'Whoops.'

Impressive, thought Magen. *Only six, and already he has the abilities of a fourth-year student.*

'Aridain, we don't want you running before you can walk and throwing your magic around willy-nilly now, do we? Just listen to what I tell you. It's relatively easy to fling rocks around. Control is the key.'

This was Aridain's fourth lesson; during the initial lesson she had simply asked him to show her what he could do, while the subsequent two were teaching him simple techniques; however, this was the first time she'd allowed him to manipulate solid objects.

'Aridain.'

Gesturing dramatically with his hands, his tongue working overtime in and around his mouth, as he slowly lifted the stones and guided them back to where they stood, he replied, 'Yes, Auntie Magen.'

'Do you trust me?'

'Of course, Auntie Magen.'

'Do you trust me to help you?'

'Yes, Daddy told me Auntie Magen is the bestest sorceress in the land of Durbah!'

Do not trust her Aridain, she is not what she appears.

Oh, hello voice, I haven't heard from you in a while. It's all right, this is my Auntie Magen, she wouldn't do anything nasty.

'Very well, could you tell me, has anyone been tampering with your head recently?' continued Magen.

'What do you mean?' asked Aridain innocently, the stone dropping back to earth with a thud.

'How can I put this? Has your grandmother put anything in there, perhaps for safekeeping?' she asked, pointing to her own head, 'like, oh, I don't know, a secret memory or a special word.'

Aridain no, your auntie is very clever. You mustn't tell her anything, said the voice.

'Ok, I'll come straight out with it. Aridain, is there anything or anybody in your head?' Magen reiterated.

Concentrating once more on the task at hand, Aridain chuckled. 'That's just silly, Auntie Magen, why would there be anyone in my head?'

Magen regarded her nephew closely. Either he was a very good liar for a boy his age or, as was more likely, he simply didn't know. For some reason, her meeting with Gradine earlier that day suddenly intruded into her thoughts. Magen had known Gradine for a while now. Wielding power was what Gradine lived for and once she'd basked in that power, she would trample over anyone in her quest to retain it, regardless of the consequences or who got in her way or who she had to manipulate, be it grown-up, or… child…

'What have you discovered regarding the boy, Magen?' Gradine had asked darkly, studying reports while sat at Kuelack's desk.

'I believe there is another presence in his mind,' she had replied. 'This presence, it comes and goes, for when I think I'm close, it disappears.'

'Then do what you have to. I don't trust that conniving Mind Master…'

'Mass Martin, why do you say that?'

'Well, who else can it be? If the youth is as powerful as we suspect, Mass would have a powerful ally. That is why I'm ordering you to get him on our side, before Mass does.'

'Do you think Alfic and Lascana will just stand by as you attempt to subjugate their son?'

'Oh, I certainly hope so as I have several bones to pick, especially with Lascana…'

Her brother's son was talented, his gift immense, and if Mass could have, he would have already overpowered him. No, something else was going on here.

Her focus returning to the present, she thought about who it could be. Who had the most to gain? Was it Vara? Had she the skill needed for such a complex spell? Normally magic held a residue, a footprint, so unless this teacher at the school had learnt to mask their footprint, which was highly unlikely, it was someone new. Deciding to be more direct, she said, 'Aridain, listen to me. I want you to become a great wizard, but I think you're in danger. I think someone nasty is in your head. So, I want you to help me see who it is? I'm going to kneel in front of you and place my hands on your forehead. It's a way of seeing into your mind. It doesn't hurt.'

'Ok.'

Aridain, say nothing, lie if you have to, said the voice urgently.

It's okay voice, don't worry, Aridain said confidently.

As Magen was about to position her hands, her nephew looked at her shrewdly. That shrewdness turned to disappointment, and that disappointment turned to certainty. His look of embitterment shook her to the core, causing her to feel forlorn, underhanded and worthless. It was then that she realised he'd somehow seen through her deception.

Just then, with a hiss and a jet of fire, the dragonlet burst through the trees that surrounded the cottage's garden. The dragonlet, alighting on Aridain's shoulder, glared at her.

'Hello, Sabra,' greeted Aridain forlornly.

It's fortuitous that you should suddenly appear at this time, Sabra, said Magen, eyeing the dragonlet guardedly.

I sensed something was wrong.

Did you? I have a feeling it was something else.

I am the youngling's guardian, his guiding voice.

Keep out of this, fire breathing Squill. I am the only person able to teach Aridain at this time; his parents know that.

You may have pulled the wool over their eyes, but not mine.

Glaring at the dragonlet astutely, Magen thought, *Very perceptive Treerinks. I am intrigued, however. Is your honour that important that you would risk your life for this child?*

The Youngling has a dragon's heart and a dragon's nobility, something you sadly lack.

Squaring her shoulders, her eyes fixed on the dragonlet with dangerous intent, Magen, for the world to hear, warned, 'I also have a duty to my children and their safety. Nothing will stop me from fulfilling that responsibility. Do I make myself clear?'

The dragonlet, fixing her with an equally intense stare, replied, 'Perfectly! Youngling, it's time to go.'

'Sabra, you can talk.'

'Of course I can talk. It's just easier not to.'

Following the dragonlet, Aridain asked, 'So, where are we going?'

'Away from this skulking Bantu.'

'What's a Bantu…?'

Standing alone under bronze and auburn leaved trees in the late autumn sunshine, Magen looked up at the candyfloss clouds racing across the sky, and felt no comfort as she watched her nephew, his face a picture of betrayal, follow the dragonlet into her brother's cottage.

This conversation would make extracting information from her nephew so much more difficult. Anyway, what did a dragonlet know of the ways of men? It couldn't possibly perceive human politics or the social complexities involved here.

Taking consolation in the fact that she didn't have a choice, she called, 'Don't forget Aridain; be here at the same time next week.'

A crystal tear rolling down her cheek, her heart as empty as her words, she walked with as much dignity as she could muster out into the lane, her solitary footsteps as empty as her soul.

Shading his eyes against the low autumn sun's rays that had turned the underneath of the high-altitude cirrus clouds a luminous bronze,

Kale looked back towards the school towering over the majestic bronze beech and sweet chestnut trees, now all but bereft of leaves. The sun, reflecting from the school's windows, spires and ramparts, gave the fortress a magical, ephemeral quality, as if the enchantments weaved into its structure during its construction still resided somewhere deep down in its foundations.

Armed with his new knowledge, he had come to know the creature intimately, watching as it returned to the woods on a regular basis. When he wasn't attending Perak's lessons, he had tracked the creature that, growing at an unnatural rate, had doubled in size. He had watched as it took on the guise of the things it consumed; the creature becoming bolder day-by-day, tainting everything it touched, like an animal marking its territory, turning the grove from a garden of life to a place of death. Just as disturbingly, he had discovered Tallus tracking the creature and, on more than one occasion, found him staring intently through the trees as young Aridain played in his garden. However, he had resisted the urge to confront Tallus or the creature; that was, at least until he was sure he could give a good account of himself.

If I had kept my promise to Lascana..., if I hadn't recommended Magen to be Aridain's teacher..., if I hadn't apposed Tallus, none of this would be happening, he thought.

Deciding it was high time he found out who was residing in Aridain's head and determined to right his wrongs, Kale, using the trees beside the brook as cover, strode determinedly along the bank of the stream. Waving away the unwanted attentions of a flutter of agitated water imps, he was about to break cover when he heard the sound of a gate's latch being thrown. Watching as Magen closed the gate to the cottage behind her, he waited until she had disappeared from view, then, peering left and right, he broke cover and quickly, silently, approached the cottage. He knocked loudly on the door.

A call issued from inside. 'Who is it?'

'It's Kale, Kale Sim,' he answered nervously.

The door opened to reveal Lascana looking at him stoically. He smiled apprehensively and said, 'Hello, Mrs Bruin, I mean Lascana.'

'Don't just stand there, you idiot.' Grasping his arm, Lascana pulled him violently inside. 'What are you doing here? You're a wanted man.'

'A wanted man who broke his promise.'

Regaining his dignity, Kale, straightening his clothes, said, 'I'm sorry I took so much time coming back.'

'Don't be; Perak explained.'

'Do you remember what I said last time I was here?'

'How could I forget! You scared me half to death! You said that when you probed Aridain's mind that someone else was in there with you.'

Just then there was a squeal of delight from the doorway, and Aridain, shadowed by Sabra, ran into the room.

'Kale!'

Disengaging from Aridain's fearsome hug, Kale smiled, 'Hello Aridain, it's good to see you.'

Then, to his astonishment, Kale heard the dragonlet and Aridain talking as though it were an everyday occurrence.

He has the name of a green curly vegetable.

Sabra, be nice, Aridain admonished.

Kale eyed the dragonlet warily. 'So, this is your new pet, Sabra. Perak has told me all about him.'

'Yes, you know how Aridain is with animals,' Lascana said blissfully.

'Don't say pet,' hissed Aridain seriously. 'He doesn't like that word. He gets all prickly.'

I apologise, Sabra, or should I call you Treerinks; my name's Kale.

'You can talk to him too,' Aridain said gleefully.

'I wouldn't be a very good animistic if I couldn't.'

Suddenly, the dragonlet turned a vivid red and crimson and, hissing dangerously, it advanced across the tabletop. *He's a controller! You know they can't be trusted, youngling?*

Sabra, Kale's my friend, thought Aridain. *He won't hurt you. He's not like the man at the fair.*

I mean you no harm, thought Kale, holding out his hands in an attempt to quell the dragonlet's anger. *Fairy, and especially dragon kind, are proud and honourable creatures, and too many people get away with mistreating them.* Kale then said solemnly, 'That stall owner was no animistic; I don't know what he was, but he deserved his fate.'

'Sabra has obviously latched onto Aridain for some reason,' Lascana interceded, totally unaware of the ethereal conversation. 'As well as being the perfect replacement for Chipper, he's proved to be an invaluable ally; he's also very cute,' crooned Lascana, issuing cooing noises and scratching the dragonlet behind the ears.

Its demeanour relaxing, its skin once more turning a tranquil green and turquoise, the dragonlet hissed, *Youngling, your birth mother does know that I can hear what she's saying. Please tell her to stop calling me cute!*

'Muuum Sabra say's....'

The dragonlet, now slumping contentedly onto the kitchen table, purring like a cat that's got the cream, thought, *not so hasty youngling, perhaps being a replacement pet has its advantages.*

'Says what, dear.'

'Never mind.'

'Anyway,' continued Lascana, 'explaining to the school, its teachers and students that the dragonlet is only a pet will be a problem. They'll say the protection of one pupil is not reason enough to allow a dragonlet onto the grounds, especially when Kuelack becomes first on the council. He'll want Sabra killed out of hand or, at the very least, driven away.'

That will be the day, purred the dragonlet, now in raptures under Lascana's tender attentions.

'But teacher Ramus has lots of dragonlets; I saw them at the fair.'

'Aridain has a point Lascana, although where they're kept is another matter.'

Sitting down at the dining table, Kale sat back in one of the polished oak chairs.

'Aridain, I need you to answer a question for me?'

'Okay!'

'Have you been communicating with the creature?' asked Kale.

Screwing up his face, Aridain said darkly, 'I try not to. It says nasty, horrible things.'

'I didn't know this young man.'

'If I'd have told you, Mum, you wouldn't have let me go out, even with Sabra,' Aridain moaned.

'Does your Auntie Magen know this?' Kale asked.

Aridain shook his head. 'The voice tells me what to do. It tells me what Auntie Magen is doing and if it's appro... approp..., it says not to let Auntie Magen read my mind.'

'Magen is trying to read your mind!' said Lascana, outraged.

'Yes, that's what the voice said,' stated Aridain, nodding vigorously.

'And right under my nose,' cursed Lascana. 'When I see her, I'll…'

Ignoring Lascana's outburst, Kale asked, 'Aridain, has the voice revealed its identity? Has it told you its name? This is important now.'

'No, it said, it's too dangerous at the moment.'

'Can you ask…?'

Suddenly, Aridain grasped Kale's hands. Kale tried to pull away but instead found he couldn't move. He then found himself pulled from his body and catapulted into a kaleidoscopic world of colour and form, plummeting and tumbling, his senses unable to distinguish up from down. Abruptly, he came to a stop and looked around. Colour and light twisted, came together and then pulled apart, swirling and gyrating. He had been here before… it was Aridain's mind. Then a voice boomed…,

'Hello, Kale Sim. I'm Pellagrin.'

'Yes, yes, you are; I don't know how, but I can sense it. How is this possible?'

'It wouldn't be without Aridain's remarkable spirit to sustain me.'

Determined to keep the panic from his voice, Kale asked, 'Why are you here?'

'My purpose is to guide and protect Aridain from the people who would cause him harm.'

His mind whirling with the enormity of what he had discovered, he said, 'So, Aridain, is that important?'

'He is.'

'Why reveal yourself to me?'

'Because you, together with a handful of others, are charged with protecting 'The One' who will restore balance to the world.'

'You're entrusting the safety of the youngling to a human who has a name like a vegetable?' interceded Treerinks.

'His intentions, Treerinks, are honourable.'

'The dragonlet! Now, I understand; now it makes sense,' said Kale.

'We have been communicating for some time.'

'Some would say it's meant to be,' alleged the dragonlet.

'So, what's the catch?' Kale queried.

'The one teaching Aridain, the one called Magen. She has been delving and not without success. Treerinks has done his best to dissuade her, but she needs a more forceful form of dissuasion! You must find a way to stop her from discovering Aridain's true destiny.'

'This is a bad idea,' said the dragonlet.

'Why me? I'm no match for her. Surely there are better candidates?'

'Kale Simm, you must find a way. Now, I have lingered too long; we will talk again Kale Simm, promise me you will not reveal my presence here, not yet.'

'Wait, I have more questions. What do I tell his mother? Of what destiny do you speak?'

'That is for another time...'

Catapulted suddenly from the kaleidoscopic fantasy world into sunlit reality, Kale, as if waking from a vibrant dream, stared up at the ceiling and Aridain and Lascana's concerned faces.

'Really, Mr Kale, I don't think you're very good at talking to my voice,' said Aridain, seriously.

Kale smiled. 'I think you're right, Aridain.'

Helping Kale to his feet and peering at him with innocent eyes, Lascana asked apprehensively, 'So?'

His conscience battling whether he should tell her the truth, Kale didn't answer at first. Why didn't Pellagrin want his presence known? What would the consequences be if Pellagrin revealed himself? Pellagrin may have been frugal with his answers, but it was also unfair to keep Aridain's parents in the dark.

The Dragon Lord trusted you, Kale Sim, the dragonlet thought darkly. *Think what you're doing.*

Don't you think the Bruins at least deserve to know the truth, Treerinks? Telling them now might give them a chance to prepare for the future; they deserve that, at least.

And the youngling's task?

In the words of Pellagrin, "that can wait for another time". Let's give the Bruins time to absorb this revelation first.

Kale looked Lascana in the eyes and said, 'The voice in Aridain's head is Pellagrin.'

'Pellagrin! 'The' Pellagrin, who built the school! Pellagrin... Pellagrin the Brave...'

Holding up his hand to curtail Lascana's disbelief, Kale took hold of her shoulders and looked into her eyes. 'The very same. Look, I know it seems impossible, but trust me, it was him. Together with Sabra, he is here to protect and guide your son.'

'Who's Pellagrin the brave?' Aridain asked innocently.

'It's the name of the voice in your head, Aridain.'

He looked at them seriously. 'Yes, I know, you just said that?'

'He was a brave and noble dragon lord who fought against the despots of this world a long time ago. But you mustn't tell anyone. Do you understand, Aridain? You mustn't let anyone take that name from you. It's imperative.'

'I can tell Alfic, can't I? After all, he is his father.'

Kale looked over at Sabra, who stared back with a 'don't ask me,' kind of look, then said, 'Of course, Lascana, but no one else.'

It was late when Kale left the cottage, and apart from an evening rainstorm that had darkened the sky briefly, the clouds had disappeared, releasing the stars from their daytime slumber.

Hearing a noise behind him, he quickly squatted, and listening, peered through the undergrowth into the gathering darkness. Hearing nothing but the trickling of water, bush grasshoppers, bullfrogs and echo bugs chirping in the stillness, he resumed his cautious approach along the stream's bank, his footsteps releasing all manner of earthy autumnal smells. Approaching Keegan's shack, however, he stopped still in his tracks. He cursed as the light from several torches issued from within, accompanied by voices. One of them he recognised as Cordovan Harker, and another was the complaining Drench. He cursed again. Everything he owned was in that shack except for what he was wearing and carrying.

'Weak minded fool.'

Recognising the voice, he turned, but not quick enough as a powerful bubble of force impacted with his chest. He felt himself lifted off of his feet and driven through the air, impacting with the trunk of one of the pollarded willow trees. Stunned, he laid still, the darkened trees of the stream's margin dancing and pirouetting wildly across his vision.

'It was only a matter of time before I outsmarted and humiliated you. Did you really think your skulking and innate fumblings in the dark would fool me, that you could follow me around without my knowledge? Before I kill you, I want you to know that I have enjoyed teaching Torsk's students the real meaning of power, and I have especially enjoyed giving you and your friends the run around.'

Feeling blood on the back of his skull, Kale watched as Tallus emerged from the shadows. Trying to get to his feet, his world spinning and dancing in front of his eyes, Kale swore profoundly, 'You give yourself too much credit, you pathetic excuse for a human being.'

'Your words mean nothing, traitor,' spat Tallus. 'I have tracked your every movement while you followed me, watched while in desperation you allowed that, that grounds man to give you lessons in animal calling, as if it wasn't enough to have to listen to Torsk's innate mumblings.'

'Torsk was a good and honest teacher. He taught Perak resilience and resolve.'

Pausing, his hands raised to strike, Tallus hissed, 'Resilience and resolve, pah, they are no match for dark power.'

'At least they didn't have to turn to dark magic,' spat Kale. 'Twice you tried to kill me with winged insects, and twice you failed.'

Tallus thought for a moment, his forehead creasing in thought. 'The hornet flies at Keegan's cabin. You think I put them there, didn't you? Who needs insects when I can control raging beasts?' Tallus said self-importantly.

The animistic's smug face, reminding him of a grinning Shadow cat, Kale growled, 'Still thinking in terms of bigger is better, you never did get it, did you, you still don't. Detail is the key. Perak taught me that.'

'Stalling for time, very clever, but now your time is over. Goodbye, Kale.'

Kale closed his eyes and gestured, more in hope than expectation, and braced for the searing pain to come. When nothing happened, he opened one eye and then the other.

'Are you all right?'

Kale concentrated on the voice. 'Perak!'

'I'd say our next lesson is cancelled.'

Seeing Tallus lying comatose on the grass verge, Kale asked, 'How did you find me?'

'Cordovan and a contingent of soldiers are searching the cabin. Fearing for your safety, I came to find you and just in time, it seems.'

'Thanks, I owe you one.'

Perak, making a face, hissed, 'Oooh, that's a nasty cut on the back of your head.'

'It's nothing, just a bit of bloo…' The world span once more and his legs gave way. As his world turned black, the last thing Kale felt was damp earth against his cheek.

CHAPTER FIFTEEN

LASCANA'S GAMBIT

It was very early in the morning. Alfic had gone to work and Aridain was still asleep. Rekindling the embers of the fire, Lascana placed the kettle on the range and then, pouring some water into the large ceramic sink, splashed clear, cool water over her face in an attempt to wash the sleep from her eyes. Running her hands through her hair, Lascana sat down in an effort to calm her racing thoughts.

Are you sure you want to do this? she asked herself. *If you're caught, it's the death penalty.*

To quell her nagging doubts, she once more pictured Perak's and her husband's drained and weary faces. Gritting her teeth, she rooted out the necessary apparatus and implements and then threw the ingredients, purchased from Lawna's apothecary, onto the table. While heating the kettle of water on the range, and with clarity of purpose, she emptied them into a pestle and began crushing and grating.

'What are you making, Mummy?'

Flinching, Lascana spinning around, saw her son at the bottom of the stairs, accompanied by the dragonlet, rubbing at his sleep-filled eyes.

'Aridain, you scared me half to death. How long have you been standing there?' she barked. Then, calming her outburst with an effort, she said, 'It's a surprise for someone at the school.'

'That's powdered Navarian orchid, isn't it?' Aridain said, matter-of-factly, crossing to the kitchen table and grasping a paper sachet full of dark powder.'

'Put that down right now!' she exclaimed.

'Grandma uses that in poisons. She said that in the correct amounts, it attacks the nervous system,' said Aridain, studying the other ingredients.

'It's also used in tonics for anxiety.'

'And that's Wormwood,' he pointed out proudly. 'That's poisonous too.'

Emptying another paper sachet containing white granules into the pestle, she declared, 'Is that so? Did Vara also tell you that, if diluted, it also makes vinegar and can be used as a flavouring in spirits?'

'Yes, I know, but that's boring. Is that Lily-of-the-Valley?' he asked excitedly, dipping his middle finger into the pestle.

'Yes, to make soap,' Lascana lied.

A searching look upon his face, Aridain declared, 'Mummy, Sabra says you're lying.'

'Yes, all right, that's quite enough of that. Are you going to believe a dragonlet or your own mother? Go and make yourself some breakfast. There's some bread and honey on the shelf,' she snapped.

'But I want to see what you're making.'

'Do as you're told now!'

'Nan would let me stay and watch,' grumbled Aridain.

She shook her head ruefully. 'Sometimes that dragonlet is far too clever for its own good', she mumbled under her breath.

She was apprehensive, she knew, but it was no cause to snap at her son. Had Lawna been paying attention, instead of gossiping, she may well have questioned Lascana's choice of ingredients.

Startled by the kettle's shrill cry, she emptied the ingredients into the bowl; she then poured over the hot water and began mixing.

Stood beside the old fortress wall, Lascana wound a second bucket full of water from the well. Glancing nervously into the dense, oppressive fog that overnight had enveloped the school, she attempted to discern friend from foe by the voices of figures as they ghosted past.

Lifting the bucket now full of water onto the well's rim, she stroked her abdomen, and wondered what kind of world her second child would be born into, and what his destiny would be. Silently promising her infant that it would get the chance to grow up safe and secure, she pulled the dangling container full of water to the edge and emptied it into her bucket.

'Morning Lascana, real pea-souper, isn't it?'

'Morning Harold, collecting water for her majesty?' said Lascana nervously, knowing full well who the water was really for.

'No, this water's for Mass Martin,' he replied, releasing the ratchet and watching as the pail dropped into the darkness with a loud splash. As he wound the now full bucket upwards, he drew close and whispered, 'I happened to talk to Casey Defray recently. Casey revealed that Gradine walked into her shop the other day and tried to buy some wool.'

'Nothing strange about that,' replied Lascana.

'I agree, it was her method of payment that was strange; That she wanted to pay with a silver dektar.'

'For a bundle of wool!' exclaimed Lascana.

'Not only that, Casey mentioned that it wasn't the first time. Once she'd handed over the coin, Gradine began asking questions regarding certain events taking place at the school. When Casey pleaded ignorance, Gradine took back the coin before walking out.'

'Intriguing. While at the stallholders' meeting, both Casey and Elias mentioned Gradine offered them silver coins, while none of the others did.'

'Anyway, Casey investigated further. It seems she's been handing out silver coins at will. Those that accepted the silver coins are now firm supporters of Gradine; if you ask me, Lascana, she's paying for information and loyalty.'

'I don't think it's that simple, Harold. I know our friends; none of them would give in to bribery, especially Bern and Gable.'

Then it hit her; silver has an allure all of its own. The coins must be charmed. Her mind working overtime, Lascana thought back to the stallholders' meeting and Casey, studying the room with a cool, calm, cat-like persona before the wool merchant realised Lascana was watching her. An enigma; it seemed Casey resisted silver charms as well, and what of Elias? What made these two so special?

Lascana was brought back to reality by Harold's cursing as the bucket hit the water with a loud splash.

137

Peering over the edge to check the container had survived, Harold, rubbing at his fingers, said, 'Curse this damned joint rot.'

Helping the friendly butler draw the bucket, now full of water once more, Lascana, securing the vessel, said, 'I'll tell you what Harold, in return for your invaluable information, I'll deliver Mass's water for you.'

'Are you sure, especially in your condition?'

'My condition.... oh, you mean... But how can you tell? I'm not showing, am I?' said Lascana, looking down and caressing her stomach.

'I can tell,' smiled Harold, 'you have a certain glow. You don't get to be my age without knowing a few things,' he said, tapping his nose.

'Harold, go see Areca, get something for your joints. I'll see to the water.'

'Lascana, Areca's under investigation. These last week's Beria's been treating me.'

'So, it's true, Lawna mentioned it, but I figured it was Lawna being Lawna, poor Areca.'

'I don't understand it, Lascana. Why would Areca do that?'

'She wouldn't, the investigation, the coins, it all reeks of Gradine,' said Lascana angrily. 'Go Harold, go see Beria, I'll take care of teacher Martin's water.'

'Ok, but only if you're sure Lascana.'

'I'm surer now than I've ever been,' said Lascana darkly.

Her anger bubbling just below the surface, Lascana secured the two buckets full of water to the yolk. Then, squatting and balancing the yolk across her shoulders, she stood up. With renewed purpose, born of frustration, she approached the betrayer's door, with its vine and leaf embellishment set into the fortress wall, and the soldier guarding it. Allowed to proceed, she marched past the herbaceous borders, oblivious to the Chrysanthemums, Delphiniums and Red-hot pokers now in autumn's final flush. So angry and focused on the task at hand was she, that she totally ignored people's greetings as they materialised out of and then disappeared into the fog.

However, as she approached the door at the fortress's rear, it opened and from within Gradine appeared, pushing a lavishly furnished pushchair. Mustering all of her dignity, Lascana stared straight ahead, determined not to engage Gradine in front of the staff and students, going about their daily routines.

'Ahh good, you're finally mindful of your place in the world. After you've delivered my water, my privy also needs emptying,' Gradine said loudly, so as everyone could hear.

Seeing red, Lascana, forgetting her task, set Harold's buckets down. With fists clenched, she turned and locked eyes with Kuelack's conceited spouse, who stood imperiously, a smug look upon her face. Ignoring the sniggers from the soldier stood beside the solid oak door, Lascana, now calmness personified, stood toe-to-toe with Gradine and announced calmly, 'It's against my principles to serve someone who can't even wipe her own backside without help!'

'How dare you..., you..., dung shovelers wife! Who do you think you are?'

'Someone who has no intention of being spoken to like that, be it by a King or a Princess, or a jumped-up socialite like you.'

'Why you... you..., arrogant pig herder,' Gradine spluttered, her pasty skin taking on the colour of beetroot. 'You will regret your words, Lascana.'

Her anger smouldering Lascana, glaring at Gradine, growled, 'I'd rather live in a pigsty than sink to your level.'

She glanced at the guards with intent. 'People like you have no backbone and always have others to do your dirty work for you. If you can't succeed by fair means, you succeed by foul. Isn't that right, Gradine, like charming my friends with silver coins or trying to blame poor Areca for your illegitimate dealings?'

As the smile drained from the guards' faces, Lascana knew she'd already said too much, but she continued anyway, 'Yes, Gradine, I know about your underhanded activities.'

Gradine, her eyes narrowing dangerously, hissed, 'It's not my fault your friends value money over loyalty.'

'Apart from Casey and Elias, that is,' said Lascana, smoothly.

'What can I say? They are from Calabash, after all!'

Gradine had virtually admitted it, but when all was said-and-done, Lascana could do nothing about it... yet.

When Lascana remained silent, Gradine, her composure reinstated, sneered, 'Power and privilege, Lascana, people crave what they can't have

139

and will do anything or sacrifice everything to have it. It's something you could have had, had Alfic emulated my husband; instead, you chose the path of deprivation and squalor.'

'And your weakness, Gradine, is that you measure your life by your possessions, your position in society. There's more to life than that.'

Smiling wickedly, Gradine continued, 'Oh, power and wealth are much more than that. They can gain you all sorts of information; take Harold for instance.'

Lascana baulked at the mention of the retainer's name, and her heart sank.

'Oh yes,' smiled Gradine, 'I know of his treachery.'

Her fists curling, she replied angrily, 'I don't know what you're talking about.'

'Please Lascana, do you think I'm so naïve?'

Her mind awhirl and her carefully laid plans collapsing around her, Lascana struggled to make sense of how this had happened. Then clarity dawned and looking up abruptly at Gradine's confident, grinning face, she said, 'Lawna told you.'

'Yes, she informed me of your visit, and of the suspect ingredients,' said Gradine smugly. 'She felt it was her duty to the school.'

'But Harold had nothing to do with the ingredients I purchased. He wasn't even there.'

'Because you involved Harold in your web of deceit, the sweet, naïve butler's life is now forfeit.'

Lascana closed her eyes in despair, took a step backwards, then shook her head. 'Please, he didn't know about my plan.'

'Oh, pray tell, what plan was that?'

Lascana flinched. She had walked straight into Gradine's trap.

'Please, I'll do anything. Harold had nothing to do with this; he's a sweet honest man; don't punish him, punish me if you have to, he need not die.'

With a flourish, Gradine turned and attended to Gabion, who had begun to cry. She then leaned close and hissed in her ear.

'Lesson's need to be learnt, Lascana. You and your friends need to see that you're in way over your heads, that this is a fight you cannot win.' Then, in a loud voice, Gradine, sporting a self-satisfied grin, announced, 'Guard, arrest her for the murder of Harold Hunt.'

Stifling tears, Lascana stood mute as the guard seized her arms and escorted her inside. Because of her arrogance, the sweet natured retainer would pay the ultimate price.

Opening her eyes, Lascana looked around in confusion. From every angle a myriad of grotesque faces, some angry, some miserable, and some just downright barmy, glared down at her. Her befuddled senses slowly clearing, she realised that she was laid on a luxurious bed in a dimly lit room full of soft dark furnishings, warmed by a roaring fire, and that the grotesque faces were, in fact, masks, hung upon the walls. Some were skeletal in nature; some were bulbous, and many were colourful. Others, she noticed, were framed with long strands of reeds and manes of feathers for hair, while even more were demonic and sported tusks, spikes, horns and long pointed teeth.

'Hello, Lascana, you're well, I see.'

Lascana instantly recognised the small, weaselly voice.

'Do you like my collection? The masks are fascinating, don't you think? They're from all over Aymara. They represent our diverse nature and mirror the soul at its most intense, most vulnerable. The masks give us a glimpse behind the façade we project to the world. They represent our passions in their basic forms...'

Climbing unsteadily to her feet, she demanded, 'Mass, where am I? What did you do?'

'You're in my apartment. I ordered the guard to bring you here.' Then, as if they were at a garden party on a warm summer's day, Mass, holding up a decanter of Navarian Brandy and two glasses, offered casually, 'drink?'

'The guard?' queried Lascana, shaking her head.

'He does as I tell him; as they all do, he will retain no recollection of these events, nothing to report.'

Changing tact, he then said seriously, 'Your scheme was a good one; kill me and then kill Tallus.' He held up his hand. 'Don't bother denying it. Underestimating me was the flaw in your plan.'

'I won't betray my friends or family willingly, so if you're going to kill me, then get on with it,' she spat defiantly.

'Kill you! Oh no, you misunderstand. You have nothing to fear from me,' said Mass, 'and neither does your son.'

'What are you talking about?'

'Gradine has ordered your death, together with your friends.'

'Keegan and Mace?'

'Yes, the charge is "treasonous acts against the school", I believe she said; only your death is something I cannot allow.'

'So, why am I here?' queried Lascana, her mind awhirl with speculation.

'Straight to the point, I see.' Pausing and placing his drink on one of his mahogany inlaid tables, Mass turned, then announced, 'I know your son is special, very special. I also know that Magen has been tasked by Kuelack to…'

'We know of Kuelack's intentions; it suits our purpose for now.'

'Once Magen has him trained, Kuelack will take Aridain away from you, his revenge for his perceived suffering at the hands of his brother, your husband. He also suspects that Aridain is more than just an ordinary boy.'

'His suffering…? Kuelack doesn't know the meaning of the word.' Regaining her composure, Lascana said, 'If I find out that what you say is true, then the arrangement will be terminated.'

'Your control is impressive, especially as this concerns your son. However, if you fight Magen on this, Kuelack will have your friends and family killed and take your son now.'

'Then I will take him from this place. I don't care where…'

'There is nowhere you can hide. Kuelack will find you, Magen would have seen to that.'

'Why are you telling me this? Your intentions are no more honourable than Kuelack's,' spat Lascana.

Mass began pacing up and down. 'I will tell you a short story; it involves Alfic's sister who, in an attempt to placate Kuelack, informed him of Aridain's talents. Since discovering that Kuelack had tasked Tallus to scan Aridain, I have been watching your son while at play; while he and the farmer's daughter laughed and played at the fair, for instance. However, when I tried to probe his mind, his primitive, unrestrained power nearly killed me. It was then that I realised how special your son is.'

'Pity he didn't succeed!'

'Oooh, so much passion and defiance, I love it,' squeaked Mass, his body shaking, seemingly in anticipation. He then continued, 'After that, I trod very carefully. I then realised that Kuelack's fleeting concern didn't do your son justice; his resemblance to the creature, his blossoming abilities, it all added up; but to what? I intended to find out, so gradually I managed to burrow my way past those defences. Then, one sunny morning, I discovered quite by chance a mental blockade, a barrier, that no matter how hard I tried, I couldn't penetrate. I was intrigued. The barrier wasn't Magen's, because as good as she is, she is no match for me. So, Lascana, how could a boy his age prevent me, the Master of Minds, from plundering his secrets?'

'Careful Mass, soon your head won't be able to fit through the door.'

His beady eyes narrowing, Mass concentrated. 'Don't make me take the information by force, Lascana.'

Realising her knowledge of Pellagrin could jeopardise them all, Lascana took a deep calming breath and insisted adamantly. 'I don't know what you're talking about?'

Suddenly, the weight of Mass's mind was upon her, crushing and squeezing, until, all too briefly, Mass was sifting through her mind as if sifting through the pages of a book. When his consciousness departed, it left a void and a feeling of being utterly violated. The apartment's nauseating, in-your-face decor swimming in front of her vision, Lascana endeavoured to focus her mind.

'So Pellagrin travels with your son, in here,' exclaimed Mass triumphantly, pointing to his head. 'Special indeed?'

Mass's onslaught leaving Lascana's mind giddy, she said, 'You're afraid of my son, of what he can do; you also mean to challenge Kuelack when he returns.'

Mass span around, and with a look that sent Lascana back to her knees, bellowed, 'How did you...?'

'I saw it when you took the information from here,' Lascana groaned, pointing to her head. She then took a sharp intake of breath. 'It was you who betrayed Harold; you told Gradine he was passing us information, you pathetic excuse for a human being.'

Lascana groaned then, as Mass squeezed her mind once more.

'Human, I am not human,' he roared. 'I'm better; I am the next step in evolution.'

'Then... I weep... for the species,' gasped Lascana.

His hairless brows creasing in rage, Mass turned and raised his fist in a gesture of anger. He relented and, taking a deep breath, smiled and said calmly, 'You do like living dangerously, Mrs Bruin.' Regaining his composure, Mass said serenely, 'But you are correct, I told Gradine about Harold in order to maintain the façade I'm still working for Kuelack, and yes, I do intend to challenge the Dark Lord, 'if' he returns, but that is none of your concern. Your son's power, however, what I've seen of it, is daunting; it must be harnessed and controlled now before he grows much older.'

'Just like my deranged brother-in-law, what you can't control, you destroy, and what you can't destroy, you control.'

'Personally, I'd prefer to gain the boy's trust with his mother at his side. However, should his mother prove uncooperative, I'd be forced to kill her, her unborn child, and the boy's father before taking him under my wing; then I will become the father he needs, and he will rule by my side.'

Lascana, unable to picture her life without Alfic, without her family, blinked back tears. Her mind awhirl, she turned and said savagely, 'You would kill my unborn...! You monster!'

'Understand this, Lascana. For your husband, your family and your friends, there is no future. You can die along with them or you can live and nurture your son by my side. Your choice Lascana.'

'This is madness,' she despaired, wiping away tears of frustration. 'You're asking me to abandon my family and friends?'

'Kuelack will tolerate no challenge to his rule, and your family will not tolerate me taking your son. You will be killed and your son taken to be fostered by Magen. Some sacrifices will have to be made, but my way, at least I can save you, your son and the life of your unborn child.' Staring into her eyes, Mass insisted, 'Oh, and one more thing, no more unnecessary risks. Now go back to your humdrum life. I will be watching...'

Standing outside the admin building once more, Lascana looked down towards her unborn child and, caressing her abdomen, she sobbed, 'I'm sorry. Don't ever listen to a mother who can't keep her promises.'

Despairingly, she hoisted her water buckets across her shoulders and, with the feeling she was carrying the weight of the world in those buckets, she traipsed dejectedly across the grass towards her small bric-à-brac stall.

Dressed in a brushed dark blue and orange stitched cuirass, bodice and matching tight-laced boots, Casey Defray, her dark, free-flowing hair now tied in a ponytail, locked the door to her store for the last time and peered into the night. Making her way noiselessly towards the stables, she checked one more time to make sure she wasn't being observed. Adjusting her dragon scaled shoulder armour, she slipped her gauntlets over her hands, making sure they were secured properly, then tied rags around the horses' shoes in order to muffle the sound of their hooves. Then, looking and listening intently for any movement, she led her mounts quietly across the courtyard.

Soon I'll be far from here, she mused in an effort to conciliate herself. *It will be good to finally get back home.*

As was the way of Durbarians, they would speculate for a time, postulate why she had left suddenly in the night, then they would forget about her. Still, when she recalled the faces of the people she had come to know, she felt sad, as some of them she even thought of as friends, which annoyed her. She shook her head angrily, as if the action would purge the memory of their faces and her time here.

"The Sovereign, the realm, the Korda, defend these pillars of our society with your life, your very being, and you will be rewarded in this life and the next."

There was more to the recital, but strangely, she could not recall the words. It was yet another reason why she should leave.

Yes, better to not get too familiar in the first place; dedication and devotion were the way; fondness and friendship were weak-minded notions and a passing fancy, she thought, in an effort to reinforce her allegiance, *still they had been kind.*

The store holders' friendly faces flashed before her eyes once more.

'What is wrong with you?' she hissed savagely. 'You have an assignment to fulfil; you have orders. I passed on what I knew to the manservant Harold. What more can I do? These people are my country's enemies, after all.'

But she knew deep down the reason for her reticence. She felt guilty, for despite knowing what she had learned, she was abandoning them.

Focus, fulfil your mission.

She forged ahead, determined not to drown in the overrated concept of nostalgia, and turned her mind to the task ahead.

The sleeping draft I administered should have taken effect by now, so it's a simple matter of collecting my charge and returning home.

The smell of baked bread assailing her nostrils, she hid the horses in the alleyway beside the bakery and lifted a coil of rope from her saddle. When she tested the door, however, Casey discovered it was already unlocked. Drawing her knife from its pommel strapped to her thigh, she pushed gingerly against the door and then peered cautiously into the interior of the bakery, which was lit by the embers of the cooling ovens. Stopping and listening, and detecting no movement, she crept with the grace of a cat across the shop front and into Elias's rooms beyond.

Too late, she realised her mistake and before she could react; she was bundled to the floor. Before her attackers could restrain her, she twisted her cat-like body, her hand sweeping around in an arch, her exertions greeted with a satisfying yelp of pain as her knife ripped through flesh.

'Hold her, you morons,' a woman's voice hissed angrily.

With her face forced onto the wooden floor, she continued to struggle, screaming like a wildcat. Rough hands grasped her arms, and they were twisted painfully behind her back. Her hands now bound, they twisted her onto her back but, before they could bind her legs, Casey kicked out. Again, she was rewarded with a high-pitched yelp as her foot connected with a soft bundle of flesh. But her three aggressors were stronger and, as hard as she struggled, her legs were forced together and bound with rope.

'Stand her up!'

Dragged painfully to her feet, Casey came face-to-face with the grinning facade of Gradine Bruin bathed in flickering torchlight.

'Well, judging by your attire, you're no seamstress. So, tell me, assassin, what do you want with the baker?'

'If you know of our kind, then you know you will never get me to talk.'

'Bring him in,' Gradine barked.

She watched as the two guards dragged the unconscious Elias Tan into the room and sat him roughly in an old wooden chair.

'If you won't talk, then maybe he will. Wake him up!'

'He won't wake up mistress, we've tried.'

'Very well, bring him along. When he awakes, we'll ring the truth from him.'

CHAPTER SIXTEEN

COLLARD-RAY

As Ramus flew Kuelack northwards along the spine of the Monad Mountains, a winter chill had replaced the autumnal air and frosted snow increasingly covered the countryside below.

'Look down there, Kuelack. Is this also part of your plan?' Ramus declared as they flew northeast over the Salamis pass, a wide valley separating the Monad and the Mycean highlands that marked the border between Srinigar and Durbah.

Down below, lines of refugees clogged the roads as they fled south.

'Those people are worried for their lives.'

'Our armed forces are simply responding to the concerns of Durbarian citizens. The Zapatian military would be wise to keep its forces north of the border.'

'It is not our forces you need to worry about; there are reports that Durbah's soldiers are ranging northwards into Zapatian territory.'

'They are ranging northwards to nullify the barbarian threat, to keep our borders safe,' insisted Kuelack belligerently.

'Have you learnt nothing from the past? Power and greed lead to war, devastation and suffering.'

Kuelack said dismissively, 'It's the way of things, Ramus, the rich triumph over the poor and the strong triumph over the weak; you either profit by it or suffer beneath it.'

'My father always argued that conflict achieves nothing; dialogue and communication are the way forward. Secrecy and lies are the evils that besiege us,' he always lectured, 'and the need to obtain that which we cannot have. It's the reason the protectorate, along with their riders, attacked my home while my family lay sleeping; they wanted my father's dragons, dragon riders and his numerous Sprawls. And now that they have seized power, they sit by and watch as Durbah's forces encamp themselves in Zapatian territory? The more I think about it, the less sense it makes. It's almost as if…'

'If presented with a lucrative opportunity, very few people refuse,' Kuelack said simply. 'Now, no more discussion; the fortress of Collard Ray awaits.'

In silence, following the wide valley northwards, Ramus flew above the glittering ribbons of the rivers Undine and Storna, the headwaters of which had their origins in the high peaks of the Monad Mountains. Then, they continued northeast, taking care to avoid patrolling Dragon riders as they crossed the border into Zapata. Later that day, having passed safely over the demarcation lines, Kuelack, above the whistling of the chilling wind, grumbled, 'How can you call this cold, barren, moss ridden tundra home?'

'We dragons crave wide-open spaces and freedom. The further away from Gonda's politics and those pompous fops in the civilised world, the better; that life is anathema to our kind. Civilisation…' he shivered, his body shaking violently, 'the very word makes my skin crawl. Pellagrin's and its politics are as much as I can stomach.'

Continuing on in silence, Ramus soared over the Zapatian foothills, the rising ground below dusted in a layer of snow, like frosting on a cake. Now, bearing an intense loathing for his passenger, Ramus glanced back at the dark mage sat astride his back, who now firmly believed he was destined for greatness and displayed a singular sadistic determination to master the stone's power. This determination, however, came not from him, but originated from the shards that now affected every aspect of his behaviour to the exclusion of everything else - demonstrated by his callous determination to kill the Hasp.

Taking a deep breath of sulphurous Zapatian air, Ramus roared above the whistling of the wind, 'How does a man come to be so full of hate, to loathe his family enough to want to kill them?'

'It's simple, families make you weak and vulnerable; families generate sentiment, and sentiment gets in the way of greatness; they become an unnecessary distraction, a burden in point of fact.'

'Like the Hasp, whose only purpose was to serve you?'

'They were unnecessary, surplus to requirements,' Kuelack replied simply.

'As am I, no doubt, once we reach the school.'

'Then, you had best serve your purpose and not anger me.'

'I pity you, Kuelack. Without family, life loses its purpose. I would give anything to have my family back,' Ramus roared wretchedly.

'Family, pah, money and power, they are the only things worth having.'

As the miles passed, the pines and spruce disappeared altogether as they flew higher and higher across Zapata's volcanic plateau. Plumes of smoke and gas appeared on the horizon, filling the air with its metallic earthiness, but to Ramus and his dragon senses, they meant much more.

'The Hasp told the truth. Monarch Mountain is a fresh eruption; it's a scent I've not encountered before. Arrowhead is situated just beyond.'

'Then, let us make haste; the slightest delay could see the remaining shard slip from my grasp and stay away from those plumes; I've read dragons are predisposed to immersing themselves.'

Veering between snow-capped mountains, Ramus crested a ridge. Alighting upon a spur of volcanic rock, on Arrowhead Mountain's razor edge, they gazed down through the acrid atmosphere into the tortured valley below, now a viscous river of lava. With a sudden down-draught, the clouds parted and there, balanced on an outcrop, stood the ruins of Collard-Ray, a gargantuan fortress built, it was rumoured, by strange one-eyed giant folk, long before the great devastation. After scrutinising their surroundings one last time, Ramus flew out over the spurting lava fountains and plumes of choking gas, alighting upon one of the many toppled-down towers that could easily have been mistaken for a jagged mountain spur.

With a word and a flick of his hand, Kuelack once more produced a small globe of light. Preceded by the fiercely glowing ball and accompanied by the three shards' ever-increasing emerald green radiance, Ramus descended through one of the many towers, broken and faded with time. Into the bowels of the mountain, they flew in ever decreasing circles, finally alighting at the base of a giant curved stone stairway, designed for a gait far wider than any mans.

With every groan and shudder, rocks fell from all around the vast chamber, ranging in size from pebbles to the size of horses. 'We haven't much time, Kuelack,' warned Ramus, glancing around.

'Don't you think I know that, you fool? Now lower me to the ground,' ordered Kuelack.

'I think, after our previous encounters, I should accompany you,' hissed Ramus.

'I give the orders here,' commanded Kuelack. 'Now, do as I say.'

Powerless and bound by Kuelack's command, Ramus crouched low to allow Kuelack to dismount.

'Now, wait here.'

Despite the volcanic nature of the terrain above, the interior of the chamber was wet and humid. Water dripped from large curtains of multi-coloured moss that hung from the walls and disappeared into the blackness above, where piranha bats and firethorn lizards screeched their radar song in the darkness.

His dragon eyes, piercing the gloom, Ramus watched as Kuelack, accompanied by the shards' combined radiance now a green concentrated beacon of light, climbed the ancient stone steps one by one. Sensing movement in the empty silence, he issued a warning hiss, 'Hurry up mage, we are not alone.'

'Do not display any false anxiety on my part, Ramus. We both know your concerns are purely selfish.'

However, the globe's light increased to reveal ghastly, unsightly creatures that lingered briefly before scampering away unseen into the darkness, odious things that would not venture into the light to challenge him or the dark sorcerer.

Ramus thought, *it almost beggars believe that this last segment, joined to the other three, could possess so much power.*

He wondered at the wizards of old who had failed to realise the force in their midst, and instead of embracing said power had, in their fear and trepidation, chosen to split and consign the Firebrand stone to obscurity. *With just one piece, it will be a simple matter to avenge my family, but with four, I dread to think about what might happen.*

He watched as Kuelack climbed the final step of the stairway to stand before a strange stone dome with a smaller inverted dome on top. The sculptures that sparkled in the intense green light were decorated with worn and half-obscured scriptures and writings which had become fractured and worn over time. Sat on top of four out-turned, leaf-shaped plinths were four giant bipedal statues, possessing two horns that protruded from either side of their foreheads and a single eye. Ramus had heard of such creatures that had once inhabited Zapata, and he often wondered if this Cycloidian race still roamed the barren volcanic northern plains.

Another rumble shook the cavern as Kuelack, now on his hands and knees, disappeared out of sight into a recess below the sculptures. Abruptly, a change permeated the air and a green mist appeared from the ancient structure, coalescing and undulating as if alive. Reappearing, suddenly, Kuelack jumped backwards as the broiling vapour enveloped his body in a sinuous embrace. Kuelack, his body contorting in pain, spread his arms and began chanting rapidly. For an age, it seemed, he chanted as the mist twisted, convulsed and squirmed around him. The living fog then froze abruptly, statue-like, its appearance sparkling like glass. Then Kuelack clapped his hands and the statue of frozen fog shattered with the sound of a thousand icicles that echoed loudly in the vast chamber. Now alone on the stone steps and breathing heavily, Kuelack, after what seemed like an age, stirred. On hands and knees once more, Kuelack slowly crawled into the dark recess. However, in the chamber, as he disappeared once more, the atmosphere changed again. Ramus turned at the sound of chittering and clicking. Peering into the darkness, he saw the misshapen creatures that so far had kept to the shadows, scurrying and scampering towards him, possessed of a renewed bravery and buoyed by ever-increasing numbers. Too preoccupied now to follow Kuelack's progress, Ramus danced and pirouetted, slashing with his tail and talons, reducing to ashes a myriad of creatures that leapt, crawled and flew towards him; biting, stinging and clawing at his leathery skin.

Ramus caught sight of Kuelack as the Dark Lord, clutching another small silk bag and wavering on his feet, reached the last few steps, pursued by hundreds of grotesque, misshapen creatures. Ramus knew that Kuelack and the shards had mere moments left. Before he could act, however, Kuelack ordered, 'Ramus, to me, now!'

With a frustrated roar, Ramus engulfed himself in flame. Then, taking to the air, he flew through the fireball, frying the mass of flying and crawling things, ripping and tearing at his armoured body.

Followed by a myriad of misshapen winged creatures, Ramus, clasping the wizard in his talons, ascended towards the great rent in the ceiling, accompanied by a renewed shaking of the mountain. With a roar, Ramus burst from the collapsing tower as it, together with the great fortress, collapsed slowly into the lava-filled valley below.

'It is done. Return me to the school, Ramus,' commanded Kuelack.

Despite his efforts, despite his desperate opposition, he could not disobey Kuelack's last command.

'What about your promise - my revenge? My home is but a short flight from here, Kuelack. You said that once we had the shards, you would help me avenge my family. We had a deal!'

But his agonised words fell on deaf ears. Kuelack now lay unconscious in his talons.

It was then that the truth dawned. The baron's uprising, the deployment of Durbarian troops; it was all Kuelack. He had never intended to help him; it was just one of many broken promises.

Having left their winged assailants far behind, Ramus soared south across the Zapatian sky on crisp night-time winds. The familiarity of home and the dragon sprawls, the all-pervading tang assailing his nostrils, calling him home. At the same time, the shards' insistent whispers struck fear into his very soul, their unrelenting murmurings exploring and infusing his dragon mind while numbing his senses; a mantra that prevented him from disobeying Kuelack's last command.

'Where are we?' enquired Kuelack.

Perceiving Kuelack's enquiry through the whistling of the wind, Ramus sneered, 'We're over the Mycean Highlands, following the River Seddon south. That's three times I've saved your skin, mage,' Ramus scorned, and you repay me with betrayal; you have no honour. But you knew I'd be compelled to obey you; despite my diluted blood, you banked on the shards' influence over my kind. It was you who bribed the Barons, ordered my family killed, wasn't it? You used my lust for revenge as leverage to help you retrieve the shards. It has always been you; everything that has transpired has been of your design,' Ramus bellowed.

'Don't act so righteous,' Kuelack grumbled. 'It was a necessary deception to stop you from killing me, stealing the shards and leaving my body for the crows.'

'You're right, I should have killed you. Killed you while still in control of my own senses.'

'But now it's too late. The shards will be mastered, and their power harnessed, and in time, your concerns will disappear. When we reach the school, you will embrace the Master of the Firebrand stone; you will serve me, Dragon Lord,' said Kuelack, the scorn in his voice unmistakable.

'You will never master the stone, no one can,' Ramus hissed angrily, 'and in the end, you will be but a servant, as will we all.'

CHAPTER SEVENTEEN

CHOICES OF THE HEAD AND HEART

Secreted in the darkened alleyway between the perimeter wall and the student lodgings, the sun having dropped below the horizon hours ago, Beria Dearing sniffed at the tang of wood smoke in the chill night air. Starting at a hand on her shoulder, Beria turned hesitantly and came face to face with the reason for this dangerous liaison.

'Do you have to do that?' hissed Beria. 'I nearly had a heart attack.'

Ramus, dressed all in black, his head bowed against the wind, whispered, 'Keep your voice down.'

'I must say, I was very surprised to receive your note.'

'Does anyone else know you're here?' he hissed.

'No!' Beria said derisively. In the silence, she looked at him quizzically. 'If I'm not mistaken, I'd say you look betrayed, or it could be regret.'

Ramus glared angrily at her and in his deep resounding voice hissed, 'How can an order of witches, deemed to be so wise, add two and two and come up with five?'

'Is this a joke to you? I'm risking a great deal by meeting you here, Ramus. If caught, we'll end up in the dungeons, or worse.'

Taking a deep breath, Ramus said in a more controlled tone, 'Your reticence is understandable, Beria Dearing. These are unprecedented times; suspicion and uncertainty are affecting everybody and everything.'

Wrapping her shawl more tightly about her person, Beria urged, 'Stop talking in riddles, Ramus. What do you want?'

Furtively Ramus then looked around the small grassy area, then indicated Beria to follow. Beyond the grassy area, in the corner of the old perimeter wall, was a walnut tree. Next to that, beneath its branches, was another small sturdy oak door that also retained its magic.

In gloomy silence, Ramus pressed his hand to the lock, then hissed, 'Dralmoren.' There was an audible click and then the door opened; he led the way out into the lane beyond. Checking all was quiet, he turned abruptly, then said seriously, 'Beria, I'm afraid. Afraid of a man whose exceptional raw power no-one can match.'

'You talk of Kuelack?'

Ramus nodded. 'He's becoming more obsessive with every passing day. Take the increased military presence at the school, for instance.'

'It's rumoured, Ramus, that Mass is also after the shards,' enquired Beria.

'He is,' replied Ramus, holding up his hand to halt the question he knew Beria would ask, 'and to my shame, I made a deal with both.'

'Sounds to me like you were hedging your bets?'

'The plan was to dispose of Kuelack and return the shards to Mass, but I made a secret deal with Kuelack. In exchange for helping Kuelack acquire the shards, he would help me exact my revenge against the Barons who killed my family and took my lands.'

'I don't understand,' she asked, perplexed. 'It's not as if Mass could unite them. His power doesn't work that way.'

'I didn't count on Kuelack using the stones' influence over my kind; it's repugnant to dragons, and it's our doom.' Ramus shivered noticeably. What I saw him do, what he made me do, I knew it was imperative to deny him the shards. But, despite my opposition, Kuelack compelled me to return him to the school.'

'So, the double-crosser became the crossed,' she smiled. 'I must say, that has a satisfying symmetry to it.'

'Please, Beria, if you saw what I saw, you would not wish the shards wielded by Kuelack loosed upon the world.' Ramus then looked up at the spires and domes of the school, stark against the chill night sky. 'I have no excuse for my past behaviour. However, I do see things more clearly. Should Kuelack possess them, all this...' he insisted, indicating their surroundings, 'Our lives, our petty worries and concerns; we can kiss it all goodbye.'

'Agreed, but I still don't see what…'

'I switched them for fakes, Beria. I swallowed the real shards and when we returned to the school, I hid them beneath a tree in one of the school fields.' He visibly shuddered. 'The very memory of it turns my stomach.'

'So, Kuelack thinks he has the real shards,' Beria said abruptly.

'Yes,' exclaimed Ramus, 'were you not listening?'

'But hold on, couldn't he tell?' continued Beria, ignoring the Dragon Lord's jibe.

'No, he's deluded, you see. He thinks he's immune to their power, as do all who possess them.'

Beria looked at him shrewdly. 'So, you want me to take the shards and do what…, hide them?'

'Yes, you're a Balefire; I know the stones have no influence on your order, not anymore. Safeguard them, take them away from here, hide them once more.'

'I cannot hold them, only Balefire elders possess the magic, them and the Hasp,' said Beria darkly.

Ramus said desperately, 'Then call your clan or whatever you call it, tell them my story, you have to help me.'

Shaking her head, Beria said softly, 'No!'

'Why not?' demanded Ramus.

'Because,' said Beria thoughtfully, 'I have a better idea.'

Placing the delicate mask that he'd been restoring on the table, Mass Martin rubbed at his eyes and drank a beaker of water infused with white Horehound. He then lit the candle in front of him, scented with its opposite - black Horehound root, a plant used to purify and focus the thoughts and famed for its trance inducing qualities. Then, using a technique taught to him by one of his old clairvoyant teachers, he immersed his hands in the candles lingering smoke and slowly, methodically drew it up across his face, over his clean-shaven head and down the back of his neck. Then, closing his eyes in the warm, comfortable atmosphere, the room took on a shifting, dream-like quality and his consciousness wandered. But, despite his desires, a singular vision gradually invaded his mind. It was a memory from his school days involving three boys, their faces beaten and blood stained, leering at him from the fog of the past; it was a memory that always lurked on the periphery of his consciousness…

'Hey, freak, does it give you a perverse pleasure to use us normals like puppets?' the school bully, Mazzard, had threatened, levelling a large club at him. 'You're so weird, even magics stay clear of you.'

'Your statement suggests that I'm not human.'

'Shut your mouth, freak! Were here to put you in your place!'

'A freak that you and your friends beat-upon when my gift no longer benefits them.'

'Don't listen to him Mazzard, his words are poison, do him before…'

His all-consuming anger at the constant beatings and abuse had given way like a dam bursting from too much water, and Mazzard's mind, together with his two accomplices, had soaked up his rage like a sponge. The obnoxious thugs, dancing to his tune, had set upon Mazzard with their clubs, reducing his face and body to a bloody mess. Mass had then turned them upon each other…

An insistent banging at the window roused him from his fog of memories and, to stop himself toppling backwards, he cupped his foot under the table's rim, causing the intricate Bantu clay mask to fall and shatter upon the hard stone floor.

'Curses,' he hissed.

Then, searching with his mind, he sensed the tall brooding figure of Ramus waiting impatiently in the dark, outside on the balcony. Dabbing at the nightmare-induced sweat running in rivulets from his scalp, Mass opened the patio doors. Outside, his dark beard and face shrouded in shadow, his head topped by his two-pronged helm, Ramus, looking drawn and withered, glared down at him cryptically with cold frosty eyes.

'Is it done?'

'Yes, I took the shards. Kuelack now holds the replacements you gave me.'

Leading the way inside and leaving the glass doors open, Mass turned impatiently and enquired calmly, 'Then you have them?'

'No.'

'What do you mean, no? Why not? The plan was to kill Kuelack and then, on your return, hand the shards over to me.'

'Kuelack commanded me to return him to the school; he then fell into a Wizard's sleep. So, I swapped them for your replacements as you asked. I then swallowed the shards.' Ramus shuddered involuntarily.

'So, dragons ARE bound to its power,' Mass said markedly.

'They are not for mortal men; they are an abomination. Seeking them out was a mistake.'

Shaking his head, Mass mused, 'Had I kept faith with the legends, I would never have assigned you this task.' Then, turning to Ramus, he asked, 'So, where are they?'

'I hid them. Forget dreams of power and glory, Mass. When Kuelack realises he holds the fakes, his retribution will be dire.'

His squeaky voice rising with every syllable, he yelled, 'I believed Kuelack thought as I did but, like everyone else, he shuns me as a deformity to be reviled. Without me he would have achieved nothing, gained nothing, he benefits from my talents but, just like my family and friends, he refuses to treat me as an equal, so, I am done trying to live up to normals expectations. I owe the race of men nothing; I owe dragon kind nothing, apart from pain!'

Mass's eyes narrowed and with a look sent Ramus to his knees. Ramus gasped in pain as Mass's power began to squeeze his mind.

'Has your... yearning for them made you... so drunk with power?' gasped Ramus.

'I am the foremost mind master in the land. The shards will bend to my will!'

'You cannot control them... as you do men!... They are vile, repugnant things; they will only... warp your mind. Kuelack claimed he was immune..., but his... longing for the shards... affected his reasoning. Better... to forget them.'

Like a shutter being closed on a window, Mass blinked, leaving Ramus on his hands and knees gasping for air. Calming his anger with an effort, Mass picked up the pieces of broken mask from the floor and placed them upon the table.

'Unlike Kuelack, I have a solution to their addictive nature, to controlling them,' he then said ominously, 'Did you honestly think you could deceive me, Ramus? I procured this clay mask from a trader, who acquired it from the insectoid race that dwells in the Monad Mountains, the Bantu. Unlike this broken mask, we mind masters don't do unforeseen, and we never break things unless by design. Likewise, we don't make mistakes or trust in luck. However, it seems luck has played a significant role for you.'

Suddenly, there was a knock on the door.

His eyes narrowing, Mass said in a clipped tone, 'Ahh, about time, gentlemen!'

The door opened and Tallus entered the room, accompanied by the giant figure of Hogan, the half-giant's cocksure attitude and relaxed manner annoyingly evident, as always. Mass then turned his attention to the youngster, pacing back and forth, his unkempt brown hair and unshaven appearance testament to the strain he'd been under these past months.

'Sit down, boy, you're making me nervous,' Hogan said irritably.

Tallus turned with intent, but thought better of his actions when Mass shook his head.

'So, why are we here?' Hogan demanded.

'Does Kuelack scare you?' insinuated Mass, turning abruptly to look upon Hogan's scarred and pockmarked face.

'Yes, and if you had any sense, so should you be,' sneered Hogan.

'Show some respect, half-giant,' Tallus growled.

Mass smiled confidently. 'Hogan's words are of no concern; he's just chosen the wrong side is all. Tell me, gentlemen, do you revere the Dark Lord?'

Tallus and Hogan nodded solemnly.

Placing his hands upon their shoulders and gazing into their eyes, Mass said, 'Then prove your loyalty, demonstrate your fidelity and kill the Bruins, picture them bloodied and mutilated at your feet, but,' he emphasised clearly, 'do not harm the boy or his mother.'

'Kill the Bruins?' exclaimed Ramus.

'When I come to power and take Aridain and his mother, I will become an enemy of Alfic, his family and friends. The only way to rule over the school is to eliminate my enemies.'

'Kill our enemies,' chanted Hogan, compliantly.

'To placate the Dark Lord,' intoned Tallus, passively.

'As for Kuelack, no one will tell him what we have discussed here, understood?'

Hogan and Tallus nodded compliantly.

People were afraid of events they couldn't control or understand. Mass had learnt that the hard way. Mazard had been right; he wasn't human; he was better, superior, humans were beneath him. The fear in their voices, their continual self-bolstering confirmed his conclusion; Psychics were the future; he was meant to rule. Taking his hands from their shoulders, Mass ordered, 'Go, you have your instructions. Do what has to be done; I'll leave the details to you.'

When the pair had left, Mass turned to Ramus.

'I have recently discovered that Kuelack is awake but still recovering from his ordeal; it's an opportunity I cannot miss. As you've gone to all this trouble on my behalf, I will give you one chance to redeem yourself and bring the shards to me; if I have to get them myself, Kuelack's wrath will be nothing compared to mine. It's time I took my rightful place as head of this school and psychics can take their rightful place as rulers of this world.'

CHAPTER EIGHTEEN

DUNGEON'S AND GREYSWORDS

Casey Defray peered out through the grill of the fetid iron mask with sweat and blood encrusted eyes. Her hands and head pinioned by thick leather straps to a cross of oak secured to the wall, she watched as Gradine, displaying certainty and boldness, nodded to the hooded figure sat at an old wooden desk in the corner of the room. Closing the worn, leather-bound folder on the desk in front of him, the figure stood quietly and strode soundlessly from the room, leaving the two of them alone.

'Hello again, Casey,' said Gradine, grasping and tugging the leather strap around Casey's throat. 'My, you look a mess.'

Casey stared back with intense hazel eyes, then strained against the securing straps as Gradine, her face illuminated in the flickering torchlight, leered in at her through the mask's narrow slit.

Yanking on the throat strap, Gradine smiled in at her. 'Don't waste your strength trying to break your bonds. They are quite secure.'

Despite Gradine's reassurances, Casey tested them again. She then studied Gradine's face intensely, trying to gauge her mood and what she planned next; it was a face she knew masked a darker heart.

'Your man there has failed to gain anything of value from torturing me, so you may as well let me go, Gradine. Give me my prisoner and let me go, then perhaps I'll persuade my government not to reduce this fortress, you hold so dear, to rubble!' Casey demanded angrily.

Turning savagely, Gradine said, 'You're in no position to demand anything!'

'Then get on with it and kill me; I'm bored with these games,' she croaked defiantly.

'But I'm not; Elias's torture is proving to be highly entertaining.'

'Where is he? What have you done to him?' Casey demanded, straining against the straps despite the pain.

'Admirable, such concern for your prisoner.'

Swallowing against the tight leather strap, Casey croaked, 'I'd hardly call it concern. Anyway, I thought they outlawed torture in this overindulgent democracy.'

Gradine Spat, 'To achieve our goals, someone with balls has to deal with the malcontents.'

Standing, Gradine peered around the chamber. Purring seductively as if gaining a perverse pleasure from caressing the various instruments of torture, she said, 'I believe that in your backward country of no imagination, they still treat madness by cutting a neat V-shaped incision in your forehead to release a person's inner demons. Of course, because your government endorses that kind of drivel, they wouldn't question our methods, but the procedure would be very painful.'

'If you're trying to scare me, it's not work... What is going on here?' insisted Casey.

Just then a door creaked in the gloom followed by the sounds of something being dragged across the floor, and swivelling her eyes she saw two men dragging the half-conscious figure of Elias Tan through an open door, and judging by his appearance he had already experienced much more of the dungeon's painful hospitality.

Then, releasing her grip, Gradine stood and said angrily, 'About time! Sit him in the empty chair next to hers.'

Casey ground her teeth in anger. Despite being a dissident, Elias was a Calabash citizen. His baker's clothes were bloodied, as were his dark piratical good looks, soiled from painful looking gouges in his cheeks and forehead. Blood had also seeped from several missing fingernails.

'As your friend here has proved, you Calabashian lot are a stubborn race,' Gradine smiled. 'Elias Tan, dissident and thorn in the side of King Bovid the Fifth, who fled here to escape imprisonment in Quelea;

please meet Casey Defray, an active member of the Korda Halide, tasked to keep you under surveillance.'

Casey raised her eyebrows at that.

'Oh yes, we know all about you and your mission here.'

When the baker said nothing, Gradine pulled up Casey's trouser leg, revealing the Korda tattoo on the outside of her calf in the shape of a coiled viper.

Glancing at Casey with eyes drained of life, Elias croaked wearily, 'Humph, if I had known, she'd be dead by now.'

'Anything,' asked Gradine, turning to the soldiers.

With a shake of the head, one of the men said, 'Apart from a speech about freedom and democracy, this cretin provided nothing of use.'

'Then kill him. It will save my government the trouble,' Casey said dismissively.

The statement brought a muffled snigger from Elias Tan, who then coughed, 'A helpless Korda, (cough), her options taken away, I never thought I'd see the day, (cough). Admit it, Korda scum, you've been out manoeuvred (cough, cough). Now I can die a happy man,' and with that Elias passed out.

'You know, I never really thought about the name Casey Defray until now,' announced Gradine, as if passing the day while on a stroll in the park, 'a typical Calabashian name, as is Elias Tan.'

Standing, then strolling around the shadowy interior, Gradine said offhandedly, 'Haven't you worked it out yet? The reason we know so much about you? What you were planning? We and your employers have come to an understanding.'

'My government would never collude with you or be stupid enough to trust you, despite what you've promised.'

'Oh yes, all covert operations are to be made transparent.'

'I don't see Kuelack making the Quelean secret service aware of your operations in Calabash or here at the school.'

'You're right, of course,' agreed Gradine, 'but we have no need, do we, Casey? You and your network of spies do that for us.'

'As does yours. Your overconfidence will be your undoing,' scoffed Casey.

'Oh really, pray do tell,' mocked Gradine.

'You have a handful of men and a few magicians; you wouldn't dare challenge the might of Calabash; our numbers greatly exceed yours.'

'Numbers are irrelevant, especially to whoever possesses the Firebrand stone. Yes, that's right; the stone will soon be in our possession.'

'Clever men talk because they have something to say, idiotic men talk because they have to say something,' Casey scoffed. 'The stones are a fable to frighten children on cold, dark winter nights.'

'Oh, I forgot government policy. All Calabashians on pain of death are non-believers; no gods, no legends, nothing but good, solid practicality. Well, that is, everyone except the people who make the rules. Forget seeing your countrymen and contacting them with whatever information you've gathered. You're on your own here with no hope of rescue.'

'The minute I took on this assignment, I knew that. Better to be a prisoner fighting for a just cause than a disposable pawn fighting for a madman.'

'Gallant words, I'm sure,' Gradine said dismissively. She then gestured to the world at large.

'Soon, with the shards united and in our possession, we will have the power of gods, then we will be unstoppable. But that is no longer your concern; what you should be concerned with is what's about to happen to you.'

'Go ahead. I am prepared to go to my grave knowing I served my country and my people with honour,' announced Casey regally.

'Death, oh no, gods forbid we blemish those narrowed eyes or that pronounced jaw line; no, your Calabashian characteristics will serve us well, I think.'

'Don't try to scare me. Your threats count for nothing; you have already tried and failed to control me with your pathetic enchanted coins.'

Sitting down beside her, Gradine began running her hands along the inside of Casey's legs and up over her torso and breasts. 'That statement is what we expect from a citizen of a controlled downtrodden society,' she replied offhandedly. 'So patriotic and such a waste of talent; soon Calabash and the other kingdoms will be in our hands; much better to be part of our success than a victim of it.'

Trying her best to ignore Gradine's roving hands, Casey thought about this recent information. Lascana had said exactly the same thing at the tenants' meeting.

Glaring at Gradine, she said, 'You want me to work for you as a double agent?'

'You catch on quickly.'

'As you say, better to be part of the future than a victim of it. I'd be a fool to ignore your offer.'

Studying her closely, Gradine smiled. 'Really? I don't suppose your decision has anything to do with this additional information?'

'As you say, who can stand against it? Besides, your organisation could do with someone like me; my connections in Quelea could prove very useful.'

'How right you are, but the problem is, I just don't trust you. However, there is a more reliable, easier way to make you our agent. This calls for someone more specialised, someone who can bore into the mind and find a person's deepest, darkest fears.'

Casey's eyes snapped open at the implication of Gradine's proposition as a small, weasely figure entered the chamber.

'I believe you know of Mass Martin,' Gradine sniggered.

As they removed her mask and Mass Martin loomed close, she fixated on Elias's face, just visible beyond, and in an effort to counter the mental ordeal to come, she embraced the baker's pain and suffering.

Vanir walked across the old fortress's entrance hall, among unassuming teachers and staff, his knife pressed against Corporal Rondel's ribs. Stopping in front of the large reinforced oak door leading to the guest wing, he urged the Corporal to open it and then step through. Their footsteps were loud on the flagstone floor as they turned through ninety degrees and approached an old wrought-iron and oak door that looked completely out of character in the administration wing corridor.

Digging the knife more firmly into Rondel's flesh, Vanir hissed, 'Knock on the door and remember, no heroics.'

'Don't be a fool, Vanir. Think about what you're doing.'

'Be quiet! You traitorous runt,' spat Vanir. This is something I should have done long before now.'

'Traitorous runt, I call it self-preservation, you should try it sometime.'

'And what happened to integrity, fealty and your oath?'

'Old, outmoded notions. I deal in reality.'

Hearing the sound of hollow footsteps from behind the door, Vanir warned, 'Be quiet, and remember what I told you.'

A small shutter was drawn back, and a face peered through the grated opening.

'Greysword Vanir; state your business,' instructed the soldier while wiping crumbs from the corner of his mouth.

'The Corporal and I are here to escort the prisoner, Keegan Fold, to Gradine's chambers. She has plans for the groundsman, if you know what I mean,' smiled Vanir knowingly.

Silence followed, and for several seconds, the guard looked back blankly; then Vanir's meaning slowly dawned. 'Ahh, I see what you mean.'

'So, what are you waiting for, man? Open the door,' he ordered in an authoritative voice.

Startled, the Private disappeared and in quick succession they heard the clatter of locks being undone and the freeing of bolts from their iron fixings. Then, the door swung inwards with a metallic grinding and screeching.

Before the soldier realised what was happening, Vanir shoved Rondel before him. The two entangled guards fell to the cold, grey floor of the dungeon and, as swift as quicksilver, Vanir stamped down hard on the Private's arm as he tried to draw his sword, causing him to release it. In the same quick movement, Vanir brought the pommel of his knife down onto the bridge of Rondel's nose. Vanir then delivered a solid punch to the Private's chin and his body went limp.

'Bastard, do broke by dose!'

'You're lucky I didn't break anything else,' Vanir threatened resolutely.

Holding his nose, now gushing blood, Rondel said angrily, 'Are you dat naïve, Vanir. Do you dink you will det away with dis? Dink about what you're doing. When you're caught, your life won'd be worth Scarrion dung.'

Helping the Corporal to his feet, Vanir drew his sword, and pressing it against Rondel's spine, said darkly, 'They have to catch me first, and for your sake, best pray they don't.'

Retrieving a set of keys hanging from the unconscious Private's belt and throwing them to Rondel, Vanir, hoisting the guard's limp body over his shoulder, ordered, 'Get moving down the stairway. My sword will stay where it is until you're under lock and key.'

With time now of the essence, they hurried down a long flight of spiral steps to the basement, lit every few feet by torches hanging from the walls. At the bottom they came upon a chair and table sporting the remnants of a half-finished meal and a flagon of cider. Beyond, across the straw-covered floor, was another thick oak door.

Then, thrusting Rondel through the doorway, Vanir said ominously, 'Open it.'

Shivering from the cold and the damp that now permeated every fibre of his body, Mace Denobar lay upon a straw-stuffed mattress, listening to the drip, drip, drip of water in the silence.

'Do you know what I really miss? Spending time alone in my rowing boat on the lakes, feeding the fish,' considered Keegan from somewhere in the dark. 'I even caught a few, for personal consumption, you understand; it was a pleasant addition to my duties.'

His deep throaty voice reverberating in the dungeon's cold, damp, claustrophobic atmosphere, Mace said, 'You say you prize isolation and quiet, but really you love socialising, and you love gossip; you're the male equivalent of Lawna. It's what amuses you on cold winter nights.'

'Hey, if I wanted amusement on cold winter nights, I'd bed myself a woman, the fighting stick Mistress, Crystal, for instance. Now that's what I call a woman.'

'Dream on, she'd have you for breakfast.'

'A good way to go, though?'

'I heard she has a thing for Kale.'

Coughing and clearing his throat, Keegan replied matter-of-factly, 'Are you saying she'd pass up the chance to bed the hunk of loveliness that is Keegan Fold?'

Chuckling in the dark, Mace wiped at his runny nose.

'What's so funny? I'm very nice when you get to know me.'

'Oh, it's not that, I was just thinking of our card games and how much I'm going to miss stripping you of your hard-earned money,' said Mace, 'and by the way, you still owe me fifteen copper Sontars.'

'Since when?'

'The Cockrell and Whiskers in Barfleet, remember?'

'You cheated.'

'I have witnesses that say otherwise,' countered Mace.

Keegan paused, then said, 'Do you know, I was just thinking…?'

Mace, rolling his eyes frustratingly in the dark, said, 'You do this every time.'

In a voice dripping with innocence, Keegan replied, 'What?'

'Change the subject whenever I mention money that you owe me!'

'Ok, ok, don't get you gauntlets in a twist, I was only going to say that you seemed to have started a trend. Did you know that in the modern era, they have never imprisoned a teacher or Greysword in these dungeons?'

Giving up, Mace stated frustratedly, 'What I want to know is… when is the famed escape artist Keegan Fold going to live up to his reputation and get us out of here?'

'I'm working on it,' insisted Keegan.

'You're a pitiable excuse for a gamekeeper and an even worse army tracker. Do you know that?'

'Hey, there's no need for insults,' Keegan chuckled.

'Alfic's family needs us, and where are we…? Locked up in a dirty, smelly cell in the dark.'

'Hey don't take your frustration out on me. Besides, I don't hear you coming up with any plans, you grumpy old excuse for a Fighting Master.'

Just then, they heard the rattle of keys turning in the lock of the door.

'Bit late for breakfast,' mused Keegan.

Then the door swung inwards on noisy rust-covered hinges and a soldier was sent sprawling to the dungeon floor, he was followed by a hulking fellow dressed in crimson leather armour.

'Mace, Keegan, are you in here?'

Then, before Keegan could utter a clever retort that Mace knew was coming, he said, 'Vanir, yes, we're in here. You're a sight for sore eyes, my friend!'

Standing up, his body weak from lack of food and water, Mace walked over to the bars of his cell on stiff, unsteady legs. Looking over at Keegan, illuminated in the torchlight, Mace smiling said, 'Who needs a washed-up old army tracker, eh, when we have trusted Greyswords?'

Presenting his torch, Vanir looked grimly at Keegan and then Mace.

'Thank Seline, you're both all right. I thought it was time to get you out of here,' he said decisively. 'Open their cells, Rondell.' Then, fanning at his nose, Vanir exclaimed, 'Phew, you two smell like a Scarrion lizard's innards.'

'Languishing in your own piss and shit will do that to you,' said Mace irately.

'Gradine has decreed you're both scheduled for termination.'

'Termination, get me out of this birdcage now!' demanded Keegan, rattling his cell door violently in the dark.

Shielding his eyes against the torch's light, Mace said angrily, 'She really is a piece of work.'

'Agreed. With Kuelack absent, power's gone to that woman's head.'

Dropping the comatose private onto the primitive bed, Vanir, encouraging Rondel into Mace's cell, said, 'Right in you go.' Locking the cell door, Vanir offered Mace a large leather holster and inside was his sword. 'This is yours; I believe.'

Mace strapped the holster over his shoulders and drew the dark grey blade.

'Hello, Rage, old friend,' said Mace, feeling its familiar weight and wrapping his hand around the pommel of the dark grey sword, longingly.

'What do you think, Vanir? Should we give them some privacy?' chuckled Keegan, his amusement turning into a fit of coughing.

'It's a Greysword thing,' said Vanir, seriously.

Seeing the concern in Keegan's eyes, Mace said, 'I'm all right, my friend. The connection with my sword will sustain me for a short while; however, you need to see a healer.' Then, taking a deep breath, Mace said, 'For this, Vanir, I thank you.'

Smiling, Keegan, desperately holding on to Vanir's shoulders for support, asked cheekily, 'So, nothing for me, dear?'

'I believe a Korda knife is your weapon of choice,' said Vanir seriously, pulling a large serrated blade from his belt.

'Why, thank you darling,' Keegan smiled, the attempt at levity only emphasising their desperate circumstances.

Leaning against one of the dungeon's thick, supporting pillars for support, Keegan asked, 'What are you going to do with them?'

'I know what I'd like to do with him,' growled Vanir.

Suddenly, fuelled by rage, Mace grasped Rondel, who'd been glaring at them with ill intent, by the throat and thrust him roughly against the cell's iron bars.

'I'll teach you to throw me in a shit-ridden dungeon, you pathetic excuse for a human being. I thought you were our friend, our colleague. How many more of you have gone cowering to Kuelack with your tails between your legs?' Mace's face, only centimetres from Rondel's terrified face, hissed, 'We have a maxim, my friends and me; "one more dead, one less to fight!".'

Keegan hobbled over to his friend and, laying his hand upon his friend's shoulder, leaned close. 'Mace,' placated Keegan softly, 'we haven't time for this!'

'Oh, I think there is. It's definitely time for some payback.'

'Those days are passed, my friend. I know you're angry, but we have to be better than them.'

Looking from the hapless Corporal to Keegan, Mace said incredulously, 'Keegan, this is coming from you?'

'I know my friend, I can't believe it either, just old age, I guess.'

His adrenalin fuelled rage spent, Mace released Rondel and spat, 'This is your lucky day, Cockroach, and I think it's only right that you should sample the dungeon's exquisite bouquet and ambiance.'

'You are a tool, Rondel,' offered Vanir, 'remember that. Once you've fulfilled your purpose, Kuelack will discard you like a blunt saw. Now, it really is time we were going!' insisted Vanir, leading them from the chamber.

'You are all guilty of treason!' shouted Rondel. 'And when you are caught, you will all be executed.'

'Executed while fighting for freedom,' shouted Keegan, 'And not like a skulking Bantu.'

A flaming torch held high in one hand and the other clutching his sword, Vanir led them out of the cellblock and back up the stairwell. It was then that they heard Karnack's familiar rasping tones shouting orders in the corridor beyond.

'Curses, I thought we'd have more time,' hissed Vanir, angrily.

Holding on to Mace for support, Keegan turned accusingly to Vanir and croaked, 'Now what do we do? The cellblock's a dead end.'

'Live to fight another day, I say,' stated Vanir, searching the darkness with his torch.

'Agreed,' rasped Mace.

'Hold on, just hold on. I can't believe this is a dead end. What about that door?' pointed out Keegan. Where does that lead?'

Then, as one, the friends turned at a shout from the top of the stone stairway.

'Stay where you are and lay down your weapons.'

Attired in his distinctive midnight-blue leather armour, Karnack stood with his sword in hand and with several soldiers at his back. The three Greyswords locked eyes and for a moment they stared accusingly at each other, each realising in that instant that the bonds that bound the Greysword brotherhood in fellowship were now broken.

'Surrender yourselves and your weapons now!' Karnack rumbled menacingly.

'And hang for crimes we haven't committed; I don't think so,' Mace replied with conviction.

'As the school's Chief Greysword, I have the authority…'

'We don't recognise the authority of the dictators you work for. You're a Greysword Karnack; your allegiance is to the Sivan and this school, not one man,' scolded Mace. 'We serve a higher cause.'

'What I find intriguing is why an honourable Greysword, who has done nothing but good, follows the orders of a despot who is clearly insane with power,' shouted Keegan.

'One man's despot is another's visionary,' grumbled Karnack, unconvincingly.

'Then you're a moron,' coughed Keegan.

Annoyed, Mace and Vanir looked at Keegan and shook their heads, frustratedly.

'Hey, I can't make it any worse than it is, so if we're going to die, I might as well get a few insults in,' smiled Keegan.

Karnack, looking decidedly irritated, ordered, 'Don't let them escape, take them alive, if possible; if not, I want them dead!'

At a silent signal, Keegan, the keys now firmly in his grasp, stumbled down the stairs as the knot of soldiers at Karnack's back suddenly charged down the stone staircase. Fighting a retreat, Mace and Vanir slashed, parried and lunged, the flickering torchlight projecting their struggles like staccato stick figures upon the walls. With a shout of triumph, Keegan found the key to open the door. Leaving one soldier dead and two more badly wounded, the Greyswords turned and bolted from the opening. Slamming it shut behind them, Keegan quickly locked it before the sheer weight of numbers could force it open.

Suddenly, Karnack's scarred and pockmarked face appeared at the window grill, like a harbinger of doom, his one eye peering about the chamber.

'Curse you Mace, open this door. You've nowhere to go. Surrender, and I promise I'll kill you all quickly, painlessly.'

'An offer we can't refuse, very kind of you, I'm sure,' spat Keegan.

Just then, the door reverberated to a solid blow, followed by a second and then a third.

'It won't be long before they're through,' urged Keegan.

Searching the half-lit corridor, Vanir exclaimed, 'You're right! Here, help me with this wooden winch. It may be old and rotten, but it will hold them for a time.'

With grit and determination, they dragged the obsolete device across the straw-covered floor to block the doorway. Then, exploring their surroundings, Mace said urgently, 'Let's look for that exit.'

Alert and mindful of anything unusual, they hurried through the oval brick-built storeroom containing forgotten dusty torture equipment, now stacked alongside the walls, until they reached a door at the far end of the chamber. Pushing through the door, they looked around with a feeling of revulsion.

They had emerged into a large, vaulted, candlelit room and all around were dark instruments of torture that showed recent signs of use. A blooded, slatted wooden bench stood in the centre of the room, next to a large wheel on which victims could be tied spread-eagled. In the far corner, fixed between two vaulted pillars and the far wall, was a large metal cage.

Searching the gloomy surroundings, Vanir said incredulously, 'This was an old storeroom.'

'And now it's been turned back into a dungeon,' exclaimed Keegan dourly.

'Hey you, yes you, is there another way out of here?' growled Keegan forebodingly.

Sporting a leather head mask, boots and gloves, a portly leather-clad man with cloth underclothes looked up from sharpening a wicked-looking knife upon a granite wheel. Without a word, the man picked up an axe and, raising it above his head, charged.

The two Greyswords brought their swords to guard but, before they could strike, Keegan ducked and lunged upwards with his knife. The man doubled over and stared at Keegan in complete surprise before Keegan thrust upwards one more time. Retracting his knife, the portly, grubby-looking man fell to the floor, dead.

His head spinning from fatigue, Keegan collapsed on top of the sweaty, fetid man and ripped the mask from his head.

'That's Label, you've killed Label. He works in the kitchens; he's one of Amy's cooks!' exclaimed Mace.

'This is intolerable,' roared Vanir, peering about the chamber. 'This demands vengeance.'

Mace, following behind Vanir and Keegan, spat, 'The people involved will pay for this profanity.'

'Hello, is someone there?' a voice croaked.

Draped from the wall in chains and stocks hung two lifeless bodies. With barely controlled anger, they approached the beaten and blooded figures and lifted their faces. Through the dirty smears and rivulets of dried blood, they recognised the school's baker, Elias Tan, wearing nothing but his underwear and an old tattered shirt. Shackled in the other was the seamstress, Casey Defray. The leather bodice she'd been wearing was now undone, exposing her bloodied breasts, her leather trousers shredded and torn as if attacked by some rabid beast.

'Stand back,' ordered Vanir irately. Unsheathing his sword, Vanir swung his weapon; the shackle's shattering one-by-one in a shower of sparks.

Carefully buttoning up her bodice, Keegan, his voice wavering, asked, 'Casey, are you all right? What are you and Elias doing here?'

Casey slowly opened her eyes and looked up. 'Keegan Fold, this is a surprise! she slurred deliriously.

'Vanir, help me here?'

'No,' said Casey wearisomely, 'tend to Elias; he has suffered more than I.'

'You don't look so good yourself,' said Vanir, attempting without success to revive the comatose baker.

'Well, isn't this a pretty pickle?' offered Keegan, helping Casey to her feet, while at the same time attempting to keep her conscious. 'All of us, victims of Gradine's ambitions...'

'I've found a door!' announced Mace, holstering his sword while standing in front of a pile of what used to be torture equipment, interspersed with wooden boxes. 'We just have to move this old equipment.'

'Here, hold on to Elias,' said Vanir, handing the baker and his torch over to Keegan and Casey.

With the torch held high, Vanir and Mace began dragging and pulling the old debris away from the doorway. Testing the door, it refused to budge, so, using their shoulders, the two Greyswords, after several attempts, forced the door open, that ground inwards on rusted hinges.

Hoisting the baker over his shoulder, Vanir, taking the torch, said, 'Ok let's go!'

With Mace leading the way, they climbed down a set of small, wooden steps. Abruptly, the surrounding space flooded with light.

'Does anyone know where we are?' asked Keegan.

'We're in a tunnel!'

'Ha ha, it seems Mace is a comedian,' scoffed Keegan.

Vanir stared up at a series of soft glowing globes of light hanging at regular intervals from the walls.

'What are they?' he asked.

'I don't know,' replied Mace. 'But they emit light.'

Lifting his torch, Vanir insisted, 'That's all very interesting, but which way?'

'Straight ahead,' Mace said decisively.

'How do you know?' wheezed Casey.

'I don't, but it's as good a direction as the other.'

To their relief, as they ventured along the tunnel, the globes brightened and then dimmed as they passed, lighting their way.

But their progress was agonisingly slow as Mace, helping Casey and Keegan from the dusty floor for the umpteenth time, encouraged, 'Come on, up you get, Casey. Karnack and his men won't be far behind; we have to keep going.'

'Don't worry on my account, Greysword,' Casey hissed, gritting her teeth.

Then, true to Mace's words, silhouettes of soldiers danced down the corridor, accompanied by insistent voices. It was then that Casey, gasping for breath, again collapsed to the tunnel's dusty floor. Grasping Casey's shoulders roughly, Mace lifted her to her feet and insisted, 'Get up, Calabashian!' When she didn't respond, Mace bellowed, 'Master race, ha, don't make me laugh. What would your countrymen think of you, giving in to us inferior Durbarians?'

Casey slowly lifted her head and hissed, 'I know what you're trying to do, Greysword.'

'Then get up and prove me wrong.'

'Don't worry on my behalf. I'm not done yet.'

The small party continued on, stumbling and tripping down the dusty tunnel.

'It must end sometime,' insisted Vanir, glancing backwards towards the soldiers that drew ever nearer, their harsh guttural voices giving the illusion they were closer than they really were. Then suddenly, out of the gloom, materialised a solid wall and a set of steps.

'No time to delay,' Vanir urged, the relief palpable in his voice. 'They're nearly upon us. Here, Mace, take Elias. I'll cover our retreat.'

Climbing the stairs, Keegan, followed by Casey, and Mace, carrying Elias Tan, came upon a trap door fashioned from lead. Debris dropped upon Keegan's head as he pushed the cover aside, revealing a cool crisp night sky full of stars through a stark tangle of brambles and branches.

Climbing up through the hole, he helped Casey, who then helped him and Mace pull Elias out through the opening.

Gratified that his friends were safe, Vanir, his sword drawn, backed towards the steps. He then turned and began to climb.

'Stay where you are, Vanir,' shouted Karnack.

Vanir turned to see Karnack, his sword raised, racing towards him. Vanir then began climbing urgently towards the opening. It was then that the old wooden steps reverberated with three solid thumps. Glancing downwards, three arrows sprouted from the steps where his feet had been moments before. The steps now crumbling beneath his feet, Vanir doubled his efforts. Just as the stairs collapsed beneath him, he was helped up through the hole by Mace and Keegan, who hauled him up and out into the open.

Vanir stood side by side with Mace, looking down upon the calm but no-less angry Karnack.

'This isn't the end of it,' spat Karnack. 'I will see you all at the end of a rope.'

Glaring at Karnack menacingly, Mace swore, 'And I promise in Pellagrin's name that for your part in the murders of Sergeant Darin Ormstrode, Head Wizard Almagest and Tad Grearson that the next time we meet, I will send you to Fornax's realm,' growled Mace.

Moving sprightly for his advancing years, the old Greysword's head of greying hair disappeared from view to be replaced with two men wielding crossbows. Quickly throwing the lead cover over the hole, Vanir, smiling half-heartedly, said, 'I think you've pissed him off.' Then, looking around, he queried, 'So, where do you think we are?'

'Higher wood,' said Keegan wearily.

'And you know that how?' asked Vanir.

Stood beneath the stars, their breaths clearly visible in the chill night air, Keegan exclaimed, 'It has a certain smell!'

'Then Alfic's cottage is on the up slope across the stream, which means the road is over there,' gestured Vanir.

'Correct,' smiled Keegan.

Grasping Mace's shoulder for support, Casey watched Vanir, who with Elias draped over his shoulders, forged ahead once more.

'We can't stay at Alfic's cottage! Karnack will be rounding up a contingent of soldiers as we speak; it's the first place they'll look.'

'Right now, Lascana is Elias's only hope, but don't worry, we'll stay only as long as we have to.'

Beneath the stark, skeletal beech trees, Keegan and Casey, with Mace's help, made their way slowly down the slope. Coming upon the stream, its sinuous waters loud in the silence, they followed its course through the dormant undergrowth until suddenly they came to the tree line and the roadway just beyond. Checking the way was clear once more, Mace then helped the pair stagger and limp down the track. Approaching the cottage, they turned beside the barn into the back garden and then knocked on the door.

'Who is it?' a distrustful male voice demanded.

'It's Mace, you fool.'

The sounds of bolts sliding from fixings could be heard from inside, and Alfic appeared brandishing a sword.

'Can't be too careful,' whispered Alfic harshly. 'Quickly, inside.'

Once inside, the friends clasped hands and embraced. 'It's good to see you're both all right. Here, let me help you, Casey.'

'Brave, to take on your brother; foolish to think you could win.'

'We all attempt foolish things, Casey,' said Alfic…

'Like you, Casey, staying at the school, and thinking no one would notice you were a Korda agent,' said Keegan.

'A Korda agent?' balked Alfic.

'Yes, she has the tattoo on her ankle. Not very smart having the tattoo so low down, another inch higher and I wouldn't have noticed.'

They made their way into the dining room where Lascana and Vanir were endeavouring unsuccessfully to revive Elias laid upon the kitchen table.

'Mace, Keegan, thank Seline,' sobbed Lascana, throwing her arms around them. 'Gods! Look at you both. Are you all right?'

'We're fine,' smiled Mace wearily.

'But you should see the other guy,' joked Keegan.

'Vanir told us everything.'

'Sorry Alfic,' apologised Mace. 'We'll be out of your hair as soon as we can.'

'Think nothing of it.'

As Alfic disappeared into the kitchen, Casey, examining Elias curiously, asked, 'How is he?'

Lascana, leaning close to the baker's inert form, shook her head sadly. 'I'm so sorry, Casey, but he's close to death; saving him is beyond my skills.'

'He's still alive; we can't just give up on him,' despaired Casey.

Putting her hand upon Casey's shoulder, Lascana said sadly, 'There's nothing I can do.'

'So, what were you two doing down there in the dungeons?' interrupted Mace gently.

'Yes, I think you owe us an explanation,' insisted Mace. 'After all, we saved your neck.'

'Very well.'

Sitting down wearily on a dining room chair and drinking deeply from a tumbler of water, Casey looked up wearily.

'I was charged by the Halide with tracking down Elias. A dissident escaping from my country, I was charged with discovering his purpose here in Durbah. I was then to return him to Calabash, where he would answer for his crimes.'

'Don't tell me, he spoke out of turn,' said Alfic, critically.

'Yes, crimes that in this land pass as free speech or freewill.'

Mace, shaking his head in bewilderment, said, 'Such a paranoid dictatorship.'

'Elias is a rebel, wanted for acts of terrorism; we feared he was coming here to recruit help.'

'What is this, Halide?' Lascana asked, dabbing at Casey's numerous cuts and bruises.

'The equivalent of our central intelligence, Guild of Spies,' offered Keegan. 'She's a Korda assassin.'

'Well, this explains why you were acting so strangely at the stallholders' meeting,' Lascana mused.

'The Halide had also heard rumours that Pellagrin's was training young Wizards to use against Calabash. So, when I picked up Elias's trail and found him here, it was the perfect opportunity. I could keep an eye on Elias while reporting on the school, killing two birds with one stone, so-to-speak; it was a task I thought I would relish,' she mused.

'Thought?' Lascana queried.

'To my chagrin, my government was wrong. I was wrong.'

'Wow, that's some admission coming from a Korda!' Keegan exclaimed.

'Contrary to popular belief, we can be wrong, now and again,' Casey insisted, the hint of a smile crossing her lips. 'I see now. Elias only wanted a new life here.'

Mace stated, 'But still, you were going to take him back to Calabash?'

'Despite my regrets, I am still a Korda agent and my orders were specific, to return Elias to the homeland if my cover was ever compromised, and besides, if we let every citizen leave whenever they chose, there would be no one left, and my country would descend into chaos.'

'That says everything about the reign of King Bovid "the Just",' spat Lascana.

Keegan queried, 'So, who compromised you?'

Casey took another long drink of water. 'Gradine, she and Kuelack are communicating behind your government's back with my government; that's how they knew who I was, who Elias was. Twice she tried to persuade me and Elias to her way of thinking with her enchanted silver coins, and twice she failed.'

'Enchanted silver coins?' asked Mace.

'We'll tell you about that another time,' promised Lascana.

'She couldn't control you, so I'm guessing Gradine locked you up to prevent you exposing her and Kuelack's activities to whoever it may concern,' said Keegan, knowingly.

'Yes.' Casey looked around at the friends gathered beside Elias, laid upon Lascana's dining room table. 'Now I see the Durbarians' true nature; it's no different from my own countrymen,' stated Casey. 'We are all made in the Gods' images and the plain fact is, that people don't know what's happening until shown.'

'In another time and another place, I may have acted differently toward a Korda,' said Mace, 'but now...?'

'King Bovid won't understand. Better you stay here, help us fight Kuelack's threat from the inside,' smiled Keegan.

'We must all fight in our own way. Pellagrin's is gearing up for a war my country isn't expecting. I must return to my homeland, share with them what I've learnt.'

'But you've lived here for so long now, surely you trust us?' Lascana insisted.

'I admit I do think of you all fondly as my friends, but...'

Reappearing with supplies packed into a knapsack, Alfic said, 'Mace, they're coming; it's time you left. Here, take these supplies.'

'Alfic, did you pack Vara's cure-all tincture I prepared?'

'Yes, plus some bandages and infused moss for their wounds; it should help. I've also thrown some food into a bag and filled a canteen with water.'

'What of Elias?'

'Don't worry Casey,' Lascana said sadly, 'we'll do what we can to ease his last moments.'

Just then, they all turned at the sound of soft footsteps and the flapping of small, leathery wings from the base of the stairs.

'Aridain!' exclaimed Lascana. 'What are you doing down here? You should be in bed.'

Then, to everyone's surprise, Aridain ignored their astonished looks and, shadowed by the ever-present dragonlet, shuffled zombie-like from the stairs towards Elias. Frozen to the spot, they all watched as Aridain, closing his eyes, placed his small hands upon Elias's brow. To their astonishment, the colour began slowly returning to the baker's cheeks; his wounds became less fierce and inflamed, and his breathing became easier.

'He'll be all right now,' announced Aridain matter-of-factly, who then walked over to Lascana, curled up in her arms and fell back to sleep.

CHAPTER NINETEEN

THE UNRELENTING DARKNESS

The morning air was cold and clear, and overnight, the first snows of winter lay in waves across the frozen ground. Unconcerned with the school's politics or the concerns of the adults who dwelt there, Aridain, Selva and Duran played in the fields, more concerned with what game to play next, like climbing trees, jumping the stream or, what was hiding beneath that log.

Shaking frosted snow from her hair, Selva shouted, 'It's not fair, two boys against one girl.'

'Ok then, let's get Duran,' yelled Aridain, who, together with Selva, suddenly turned towards Duran with armloads of snow.

'Hey, boys should stick together,' complained Duran. He then picked up a handful of snow and threw it until, very soon, all three looked like miniature snowmen.

All too soon, the three of them, worn out and hot from their games, fell flat onto a snowdrift, looking up at the crisp blue winter sky.

'I'm bored now. Let's play something else,' said Duran.

'Ok, how about follow-the-leader?' suggested Aridain, giggling excitedly. 'Try to follow in my footsteps.'

'I've got a better game,' said Duran. 'Let's climb a tree and pretend we're Jarawapes.'

'Yey,' yelled Aridain, following Duran towards the walnut trees, stood stark beneath the weak winter sun.

'I'm not climbing a tree like a smelly furry thing that has a face like a rat,' complained Selva. Then, smiling sweetly at Aridain, she cooed, 'I'm a lady that has better things to do.'

'Then stay on the ground,' scoffed Duran.

'I'll stay with you,' said Aridain, gallantly.

'Come on, Aridain, don't be a sissy,' teased Duran, scrambling up the nearest tree.

In a very grown-up voice, Aridain announced, 'I'm not a sissy, I'm Pellagrin the Brave and I have to protect the Princess against a Jarawape, that's been taken over by an evil curse.'

'Where?' screamed Selva.

'It's Duran, silly, up the tree. You're not much good at this, are you, Selva?'

'Ha, ha, I have you now, cowardly Pellagrin,' shouted Duran, leaping from the lowest branch. Pinning Aridain to the ground, Duran attacked him with a stick for a make-believe sword.

'Phew, what's that awful smell?' Selva complained, screwing up her face.

'Urgh, it smells like rotting meat!' said Duran, holding his nose.

With a look of determination, Aridain threw Duran from atop him as if he were a feather pillow and ran in between one of the walnut tree's armchair-like buttresses.

'Hide,' Aridain hissed, urgently.

'That hurt!' shouted Duran, stomping towards Aridain, angrily. 'There're stinging nettles and everything over there.'

'Be quiet, Duran, hide.'

When Selva saw Aridain's frightened face, she began to cry. 'What's the matter, Aridain?' she asked anxiously.

'I'm not sure.'

'Is it the creature?' Duran exclaimed, looking around nervously. Then, when nothing appeared, he said, 'It's all right, there's nothing there, Aridain's pulling you're…. hey, there is something under the trees,' said Duran, peering towards the stream.

Cowering behind Aridain, Selva whispered urgently, 'Duran, stop it. I know you're trying to scare me like you always do.'

In that moment, Aridain's fingers touched something soft lodged beneath the roots of the walnut tree. Intrigued, Aridain looked down to see a small black silk pouch nestled in among the leaf litter. Opening the drawstring, he emptied its contents into his hand and then stared, mesmerised, at four beautiful green-segmented stones that tingled in the palm of his hand. Then suddenly and without warning, images pervaded his mind, depraved, strange, abhorrent images filled with blood and rage and malice that stabbed at his mind like hot pins and needles. Thrusting the stones back into the bag, he drew the strings taught and to his relief; the images disappeared. Then, for no particular reason, instead of putting them back where he found them, he secretively thrust the bag into his shirt pocket.

'Well, whatever it was, it's gone. You can come out now, scaredy-cats.'

'Are you sure, Duran?' asked Selva apprehensively.

Standing in the field and crossing his arms, Duran announced bravely, 'Yes, of course, I'm sure!'

'Then I'm going to look for mushrooms,' announced Selva haughtily and stomped towards the tree line. 'I don't need to play with two boys who are always scaring me.'

'Yay, come on Aridain, let's climb the tree,' urged Duran.

Ignoring Duran, Aridain said fearfully, 'Selva, we have to go.'

Smiling smugly, Selva glancing back said, 'Go away; I've had quite enough of boys for today, thank you.'

'Come on, Aridain, you heard my sister; she doesn't want us around.'

'If she meets the creature and dies, they'll blame us.' Then, in a loud voice, Aridain announced, 'It's as you said Duran, girls are silly and we men must look after them.'

Selva turned on Aridain angrily, 'Well actually, I'm not afraid and I know there are some mushrooms in, 'there',' she announced, pointing and walking indomitably towards the trees lining the stream's bank.

'Selva,' Aridain hissed, frustratedly, 'come back here.'

It must be one of those girl things my mother told me about, thought Aridain, grumpily, *a woman's perog, prero...*

Prerogative corrected the voice.

Yes, that's it, thank you, voice. 'Prerogative,' announced Aridain, grumpily.

Looking fearfully left and right and followed by a morose Duran kicking petulantly at the hard-ploughed earth, Aridain broke cover and hurried across the field as Selva disappeared into the trees lining the stream's bank.

Everything was quiet for a while, then abruptly a shriek of fright issued from the stream's direction. Aridain turned and watched as a pheasant, flushed from its hiding place, burst noisily from the undergrowth. Then, Selva suddenly disappeared from view, and Aridain, with little regard for his own safety, plunged headfirst underneath the bare branches, followed by Duran.

'Selva, are you all right?'

Covered in soil, Sabra poked his head out from an old rotten log.

'Sabra, what did you do?'

Nothing youngling, it's not my fault the she human fell into the stream, Sabra hissed irritably. *More importantly, the young female has just lost me my dinner.*

Just then, Selva, with as much dignity as she could muster, emerged from the water, dripping wet. The boys laughed as they helped her up the bank.

'It's not funny,' she squealed angrily, stamping her feet. 'I'm all wet and cold thanks to your pet; he's always scaring me.'

'Yes, can't you shoo it away or something?' said Duran.

Chuckling softly, Aridain turned to see Sabra feasting on a tasty beetle that he'd discovered overwintering in the log.

I think you should get out of sight for the moment, Aridain advised.

Have I done something wrong, youngling? Sabra enquired innocently, completely missing the point of the request.

Something's wrong, Aridain.

What is it, voice?

'Did you hear that?' whispered Duran.

'Sure did,' replied Selva. 'Now be quiet,' she admonished.

Ducking behind the decaying tree trunk, they stopped and listened. At the sound of snapping twigs, a shadow moved through the woods to their left.

It's the creature, Aridain; it's returned and grown strong; run home, now!

But why voice?

It's here for the shiny stones in your pocket.

I'll leave you younglings alone then, said Sabra, self-importantly.

Sabra, no, insisted Aridain. *We're scared!*

Then, its demeanour changing, the dragonlet, now all heat and quivering sinew, settling next to Aridain, hissed menacingly, *Apology accepted.*

Cautiously, they peered above the rotten log. Before he saw them, Aridain felt the menacing yellow eyes staring back at them intently, only now they were more mature. As the creature drew near, Selva, sat with her back to the trunk, began to cry.

'Aridain, I'm scared.'

Aridain, I implore you, beseeched the voice. *Flee, run, you must go, now!*

It was then that Duran, with a frightened yelp, bolted from cover.

'Kale, it's good to see you,' exclaimed Keegan, emerging from between the trees by the stream.

'Keegan,' shouted Kale, embracing him fiercely. 'You look as if you're about to keel over.'

'Oh, I'm all right, let's get undercover before another patrol comes along,' urged Keegan, leading Kale to a depression beside the stream's bank.

Keegan then turned to him and said, 'Phew, you smell like a warthogs wallow.'

'I was nice and cosy in your shack with Drench; that was before Gradine turned up. Since then, I've been moving around avoiding the patrols while keeping an eye on our young prodigy over there, then holding up where I can during the night. This,' smiled Kale, indicating his new look, 'is all part of my disguise.'

'Hey, I'm not judging,' said Keegan.

In the silence that followed, Kale listened to rooks squawking from a rookery somewhere in the woods and a robin, trilling eagerly to proclaim its territory, from a nearby holly tree, its cheery lilting song completely at odds to the mood he was in.

'I heard what happened, pretty ballsy of Vanir.'

'He's a Greysword.' said Keegan, as if that explained everything. He then plucked an old grass stalk from the rough margin and chewed on it contentedly, causing Kale to smile, the gesture as familiar as the rising of the sun and the waning of the moon.

'Who'd have guessed we'd all be wanted men, creeping around the grounds of a place we all served so avidly,' said Kale, swatting at an annoying flutter of Water Sprites.

Suddenly, they turned at a high-pitched scream. They watched, as further along the stream's bank, a pheasant, cackling loudly, took to the air, flushed from the stream's scrubby margin.

'That sounded like Selva,' declared Keegan.

'It did,' said Kale.

Racing to the bridge, they crossed the stream, then scanned the snow-covered fields. Suddenly, two of the children, followed quickly by a third, bolted out from the tree line across the open field. Behind, leaping in long arching bounds on long spindly arms and legs, was a black ape-like creature, pursued by an irate dragonlet squirting jets of white-hot flame.

'It's the creature!' exclaimed Keegan. 'How did it get so close without us noticing, some guardians we are?'

Sprinting across the field after Keegan, Kale said, 'But I don't understand.'

'What don't you understand?' shouted Keegan infuriatingly.

'It doesn't like sunlight; it can only move at night!'

'Tell it that,' barked Keegan.

'Uncle Keegan,' screamed Aridain. 'Help us.'

'We're coming, Aridain!' Keegan bellowed.

They closed the gap quickly, but it was clear the creature would reach the children first.

'What are you waiting for? Do something!' bellowed Keegan.

'I'm working on it; running is not conducive to spell forming.'

Kale watched helplessly as the Dark Creature, ignoring the dragonlet's searing bursts of flame, pounced, flattening Aridain into the soggy soil and then stood directly over the terrified youngster. The creature hissed a nightmarish shriek, and with the dragonlet tearing ferociously at its back with needle-sharp teeth and claws, opened its gaping maw.

All of a sudden there was an anguished cry and the dark creature, together with the dragonlet, flew backwards across the field.

Reaching the children, Kale, his heart in his mouth, bent over a terrified Aridain. Searching the youth's face; he asked apprehensively, 'Are you all right?'

'Yes,' panted Aridain, looking like a startled owl.

'Good.' Heaving a silent sigh of relief and helping Aridain to his feet, Kale asked, 'What did you just do?'

'Tele..., tele...'

'Telekinesis?'

'Yes, that's it. Aunt Magen taught me.'

'So, Magen's lessons have done some good after all,' he murmured, keeping one eye on the creature that climbed to its feet once more. 'Keegan, get the children to safety!' ordered Kale.

'What about you?'

'Don't worry about me; it's time I made up for my mistakes.'

Then, with intricate hand movements, Kale began drawing the light from the surrounding air towards him and, for an instant, everything turned to shadow. With an intense white glowing ball now forming in his hands, he gestured, thrusting the blazing miniature sun towards the creature. Engulfed in the bright light, the dark child howled with a nightmarish scream, squirming and writhing in pain.

Encouraged by his success, Kale gestured again and drove the creature back into the scrub with a bubble of force, its passing accompanied by the sound of splintering wood and snapping branches. Turning, he smiled, then setting his jaw, Kale disappeared into the tree line after the creature.

'Why is it chasing us?' asked Selva miserably.

'Will it come back?' queried Duran, eyeing the cruel-looking knife in Keegan's hand eagerly.

'I don't know,' said Keegan.

'I do!' Aridain stated abruptly, then said miserably, 'It's after me; it told me it's doing what it must.'

'Do you know why it wants you?'

'It didn't say.'

His jealousy overriding his fear, Duran said, 'You said the same about 'your' dragonlet.'

Did someone mention me?

Keegan quickly span around at the flutter of leathery wings.

'Don't be scared, Uncle Keegan, this is Sabra,' said Aridain proudly. 'He's...'

Not a pet, Sabra emphasised, alighting on Aridain's shoulder and peering at him smugly.

'My friend,' Aridain said proudly.

'Hello, Sabra,' said Keegan, curtsying and inclining his head flamboyantly, which incited Selva and Duran into silent giggles. Then, studying the dragonlet closely, Keegan asked, 'Do you talk to Sabra as well, Aridain?'

'All the time!' he smiled.

Watching the dragonlet fearfully, Duran said decisively, 'Aridain can't talk to animals.'

'How do you know?' said Selva.

'He just can't,' insisted Duran.

'Can too!' said Selva.

'Stop it, you two,' hissed Keegan, looking up at the sound of breaking branches and boughs, accompanied by a thunder-like sound that reverberated across the fields.

Oh, and next time you decide to defend yourself, youngling, warn me first.

Sorry, Sabra, I didn't mean to hurt you, but I didn't know what else to do... thought Aridain frantically, *I thought the creature was going to kill me... you couldn't stop it... and I was worried about you and my friends and...'*

Ok, ok, youngling, don't strain yourself, the incident is forgotten. Oh, and by the way, your Animistic friend won't be able to stop it.

'Sabra says that Kale won't be able to stop it,' said Aridain gloomily.

After a few moments, Keegan, making up his mind, said, 'All this noise is bound to attract attention, so we have to go.' He then turned to Selva and Duran. 'You two need to run home; it's too dangerous.' He then looked at the dragonlet, 'Sabra will look after you. You'll be perfectly safe, right, Aridain?'

'You heard him, let's go Selva,' urged Duran, and he led his sister across the field towards the farm.

Keegan watched as Aridain turned and stared at the dragonlet for what seemed an age; the dragonlet then took to the air and flew after the fleeing children. Grasping his shoulders gently, Keegan span Aridain around and looked into his tear-filled eyes, then, brandishing his knife, said, 'Be brave now and stay close to me.'

Aridain, his expression having taken on the resolve of someone much older, nodded determinedly.

'That's the spirit.'

Another explosion ripped through the air, followed by an ear-piercing shriek. The sound of more splintering wood followed almost immediately, and the trees shook and quivered as though grasped by some giant hand.

'Now's our chance, Aridain; let's go!'

With his hunting knife grasped firmly in his right hand, Keegan, keeping Aridain close, sprinted across the field. Crossing the bridge, Keegan was met by Lascana, who stood anxiously outside the cottage, holding a crossbow.

'All this noise. What's happening, Keegan?'

'The creature's back. It attacked the children.'

'Attacked the children! Are Selva and Duran all right?'

'I sent them home. Sabra's watching over them. A crossbow?' queried Keegan, eyeing the weapon.

'I found it in the cottage.'

'Some find.'

'Yes, it's a mystery how the crossbow and the full quiver of bolts appeared, but it will certainly come in handy, that's for sure.'

Just then, another inhuman squeal split the air together with an altogether more human cry.

Lascana demanded, 'Who is that?'

'It's Kale. Don't look at me like that; what was he supposed to do? I couldn't have stopped him even if I wanted to. Now, take Aridain; Kale needs my help.'

'Don't you dare, Keegan Fold!' Lascana said fiercely. 'You're staying here to help keep Aridain safe,' ordered Lascana, with a look that brokered no argument.

Without speaking, they both began locking the premises. Then, under Keegan's instruction, they waited anxiously in the hallway, watching and waiting for the creature they knew would appear, the silence akin to an audience-filled auditorium anticipating an orchestra's opening notes.

'Is Kale going to be all right?' Aridain enquired.

Tears stung Lascana's eyes, and she held her hand to her mouth as Keegan returned her desperate look and shook his head, the simple gesture conveying a horrific truth.

'You both think he's dead, don't you?' Closing his eyes for a moment, Aridain then opened them again and said, 'No, he's not, but he's hurt.'

'Aridain, how do you know that?' insisted Keegan.

'My friends in the woods told me.' Then, pointing towards the window, Aridain announced suddenly, 'It's in the front garden!'

Peering apprehensively out through the window with Keegan, Lascana, her nerves now at breaking point, watched Aridain's grown-up dark twin as it crept like a cautious Virion cat through the front garden, its claws unsheathed and its teeth bared.

Glaring in through the window, a sharp-toothed grin splitting its face from ear to ear, it hissed, 'Arriddaaain, join wittthhh me, it is our dessssstiny, our caaalling.'

'We have to go to the woods,' announced Aridain suddenly, tugging at Lascana's arm.

'Why?'

'Because my friends live there, they'll help us.'

'How do you know this?'

'The voice told me.'

'No, it's too dangerous. This thing wants you! We have to get away, far away.'

'Mummy, it's our only chance. If we don't, the creature will find us and we'll all die.'

Looking deliberately at Lascana, Keegan said, 'I've learnt to heed Aridain's words at times like this; he wouldn't say that for just any reason.'

'What, just like that?' stated Lascana. 'Trust the word of a six-year-old boy; and then what?'

'There is no other choice, Lascana,' stated Keegan. 'You have to go.'

Suddenly, there was a sound of breaking glass and, with a look of determination, Keegan turned, then, sprinting from the kitchen, he said resolutely, 'Go, NOW?'

Charged with adrenalin-fuelled fury, Keegan rushed to the living room.

'That's for Kale, you slimy pigskin,' he roared, slashing at the creature's face.

The creature recoiled from the blow but quickly recovered as Keegan swung his knife again, only this time unsuccessfully.

Unaffected by the gaping wound across its cheek, the creature grasped the blade and then leapt, forcing him into the hallway. It then leapt upon his chest. Bewildered by the creature's strength and speed, Keegan, unable to rise, gasped, 'What the hell are you?'

'Sssuffice to sssay Mortal, weaponsss and mortal magic cannot kill me, and what cannot kill me only makesss me ssstronger, the Animisssstic realisssed thissss.'

The wound across its cheek closing before Keegan's eyes, he pulled another knife from his opposite bicep and slashed for its throat. However, the creature, with unworldly speed, grasped Keegan's arm and, with a strength that could only be born of magic, twisted the weapon from his grasp. In desperation, Keegan wrapped his legs under the creature's arms and, with strength he didn't know he possessed, propelled it backwards across the kitchen.

Landing on its feet with the agility of a cat, the creature said calmly. 'Your attemptsss to delay me will only end in failure, Keegan Fold.'

'Not if I sever that ugly spud that you call a head from your shoulders!' bellowed Keegan.

He then leapt with the swiftness of an acrobat and swung his weapon. But for all his speed and skill, he was too slow as the mercurial creature twisted and kicked out. Propelled through the air, Keegan felt a jarring pain in his back, followed quickly by a burning sensation. Rolling away from the wood burner, he got to his feet and brushed at the hot cinders singeing his clothing. Trying his best to ignore the pain, he spat, 'You can gloat now, you evil abomination, but when Aridain reaches the grove, your days are numbered.'

Abruptly, the creature spun around and headed for the broken window.

It seems I've hit a nerve. 'Oh no you don't,' Keegan cried, striking outwards and down with his knife as the creature attempted to exit the cottage. With the Korda knife buried firmly in the back of its leg, the creature began squirming and twisting, tearing at Keegan's face and leather clothing in an attempt to escape his grasp. Despite the creature's fury, Keegan held on, but inevitably, despite his determination, the creature pulled itself free, his knife tearing through muscle and sinew. Now loose, the creature, despite the gaping wound in its leg, disappeared like quicksilver out the kitchen window and into the woods.

'Curses,' he spat.

Reaching the Kitchen's open window he bellowed towards the woods, 'LASCANA, IT'S COMING, IT'S COMING!'

CHAPTER TWENTY

THE GREY AND BLACK WILDERNESS

With Aridain's hand clasped in hers, Lascana fled the cottage. Outside, rooks cawed, sheep blared, and all seemed normal beneath the clear blue winter sky. However, when they crossed into the woods, all was silent, grey and oppressive, making her feel decidedly uncomfortable, like the feeling you get when walking into an unfriendly tavern. An evil, treacle-like blight covered everything and a cloying mist, smelling of rotting vegetables and something else that she immediately recognised as decaying flesh, shrouded the woodland.

'Phew, what's that smell?' stated Aridain, putting his arm up around his nose. 'It smells like rotting garbage.'

Then, suddenly, from the distance, like the desperate cry of some bizarre beast, Keegan's voice echoed through the trees.

Trying not to show her fear, Lascana loaded the crossbow and pulled it into her shoulder.

'Aridain, keep going. Don't stop, go and find your friends.'

Seeing his look of concern, she placated, 'Don't worry, Munch kin, I'll be all right; I'll be right behind you.'

Lascana watched anxiously as Aridain, disappeared into the mist. She then turned and scanned the grey haze. She didn't have to wait long before the dark ape-like creature appeared. Dropping to one knee, she focused and loosed an arrow that, to her amazement, hit its intended target; but to her chagrin, the creature merely looked down in curiosity at the projectile protruding from its chest. Casually pulling the bolt free and casting it aside, it continued to sprint towards her. Before she could load another bolt, however, it pounced with lightning speed, thrusting its claws into her shoulder. It then pulled her close and opened its maw, its fetid breath filling her nostrils.

'Why do you perssssissst, Mother? You didn't really think that your friend's and that fire breathing sssquill could ssstop me, did you? Your futile efforts are nothing but an irritation now.'

'Don't call me Mother, devil creature. I could never give birth to something like you.'

'Soon you will have no choiccce but to acknowledge who I am.'

Then, abruptly, the creature heaved her aside as if she were made of tinder-wood and bounded into the trees. Mumbling thanks to the gods for watching over her, Lascana got to her feet; it was then that she felt a fiery pain erupt from her shoulder. Gingerly, she pulled down her bodice to reveal several inflamed gashes. *Toxin... its claws are poisonous.* Taking a deep breath, she thought, *No time for that now. My son's safety is all that matters.*

Steeling herself and gaining her feet, Lascana, holding her sleeve to her nose and mouth against the stench, plunged headlong through the trees. Following her son's tiny footprints in the blight, she scanned the miasma for any sign of movement, and it soon became clear that the trees were fighting a losing battle. The further she ventured, the more emaciated the forest appeared. Abruptly, the hissing of flames echoed amongst the trees, followed immediately by a terrible screeching sound and then a mournful howl. Lascana, her breath coming in short gasps, stumbled into the grove.

The sight that greeted her nearly broke her heart. A thick soup-like miasma had settled over the grove like a blanket, and dead and diseased plants, bushes and trees lay everywhere covered with decay. The only thing remaining was the cherry sapling, and even that had been infected. Panting heavily from her exertions, she hissed, listlessly, 'Aridain, Mummy's here. Where are you, Munch kin? Please talk to me.'

Hearing an almost inaudible cry to her right, Lascana, heaving a silent sigh, dropped down next to her son, who was hiding in a depression beside an old rotting log. Embracing him tenderly, she whispered, 'Thank Seline, you're all right. Where are your friends?'

'We're too late Mummy, the nasty has scared them all away,' sobbed Aridain, 'and Sabra's going to die,' he cried, pointing to the dragonlet that lay unmoving among the rotting vegetation. 'The nasty has hurt him really bad.'

Wiping at her cold, clammy forehead, she stared into the eyes of the enigma that was her son, now covered in the black slimy gunge. Suddenly, his demeanour changed, and he stared serenely off into the distance. Then, looking up at her with innocent hazel eyes, Aridain, pointing, said, 'It's over there, the nasty, it's watching from the trees.'

Then, through increasingly hazy vision, she saw the creature emerge from the tree line and advance across the grove; its malicious yellow and black-streaked eyes fixed on her son. Its teeth set in a feral growl, the demon turned towards her and snarled a warning, causing Lascana to stumble backwards involuntarily as she tried once more to rise and present the crossbow.

'Forget Mothhher and Fattther, Aridain, for they will fail you in the end, aasss they have me. Forget dreamssss of love and belonging, those petty concernsss are for mortalsss. Joined with me, the pain of disssappointment and sssorrow will be forgotten, wiped away together with the petty concernsss of thessse insignificant humanss. A gloriousss future awaitsss usss, if you would only embracccce the shards. You could feel strong, exhilarated, in the absssolute ccertainty of your power. Joined, we will live forever.'

Lascana despaired as the creature advanced, confident in its knowledge that she couldn't stop it.

Alfic, where are you? she thought despairingly, rubbing at her painful, throbbing shoulder. *My son needs you; I need you.* Then, plucking up what courage remained, in a voice filled with loathing she demanded, 'You said "when you are joined". What do you mean?'

'I have been tasssked to kill my sssworn enemy, the Champion of Light,' it hissed in a voice full of menace. 'But now I realissse there is so much more. I want to experienccce the pleassuress of this reality, and the only way to do that is to join with the Elemental.'

'Champion of Light, Elemental. What…?'

'The Elemental'sss fate is unavoidable, hisss pain and yourss will be brief, but do not fret Mottherrrr, for he will ssstill live through me.'

'NO, NEVER,' cried Lascana. 'I would rather see him dead than joined with you!'

She nearly faltered when she looked down to see the concern etched on her son's face.

'Are you and Sabra going to die?' queried Aridain, all of a sudden.

The woods spinning about her, she tried to reassure him, but before she could, Aridain bolted.

'Noooo, come back here!' she screamed desolately.

She held her breath as Aridain ran, stumbling and slipping through the rotting foliage and blight-covered underbrush, towards the dragonlet. At the same time, the creature with otherworldly agility leapt through the air directly towards Aridain. Notching another bolt and ignoring her pain, Lascana dropped once more to her knee and, praying to the gods for guidance, pulled the crossbow tightly into her shoulder and fired. The bolt struck true, entering through its ear and exiting through the side of its head.

Surely it was dead this time? she prayed. *Surely?*

Notching another bolt, she ordered Aridain, who cradled the sick dragonlet, to stay put. Pulling the crossbow into her shoulder, she stumbled wearily towards the comatose creature. With her racing pulse pounding in her ears, she heaved a grateful sigh as the crazed yellow eyes darkened and the demon lay unmoving on the slime ridden floor. She turned to Aridain and caressed him affectionately, noticing that the dragonlet's breathing was very shallow. She also noticed several deep red gashes about its small body that had turned an insipid grey.

Holding her son at arm's length, she cried, 'What were you thinking?' Then, closing her eyes, she pulled him close.

Aridain, stroking the dragonlet affectionately, looked up at her with a worried expression and then pointed to the creature.

She watched wretchedly as, like a phoenix from the flames, the inky black creature pulled the crossbow bolt from its head and climbed to its feet once more. Cradling Aridain's face in her hands, the creature's poison coursing through her veins, Lascana slurred, 'Close your eyes, Munch kin.' Then, wrapping Aridain, together with the dragonlet in her arms, she curled up on the woodland floor.

Alfic turned as the double doors to the plant house burst open, the vegetation shaking as if caught in a savage wind. Then a deep guttural voice boomed his name. Hurrying along the aisle, Alfic peered through the foliage.

'Elimi! what are you doing here? What is it?'

'There's smoke rising from the woods,' he huffed. 'I think it's your cottage.'

'What do you mean, my cottage?' exclaimed Alfic.

'Come, take a look.'

Discarding his trowel, Alfic leapt to his feet and barged past the labourer. Slamming the door behind him, he ran outside into the winter sunshine. Skidding to a halt across the icy ground, Alfic looked towards the woods and sure enough, beyond the stream, black smoke billowed into the clear, ice-blue afternoon sky.

Throwing his leather apron to the ground, Alfic, noticing Elimi had followed him outside, ordered, 'I know you want to help, but don't. Too many of my friends' heads are for the chopping block because of me.'

'But...'

'No buts, Elimi, I'll handle this.'

Then, turning quickly, his legs fuelled by fear and concern, Alfic sprinted across the playing field with determination. Through the orchard he ran, vaulting the fence and racing across the fields.

Burning straw floated down all around him as he reached the bridge and, slowing to a walk, he watched in disbelief, through air thick with smoke, as flames consumed his home; the sounds of popping and spitting accompanying the cottage's destruction. Dropping to his knees, he held his head in his hands; he was too late, his wife and children were gone, his whole world taken from him in one foul swoop.

'Rest easy, Alfic, they're not in there.'

He looked up through smoke-filled tears and saw the bedraggled and bloody figure of Kale sat against the wall, burnt and blackened and harbouring numerous injuries.

'What did you say?'

'There's no-one in there, I looked.'

Alfic, wiping at his tears, smiled and heaved a silent sigh. 'Thank Seline. What happened here?' he asked, watching forlornly as flames raced up the tinder dry thatch of his fiercely burning home.

'The creature; that's what happened?' Kale answered painfully. 'I followed it into the trees. It was after your son,' he said desperately. 'I tried... but I couldn't stop it, it just became stronger. So much for my fancy theories,' he murmured forlornly.

'Where are they? Where are my wife and son?' Alfic asked, determinedly.

'The Grove. I'm convinced of it. Aridain's fairy friends are there; he'll try to find them.'

In silence, Alfic turned determinedly towards the woods.

'Wait,' exclaimed Kale, 'I'll come with you.'

'Stay here, you're in no fit state...'

'... Fornax's fires I will; I'm fit enough,' said Kale, looking up at Alfic resolutely.

'Then let's go, but I'm not waiting for you.'

CHAPTER TWENTY-ONE

ARIDAIN, MAGICAL WATERS & SAPPHIRE SPRITES

The undergrowth tugging at his clothing and skin, time seemed to stand still as Kale, his breathing laboured, his legs feeling like lead, followed Alfic determinedly through the woods, knowing the cost of any delay might mean the death of his friends.

His body complaining bitterly now, he cursed as Alfic increased the pace, leaving him trailing in his wake.

Stopping for breath, his head swimming and his body on fire, Kale gritted his teeth, determined not to let the steely, indomitable groundsman out of his sight. Ahead through the dark miasma, the grove appeared little by little, and hearing frenetic shouting and cursing, he burst through the surrounding thicket and scanned the clearing.

Off to one side, covered in the dark, slimy sludge, Alfic picked himself up from the ground. As he watched, the handyman found a large wooden log then, with a look of savagery, he advanced upon the creature that had Keegan pinned to the dark, slimy earth, despite the gamekeeper's struggles. It was then that Kale saw Aridain, cradling the comatose body of the dragonlet, laid beneath an old tree trunk on the far side of the grove, looking desolately at the curled up and unmoving form of Lascana.

'Kale, don't just stand there, do something!' bellowed Alfic frantically.

'Ahhh, Kale Simm,' hissed the creature deviously. 'You survived our encounter.'

As if recovering from a seizure, Kale growled angrily, 'Our attempts to defeat you may make you stronger, but we will never stop opposing you! Evil will never flourish here, not while I have breath in my body.'

With a demonic grin on its ghoulish, grizzled face, the creature raised its razor-like talons to strike, and in that moment, Kale realised that if he didn't act, Keegan was going to die. Gesturing, a powerful force, accompanied by an audible thump, span the creature and Keegan across the woodland's slimy, liquorish covered floor. He then stood ready and watched as the creature climbed to its feet once again, as he knew it would. But to his surprise, it stood motionless. It then turned and disappeared into the trees.

Helping Keegan to his feet, Kale asked, 'How are you doing?'

'I'll let you know when my head stops spinning.'

'Did it scratch you with its claws?'

'I don't think so. Why?'

'Thank Seline.'

'Why?' Then understanding crossed Keegan's face and he looked into Kale's pain-filled eyes. 'Your infected, aren't you?'

'I'm fine for the present; my magic…, is holding the poison at bay.'

'So, will it come back?' said Keegan, holding his head and looking around groggily. 'Perhaps it's had enough. Perhaps it's gone to find another host; perhaps it's badly wounded and has gone off to die,' said Keegan optimistically.

'It will be back,' Kale informed Keegan with certainty.

'Oh, excuse me for injecting a bit of optimism,' Keegan said sarcastically. 'So, any idea why it took off like that?'

Kale, gesturing cluelessly with his arms, shook his head.

'Fat lot of good you are, Animistic.'

The pair of them then joined Alfic, who knelt beside Lascana, was examining her pale features, concern etched upon his face. 'Thank you, Kale,' he said concernedly.

'You're welcome.' Kale then looked sideways at Keegan. 'A certain someone told me once that the time would come when my skills would be needed.'

'Hey, I'm not all good looks and charm,' smiled Keegan, 'impossible odds, no escape; feels just like old times.'

'Really!' declared Kale. 'We're all about to die and all you can think of is how battling a demonic creature makes you feel more alive!'

'Hey, it's what makes life worth living,' said Keegan, looking at him quizzically. 'Live for nothing; die for something, that's my motto.'

'How is she, Alfic?' asked Kale.

'She's in a bad way.' Alfic then shook his wife's shoulders gently and said tenderly, 'Lascana wake up, Lascana we have to go.' Receiving no response, he said, 'We need to get Lascana to a healer; we need Alsike. Keegan, help me here.'

'Alfic, I guarantee the creature won't let us leave, not with the thing it desires,' said Kale, ignoring Keegan's censorious stare.

'My son,' confirmed Alfic darkly.

Aridain, you can save them.

'Voice,' Aridain cried.

'Voice? Where? What voice?' questioned Alfic.

'The voice in my head,' said Aridain. *Voice, where have you been?* Aridain thought angrily.

That's not important right now. Saving them is.

We need a healer.

You are the only person who can save them. Remember what you did at the cottage? You only have to believe.

Will it stop the nasty talking to me?

Yes, if you're prepared to learn.

'This is ridiculous, we have to go now!' insisted Alfic, becoming more and more agitated. 'We have to get Lascana to the infirmary.'

'No', insisted Aridain vehemently.

'No, what do you mean no?' said Alfic angrily.

'Alfic, I think you should listen to your son,' said Kale.

'Kale's right,' said Keegan with certainty.

'You should know by now Alfic, that in desperate circumstances, Aridain always seems to know what to do,' said Kale knowingly.

'I think I know my own son.'

'He did save Elias Tan,' added Keegan.

'But that was different. I'll be placing my wife's life in the hands of a six-year-old boy.'

Aridain, silence your father. It's vital you do as I say.

'Daaad, quiet, I'm trying to learn,' chastised Aridain, pressing his finger to his lips.

'Aridain, I want to know about this voice, and what do you mean by learn?' Alfic demanded angrily.

'Alfic, be quiet, calm down,' hissed Keegan.

'No. I...'

'You're not helping,' barked Keegan.

'And I need to be sure,' snapped Alfic, who turned desperately to Aridain and said, 'Son, are you sure you can do this?'

But Aridain wasn't listening to Alfic. With his eyes closed, he listened to the voice.

Aridain, first I want you to picture a wall; the thicker, the better. Build it brick by brick in your mind until you can no longer see the nasty through it.

How?

Concentrate, like when you paint one of your pictures or drawings. Once you've done that, then you can heal them. Yes, that's it, said the voice, as Aridain began to build his imaginary wall, the thought of his mum and Sabra dying spurring him on.

His heart now beating ten-to-the-dozen Aridain quailed, *It knows what I'm doing. It's getting angry.*

Because it realises you're not so helpless, but don't be frightened...

It was hard at first as with each stone he placed, the creature with almighty psychic blows knocked them down again. Nevertheless, as the struggle continued and his confidence grew, Aridain's wall slowly took shape.

Good, good. Now, quickly place a hand on their wounds.

But you said ...

Aridain, you must do as I say. Right now, your magic simply isn't strong enough to sustain the wall in your mind as well as heal your mother and the dragonlet.

Placing one hand on Lascana's arm and the other on the body of the dragonlet, Aridain gritted his teeth and concentrated.

Lascana stirred to a low thrumming noise, the sound causing her head to throb painfully. Her lips and ears felt numb, and her nose itched. She sat up and scratched at the itch and noticed the dried-on gloop that covered her hand. Then, sitting up abruptly, she realised she was covered from head to toe in the tar-like substance, and that what had just happened hadn't been an intense nightmare.

'Mummy, you're alive.'

Hugging him fiercely, Lascana said jadedly, 'Hello, Munch kin.'

Smiling, she looked down at Aridain cradling the dragonlet, and although its pallor still looked like death, the small creature was now breathing easily.

'Dad. Mum's alive!'

'I can see, well done, Son,' said Alfic, hurrying over and kneeling beside them, relief written all over his face. He then hugged them both firmly. 'I don't know what you did, but I'm glad you did it.'

'Welcome back to the world of the living Lascana,' smiled Keegan.

'And where the hell were you?' barked Lascana. 'We nearly died!'

'I..., the creature..., I tried to..., oh, I give up,' stated Keegan, exasperated.

'And as for you, Alfic Bruin, don't you ever be late again.'

'I was detained,' apologised Alfic, as if that explained everything.

'And what do you mean, "Well done, Son."?' she queried. 'Are you telling me that Aridain cured me?'

'Ah, I think the penny's dropped,' said Keegan, watching her curiously.

'I saved Sabra too,' said Aridain proudly.

'This is a conversation for later. Right now, we have to go,' ordered Alfic, 'Before...

Suddenly, the dark creature appeared. Mesmerised, the friends scattered about the grove. They watched as the creature landed atop Aridain's shoulders and forced him to the floor. Before the friends could react, Aridain issued an intense agonised scream as the creature sank its black claws into his forehead and jaw, and with a malevolent hiss, wrenched open Aridain's mouth. Its evil, yellow eyes glinting in anticipation, the creature turned its lithe, sinewy, black quicksilver body into liquid obsidian.

It then flowed into Aridain's eyes, nose, and mouth. It was the strangest, most bizarre and obscene thing they'd ever seen.

Stumbling towards her terrified son, Lascana screamed, 'Alfic, Kale, do something!'

Kale barged past, a large glowing ball of light forming in his palms. Pressing his hands against the now fluidic creature, Kale manipulated the ball of light which grew, engulfing him and Aridain. He then detonated it with an intense burst of light.

Her eyes adjusting after the sunburst glow, Lascana saw Kale laid prostrate on the slimy woodland floor. She then watched apprehensively, as Aridain blinked in confusion, then slowly looked around in wonder and clarity.

'Did it work?' asked Keegan, looking to Alfic.

'How would I know?'

'Well, you have magic, don't you?'

Holding back, they watched, unsure, as Aridain walked up to Kale and reached down to him. But instead of helping him to his feet, he wrapped his tiny hands around Kale's throat and lifted him onto his knees.

His voice now dripping with malice, Aridain slurred, 'Foolish Animistic, this body has no aversion to light, I have the advantage now,' and like a child playing with a limp rag doll, Aridain threw Kale across the grove into the rotting undergrowth.

Then, grinning like a Cheshire cat, Aridain sneered, 'I like thisss, thessse new ssensssationss, thiss magic. Now that I have the ssshardsss; I want more.'

'Alfic, Keegan, do something!' screamed Lascana.

'Like what Lascana?' Alfic shouted despairingly as he ran towards the creature. 'I'm open to ideas.'

'Trying to stop this thing is like pissing into the wind,' agreed Keegan, close on his heels.

Suddenly Aridain, turning his gaze upon Keegan and Alfic, gestured, creating black, inky tendrils that snaked across the grove and the pair were flung through the air and up into the branches of the poisoned trees.

Struggling forlornly to her feet, Lascana stumbled towards her husband.

Suddenly, Lascana screamed as Aridain, with otherworldly stealth, suddenly appeared before her. A lizard-like tongue slathering around Aridain lips, the creature hissed with intent.

'Do not fret Motthhher, as I said, now we will alwaysss be together, and in time you will come to ssee me asss your ssson. Take comfort in the knowledge that you will be ssserving uss, like a loving mother should, and in doing sso sssserve a higher purpose.'

'And what higher purpose is that, to destroy this world?'

'Oh no, I will turn it into my world.' Then, in a voice filled with intent, it demanded, 'Now, kneel, and give yoursssself over to me.'

Sweating, shaking, and struggling to move, as the dark magic still coursed through her veins, Lascana, spittle dribbling from the corners of her mouth, threatened, 'Never, we'll never give in to you.'

'Foolisssh humans, he wass but a boy, a boy never ready for the burden placed upon his inadequate sssshoulders. My brother and I are now one, there'sss nothing you can do to stop me, to stop us. Hissss destiny, asss doesss yoursssss, liesss with me now.'

Lascana looked at her son, at his now darkened complexion and his citrine-coloured eyes. It was at this moment that she realised there was only one way to keep her family safe.

'You are right,' agreed Lascana, rising unsteadily to her feet. She then approached the creature. 'We are beaten.'

Taking Aridain's small hands in hers, Lascana looked into those evil, pallid eyes.

'But first, before we join, I want to show you something.'

'Where are we going?' Aridain hissed.

'To a place that will benefit us all,' smiled Lascana.

'No deceptions, Mother, and no tricks. You know they will do you no good.'

Lascana smiled, 'I know now what a fool I've been. Better to trust in fate; it's easier that way.'

Leading Aridain from the grove and out through the woods, she said, 'Will you allow me to talk to my other son one more time?'

The creature then stopped and leaned close, cradling Lascana's face with Aridain's childlike hands. 'Tears Mother, I know they are not for me. Very well, call it a reward for your compliance.'

Lascana grasped Aridain's hands fiercely and then stared into those citrine eyes as if searching for something. Aridain tried to take a step back and to disengage from Lascana, but Lascana held on.

'I told you no tricksss…,' hissed the creature menacingly, 'release me!'

'I'm here Aridain, Mummy's here,' cried Lascana. 'I know you can hear me; I know you are there. Fight Son with all your strength…'

Suddenly, without warning, the creature paused. Releasing its hands, Lascana watched as the citrine eyes glazed over, and confusion played across its features.

'Noooo,' it hissed, 'thisss isss imposssssible.'

The creature then collapsed to the floor, shaking and moaning in agony. In desperation, Lascana bent over and picked up Aridain's small body in her arms.

'Keep fighting, Munch kin. It's time to find your friends,' she said fervently. Then, looking to the heavens, she prayed, *Please, let me be right.*

Gritting her teeth and cradling the small, squirming body in her arms as it threatened to extricate itself from her grip, Lascana staggered to the stream.

Where are you going, Mother? The dark child screamed in her mind. *You cannot escape me, neither can my brother.*

'Go to hell,' raged Lascana defiantly. 'You may be in my head, but I won't listen to you!' *Stay strong now, girl. Only a little further,* she thought sternly.

Desperately trying to ignore the creature's perverted thoughts and holding onto the now frantically wriggling body, Lascana arrived at the stream's bank. Without a thought, she plunged into its cold, clear waters.

Stay strong, Munch kin, she thought. *The creature struggles because it knows the waters can kill it!*

Then, staring into Aridain's panicked eyes, she firmly and urgently pushed the desperately squirming body under the water.

Abruptly, Aridain's head snapped backwards and power exploded through Lascana's veins like a raging river over a bed of hot coals, coursing through her arms and hands, leaving her weak and disorientated. Sobbing uncontrollably, Lascana, clinging to her son with all her might, watched as he glared at her with a look of incomprehension and terror. The waters then began to boil and bubble and Lascana, holding her son close, stared in amazement as six blue shining pools of swirling water formed around them. Then, the blackness that was the creature gushed from her son's mouth, nose and eyes, coiling and twisting about them as Aridain's small body began to convulse and shake uncontrollably. It was at this time that a shimmering chiffon curtain that Lascana realised was her son's essence, mingled inexorably with the undulating curtain of dark fluid above her head.

'That's it, Son,' Lascana sobbed, 'don't let it escape, let the stream and your friends' magic kill it.'

Contorted and twisted, the dance of light and dark continued until an ear-splitting howl of despair, accompanied by a tremendous clap of thunder, shattered the stillness. Then, six sparkling azure blue lights in the form of the Sapphire Sprites broke the surface waters, and hovered around them briefly before disappearing into the trees.

Blowing air into Aridain's lungs, Lascana held his head above the water and shook him vigorously. 'Breathe, Aridain, please wake up, FIGHT!' she wailed.

When, after a few minutes, nothing happened, Lascana held him close and began crying inconsolably. *I'm sorry, my precious boy. Better dead than under the creature's control.*

Do not worry, Aridain's birth mother, this day is not yet over.

She looked up with tear-filled vision at the flapping of small leathery wings to see Sabra perched upon a branch overhanging the stream.

Lascana then looked around in wonder as her son's sparkling essence flowed through her, imparting her with a sense of abandon and euphoria. Aridain then took a deep breath and, with tears of relief, she hugged him tightly.

'Are you both all right?'

Elation mixed with relief, Lascana looked up to see the young animistic, battered but alive, leaning against a tree. 'Kale!' she screamed. 'Thank Seline. It worked!'

'The stream was the answer, wasn't it? It possessed the ambient magic of the Sapphire sprites.'

'Yes,' she nodded frantically, 'All the signs, all the clues led me to this.'

'Daddy, Uncle Keegan,' yelled Aridain excitedly, who, having miraculously recovered, wriggled from Lascana's arms and splashed through the water excitedly to join his father and Keegan as they hobbled towards them from the woods. 'We beat the nasty.'

'Well done, Munch kin,' smiled Alfic kindly.

'I knew you'd be ok Daddy. You had uncle Keegan with you,' smiled Aridain.

'Did you hear that? I'm his favourite uncle,' beamed Keegan.

'Soldiers are coming,' said Aridain, 'Sabra told me so, and that they are led by a man with one eye.'

'I hope Kale and Keegan got away all right?' whispered Alfic.

'Sabra says that they weren't seen,' informed Aridain happily.

'Still think the dragonlet is a bad idea?' said Lascana, looking keenly at Alfic while wringing the water from her saturated clothes that now weighed almost as much as her.

Alfic, saying nothing, turned and looked sternly up at the small lizard, looking uncannily like a contented cat, as it sat gnawing on a large toasted Timber rat on a branch above their heads. Forgetting the dragonlet, Alfic then waited with Lascana and Aridain as six soldiers, their armour glinting in the late winter sun, appeared through the trees led by Karnack.

'Alfic, Lascana, stay where you are; you're under arrest!'

'On what charge?' Alfic demanded seriously. 'If it's because we have just destroyed the creature; or for fighting against an unjust regime here at the school; then yes, we are guilty.'

'You are accessories to breaking Keegan and Greysword Mace Denobar out of jail; and plotting against the Sivan,' announced Karnack.

'Me and my family had nothing to do with breaking our friends from their unjust imprisonment in the dungeons. As for plotting against the Sivan, since when was freedom of speech a crime?'

The grizzled warrior then looked at their bruised and battered bodies, and then at their surroundings.

'Go,' ordered Karnack, looking at the soldiers, 'search the area for the fugitives, while I get to the bottom of this. I'll be along shortly.'

'Do you take me for a fool, Alfic?' grumbled Karnack. 'Tell me what really happened.'

'It's true Mister Karnack,' said Aridain seriously. 'Mummy lured the creature into the magical stream and, together with the sprites, they helped me kill it.'

'Something happened here, Aridain, but I don't believe for one moment it had anything to do with Sprites and magical streams.'

Lascana smiled down at her son and said, 'I knew he wouldn't believe us, Munch kin.'

'You're damn right I don't believe you; I never knew your family had such overactive imaginations, Alfic,' mocked Karnack. Then, producing two sets of manacles, he ordered, 'Now hold out your hands. You can contemplate your stories while in the dungeons.'

Staring at Karnack intently, Aridain insisted angrily, 'Mr Karnack, we're telling the truth.'

Stepping in front of Lascana and Aridain, Alfic said, 'Please Karnack, we are a good family. You know we are devoted to the school, and we would never invent a story like this.'

'Don't make this any harder than it is, Alfic,' said Karnack stoically.

'Conflicted? What happened to the famed levelheadedness of Karnack "the ferocious"?'

'Do not mistake broad-mindedness for apathy, or comradeship for charity, Alfic,' growled Karnack.

The old grizzled warrior looked down at Aridain in confusion as the youth stared back with eyes now the colour of black opal; blinking, his features softening, Karnack looked towards Lascana and Alfic.

'I've known Perak a good many years now; it's true. He's a good man.' Then, raising his sword, he pointed it threateningly at Alfic's chest and warned menacingly. 'But know this Alfic, the balance is changing and reprieves through association will no longer hold sway. This is the last time; now go home.'

Watching in silence as the old Greysword disappeared into the gathering gloom, Alfic said loudly, 'Well, thanks to your employer, my brother, I now have no home to go to.'

Then, together with Lascana and Aridain, he made his way through the rot towards the burnt and blackened ruin that was their home.

CHAPTER TWENTY-TWO

THE HORNS OF A DILEMMA

Her footsteps loud in the silence, Magen made her way between the assembly hall's rows of empty pews, as the sun striking the lead-lined roof above, reflected through the tall, imposing arched windows, throwing the thick oak rafters and beams into stark relief.

Stepping up onto the dais, having passed the busts and portraits of teachers and Wizards, past and present, their studious likeness's silently watching from recesses set into the walls, Magen climbed the wooden steps then skirted the Sivan's imposing black onyx table. She then parted the thick richly embroidered gold and crimson trimmed tapestries and opened a plain wooden door that led into the council chambers beyond. The door's hinges creaking noisily in the silence behind her, she sat at one of the tables next to Exedra, who said vaguely, 'Ah, Magen, there you are.'

'Exedra,' acknowledged Magen with an incline of her head.

'Your injuries are healed, I see.'

'Yes, thank you, Exedra,' smiled Magen, having reinforced the lie that the cuts and bruises (inflicted for her defiance at the spring fair) were acquired while separating her brothers.

Shaking her head disapprovingly, Exedra stated, 'Good, I hope these ridiculous family squabbles are a thing of the past. Your brothers can be intolerable sometimes. Talking of your brothers; has Kuelack returned yet? He does know we have a school to run!'

'Oh, believe me, the school's welfare is the reason for his absence,' stated Magen.

'Tolerance and understanding, Exedra,' interceded Mass in his thin, reedy voice while staring at Exedra intently. 'It's the school's motto!'

'Yes, of course, forgive me,' said Exedra, looking somewhat confused.

'It's a joke, don't you think?' said Mass, staring towards the alabaster, aquamarine and white marble vista, set into the wall at the far end of the small panelled room, atop two small white marble columns.

'What is?'

'The school's motto.'

'And take that fresco, for instance; it depicts Pellagrin as a saintly, heroic figure preaching to a group of pilgrims, consisting of all manner of beasts and people; but the man was a hypocrite. Why anyone would revere a wizard who would not tolerate what he had called 'evil practices', is beyond me? That scene is a self-serving mockery, a panorama stretched to the realms of incredulity.'

'I doubt that he commissioned the carving,' Exedra challenged.

Then placing her quill into the ink well and spinning around in her chair towards them, Exedra, in an effort to make light of Mass's allegations, said, 'It was of its time, meant to inspire the school's residents, teach them that if they set their minds to a task, the possibilities are boundless.'

'That's the most pitiable defence of the school's founder I've ever heard,' argued Mass.

'Pellagrin imbued the school with magic to detect and prevent anyone with the slightest hint of evil from entering. It was in the school's interest,' asserted Exedra forcefully.

'And should they try to gain entry, the school would dispatch gargoyles to deal with them,' Mass said contemptuously. 'I know of Pellagrin's so-called "safeguards".'

'Those safeguards, along with Pellagrin's magic, have long since faded, so the point is mute,' Magen remarked, while regarding the saintly panorama. 'I admired his strength of character but, for my part, I could not understand his aversion to change. The idea of any Wizard trying to bring order to a new world, but purge variety, is condescending in the least.'

'I find that point of view very surprising, coming from the woman who's barely left the school grounds in the last ten years,' stated Exedra.

'As far as I'm concerned, it's a self-righteous contradiction in terms from a Wizard and an era thankfully long dead,' stated Mass. 'Now, Wizard Rueben on the other hand, he was a visionary, seeking variety and the bizarre in this world. Forward thinking leaders like him established a new order, uncompromising and resolute in its goals.'

Pushing Mass's rhetoric from her mind, as hard as Magen tried not to, her chance encounter with Beria, nearly a week ago, pushed itself to the forefront of her mind...

Having finished teaching for the day, she had heard Beria's familiar voice calling to her from the teaching centre's entrance. Ignoring Beria's hails, she had sped up, but the novice Balefire Witch had caught her, nonetheless.

Spinning around, she had said savagely, 'Please Beria, leave me be. I can't talk to you.'

Beria had ignored her outburst and demanded, 'Why? We've been friends since childhood; why won't you talk to me?'

Glancing around nervously, she had replied, 'No particular reason.' Then, in a voice devoid of warmth or fervour, she had asked, 'What can I do for you, Beria?'

'I'm concerned for my friend.' Then, in earnest, Beria had asked, 'Where have you been? What's happened to you? You've lost so much weight and your clothes hardly fit; and your face, why..., its gaunt and drawn.'

She had looked up and, staring into her friend's eyes, had said, 'Please understand that I always looked forward to our walks around the grounds; it was an opportunity to air grievances, compare notes and wear our finery; separate us from the rigours of teaching. But those days are gone, Beria; now it's time to put aside trivial things and prepare for the future to come.'

'That's your brother talking. We cannot let absolutists like Kuelack do as they please.'

'You can say that; you have nothing to lose. You have no children, no family here at the school.'

'Perhaps, under different circumstances, I would have had children, but I took a vow and it is a decision I don't regret.'

'You don't know what he's like.'

'Oh, I think I do,' Beria had replied.

She had turned to go but had faltered when Beria had insisted, 'Magen, stay, please. It's been so long since we walked together and just talked.'

'Very well, as you wish,' she had said reluctantly.

Walking in silence around the combat field, it wasn't until they reached the outstretched branches of the copper beech trees that she had asked, 'How are Mother and Father?'

'As stubborn as ever,' replied Beria.

'Still at each other's throats?' she had asked accusingly.

She had taken Beria's silence as a conformation.

'You know they still enquire after you,' then, smiling apologetically, Beria said, 'Well, Perak mostly, Vara, well, she's just Vara.'

'All I remember are the arguments and disagreements, which only became worse as I grew older, until me and Mother stopped talking all together. I was so glad when I left; we're just too much alike, although we kept in contact after a fashion, through you.'

'I remember the situation better than you think; I virtually grew up in your household, remember? Have you contacted Beaty recently?'

'I can't afford any affection for my husband right now, I have to be strong for my children, if I drop my guard even for an instant... besides, his job as a travelling salesman is for the best, it takes him away from the school, away from all this.'

'You have friends, Magen, friends that can help you if you allow them to, you know that.'

'No one can help me, you, Alfic, no one; Kuelack is too strong. The only person who can help me now is me. Besides, soon none of this... the school or our way of life, will matter anyway,' she had said, looking around furtively. 'Now I have to go. I've said too much already. I fear we won't meet again.'

As she had turned to go, Beria's voice followed her; it had caused her to feel even more wretched than she already did.

'You don't fool me, Magen Breed, you gave the diary to me because you still care, there is still good in you...'

Am I a coward? Am I a fraudster, sat unwilling to intervene? She hadn't really considered her actions in that context. When Keegan and Mace were brought before them, charged with the murders of Sorensen and Darrel, she had sat mute and numb as the horror of the situation had dawned. Instead of intervening, she had listened in mute silence to Exedra's denial that anything so disdainful could take place at the school; her thinking process bolstered by Mass's prodigious mind. She then pictured her children, Linden and Ferula, writhing in agony if she resisted her brother again; that thought was too much to bear.

'Magen, Magen, are you listening to me?'

She looked up, returning the audacious stare from Mass and the strange look from Exedra.

'Yes, yes, of course.'

'Magen, are you all right?'

'Fine, fine, just fatigued, that's all.'

'Good, then in your brother's absence, it falls to you to help us fill out these forms.'

'Of course,' she said absently.

Reading through the parchments placed before her, Magen, selecting a fresh goose quill, dipped it into her inkwell and reluctantly began the arduous task of filling in forms and reports. After half an hour, however, Magen's focus shifted from the work in front of her to Mass sat opposite, confirming he was occupied filling out paperwork. She then shifted her focus to the Lightning Mistress as she conversed with her advisors, and like a mosquito searching quietly for blood in a sleeping household, her consciousness crept through Exedra's mind.

Every now and again Exedra would pause and her mind would wander, as if trying to remember something. Then, with an irritable shake of her head, the youthful school principal would continue with the task at hand, totally oblivious to her intrusions. Continuing her stealthy exploration, she abruptly encountered a dark centre that, no matter how hard she tried, she could not break or pass through, and it left no fingerprint and as to its creator. She paused. Only three people at the school could prevent her searching a mind, Almagest, he was dead, Iona, teacher and expert in astral projection and the school's chief authority in far seeing and future telling who, as far as she was aware, had so far avoided any involvement in the events unfolding at the school, and Mass Martin.

My dear Magen, did you honestly think you could penetrate my psychic implant without me noticing? Even Almagest could not break that barrier, so your feeble efforts are of no consequence.

She looked up suddenly to see Mass Martin sat opposite across the table glaring at her, a smug smile plastered across his face.

Mass, if you wish to live out this day, you will remove that dark void in her mind right now.

We both know that's an empty threat, Magen. When are you going to realise that when it comes to the mind, I am second to none?

You think you're so clever, but you are not clever enough. When Kuelack returns, I will...

You'll what? Your thoughts leak into the atmosphere like a knight grown too fat for his armour. Tell me, what do you think Kuelack would say if he found out you stole his diary and gave it to Beria? Or Vanir, sent by you to investigate Almagest's demise.

She gritted her teeth, but despite her efforts to keep him out, Mass probed deeper.

So, it was Kuelack that tasked you to probe the Bruin boy's mind and train him.

I'm curious, Mass, she countered. *I can think of only one reason why you'd place obstacles in Exedra's mind, as well as the boy's.*

The Bruin boy is mine, as is Exedra, and unless you want another beating at the hands of your brother, you will say nothing.

They all looked around abruptly as Weather Wizard Savarin flung the doors aside and burst into the chambers, his tough weather-beaten face as grim as the thunderclouds he commanded.

'What is the meaning of this intrusion, Savarin?' Exedra boomed. 'These chambers are off limits to...'

'Off limits! I am next in line for the Sivan.'

Straightening his ruffled robes into some semblance of order, Savarin, pointing an accusing finger at Mass Martin, growled, 'What is he doing here?'

'I persuaded him to sit on the council,' Exedra stated calmly.

'Onto the… but why? Oh, I get it; this is because of my disagreements with the Head Master, isn't it? We may have disagreed on more than one occasion to be sure, but my loyalties were always with him.'

Magen watched curiously as Savarin tidied his thick, straight, black hair as he studied Exedra kindly with his stark grey eyes. Then, his frenzied features softening noticeably, Savarin said, 'Exedra, I thought you… understood?'

'Understood?' stated Exedra, puzzled. 'What are you talking about?'

He then took one faltering step towards her. 'Understood that you could always count on my loyalty.'

It was then that Magen realised what she was seeing; Savarin had feelings for Exedra, only Exedra couldn't see it.

Excusing her two clerks, Exedra sat back in her chair and said pleasantly, 'Your loyalty is appreciated, Savarin, but Mass's appointment has nothing to do with favouritism or past disagreements; his appointment was the logical choice. As a psychic, he is neither of the light nor the darkness; he is impartial.'

'How many times have I heard that hogwash?' hissed Savarin. 'Exedra, things are not what they appear. Trust your feelings; only in your heart can you tell who your real friends are.'

Eyeing the Weather Wizard threateningly, Mass sneered, 'Sour grapes, Savarin?'

'That is enough! What do you want here, Savarin?' said Exedra ominously.

Keeping his eyes on Mass, Savarin said impassively, 'I've been investigating rumours, rumours pertaining to Magen's brother, rumours that cannot simply be ignored.'

Dropping her quill onto the parchment in front of her, Exedra, whose face had turned ashen, exclaimed, 'I'm sorry Savarin; I know you were close, as was I.'

'No, no, no. I'm not talking about Almagest,' Savarin exclaimed, staring at Mass.

'Then I don't know…'

'Surely, you of all people, Exedra, cannot be so naïve that you haven't noticed?'

'Can someone enlighten me as to what the hell Savarin is talking about?' bellowed Exedra.

'The only incident Savarin could be talking about is my brother's encounter at the fair,' suggested Magen innocently.

Ignoring Magen, Savarin ploughed on. 'Certain deaths at the school were not in fact accidents,' thundered Savarin. 'Take you, for instance, Exedra. Don't you think it odd that a novice, powerful as you are, should be voted onto the council in place of more experienced teachers like Merle or Areca?'

Magen watched Exedra's face as the meaning and magnitude of Savarin's words hit her.

Her face now a mask of barely contained anger, Exedra, her blond hair and blue eyes crackling with barely contained energy, growled, 'What are you suggesting, Savarin?' Exedra then looked at each of them in turn and said dangerously, 'Can someone please tell me what Savarin is talking about?'

Standing tall, having not taken his eyes from Mass, Savarin said resolutely, 'Give me the authority, Exedra, and rest assured I will get to the bottom of this!'

Sat staring torpidly at the numerous shelves built into the walls, containing row after row of books, parchments and scrolls, Magen tried her best not to meet Savarin's gaze. She knew Savarin didn't make empty threats.

Her demeanour having changed completely from a few moments ago, Exedra, regaining her composure, looked up kindly at Savarin and said sympathetically, 'If what you say is true Savarin, I promise you, my appointment will be looked into.'

'Very well.' Then, exhaling loudly, Savarin, more upbeat, said, 'It's been a stressful day. I suggest we retire to the food hall.'

Turning towards Mass, Magen exclaimed, 'For what purpose?'

'I don't know if it's come to your attention, Magen, but after all the doom and gloom, I think a night of relaxation is in order, you know… have a drink or two, play a game and socialise?'

'Don't be ridiculous…'

'I think that is an excellent idea,' exclaimed Exedra.

'Then let's go?' said Savarin, offering Exedra his arm.

Mass, looking at Magen smugly, cast his thoughts; *A 'thank you, Mass, for saving me from a potentially catastrophic fight', would be appropriate at this time.*

Returning Mass's confident gaze with one of ambivalence, she replied, *Mark my words Mass, this is not over between us, not by a long chalk.*

You, Magen, are in no position to deliver threats or defend your weakness.

Her eyes settling on the plaque hanging beside the bay window, framed by brown, red and white arched pilaster columns, she studied Almagest's falcon crest emblem above it, soon to be removed, that read;

"With tolerance and understanding, we battle sin and malice. To banish wickedness and immorality, we must overcome and defeat evil."

Who is to say what's right, and what is wrong, good and evil? Sometimes, in order to survive, we have to tolerate evil even if it resides in your own family. One thing is certain, I am no longer the frightened sorceress that turned up begging for protection on Savarin's doorstep.

CHAPTER TWENTY-THREE

THE BLACKSMITH AND
THE SILVER COIN

It was evening, and Alfic, after yet another exhausting day, sipped on a well-deserved glass of cloudy cider from a large pewter tankard. Sat at one of the long wooden benches in the food hall, he scrutinised the eclectic mix of travellers, locals, students and staff, drinking and eating, conversing in muted voices in the smoke infused atmosphere.

Sitting adjacent, were two well-dressed gentlemen gesticulating frantically to a third, sat calmly pulling on a long thin pipe. At a nearby table sat a band of boisterous Durbarian soldiers. Recently assigned to the school, and dressed in crimson leather and silver battle armour, they conversed with the Pike brothers, while noisily consuming vast amounts of alcohol. Hawking his wares to a party of thickset Dwarves, and a group of travelling merchants from Sima in the Mycean highlands, stood a finely dressed gentleman, who introduced himself loudly as a confectioner from the town of Hemlock in the east.

Scanning the room further to his right, his attention was drawn to a smaller table against the wall, where two fur and leather-clad warriors from the land of Navar talked in harsh whispers with Mizar, the school's Junior Horse Master, who was no doubt eager to hear news from his homeland in the south. But the individuals that intrigued him the most were the pair of Bantu, sat unobtrusively in the far corner of the room. Sitting quietly, these more civilised descendants of Harvestmen scanned the room distrustfully from small unblinking yellow compound eyes placed either side of a ridged, nose-less grey face. They had four arms and walked upright on two legs and carried a large grey carapace staff with a polished white opaque stone set into the crest. They also had grey, armour-like skin and wore thick grey-layered cloaks, and judging by the size of the thick curved antlers emanating from the thick ridge above the eyes, these were royal drones.

'So, what are those Bantu doing here do you think, this far from home?' asked Gable, the blacksmith, plonking himself down opposite.

'Gable, long-time-no-see,' greeted Alfic. 'Your guess is as good as mine. All I know is that they hail from the Monad Mountains and are rarely seen in this part of the world. They're a race strong in ritual magic.' He then added, 'Historically, they have always fought on the side of darkness.'

'And what of those Navarian clan leaders? Are they "fighting on the side of Darkness" as well?'

'Coming from you, Gable, that is a very naïve statement.'

'All I'm saying is, we get herders through here all the time.'

'But not clan leaders. I think Kuelack's reaching out, and in doing so, drawing evil to him.'

'Hey, watch where you're stepping, woman!'

The pair turned as one of the burly Durbarian soldiers swung his lance above his head, causing a serving girl to duck and spill her drinks tray, to the amusement of his colleague.

'Easy Gable,' calmed Alfic. 'Catia can take care of herself.'

'Hey, hands off!' she growled as one of the soldiers tried to grab her, and received a slap for his troubles.

Her rebuke was met with raucous laughter.

Raising his glass to two more of Pellagrin's guards, sat a couple of tables away, Alfic murmured, 'Amateurs, they've been following me for a week now. When are they going to realise that I don't know where my friends are hiding? Even if I did, I'm not stupid enough to contact them.'

'They're only following orders, Alfic.'

'Orders! I'm all for following orders, Gable,' growled Alfic, 'as long as those orders make sense, but loyalty and common sense have flown away on the wings of fear; those soldiers fight for Kuelack because they're scared, as are many others who have had their minds made up for them. However, others hedge their bets and back who they believe to be the winning side when things go belly up. No one seems to know what's right anymore.'

'Alfic, your dislike for Kuelack is no secret. But it seems you're prepared to destroy the world, destroy your family; even bring Pellagrin's to its knees to quench that hate. I've had my eyes opened and like many others at the school can see the madness in your resistance.'

'Have you got an itch?' questioned Alfic irritably; pointing to Gable's hand, fondling restlessly with something in his pocket.

'No, why do you ask?' replied Gable, innocently pulling his hand from his pocket.

'You were doing that at the stallholders' meeting.'

Taking a long swallow of his cider, Alfic, annoyed at his friend's increasingly adversarial attitude, looked at Gable keenly, 'What's happened to you, Gable? I thought my friend, the blacksmith, would see sense; see my brother's madness for what it is.'

'Alfic, please,' placated Gable, 'all I'm asking is that you take time to contemplate what you are doing. Go to Gradine and your brother, talk to them; that way, you will see the error of your ways.'

Staring at Gable incredulously, Alfic hissed angrily, 'Contemplate what I'm doing... apologise...! Now I know something's wrong with you.'

Alfic watched his friend, perplexed, as the Blacksmith, mumbling under his breath and shaking his head irritably, began fumbling with something in his pocket once more.

'What is that in your pocket?' Alfic demanded, his curiosity getting the better of him.

'I don't know what you're talking about?' said Gable nonchalantly, his denial suggesting straight away to Alfic that there was something he didn't want him to see.

Alfic observed as the blacksmith, while absently staring around the smoke infused tavern, continued rummaging around in his jacket pocket.

'You're doing it now!'

Waiting until Gable took his hand from his pocket once more, Alfic, in an attempt to solve the mystery lunged, and a flash of silver spun through the air. As one, the two men leapt across the bench in an effort to reach the object that had rolled among the many feet of the people sat at the table; scattering plates of food and goblets full of drink in all directions.

Unable to locate the object, Alfic elbowed Gable in the stomach to gain the advantage, but the giant blacksmith persevered, seemingly unfazed by the blow, so fixated was he on retaining the article.

'Looking for this?'

In desperation, Alfic poked his head up above the bench as his sister, holding up a silver coin with her forefinger and thumb, approached through the disarray of food and drink spattered people.

'Sister!'

She was accompanied by Exedra, looking more regal than ever, and Savarin, who looked upbeat and jovial.

His gaze returning to his sister, he stared; sickened at her gaunt appearance, the outlandish, colourful clothes that normally fitted her so snugly, now sagging in places from weight loss.

In an effort to hide his surprise, he stood up and said, 'The coin, Magen, give it to me, please, you don't know what...'

'Why? What would you be doing with a silver coin?'

'Give me my coin, it's not his,' said Gable vehemently.

'I don't think so; this is more than a blacksmith makes in six months! I think I'll hang onto it.'

Alfic watched Gable closely. He realised that the hulking blacksmith, now sweating profusely, couldn't keep his eyes off of the pocket in which Magen had secreted the coin.

'Gable,' Alfic bellowed, 'GABLE, NO!' and he grabbed the blacksmith's thick, trunk-like arm.

Gable looked down at him as if from a faraway place, then, turning towards Magen once more, snarled, 'Let go of me!' and ripped his arm from Alfic's grip. Then, curling his hands, he grasped Alfic around the throat and began to squeeze.

Gasping for breath, and helpless in the grip of the blacksmith's shovel-like hands, Alfic brought his foot up into Gable's groin.

Gable yelped in pain, and he abruptly let go. Caressing his pain wracked groin, the moaning blacksmith looked up and blinked in surprise.

Rubbing at his throat, Alfic wheezed. 'Gable, welcome back buddy, you had me worried there for a moment.'

'What do you mean, welcome back?'

'I'll tell you later, my friend.'

Approaching Alfic, with a forbearing look on her face, Exedra said, 'I hope you're not intent on spoiling what has the potential for being a thoroughly enchanting evening.'

'Of course not,' then, rubbing at his throat and staring at Magen scornfully, he added, 'By-the-way, thanks for the assist, Sis. So, what's the occasion?' he asked, wiping at his gravy, custard and beer plastered face and clothing.

Looking at the pair disdainfully, Savarin said, 'Exedra and I decided it was time to take a break from the rigours of running the school; although Magen was quite insistent, we stay away.'

'Believe you me, that's not so surprising actually,' said Alfic awkwardly.

'Yes, a game of skittles and a couple of drinks will do us all the world of good,' Exedra said excitedly. 'Savarin, Magen, shall we go?'

'Magen will be there shortly,' said Alfic, throwing Magen a meaningful glance.

When Exedra and Savarin had left, Alfic turned to Magen. 'So, you've made your choice. You've thrown your lot in with our monster of a brother?'

'My children are all that matter to me now. Perhaps I have more in common with our mother than I previously thought. I was, after all, a child torn between two parents.'

Shaking his head, Alfic said in a harsh voice, 'That's an answer born out of compliance and obedience. I would have thought you'd accrued some morals from our father, some sense of right and wrong.'

'As you have often implied, I'm not as strong as you.'

'And your search for Almagest?'

'That was before. I am grateful for Vanir's efforts, on my behalf, but now he is a fugitive, his releasing of Mace and Keegan has seen to that.'

He looked at Magen's severe face. 'You say you don't care, but you saved my life; proving that beneath that hard exterior you still have a good heart.'

'A good heart means only one thing; pain and suffering. Forget the sister you knew, Brother, she will not come to your aid again.'

With a heavy heart, Alfic watched his sister join Savarin and Exedra. The realisation that she was truly lost felt like a hammer blow to his soul.

He then stood silently and observed as a laughing and smiling Exedra, with Savarin and Magen looking on, rolled a wooden bowling ball along the floor towards a triangle of skittles, scattering them across the floor. Then, with a joyous giggle, she skipped away and clapped her hands.

'It's good to see Exedra smiling again,' said Gable, joining him.

'Yes, it is,' said Alfic, stoically.

'So, mind telling me what that was all about?' asked Gable.

'I was just asking Magen why she has no interest in skittles?' replied Alfic, wearily. 'Let's just be thankful Savarin has a head for games.'

Then, looking down in disgust at his clothes, Gable asked, 'Alfic, can you explain to me why I'm covered in beer and beef stew?'

CHAPTER TWENTY-FOUR

PSYCHIC'S PAWN

Magen heaved a sombre sigh and shook her head in sadness. Innocent, Exedra was totally oblivious to the events occurring about her. She had been manoeuvred into position on the Sivan to replace the murdered Cardia. Exedra, the one person who could oppose Kuelack tooth and nail, now stood laughing and joking with Savarin, more relaxed than she had been in many months. They could have been good friends if circumstances had been different, but her brother's orders were explicit; if there was an inkling that Mass or anyone else had compelled Exedra into their way of thinking, she was to be killed.

She looked up suddenly at Exedra's laugh.

'I respectfully suggest you show the proper respect due to a senior member of the council,' Exedra chuckled.

'I apologise for your defeat,' beamed Savarin. 'I've a mean right arm; ask Merle or Karnack or Almage...'

The pain of his friend's recent demise plain to see, Exedra said hurriedly, 'Another game?'

Smiling half-heartedly, Savarin, nodding consciously, replied, 'Of course.'

Judging the wooden skittle ball's feel and weight, Savarin asked, 'So, tell me Exedra, what about you, your desires? A young woman like yourself, shouldering all of this responsibility, must wonder sometimes what you're missing? Your commitments to the school have buried a woman who I knew loved to have fun, like your love of the arts, sculpture and dance, for instance.' He launched his ball at the skittles, scattering all but one.

'How did you...?'

'You told me, remember?' smiled Savarin.

'Oh yes, so I did. How could I forget?' Looking over at Magen curiously, Exedra smiled. 'I must admit I was surprised when you joined us, Magen. I know we've never been close, but...'

Smiling reluctantly, Magen replied, 'I just wanted to see you enjoy life again. It's been too long.' She then hefted a polished wooden ball of her own and watched Exedra closely, gauging her mood.

'I have enjoyed myself. It's just that lately, my personal needs have taken a back seat to the needs of the school,' said Exedra morosely.

'Exedra,' said Savarin earnestly, 'I can't give you art or sculpture, but I can show you a good time!'

'Perhaps, Savarin, I'll take you up on your offer. I think the school would function just as well, despite me not doing the paperwork now and again. My mind has felt like lead lately.'

'Everyone needs to let their hair down, once in a while, otherwise life is just... well... dull. Isn't that right, Magen?'

Forcing a smile and inclining her head slightly, Magen stared at Savarin with intent. She then threw the wooden ball, which hit the outside rail and skipped out and across the floor.

'Oh, bad luck,' smiled Savarin, lining up his ball, fashioned from oak wood, for a second throw.

Choosing another polished wooden ball, Exedra asked, 'You said something at the council meeting that I've not been able to get out of my head, Savarin; "things are not what they appear. Trust your feelings; only in one's heart can you know the truth." What did you mean?'

Looking at Exedra affectionately, Savarin said, 'Only that people must think for themselves; that if you look hard enough, the truth is right under your nose; take the recent events at the school, for instance.'

Exedra looked up intently at Savarin, 'Magen assures me these "events" are nothing to be concerned about, and I concur. These disturbers of the peace, led by people like Alfic for example, are determined to cause trouble. If we pander to his like, it only makes them stronger.'

Returning Exedra's puzzled look, Magen, smiling ruefully, said, 'With authority comes responsibility!'

Shaking his head, Savarin admonished, 'Really, Magen, no wonder the school is so dire these days with rhetoric like that.'

Then, Exedra turned to Savarin and looked at him earnestly, 'I know that sometimes I can appear callous and cold, Savarin, but...'

'Nonsense,' smiled Savarin fondly. 'I've never thought of you as callous or cold. In fact, given the chance, I think you're considerate and caring.'

'And what's that supposed to mean?' replied Exedra guardedly.

Realising that Magen was staring at them, Savarin, in order to make light of the situation, beamed, 'What do you say, Magen, am I right?'

'I couldn't possibly comment,' Magen said dryly.

'No, I suppose you couldn't. I reckon it's been a while since you enjoyed anyone or anything,' replied Savarin dryly.

Magen could feel her hold on Exedra's mind slipping away as Savarin's suggestion of fun and relaxation slowly steered Exedra's mind from her control; his upbeat and infectious demeanour persuading her to let her hair down even further. Rubbing at her sweaty palms and swallowing deeply, Magen realised that she might have to carry out her brother's orders after all.

'You're up, Mrs Breed. You will find that this wizard isn't as unprepared as you thought; prepare to be humiliated.'

'Nor is this Sorceress,' she said stoically. 'I fancy embarrassing the school's Weather Wizard in front of the Head of the School.'

As Magen bent down to pick up another of the polished wooden balls, the Lightning Mistress leaned close and whispered, 'I didn't know Savarin could be so charming. He's far from the tyrant he's made out to be.'

'Yes, a pretty face can turn the most sombre of men into putty, Exedra, but if I were you, I'd stay away from that one.'

'That's a negative view. I get the feeling he cares,' said Exedra, watching the Weather Wizard reset the skittles.

'Courting Savarin will only bring you trouble,' Magen warned harshly.

'Courting… I hardly think…' She then smiled, embarrassed. 'All this time, Savarin, a secret admirer; it's quite flattering, really. I wonder if I should…'

Magen stared perplexed as the Lightning Mistress blinked and stared ahead with her intense blue eyes as if she'd been gifted an epiphany.

'Exedra, are you all right?'

'I think I'll retire; suddenly, I'm feeling tired. But don't let me stop you and Savarin having fun.' With that, Exedra turned and purposefully left the food hall.

Swallowing a mouthful of ale, Savarin asked, 'Where's she going?'

'Out for some fresh air, she said she wouldn't be long,' Magen lied.

'Perhaps she's had too much ale. I'll go and see if she's ok.'

'That won't be necessary. I can do it,' and with that, Magen followed Exedra from the hall.

In the late afternoon, Gradine stood gazing through the bay window of their living quarters, out across the fields and orchards. Having taken on the mantle of the dutiful wife once more, Gradine turned and smiled as Kuelack looked up from studying the roll of parchment laid flat on his table.

'Are you recovered, my husband?'

'My husband, how pathetic,' replied Kuelack, 'and you can take that ridiculous look of sympathy off of your face; we both know your concerns are nothing more than a well-rehearsed performance.'

'As you wish,' she replied stoically.

In the time since Kuelack's return, she had managed his affairs and handed him regular updates and reports, delivered by trusted students through a partially opened door. However, this morning, while going about her daily tasks; he had emerged from his private chambers looking withered and drawn, but more alert and coherent.

'Where's Delran? I need a message delivered!' he snapped.

'He's not here.'

'What about Gavin?'

'Delivering a message. I can deliver it for you if you like?' she said helpfully.

'I have people for that!'

Disappointed, she said, 'Underlings, why, husband, do you rely on them so much? We don't need them.'

Kuelack looked up slowly, menace clearly visible in his steely grey eyes, 'You, high-borns,' he sneered scathingly, 'you just don't get it do you, your wealth is built upon the bones of people like Ryan Delran and Gavin Torn, without them, you'd be nothing, I would be nothing.'

'Sympathy for low-borns,' she sneered. 'I thought you wanted more.'

'Don't you see? That's your family's failing, Gradine. Only when you come from a life where nothing is free, and nothing is available at the snap of your fingers, can you appreciate the true riches of this world. Unlike you, I believe that, given the chance, anyone can aspire to their dreams.'

'People like them will never amount to anything, they are put on this earth for one purpose, to service people with power, like us,' lectured Gradine arrogantly.

Shaking his head, he turned his attention to the paperwork laid out in front of him.

'I have read your report and commend you on your handling of the rebellious shopkeepers, as well as your discovery that Harold has been feeding Lascana information. This report also states that you discovered Kale still living here on the grounds and working with the Bruins. However,' said Kuelack, his voice lowering an octave as his finger traced Gradine's script, 'your plan to allow the Greysword Vanir to release Alfic and Mace from the dungeon, then catch my brother's family and friends in the act of plotting together, seems to have backfired.'

'We didn't count on their ingenuity,' she mumbled angrily.

'But, according to you, they have no intelligence, fit only to feed pigs, put on this earth only to service us,' sneered Kuelack derisively. 'My, my, how the mighty have fallen.'

Gradine watched Kuelack apprehensively. 'It is not a mistake I will make again!'

His face turning the colour of beetroot Kuelack boomed, 'Had Sergeant Ormstrode killed Vanir, and Tallus succeeded in his attempt on Alfic's life, none of this would be happening. As it is, Tallus failed and instead of a dead Greysword, Mass had to kill Ormstrode; these botched attempts have done nothing but result in increased sympathy for Alfic's cause, so forgive me if I don't share your enthusiasm. Because of your incompetence, we now have two Greyswords on the loose, who are both friends to my brother, that after an extended period languishing in the dungeons, one of them is now more than willing to fight. Not only are they on the loose, but the Korda and her charge are now free, and no doubt heading for Calabash as we speak.'

Gradine, looking longingly around the room at their opulent surroundings, said, 'Understand, husband, that what I did, I did for our future endeavours. As you say, the Korda and her charge are probably on their way to Calabash. But do not fret, your anger will soon turn to joy when my plan bears fruit,' declared Gradine smugly. 'The Greyswords, however, if you're that worried, seek them out, you have the shards now, kill them and have done with it.'

'Are you really that naïve? You'd risk turning the school to ashes?' Kuelack bellowed.

'We cannot give in to these thugs,' she demanded abruptly. 'If you don't have the guts, then I will do it.'

'Don't push your luck wife, or overestimate your importance. I did not travel half-way around the known world to destroy everything I've worked for. Everything we have achieved has been gained through my cunning and caution, whereas, in just over a month, you have disrupted everything I have accomplished in six years,' shouted Kuelack. 'The one saving grace in all of this is that the Greysword's and that irksome gamekeeper are still here, somewhere,' he said irritably.

'I hardy think...'

'That is your trouble, you hardly think. Those who disregard his enemies can still die by their hand. If you had any respect for my brother or his friends, you would know of the loyalty Alfic commands,' spat Kuelack. 'You also knew of our accord with the Calabash government, but you imprisoned our Calabash citizens anyway. Have you any idea of the significance of these events? DO YOU? At the moment, we're pulling the strings; but if Bovid realises he's been double crossed, he will order two million armed soldiers to cross from Calabash into Durbah. Let us hope, for all our sakes, that your plan succeeds.'

Angrily, Gradine turned and looked unseeingly out over the grounds.

So, this is how it's going to be. She mused. *I'm to be treated like a subordinate, a lackey.*

She then felt him advance from behind his desk. He grasped her arm and span her around. His face close, he grasped her chin roughly in his soft manicured hands and then thrust her up against the window.

'I find your fight intoxicating, but you will submit to my will, wife!' Kuelack hissed passionately. 'The time for action will come soon enough, but for now, I will not jeopardise everything because of your lust for power, revenge or petty jealousy.'

His hand still clamped firmly around her chin, Kuelack slowly pressed his lips to hers, and despite his aggressiveness and heavy handedness she responded to his advances, unable to deny the arrogant, surly, self-assured Mage, as his other hand explored the small of her back.

'You think playing your mind games will get you what you want, husband,' she hissed passionately, responding in kind.

Then, holding her at arm's length, he exclaimed, 'Mind games, Mass Martin!'

'You do know how to ruin a moment,' said Gradine breathlessly.

'A moment may be all we have. You wanted something to do, Gradine.'

Straightening her clothes, she nodded slowly, 'Yes?'

'Take a contingent of guards and find Mass Martin,' said Kuelack. 'Now!'

Suddenly, from the corridor, they heard an ear-shattering explosion.

'What's happening? What aren't you telling me?' exclaimed Gradine.

'Get behind me, Gradine, now!' Kuelack bellowed.

Immediately, a white-hot bolt of lightning lanced through the door, followed by another ear-splitting crack as the inner door split asunder, showering the apartment and them with lethal splinters that sprung from the walls and furniture like grotesque porcupine quills.

'Exedra!' Gradine declared, watching transfixed as the Lightning Mistress walked confidently and purposefully into the room.

Holding Gradine behind him, Kuelack sneered, 'You've been busy, Mass; I was just wondering when you would make your move.'

'Mass,' said Gradine in confusion, 'but...'

'There is no Exedra, not anymore,' hissed Kuelack. 'Mass controls her. Isn't that right, you conniving cockroach?'

'And all it took was a word,' sneered Exedra, although the words were not her own. 'You gave me no choice, Dark Lord. I knew you would end my life, eventually; I'm just ending yours first.'

Gesturing, Kuelack hastily erected a barrier as Exedra sent a ball of lightning whirling towards them; the sphere exploding in a spectacular cascade of sparks, its blast spinning Gradine and Kuelack through the air; slamming them against the shuttered wooden panelling behind.

Gradine, dragging Kuelack behind the oak fashioned desk, screamed above Exedra's crackling energies.

'The shards, Kuelack. Get the shards!'

However, before Kuelack could open the draw, the Lightning Mistress, her blond hair a medusa-like writhing mass of power, and her lithe form now shimmering with energy, produced a second white-hot lance of power that ripped through the air. It blasted a hole in the wall and cut the desk in two; the heat searing their exposed skin and starting several small fires. A third bolt lanced towards them, scattering chairs and implements across the room, and Gradine, feeling a hot searing pain throughout her being, flew through the air once more to impact with the wooden window seat. Her vision blurring and the room spinning, Gradine tried to focus as Kuelack, grabbing the silk bag from the wreckage, emptied the stones into his palm and then climbed wearily to his feet.

Extending his hand with deadly intent, Kuelack declared, 'I knew you were ambitious, Mass, and you're right; I never did trust you. This confrontation was inevitable, but you never did stand a chance.'

Leant helplessly against the wood-panelled seat, Gradine watched as Kuelack moulded his own spinning, crackling ball of lightning. As it grew, he then sent the molten ball spinning towards Exedra. The ball impacted in a cascade of sparks, but to Gradine's surprise, when the radiance dissipated, Exedra stood smiling as resolute as before. She then watched, fascinated, as a determined Exedra reached Kuelack in a series of hurried steps and with hand extended, pressed Kuelack into the floor.

'Surprised? You should be. You wasted your time reaching for these fancy baubles.' She then stamped on Kuelack's wrist.

Crying out in pain, Kuelack released the stones that Exedra proceeded to crush underfoot.

'You said you were so powerful that the shards wouldn't affect you. How conceited you've become, how naïve, time to end you and your pathetic plans once and for all.'

Energy writhed and crackled, encasing and empowering the lightening mistress once more. 'As my reign begins, so yours ends,' Exedra bellowed triumphantly.

'Oh, my sainted britches, Magen. Magen!' screamed Merle.

Magen looked up as Merle, the elderly colour magic teacher, her face a mask of terror and her clothing all askew, shuffled along the third-floor corridor towards her, her frenzied panic matching her wild eyes and greying, untamed mop of hair.

'It's Exedra. I've never seen her like this. I tried to talk to her, but she pushed me to the ground. She's destroyed the door to Kuelack's quarters, I think she's going to kill him,' despaired Merle incredulously, as the sound of ripping and tearing wood exploded through the building, accompanied by a flash of radiant light that lit up the end of the corridor like a fireworks display.

'Magen, what's happening? What shall we do?'

'It's ok Merle, go back to your apartment and lock the door. I'll take care of this.'

Stealing herself, Magen started forwards but when her hand grasped the door's shattered frame, her legs suddenly turned to jelly.

Come on, Magen, you can do this.

Crossing the threshold, Magen stepped cautiously into the small entry hallway and then peered gingerly into the room. The luxurious wallpaper and oak flooring were charred and burnt, as were her brother's ornate furniture; now smashed and twisted beyond all recognition.

Stepping through the door into the living quarters, Magen stared in horror. Ranting in a voice that wasn't hers, her eyes flashing, the lightning mistress stood over her brother, Kuelack's priceless oak wood desk now in two halves, suspended in the air above him as he lay prone upon the floor.

'Ahh Magen, nice of you to join us,' Exedra said confidently. 'I'll be with you in a moment after I've disposed of your accursed brother.'

The sight of her younger brother, about to be crushed, unleashed a long-held frustration. Anxiety, anger and fear, coupled with years of acquiescence, turned into uncontrollable rage, and like a thunder cloud unable to contain its energy any longer, this pent-up rage ripped through Exedra's body in one untamed scythe of force.

Hands clamped firmly to her sides, Magen stared transfixed and unfeeling towards Exedra. Turning towards her, the lightning mistress, her mouth opening and closing silently, registered only shock and surprise. Then, the two halves of the desk collapsed to the floor, followed by Exedra's severed body that landed with a wet thump amongst the burning ruins of her brother's apartment.

'Where have you been?' gasped Kuelack angrily, sitting up wearily.

Her hands and body shaking with the enormity of what she had done, Magen looked up at Kuelack slowly. Her voice shaking, Magen said grimly, 'You're welcome, Brother. I told you Mass was untrustworthy. If you had listened then, this carnage, this bloodbath, could have been avoided.'

'You should have listened to your sister, Kuelack.'

They both turned to see Mass Martin, stood in the doorway, serene but menacing and dressed in his favourite blue robes. 'I underestimated you, Magen. Never in a million years would I have thought you had the gumption for a proper fight.'

Magen, standing resolutely between Mass and her brother, replied calmly, 'That's the pot calling the kettle black, using Exedra to do your dirty work.'

'That is something I'm about to rectify. Join me Magen, your psychic ability is impressive. However, your brother..., well, it's too late for him. Turn away and let me finish the job; after all, with him gone, your children wouldn't be constantly under threat, plus, the school would be a safer place.'

'And your self-centred belief that your kind are the superior race; how will that work, Mass? Everyone who isn't a psychic is to be what..., scythed? Cut down like wheat.'

'So, you choose death over life?'

She stared at Mass and realised why mind masters were so feared through the ages and why the world would be better off without this one. *Magic was one thing, but if that magic was controlled by another...* 'You may be able to enter my mind, you weasel, but I would never allow you to abuse my power for your purpose!'

Glaring at her from bright blue eyes, Mass Martin, stroking his bald head, stated loudly, 'Last chance, Magen. It is I who will rule here, join me, or share Kuelack's fate. This bumbling fool has barked his last orders, imagined his last dreams of conquest,' sneered Mass, pointing at Kuelack.

'He is my brother, family, I will not...'

Feeling her arms and legs becoming paralysed, as Mass's mind wormed its way past her considerable defences, Magen watched helplessly as the might of Mass's mind sent her brother crumpling to the floor in agony.

'Help... me..., Sister,' pleaded Kuelack.

'Ah, ah, ah, no speaking,' grinned Mass, who, with a gesture of finger and thumb, closed Kuelack's mouth shut. 'I have an idea; wouldn't it be ironic if the sister killed her brother?'

Magen grunted out loud, then sank to her knees as Mass brought all the might of his prestigious mind to bear. Blood trickled from her nose and ears as she tried desperately to summon forth her own magic, but so overbearing was Mass's authority that it took all of her power to combat it as, slowly but surely, Mass's mind blanketed her own.

'You and your brother are no match for me, Magen; you never were.'

Mass then turned to Kuelack.

'Where the great mind master Caberartus failed, I, together with my fellow psychic's, will succeed.'

She glanced sideways, painfully, at her brother, laid amongst his furniture's splintered remains twitching and groaning helplessly on the floor. Unable to combat Mass's prodigious mind anymore, she felt her control leave her. Unable to stop herself, she watched as her body stood and walked over to her brother, squirming on the floor. Her head felt as if it would explode in agonised pieces, but still she complied.

'I want you and your brother to die knowing that the shards and the Bruin boy will be mine. The gods giveth, and the gods taketh away,...'

Magen opened her eyes; clinging to the wall for support, she climbed unsteadily to her feet, her eyes struggling to focus, her head pounding as if a myriad of tiny people were stomping on her forehead. She saw Exedra's cleaved body, laying on the floor where it had fallen, and her brother, with red-rimmed bloodshot eyes, sat in his Onyx chair staring ahead unfocused, but of Mass there was no sign.

Holding her head as the room began expanding and contracting, Magen asked, 'What happened?'

Her brother turned towards her wearily, as though seeing her for the first time, and with a pained look on his face, he replied, 'It seems we owe Gradine a debt of gratitude.'

'Gradine?' it was then that she saw Mass Martin laid on the floor beside the bay window, a shaft of splintered wood protruding from his chest.

With her back to them, Gradine stood peering serenely out the window into the late afternoon sunshine, cooing and humming softly to her son, Gabion, as she replied matter-of-factly, 'He had his back turned, so I killed him.' Cut and bruised, her hair a mess and looking nothing like the daughter of a high-born family, she seemed to have taken the affair in her stride.

'Magen!' shouted Savarin, appearing suddenly at the doorway. 'I came as soon as I heard. What happened?' he asked, staring at Mass Martin's body laid amongst the debris. 'Teachers are gathering in the hallway; they all heard the disturbance; we need to tell them something!'

Examining the blood on her hands and clothing, Magen, herding Savarin from the room, replied, 'Please go and keep everyone at bay; a statement will be forthcoming.'

But it was too late; Savarin, pushing Magen aside, stared mutely at Exedra's broken body. He then shambled over and, ignoring the blood spilled across the floor, fell to his knees beside her.

'How did this happen?' asked Savarin in bewilderment. His gruff demeanour evaporating as he caressed Exedra's face tenderly.

'I'm sorry, Savarin,' said Magen sympathetically. 'Mass Martin used Exedra; he tried to take over the council.'

'She had to be stopped; killing her was the only way,' Kuelack stated gruffly.

'I brought her to this. She was my responsibility,' despaired Savarin.

Magen grasped Savarin's face in her hands and, returning his bewildered tear-filled gaze, said, 'Savarin look at me, I know what she

237

meant to you, but right now we need the steadfast Weather Wizard we all know and trust, are you up to this?'

Staring back at her resolutely, Savarin nodded. 'When am I not?'

'Then send for some guards to placate the teachers and send for Alsike. Exedra will be tended to.'

'But...'

'All will be made clear, I promise.'

As Savarin walked mutely from the room, Kuelack murmured, 'Impressive... how you cut Exedra in two, I never knew you had it in you.'

'Neither did I,' Magen said darkly.

CHAPTER TWENTY-FIVE

RENAGADES

'Did you arouse any suspicion?'

'No,' Hogan smiled, eyeing Tallus wearily as he stepped out from under the shade of the chestnut trees into the winter sunshine, 'No one to miss me.'

'Perfect,' smiled Tallus. 'This is a momentous day indeed; finally, we shall rid the school of Alfic and his interfering friends.'

Listening to the conceited youth, Hogan could recognise the same pride, the same arrogance he had had at that age. It came with a certainty that nothing could harm you or stand in your way.

Their task to kill the Bruins seemed pointless on some level and that troubled Hogan, as did the dire consequences, should they fail. In fact, every time he questioned their mission, pain stabbed at his psyche like barbed fishhooks.

He turned to look at the pompous youth, as he placed one weary foot in front of the other. The weeks of constantly controlling his winged assassins, as well as disrupting the farm animals, were plainly evident in his gaunt features. Exposing his withered skinny legs, as he hoisted his robes up above his bony knees to avoid a large puddle, Tallus continued his rhetoric... 'And when Kuelack hears of our triumph, he will reward us handsomely.'

'Will he? Are you so wrapped up in duty that you can't see... Ahhh.' Staggering forwards, holding his head, Hogan fell to his knees.

'What's the matter now, you oversized oaf?'

'Nothing,' he said with a puzzled look. 'I suddenly had a splitting headache, but it's gone now.'

'More like too much ale down the tavern, I wager.'

'Don't you experience pain when you question the validity of this task?' Hogan grimaced as pain threatened to explode in his temple once more.

'Why would I question Kuelack's will? I'm more than happy to die in his service, as you should be.'

'Dying is okay, as long as it's for the right cause,' hissed Hogan, showing two rows of grey-stained teeth.

Just remember your place, and our task, assassin,' threatened Tallus.

Perhaps it was his ancient ancestry, trying to tell him, that something wasn't right. On one level, he was unsettled by this new turn of events, but on the other, he relished the fight to come.

'You magicians are all the same; you think having power means you can do anything, say anything, but you can't, can you? Take the kid's pet, for instance, because of him, that fire breathing Squill of a dragonlet has defied you for months now,' gibed Hogan, 'and you can't stand it, can you?'

'It is a state of affairs that will soon be rectified, my mentally challenged friend,' growled Tallus. 'Those who oppose us will pay dearly for their traitorous behaviour. Now lead the way, we have a job to do.'

'Yes, today will be a good day to settle scores.'

'You can kill who you like, assassin. But remember not to harm the child or his mother.'

Making sure the coast was clear, Tallus and Hogan turned their backs on the school and made a beeline towards the willows on the far-side of the field, then followed the stream out across the meadow.

Having been taken in initially by Sorin and Celia after the fight with the creature, she, Alfic and Aridain now resided with Perak in Spalding. Despite her melancholy, Lascana hummed gently while repairing one of Aridain's old jumpers, and smiled as she thought of happier times...

She pictured Mace, Alfic and Keegan, having returned from duty on the Turkanian border, walking into Pellagrin's kitchens, where she had worked for a time; Alfic looking debonair in his captain's uniform, Mace and Keegan resplendent in their crimson and chrome livery.

Introduced by Mace, whom she had dated previously, Alfic had made the most memorable first impression. She remembered he possessed a distinctive character, his expressions and mannerisms setting him apart from other men.

Keegan had revealed that when off duty, Alfic could be found more than often helping his father tend the seedlings, herbs, and exotic plants in the greenhouses. So, determined to discover more about the reserved Army Captain, she had followed him.

She chuckled at the nervousness and excitement she had felt as she had entered the greenhouse. She remembered walking slowly along the rows of plantlets and small fruiting bushes, feeling the sensation of warm humid air upon her face while smelling the profusion of heady aromas. Reaching the furthest corridor, she had glimpsed Alfic through the foliage and watched, astonished, as with intricate movements of his hands he coaxed the young plants, which grew noticeably in size at his behest...

Walking toward him in the silence, ducking through the overhanging plants and sifting the leaves and blooms through her fingers, she had announced abruptly, 'The Sringarian rhododendrons smell divine,' then bending over and drawing a floret of black, purple streaked blooms to her nose, she had offered, 'as do these Navarian orchids.'

'Lascana, hello! You gave me a start.... uh yes, they are one of the sweeter smelling plants, just don't inhale too deeply.'

'Well, as chat up lines go, I've never heard that one before,' she had smiled, the statement, an attempt to make them both feel more at ease.

Straightening his mop of jet-black hair and wiping his hands on his overalls, Alfic had stood up and stuttered, 'Uh, well, Father... grows them for the school, but chiefly for Herb Mistress Areca as... Navarian Orchids contain one of the most potent poisons... known to man.' He had then whispered conspiratorially, 'But between you and me, I think it's because my father has a thing for her.'

'And you're all right with that?'

'You haven't met my mother?'

He had then turned red, as if he'd uttered some kind of obscenity.

'I didn't realise you had such an interest in plants,' enquired Lascana quickly.

'I always come here after a particularly intense patrol. I find working with plants relaxing.'

'And the school, are they all right with that? I mean, you certainly have a tender touch.'

Alfic, slapping his forehead, drew his hands through his hair. 'So, you saw?'

'I did. Oh, don't misunderstand me. What you can do is amazing!'

Impressed by this humble army Captain, she had removed her headscarf and then drawn herself to her full height. Then, before he could say anything, she had draped her arms around his neck and stared into his dark brown eyes.

'Don't look so scared; you have nothing to fear from me.'

'Lascana, what are you doing?'

'It's ok, no one's looking.'

Then, she had kissed him, and from that moment on knew she had found her future husband…

The sound of the glasshouse door opening, followed by the stamping of boots on the limewash floor, shook Lascana from her reverie.

'Who is it?'

'It's me, Perak.'

Hanging his winter jacket from the wrought iron hangers in the kitchen, Perak blew into his hands.

'I tell you, it's a keen frost out,' he said dolefully, sitting opposite Lascana at the table.

'Hello Father,' then, noticing Perak's troubled face, she asked, 'You sound glum. What's the matter?'

'Harold's dead!'

'Dead… Owww!' she exclaimed, missing her next stitch and pricking her middle finger instead. Then, sucking at the small wound, she inquired tentatively, 'How?'

'Apparently, his heart failed; mind you, this was nearly a month ago. I thought he was just being very cautious; no wonder he missed our rendezvous! Lascana, what is it?'

'Nothing, I'm fine.' But despite the conviction of her words, tears appeared regardless of her attempts to staunch them.

'Lascana, what's the matter?' asked Perak, walking over and squatting in front of her. 'Tell me.'

Lascana burst into tears. 'I killed Harold!' she sobbed.

There was a moment's silence, then Perak exclaimed, 'What? Don't be daft, girl.'

'It's true,' she cried. 'He died of a poison meant for Mass Martin. You and Alfic were snowed under with work. Mace and Keegan were in jail, and Vara was skulking at home in Spalding; so, I acted; I was the only one who could.' She persisted with conviction, 'I thought that if I could eliminate Mass, it would give us a fighting chance. Now Harold's dead because of me.'

'Then I take it Mass found out,' stated Perak.

'Yes,' she cried. 'He threatened me to silence with my son's life. I'm so sorry.'

'There's nothing to be sorry about, Lascana,' Perak said softly, sitting beside her and wrapping his arm around her shoulders. 'You did what you thought was right, you tried to safeguard your family, anyone would do the same, and besides, Mass Martin got his comeuppance.'

Wiping her tears, Lascana sniffed, 'I'm sorry Father, it's just that the more I think about our situation, the more hopeless our struggles seem. I try to stay upbeat, but the happy-go-lucky days of the past are fast disappearing.'

'Yes, it seems despair is engulfing the school, especially with Exedra's passing,' confirmed Perak.

They both turned around at a noise to see Mace stood in the doorway looking like his old self; the dark sunken circles around his eyes from lack of food and water during his tenure in the dungeons had disappeared, and his frame filled his armour once more.

'What are you doing here?' said Lascana fiercely.

'Well, there's a welcome for you; keeping an eye on you and the boy, of course!'

'Then you're a fool,' spat Lascana angrily, although at the same time she felt reassured by his presence. 'You, Vanir and Keegan should be hightailing it out of here as fast as you can.'

Mace smiled then and said determinedly, 'Do you honestly think we would leave your family to fight alone?'

'Then you need your heads banging together,' despaired Lascana, determined to berate them despite Perak and Mace's fortitude.

'You see, this is what I'm talking about; Kuelack is determined to turn the world upside down. Forget us, forget dreams of grandchildren, of retirement in old age, Kuelack is too strong, resistance will only lead to your deaths, Mace. All I'm saying is that fighting for what you believe in is fine, but when it concerns my friends and family making daft decisions...'

'You mean like trying to keep your plans to poison a mind master from 'said Mind Master',' retorted Mace.

'You were listening...'

Mace nodded slowly, then declared, 'Hey, it's not the first time I've faced death, Lascana, and it won't be the last. Besides, Karnack's men will never find us.'

'Well, that's debatable.'

'Lascana, I'm wounded by your lack of faith,' Mace smiled. 'Don't you see? This is what Kuelack wants, us demoralised, fighting with each other. Well, I, for one, am not going to oblige.' He then said reassuringly, 'Besides, we still have Alfic. He's a natural leader that many would follow into Fornax's fires if need be. If it wasn't for his reasoning influence and keen senses, Keegan and I wouldn't be here now.'

'I seem to remember that Alfic bailed you and Keegan out of hot water more than once,' reminded Perak.

'It's as true now as it was then. Where we would unwittingly blunder into a trap, or happily wade into a fight, your husband's common sense saved us many a time.'

'Hmmm, you were all far too happy-go-lucky when I first met you,' she smiled, now more upbeat.

'And you were a real Hellcat. You gave me a few scars I won't forget,' smiled Mace.

'It was a reminder never to upset me.'

Perak smiled and shook his head. 'Never lock horns with an ex, Mace. You should know that by now.'

Engaged to be married, she remembered vividly her shock when Alfic had announced he was quitting the army…

'Not because of me, I hope?' she had declared.

'No, I figured it was time I settled down, although Mother wasn't too pleased. She said that I lacked ambition and vision, that I could one day be a Colonel or a General, and that you had turned my head; she also went on extensively to remind me of my siblings, who'll be in charge of the school one day. I told her it's a decision I stick by.'

'I love you for who you are, Alfic. Whatever you decide, you know I'll stand by your decision.'

Smiling at her tenderly, he had said, 'I do love you, Lascana Bruin.' He had then gathered her up in his arms and kissed her soundly on the lips…

A high-pitched whistle from the kitchen announced the kettle was boiling, prompting Lascana to make the tea.

'A soppy look on her face, and tears in her eyes, can mean only one thing,' said Mace sardonically.

'She's thinking of my son again,' smiled Perak fondly.

'She's got it bad,' chuckled Mace.

'Will you two cut it out?' Then she smiled genuinely. 'Thank you both for reminding me what we're fighting for.'

'Our pleasure. I think?' smiled Mace, nonplussed.

Returning, Lascana placed a tray with three blue and white cups and saucers, a milk jug and a sugar bowl on the table. She then poured the tea from a similarly decorated teapot.

Munching on a ginger flavoured scone, Perak asked, 'So, how's that scallywag, Keegan?'

Mace, stuffing half of a whole scone into his mouth, said, 'He's doing his thing,' as if that explained everything.

'His thing?' queried Lascana.

'Scouting, tracking, you know, his thing,' explained Mace. 'Do you know, he still bleats on about his ferrets?'

'He misses them Mace, to him, they were more than just tools of the trade. Besides, Drench takes care of them.'

'I keep telling Keegan he'd be better off with a woman,' smiled Mace.

'Mace Denobar, sometimes I think you have a heart of stone.' She then looked in understanding at the two chuckling men and said, 'Very funny.'

Just then, they heard a crash.

'What was that?' exclaimed Mace.

'Mummy; Mummy...' yelled Aridain, sprinting into the kitchen.

Holding him at arm's length, Lascana looked down at the ball of boundless energy that was her son and asked worriedly, 'Aridain, are you all right, what's the matter?'

'Four large insects tried to grab me. They smashed my bedroom window. Sabra saved me; you have to help him. Sabra also said that the bad animistic, together with a giant man, are coming this way,' offered Aridain.

'Bad animistic, Giant?' queried Lascana.

'Hogan and Tallus,' Mace stated harshly. He then sprinted from the cottage.

Closing his eyes and raising his head, Perak, after a few moments, announced, 'Harvestmen!'

'Harvestmen. What do you mean, Harvestmen?' Lascana insisted. 'How do you...'

'Keep Aridain here. I'll take care of this,' Perak ordered decisively.

Sprinting down the corridor, Perak pulled up sharply as an intense glow lit up the stairway. Peering around the corner, Perak watched as the hovering dragonlet, spewing intense bursts of dragon fire, its emerald skin now a vivid flame-red, struggled to prevent the four emerald Harvestmen from advancing down the stairs.

Their antennae twitching violently, they hissed, *If you value your life human, order the fire breathing squill to stop, and bring the child to us, now!*

Staring at them intently, Perak closed his eyes and thought. *Tallus, I know you can hear me. Call off your assassins.*

Their mandibles clinking agitatedly, their insect-like heads devoid of sentiment, the creatures looked from one to the other indecisively.

Then, the Harvestmen's desperate thoughts rasped gratingly in his head. *Must find the child and his mother, must do the master's bidding.*

Then the oversized insects, twitching with expectation, suddenly flew towards them. Battling for control, Perak sensed the swirls of dark magic. For what seemed an age, the oversized insects, buoyed by Tallus's dark power, pressed ever closer, their mandibles reaching for his throat, their sharp hooked skeletal legs poised to strike. The dark forces threatening to overwhelm him.

Perak, unable to resist the impious force any longer, gasped, 'Sabra, I hope you can hear me; now's your chance!'

Abruptly, Perak felt the Harvestman's pain, as the creatures were engulfed in flame. All but spent and released from the contest of minds, Perak watched in fascination as the Harvestmen, thrashing and squealing in pain, began flying around as if intoxicated, bouncing and ricocheting from the walls, floor and the oak-beamed ceiling. Running up the stairs, Perak, together with the dragonlet, chased the Harvestmen, that, through luck more than judgement, flew back up the stairway and out through Aridain's smashed bedroom window, the angry dragonlet, pursuing the outsized insects out across the lane and into the wooded copse opposite.

Sat on Aridain's bed, amongst his grandson's models, toys, bird egg collection and animal skulls, he looked up at the sound of Tallus's thoughts ringing in his head.

Impressive Perak, but your struggles are for nought.

With the realisation of what was happening, Perak struggled wearily to his feet and staggered down the stairs.

'Father, are you all right?' shouted Lascana, concerned, while attempting to douse the many small fires that had erupted in the hallway with a water-soaked towel.

'Yes, I'm fine,' he said angrily. 'Tallus and Hogan, they're here for you and Aridain, Lascana.'

'Are you sure?'

'Yes.'

'But how did you...?'

Perak pointed to his forehead. 'Tallus told me as much. Any idea why?'

'Well... not really. Oh, wait a minute. When I was in his apartment, Mass boasted of killing Kuelack. He said my family couldn't be left alive for fear of reprisal; do you think...?'

'... that this attack has nothing to do with Kuelack.' finished Perak. 'No. I think that in order to control Aridain, Mass needed you as insurance.'

'But he's dead!'

'A Mind Master's instructions are very compelling. Even after a Mind Master's death, the persons tasked will not stop until they fulfil their mission. I think these two are carrying out Mass Martin's last request.'

Suddenly, appearing in the hallway, Mace, nodding to Perak, announced grimly, 'I need you, Perak. Tallus and Hogan are coming up the garden path.'

'The two of you can't face them and the Harvestmen alone,' insisted Lascana.

Mace smiled then and said, 'We all have to die sometime, darlin.'

Suddenly, Perak disappeared into the living room, and moments later, emerged with a sword.

'Where in Praxis name did you get that?' queried Lascana.

'I woke up one day, and it was stood against the wall in the living room; been there for a while.' Seeing the confusion mapped on Lascana's face, he said, 'You didn't know it was there, did you?'

Lascana shook her head. 'Do you think this has anything to do with the crossbow I found at the cottage?'

Perak just looked at her with a questioning shrug. He then followed Mace out into the garden.

'I wondered when Kuelack's lap dogs would make an appearance,' spat Mace.

'We know why you're here, but you're going to leave disappointed,' said Perak.

'And you know it's futile trying to stop us,' declared Tallus.

His body frail with misuse and looking like a living corpse with dark sunken eyes, Tallus, his skin displaying a noxious pallor was backed up by Hogan and two of the four Harvestmen that, now blackened, their emerald skin dishevelled, hovered in close attendance. Hogan, by comparison, grasping a large sword, looked healthy and steadfast.

'Hogan, take Lascana and...'

'Why, Tallus? This is Mass's will, and now he is dead. What's being gained by this?' cried Lascana.

'It is not my place to question,' said Tallus, 'but you, Lascana, and the youth will be taken to the school.'

'Over my dead body,' spat Mace angrily.

'A task I will perform gladly, Greysword,' hissed Hogan.

Feeling a profound sadness for the remaining Harvestmen, hovering nearby and forced by Tallus to comply against their will, Perak growled, 'You're a means to an end, Tallus, nothing more.'

Looking down his nose, Tallus sneered, 'The future of this school has no place for your like, old man. But, unlike the traitorous Greyswords, I will not betray his trust. Kuelack has shown me how much I can achieve if I believe in my abilities.'

'What happened to the boy we all knew, with dreams and aspirations of becoming a celebrated Wizard?' asked Perak.

'That 'celebrated Wizard' fell foul of grown-ups who stopped children aspiring to their dreams.'

'So, anybody who cares for your wellbeing; dies by your hand. Is that it? Children need insightful guidance, Tallus, not wrongful encouragement,' said Lascana sadly.

'There you go again, another opinionated grown up focusing on the negatives, never the positives. "Magic is evil Tallus. Stop daydreaming and face up to reality, Tallus. You're just a child, Tallus, too naïve to understand." Well, I proved you all wrong, I proved them wrong, and they paid the ultimate price for their interference.'

'Who, Tallus, who paid the ultimate price?' stated Perak, suddenly recognising the bitterness and resentment of a lonely, unloved child.

'My cursed parents,' he spat. 'Magic is a curse, they said, a disease; it stifles ambition, hard work and sacrifice.'

'So, they sent you here to Pellagrin's?'

'My parents had nothing to do with that,' he said angrily, now pacing back and forth irritably. 'No, they sent for a cleric in an attempt to purge me of my magic, because in Srinigar, magic is a curse, a contamination. So, they did what all adults do; they pronounced I was possessed by evil and that I was the cause of all their woes. The cleric proclaimed that if I didn't renounce magic, it would drive me mad, and I believed them. I thought I was cursed. Therefore, I confined myself to my room for weeks on end and prayed to the gods for absolution. Those weeks turned into months, then years!'

'Misguided, they may have been, Tallus, but, in their own way, your parents probably only wanted what was best, they wanted you to be the best you could be,' theorised Lascana.

'The best I could be without magic!' spat Tallus.

'My mother and father shunned and ignored me for fear of being "infected",' Tallus cackled. 'I renounced magic and prayed for forgiveness, and when no one answered my prayers, I even contemplated killing myself. Then, in my solitude and enforced confinement, I had a revelation; I realised that my magic was part of me, and that without it, I would die. How can you cut off someone's legs and then ask him to walk, or cut out someone's eyes and ask them to see? I realised magic was a blessing and, despite my parents' intolerance, I tried to convince them that, without the magic, I wouldn't be me, I wouldn't be their son. Do you know what they did? They disowned me and had me arrested, claiming that the magic was evil, subverting me, turning me against them, against Sringarian society. So, to purge my 'infection', Srinagar's final solution was the death sentence. That same night, I escaped across the border into Durbah, cursing my family name, and I wandered the world until I met someone who told me of Pellagrin's school. So, I made my way here, where I was accepted simply for who I am.'

'Tallus, I can't overestimate how important it is to have the support of friends and a loving family behind you,' insisted Perak. 'It's something I never had. Take yourself, for instance, lost and alone. With only Kuelack as your guide and support mechanism, it's no surprise you're so bitter!'

As a dribble of spittle ran down his chin, Tallus roared, 'I will not heed your words. Kuelack is a great man, with a singular vision; I owe him my allegiance and I will not betray him, or his trust in me. He was the only person who has ever cared or encouraged me.'

Tallus then calmed himself with an effort. 'I will become part of an order that will steer this school, this land back to greatness and rid it of the driftwood that suffocates ambition and purpose, and when my service here is done, I will do everything in my power to eradicate the Sringarian race from the face of the land.

'Those are not a young boy's words; they are my son's,' stated Perak sadly. 'When are you going to learn, Tallus, that when you threaten people's freedom, people fight back?'

'Once you and your friends are dead, who's going to stand in our way, that sword-wielding buffoon?' Hogan sneered.

'And you couldn't fight your way out of a four-sided room if there was a door on each wall, assassin,' sneered Mace.

'Mace, you're not helping,' hissed Perak.

'Strength and power are what matters,' Tallus said softly. 'The strong rule and the weak perish.'

'Power is nothing without wisdom and compassion. It's a lesson my son never learnt. His insane plans will only end in your death.'

'And what's the point of wisdom and compassion, without the power to apply it?' smiled Tallus.

'Tallus, listen to me, please. It's not too late to stop this madness,' implored Perak.

'Enough,' bellowed Hogan. 'You, Lascana and the boy, come here.'

'Stay where you are!' ordered Perak. 'You're insane, if you honestly think for one minute that my grandson and daughter are going with you!' exclaimed Perak.

'You have witnessed my power,' scoffed Tallus, 'both of you must die so Kuelack's plans can flourish.'

'And while I have breath in my body, Kuelack will not prevail, not here, and neither will you,' growled Mace, stepping forwards and facing Tallus. Then, with a roar, he charged, his sword aiming towards the animistic's throat.

Cursing Mace's gung-ho attitude, Perak having reached out to the insects of the stream and surrounding fields, began directing them to congregate around Tallus and Hogan.

Stepping in front of the Animistic, Hogan, drawing his broadsword, deflected Mace's attack, but his actions became more frenetic as insects flew into their nostrils, mouth and eyes. Then corvids, from a nearby rookery, filled the air, pecking and clawing at Hogan's and Tallus's faces.

Blinking and peering around frantically, as if trying to locate something in the dark, Tallus scoffed, 'You think a few insects and scavengers will stop me?'

'No, but it means that you can't see what I'm about to do next,' said Perak, who, with a swiftness belying his age, struck at Tallus with his sword.

'Ahh, curse you, old man,' hissed Tallus, grasping his bicep.

Confidant the advantage was still with him, Perak raised his sword to strike again, but found himself confronted by the remaining two Harvestmen. Loath to kill the forlorn creatures, he lowered his sword.

'I thought not,' sneered Tallus, 'weak, pathetic human.'

At a gesture from Tallus, the insects ignited like tiny fireflies. Then, the rooks began dropping from the sky, to lay dead and dying on the snowy ground. He then directed the remaining Harvestmen, that, with an ill-tempered hiss, flew towards Perak.

With broad strokes of his sword Perak slashed back and forth, but the Harvestmen were agile, causing him to swing at empty space, and when he paused, they would suddenly attack, biting and slashing at his head and shoulders with sharp serrated pincers and mandibles.

'What sort of animistic are you that would make the creatures of the world suffer so?' huffed Perak sadly.

'One that knows his place in the pecking order, one that can do this.'

Dodging left and then right, Perak swept about him with his sword.

'Sprightly for a dung-shoveler,' sneered Tallus.

Suddenly, Perak felt himself hoisted into the air and before he could react, he was carried through the air and smashed against the side of the stables lime-rendered wall. *I told you, Perak, your pathetic attempts to best me are feeble at best.*

Despite the aggressive fauna, Hogan still managed to parry Mace's attack. Sweeping his sword about his person, Hogan sneered, 'Is that your best, Greysword? How pathetic! I may be blinded, but I can still hear you.'

His anger renewed by Hogan's impudent disregard, Mace, cutting this way and that, drove the flailing giant back down the path and, when the half-giant left an opening, Mace thrust the tip of his sword into his gut.

Examining the blood oozing from his wound, Hogan, looking up at him, smiled and said, 'It's nothing personal, Mace, but after I'm done with you, I'm going to kill Keegan, Kale, and Vanir. Then, I'm going to kill Alfic and Vara.'

Enraged, Mace struck out with his sword, but before he could strike again, the giant grasped his sword arm and wrenched his weapon from his grip. Then, with his free hand, the half-giant enveloped his head. He had been a victim of the oldest trick in the book. He had let the giant anger him.

'Now, Greysword, I will squash your head like an overripe pumpkin.'

Kicking and struggling, his world turning grey, the last thing Mace heard through the crushing pain was Hogan's exultant laughter.

Exhausted, his sword held in two hands, Perak swung in desperation and tripped, his sword clanging against the stone floor. It was the queue for the Harvestmen to attack. Bellowing with fury and fighting for his life, Perak kicked, punched, gouged and bit at anything he could reach as the Harvestmen smothered him in a frenzied mass of claws and slicing pincers. Then suddenly, miraculously, the Harvestman's frenzied attack ceased, and Perak, swinging his sword this way and that in wide arcs, leapt to his feet with a shout of defiance. Pausing for breath, he then looked around to see the Harvestmen hovering just out of reach.

With upturned palms, as if praying to the gods, his face smiling, as if experiencing some profound pleasure, Tallus sneered, 'You're beaten, Perak Bruin, time to die.'

Perak gritted his teeth and, closing his eyes, mouthed a silent mantra, but the magic didn't strike. Instead, he heard Tallus scream, and opening his eyes, he watched the dragonlet disgorging molten fire.

The smell of burning flesh and blazing cloth now filling the air, Perak approached the Animistic, now rolling around on the floor in agony.

'That's enough, Sabra,' ordered Perak. 'Admit you're beaten, Tallus.'

His howls of pain turning to cackles of insane laughter, Tallus, discarding his fiercely burning robes, climbed naked to his feet. Tallus then looked up at Perak with an evil sneer. His skin still boiling and roasting, Tallus gestured and Perak flew backwards through the air, landing painfully in and amongst the pruned rose beds. Then turning towards the dragonlet, Tallus, his voice rising with every syllable, cackled, 'Stupid fire breathing Squill, the controlled cannot defeat the controller. Now you will witness the full power of a Master Animistic.'

But confidence turned to confusion, and then confusion to astonishment, as the dragonlet belched fire once more. Throwing up his hands in a futile effort to stop the flames, Tallus, now on his knees and holding his melting face in his hands, screamed, 'This isn't... possible! Not... possible!' Tallus turned then and spied the youngster stood in the doorway, his mother's arms wrapped around him protectively. Tallus smiled at the youth in realisation, then turned to look at Perak Bruin. The last thing Tallus felt was Perak's blade as his head was separated from his shoulders.

'A little help here?'

With the headless animistic lying dead at his feet, Perak span around to see Hogan, with Mace at his mercy.

Letting Mace's limp body drop onto the hard-packed road, Hogan turned and eyed Perak contemptibly. 'You think you're so great, you think Durbah is so great, but you're soft, just like your soft, bloated monarchy. That's why in the end, people like me will win. We grew up amongst hardship and adversity.'

'Every dog has its day; at this precise moment, it is Durbah. Once upon a time it was Turkana and before that Calabash, who knows, one day it might even be Zapata's time.'

'My ancestors had their time, long ago, before men devastated the earth, and now they are extinct.'

'So, you're pissed that your ancestors couldn't claim their birthright, didn't have their day. Cultures come and cultures go, kingdoms rise and fall, as does ancestry. The only thing that really matters is survival and comradeship and how we cope with adversity.'

Hogan smiled knowingly and nodded his head slowly. 'Let's see if you can survive for comradeship's sake.'

Taking a deep calming breath, Perak squared his shoulders, then said, 'We both know that you are more than my match. That's why I need an advantage.'

Suddenly, the half giant was engulfed in flame as the dragonlet rose into the air behind him. Then, with what remained of his strength, Perak attacked.

Hogan, his clothes now a blazing inferno, parried Perak's lunge, but it was half-hearted at best.

Perak rolled, surprised at the giant's speed and skill with a sword. Keeping low against his much taller opponent, Perak slashed at his calf with his sword; while Hogan swung his weapon in great, disjointed arcs.

'Curse you, groundsman, and curse that fire breathing squill,' bellowed Hogan, dropping to one knee, while trying in vain to douse the flames.

Perak, circling his wounded but still dangerous opponent, spat, 'Who's been training you, Hogan? How come an assassin and a bandit is so accomplished with a sword?'

'Wouldn't you like to know?'

Perak then rolled sideways to avoid the giant assassin's downward thrust, resulting in Hogan's sword point embedding itself in the frozen ground. Hogan then tried to pull his sword free, but Perak, with a reverse sweep of his sword, planted his blade firmly between Hogan's shoulder blades.

'When you imagined working for Kuelack, was lying prone with a sword buried in your back what you envisioned?' Perak hissed in his ear.

Looking down in surprise at Perak's sword point protruding from his chest, Hogan, coughing blood, croaked, 'It's a pity you didn't have the sense to join us, Perak; we could have used a man with your skills.'

Pulling the sword free, Perak stared into the half-giant's unseeing eyes.

'That was for Tad Grearson and Sergeant Ormstrode, and this is for me.' With a roar of fury, he buried his sword into Hogan's heart and then ripped his sword upwards and out.

'This isn't possible,' gasped the half-giant. Shuddering one last time, Hogan fell forwards and lay still.

Helping Mace into a sitting position, Perak heaved a sigh of relief. 'I'm glad you're ok, I feared the worse!'

'I'm fine,' hissed Mace, gingerly stretching his neck. 'It will take more than a malodorous giant to kill me.'

Helping Mace to his feet, Perak shook his head sadly when he saw Tallus and Hogan's bodies lying prostrate on the ground.

'That took some guts. I didn't think you had it in you,' queried Mace.

'I never thought I'd have to use the skills I learnt in the army again. I may have a problem killing wildlife, but a couple of self-appreciative idiots..., not so much, still, it is such a waste of life.' He then looked up at the dragonlet hovering overhead. *Thank you for your help.*

You are welcome, Aridain's ancestral father.

'Now that their souls are burning in Fornax's forges, I wonder if they think their sacrifice was worth Kuelack's approval?' surmised Mace.

'I only hope that after killing two men, that I won't be joining them,' said Perak uncertainly.

'Grand pop!'

Squatting, as Aridain ran into his arms, Perak then held him at arm's length and looked into his grandson's teary eyes. 'It's all right Aridain, don't cry, we're fine.'

'Are you all right, Uncle Mace?' asked Aridain, concern etched on his face.

'I'm fine, you little scallywag. But all that really matters is that you're all right.'

CHAPTER TWENTY-SIX

THE CIRCULATION OF EVENTS

Vara placed her hands upon the bark of Pellagrin's Oak, now stark against the chill autumn night, the revered tree stripped bare by a brisk chilly wind that whistled through the branches. Looking around one more time, she gazed upwards, then closed her eyes as a spattering of icy snow, dislodged from the upper branches in a sudden gust of wind, showered her head.

'Hear me Pellagrin,' she had pleaded silently, 'I require your council. I have followed your instructions diligently and protected my grandson for the past six years without objection or regard for my safety. And where have you been? I alone have shouldered this burden, alienating everyone I hold dear. I have withstood the contempt of friends and family in order that Aridain remain safe and achieve the future you claimed is his. With "our" protection, you said, my grandson would be safe, despite your failing to mention that I would be protecting him from a dark opposite, or my own son's evil schemes.'

Waiting silently in the dark, with her hands pressed against the bark of the ancient tree, she opened her eyes. 'I have a chance to save my grandson from a life of conflict and suffering, to let him live as a boy should, without the burdens the gods have placed upon his young shoulders. I have the chance to secure the shards and hide them once more, despite Kuelack's threats of punishment.'

You will only delay the inevitable, Vara Bruin.

'You took your time, you duplicitous spirit.'

All I can tell you is that destiny will have its way, and that Aridain is fated to destroy the stones. Even the gods themselves cannot change the path he is now upon. Your task, together with family and friends, is to ensure Aridain succeeds, and he must, otherwise our futures are lost. How you do that is up to you, farewell.

'How you do that is up to you, indeed!' she mumbled grumpily. 'It's all right for you, stood looking down from your lofty podium,' she hissed, angrily, 'directing people's lives like an overzealous conductor waving his baton. But I'm the one shouldering the burden, risking my life.'

Dressed against the cold frosty air, raw against her skin, Vara, being careful not to attract any attention, hurried along the path into the fields. She looked back, beyond the farmhouse and the paddock containing Perak's now dormant beehives, to the school, its domes and spires stark in the frosted light of the rising sun, like a scene from an imagined dream.

The cold seeping through her thick leather moccasins, she stood listening in the stark early morning light, watching the smoke rising lazily into the air from the chimney of the gamekeeper's hut. She turned with a start, as the mill's waterwheel, turning noisily, suddenly engaged, powering the mills grindstones once more. Looking around one more time to check that the coast was clear, she made up her mind, and walked across the frosted field towards a specific tree. Focusing her mind on the task ahead, she reached down into a recess beneath the buttress. Finding nothing except cold earth and leaf litter, she searched more urgently, refusing to believe the evidence her hand confirmed. Suppressing her panic, she counted the trees again, then conducted a thorough search in case she'd made a mistake.

Had Beria misheard? Had someone else found them?

Straightening, she searched beneath the two adjacent trees with the same result. Calming her racing thoughts, she placed her hand against one of the trees, caressing the bark with her fingertips in an effort to sense any recent impressions left there. Nodding her head, Vara smiled grimly; so that's what Pellagrin had meant. Fate had indeed intervened.

'Looking for something, Vara?'

Suddenly, a powerful force slammed her against the trunk of the walnut tree. She attempted to glimpse her attacker, but was picked up and thrown through the air once again. Encased in a dark bubble of force, she was slowly squeezed. Before she passed out, the last thing her fading vision saw was a thin, shrouded figure standing over her.

EPILOGUE

His mood dire, Kuelack stood looking out in watchful silence from the bay window of Almagest's old apartment, as retainers and staff, harassed by Gradine, attempted to arrange what remained of their treasured artefacts and furniture.

He turned angrily at a heavy thump.

'Careful with that chair, you morons; can't you do anything right?' He then turned as two more men walked away from his commissioned portrait, now hung upon a picture hook.

'Imbeciles, it's still crooked. Must I do everything myself?' he raged. 'Go, get out; make yourselves useful somewhere else, if that's even possible?' Then, with a wave of his hand, he straightened the portrait and then arranged his black and crimson throne-like chair behind the desk.

'I hope you're satisfied, Husband; I honestly don't understand why we have to move into this apartment. Once it's repaired, our old apartment would be perfectly adequate.'

'Moving into Almagest's old apartment has nothing to do with practicality Gradine, and everything to do with sending a message, that we are in charge, that we are in control, and besides, this apartment is on the corner and has a far-reaching outlook onto the grounds.'

'In control, is that what you call it?'

'If you're referring to Karnack, his decision to let Alfic's family go was the right one. People always blame their mistakes on anything and everything except themselves,' lectured Kuelack. 'I think your anger has more to do with your hatred of Lascana than Karnack's decision.'

'This has nothing to do with her. Every time we back down, your brother laughs at us, accrues more support. It makes people question you, question us,' argued Gradine.

'The only thing Alfic and his family have time for at present is safeguarding their son; if they dismiss Magen, they fear the consequences, so, as long as Magen continues to teach Lascana's son, Alfic isn't a threat.'

'You have nothing to fear,' said Gradine with certainty. 'You are, after all, First Wizard, and he is just a man.'

Kuelack looked up with an angry scowl.

'Ye gods, Gradine, when are you going to realise that throwing your position around like confetti, especially here at the school, is not the way? Many of our spies and supporters are returning with news of our success throughout the realm. It's only a matter of time before the opposition here at the school will have to capitulate. Remember also that you are not indispensable, and I guarantee that if you don't curb your lust for power, that lust will be your downfall.'

Smiling sweetly, and caressing his face in her hands, Gradine kissed him seductively, 'Husband, you misunderstand my intentions. I only ever have our interests at heart.'

Just then, they heard a baby's wailing coming from one of the small bedrooms.

'Now, don't fret. I have to see to Gabion,' Gradine said nonchalantly.

Waiting until Gradine had left the room, he climbed to his feet and approached one of two glass cabinets. Unlocking it with a subtle wave of his hand, he reached inside and took hold of a round mottled yellow piece of quartz, the size of a small melon, together with its black marble stand and placed them on the desk. Sitting quietly, Kuelack, for no particular reason, stared into its interior. Suddenly, the core of the stone began to change as patterns and colours swirled and coalesced, its cloudy heart combining and spiralling until it became a light milky fog. Then, as if making up its mind, the stone rapidly cleared to reveal a hooded figure whose face was back-lit, and hidden in shadow.

'Don't look so shocked, you are looking into one of the...'

'The lost knowing stones, I know. I just thought that I had the last one. So, who are you?' Kuelack questioned suspiciously.

'A benefactor. It was I who left you the diary. I take it, it's been useful?'

'It has, but tell me, what is the price for this 'assistance'?'

'I am just a facilitator; I only strive to see Durbah as it once was and see the right man on the throne.'

There was a pause, and Kuelack, staring into the back-lit interior, could almost feel the weight of the stranger's eyes gazing upon him from the haze.

'So, you have the shards?'

'I did.'

'What do you mean, did?'

'They were stolen from me.'

'Fool,' spat the figure. 'You had the most powerful objects that have ever existed in your grasp. Did not the thought of parting with them leave you desolate?'

Kuelack's eyes narrowed dangerously as he stared into the globe's swirling mists. 'Clearly you've dealt with these items before?'

'How did this happen?' said the figure angrily.

'That is not your concern. Soon they will be back in my possession. Tell me, what is in this diary that makes it so valuable?' Kuelack asked, determined not to be side-tracked.

'That is none of your concern, but I want it back. Do you understand?'

'Of course,' said Kuelack resolutely. 'As long as you remember that the shards are mine.'

Suddenly, the face disappeared and with it the swirling colours.

Placing the Knowing-stone back in the cabinet, he began placing his library of books onto their shelves. He didn't trust this newfound benefactor, however judicious he seemed. He was a man who talked a lot but said little. Perhaps the diary might give him some clue, some insight into this stranger. However, it soon became clear after placing the last remaining books on the shelf that the diary was missing. Scanning the shelves one more time, he confirmed his findings.

So, where was it?

AFTERWORD

This book came about as a result of my love of high adventure, fantastic creatures and incredible worlds; as well as my interests in geology, geography, history and self-sufficiency, the environment and its destruction at our hands. Combined with my own experiences these interests led me to create a fantasy world where the impossible becomes possible and (unlike our own world where we fail to learn from our mistakes and the circle of violence continually repeats), people can live in peace and harmony following millennia of conflict.

GLOSSARY

ABADON: Falls. Tributary of River Storna, spills over these falls and then flows into the Parang swamp and estuary and into the Eastreach Sea.

ALBAIN: Albain Woodruff, Corporal, member of Pellagrin's guard; friend to Tance, Mace, and Vanir.

ALFIC: Alfic Bruin, married to Lascana, has a son Aridain. Supervisor and head of Pellagrin's work force under his father Perak. His mother is Vara, his sister is Magen, and his brother is Kuelack.

AGRESTAL: Agrestal Mere, father of Gradine, head of Gondian Central. Intelligence, Guild of Spies.

ACUMEN: Head of Balefire Coven.

ALLONAL: Most south westerly town in Durbah.

ALMAGEST: Almagest Mere, deceased head of Pellagrin's School and the Sivan Council.

ALSIKE: Healer at Pellagrin's School.

ANIMISTIC: Title given to an animal charmer.

ARDENT: Ardent Wolf. Wolf with iridescent purple fur with streaks of orange that mate for life.

ARECA: Herbal magic teacher at Pellagrin's School.

ARHASS: Necromancer and teacher at Pellagrin's School; can enchant objects for others or himself. A devoted worshipper of Fornax.

ARIDAIN: Aridain Bruin, the First Elemental Wizard to be born for a thousand years. Balefire legend decrees he will destroy the Firebrand and Chimera stones.

ARROWHEAD: Mountain, site of an ancient fortress called Collard Ray; location of one of the Firebrand shards.

AQUAR: The benevolent god of the sea and passion.

AYMARA: Continent consisting of the seven lands: Calabash, Chondite, Durbah, Navar, Srinigar, Turkana, and Zapata.

BALEFIRE: Cult of witches whose headquarters are in the capital Gonda. They are dedicated to healing and helping others.

BANTU: Magical creature living in the Monad Mountains, descended from Harvestmen, they dress in thick grey-layered cloak and snow boots, cruel unblinking red eyes placed either side of a ridged noseless grey face, thick platted shoulder length hair; a race strong in ritual magic.

BARFLEET: Small hamlet in Durbah.

BERIA: Beria Dearing. Balefire witch and student of colour magic at Pellagrin's School.

BERN: Greengrocer working at Pellagrin's School.

BHAREST: King. Ruler of fortress located in Chondite on a neck of land on the Navas straight in the Eastreach Sea.

BISMUTH: Hills and woods south of Spalding, just beyond Firethorn hill.

BIT: Lowest of Durbah's currency in gold, silver or copper, one unit.

BLACK BROW: Outlaw, bandit leader, local smuggler, so called because of the tattoo of the poisonous Black Bistort plant across his forehead.

BLACK LOTUS: Narcotic associated with the god Fornax.

BLACK ROOT: Poisonous creeping black root that feeds off of other plants, also called Iron root.

BLINKS: Blinks Escarpment, containing remnants of ancient magical forest.

BLOCH: Milvus Bloch, undertaker at Pellagrin's School, allied to Kuelack.

BLUE: Painted devils, name given to barbarians living in Mycean Highlands in northern Durbah.

BOVID: (The Just), ruler of the Kingdom of Calabash.

BRYONY: Mining village and quarry located on the edge of the Blinks escarpment; Bryony Clay Works, suppliers of china ware to the capital Gonda.

BURDOCK: Orchid that shoots barbs in order to spread seeds, also a plant that makes a refreshing drink.

CABALA: Game played between teams on horseback with a leather ball.

CABERARTUS: Legendary Mind Master who led the first Psychic uprising.

CALABASH: Land and dictatorship in the Northeast of Aymara.

CANTLOCK: Village and home of Perak.

CARDIA: Former joint head teacher at Pellagrin's School.

CASEY: Casey Defray, seamstress and stall holder at Pellagrin's. Secretly a Korda assassin and spy working for the Calabash government.

CEALEON: Desert, located south of Chondite badlands, terminates at the Eastreach Sea in southern Aymara.

CELIA: Corvuss, wife of Sorin and mother to Duran and Selva.

CELESTITE: Dynasty, family of King Bovid of Calabash.

CHIPPER: Dog and family pet of Aridain Bruin.

CHONDITE: Sparse, rugged land south of Durbah.

COLOUR MAGIC: Magic that manipulates artwork and sculpture.

COLLARD RAY: Ancient fortress in Zapatian high Mountain plateaus, former home to two horned one-eyed giants.

COVEN: Balefire Council whose headquarters are situated in Durbah's capital Gonda.

CRESTAR: Highest Gondarian currency. One hundred units in Copper, Silver and Gold.

CULT OF FORNAX: Ancient order who worship Fornax and the Firebrand stone.

CUREALL: Tonic that helps with healing body and soul.

DAPPERLING: Half plant, half pixie creatures related to Dryads.

DARKLINGS: Also known as Bitterlings with an in bread hate of humans. Related to Pelts, a friendly race whose land (Chondite) was devastated by Dacron in possession of the Firebrand stone.

DEKTAR: Durbarian currency of ten units, in Copper, Silver and Gold.

DELRAN: Ryan, archery student and supporter of Kuelack's.

DRAGONLET: Small cousin of dragons and Fire Lizards, the size of a mongoose.

DRAGON'S VOICE: Flame projected from the mouth by a Dragon Lord.

DRUMMER: Horse belonging to Elias Tan the school's baker.

DURAN: Corvuss, brother to Selva, former friend of Aridain.

ELEMENTAL: Name given to Aridain, as well as all the fairy creatures tied to the land.

ELGIN: Pike, farm worker, brother of Elimi.

ELIAS: Tan, baker at Pellagrin's School, now a renegade and defector.

ELIMI: Pike, farm worker, brother of Elgin.

ELOHIM: Most southerly town of Durbah located in the southern wilds.

ENNUL: Queen of Durbah, wife to King Pheronis.

EXEDRA: Mane, sorceress at Pellagrin's School and joint head of the Sivan Council.

FELDSPAR: Town and vale in Durbah, located south west of the capital Gonda.

FERULA: Breed. Daughter of Beaty and Magen Breed.

FEVERFEW: Spotted highly toxic sweet-smelling plant from the Darkling lands.

FINDER: Mr Finder, ex-pirate from Navar.

FIREBRAND: Firebrand Stone. A round, dark green stone with red inclusions; represents evil.

FIRE SPRITES: Night flying sprites that give off light.

FIRETHORN: Hill, located to the south of Spalding, also a type of lizard.

FLUTTER OF: Imps, sprites, Dapperlings etc.

FORNAX: God of the underworld.

GABION: Son of Kuelack and Gradine Bruin.

GABLE: Bagley, blacksmith from Leardon, employed by Pellagrin's School.

GALBAINUM: Grain producing town in the foothills of the Mycean highlands in north east Durbah.

GONDA: Capital city of Durbah.

GRABBEN: River in Zapata.

GRADINE: Bruin, wife of Kuelack, daughter of Agrestal Mere, son Gabion.

GREYSWORD: Four swords forged with magic that allows its owners to combat evil and magic. Called Ferocity, Rage, Wrath and Vehemence.

GREYSWORDS: A brotherhood of four warriors chosen over the centuries to protect and defend Pellagrin's School and Pellagrin's Sivan Council.

HALIDE: Sect of spies working for the Calabash government, equivalent of Durbah's guild of spies.

HAROLD: Butler serving at Pellagrin's School of Magic.

HARVESTMEN: (Dreamcasters) Half dragonfly/half fury-like magical creature, primitive ancestors of the Bantu.

HASP: A derisory name given to Yellow Hags, a sect of debased Balefire witches.

HEAD CIRCLE: Ruling council of the Balefire witches consisting of eight members, The Acumen and seven Magnates.

HEARKSON: Agricultural town located in the far north of Durbah.

HEMLOCK: Town to the east of Gonda located on the border with Turkana.

HOGAN: Half giant, farm worker at Pellagrin's.

HORNET: Fly, aggressive form of wasp.

IMPS: Magical faerie creatures.

JACKAMAR: Youngest Greysword, teacher and sword master at Pellagrin's School.

JARRAH: Sprites that live in Farend woods behind Aridain's cottage.

JARAWAPE: Hairy ape-like creature, with a rat-like face, that lives in trees.

KALE: Sim, former teacher/Animistic at Pellagrin's, turned vigilante.

KARNACK: Moor, chief Greysword and teacher at Pellagrin's.

KEEGAN: Dax, gamekeeper at Pellagrin's School. Friend and ex-army colleague of Alfic Bruin and Mace Denobar, former citizen of Calabash.

KEEN: Superstitious butcher, works at Pellagrin's School.

KILLDEER: Large aggressive deer that hunt in packs possessing sharp teeth and claws.

KORDA: Halide, guild of spies from Calabash; also, a type of Knife named after the Halide.

KUELACK: Bruin; dark arts teacher, now First on the Sivan Council, sister Magen, brother Alfic, parent's, Vara and Perak.

LASCANA: Bruin, mother to Aridain and wife to Alfic, born in town of Leardon. Owns a hardware and rare items store on Pellagrin's School grounds.

LAWNA: Reedman, proprietor of the apothecary at Pellagrin's School.

LEARDON: Town built on the profits of mining on the Leader River, situated north of Pellagrin's School in the kingdom of Gonda.

LEADER: River that runs through the town of Leardon.

LEERCHER: Name of the Hasp charged with watching over the third shard, a responsibility handed down over many centuries.

MACE: Denobar, Greysword and sword master teaching combat and strategies at Pellagrin's School. Served in the Gondarian army with Alfic and Keegan.

MAGEN: Breed; sorceress and teacher at Pellagrin's School, sister to Alfic and Kuelack.

MAGNATE: A member of the Balefire head council.

MALVERN: Town in northern Durbah in the Mycean Highlands.

MASS: Martin. Master Psychic and teacher at Pellagrin's School.

MERLE: Colour magic and eldest remaining female teacher at Pellagrin's School.

MIDGE: Perak's horse.

MINDWALKER: Another name for Psychic's.

MONAD: Mountain range in western Srinigar.

MORREL: River that runs from the Cammar uplands into Lake Storna.

MYCEAN: Highlands, mountain range situated chiefly in Northern Durbah.

NAVAR: Land to the southwest of Durbah.

NAVARIAN GRAPE: A vine containing rare addictive juice.

NAVAS: Straight, narrow passage on the Navarian coast that connects the Navas Sea to the Eastreach Sea.

ORRINWELL: Abandoned settlement and old fort located to the southeast of Spalding on the road to Yarrow.

ORRIN MARSH: Marshland, southeast of Leardon.

OSCAN: Large black flightless bird, native to Navar.

OUTCAST: Race of mutated men now living in the Southern Wilds and Chondite.

PACCAR: Short wooden club use to strike leather ball in game of Cabala.

PACK RAT: Large destructive rodents.

PARANG: Swamp and delta. It is where the river Seddon flows into the Eastreach sea through the land of Cealeon.

PASSENGERING: The ability to hitch a ride in another's mind.

PELLAGRIN: Dragon Lord and founder of Pellagrin's School of Magic.

PELLAGRIN'S: School for the magically gifted, founded by the Dragon Lord Pellagrin.

PERAK: Perak Bruin, in charge of the workforce at Pellagrin's School. Married to Vara they have three children, Alfic, Kuelack and Magen.

PHETON: Village on the road to the capital.

PHERONIS: King of Durbah, married to Queen Ennul.

POUCHLING: Dragonlet's name for young human.

PRAXIS: God of the sky and the mind.

PRONGHORN: Woods near the village of Cantlock.

PROTECTORATE: A conglomerate of influential Barons that preside over Zapata.

PROVOST GUILD: Wizards headquarters located in Gonda.

QUELEA: Capital city of Calabash, land to the northeast.

RAMUS: Dragon Lord from northern Zapata, now a teacher of dragon lore at Pellagrin's School.

RASBORA: Sorceress and teacher of Elemental magic at Pellagrin's School. Formerly from the land of Zapata, situated to the north of Durbah.

REEDMACE: Moth from Navar.

ROCK STRIDER: Long legged, furry creature native to Navar, used by the Navar herdsmen to traverse great distances across the Navarian plains.

RUEBEN: Wizard, former head of Pellagrin's School.

RUMBLE TREE: Tree that vibrates, can move imperceptibly.

SABRA: Name given to the dragonlet Treerinks, by Aridain.

SALAMIS PASS: Wide valley that represents the border between Durbah and Srinigar.

SAPPHIRE SPRITES: Sprites enriched with magic.

SAVARIN: Destro, wizard and teacher of Weather magic at Pellagrin's School, from the town of Trover in the southern wilds.

SCARRION LIZARD: Species of aggressive scavenger lizard.

SEDDON: River that originates in Zapata and runs south through Durbah and the capital Gonda, south to the Eastreach sea.

SELINE: Goddess of the earth and the heart.

SELVA: Corvuss, playmate of Aridain, her brother is Duran, her parents are Sorin and Celia.

SHADRACK: Village to the south of Pellagrin's School in the Kingdom of Durbah.

SHAN: River in eastern Zapata, joins with River Seddon and forms the border with Calabash.

SHORAN: Taro, Colonel in the Gondarian army. Married to Umbra, they have three daughters, Lascana, Valeria and Neruda.

SIAMANG: Dragon name for Firebrand stone.

SIMA: Town in northwest Durbah located in the Mycean highlands on the Zapatian border.

SIMON: Tubney, farm worker at Pellagrin's School.

SIVAN: Ancient council of four at Pellagrin's School.

SONTAR: Gondarian currency of five units; in copper, silver and gold.

SORIN: Corvuss; runs the farm at Pellagrin's School and is married to Celia. They have a son Duran, and a daughter Selva.

SOUTHRON: Town in south western Durbah.

SPALDING: Village, home to Perak and Vara Bruin.

SPRAWL: A dragon nesting ground.

SPRITE: Magical imp-like creatures, species include Fire, Sapphire and Jarrah.

SQUILL: Derogatory name for any fire breathing animal.

SRINIGAR: Fanatical religious land to the west of Durbah.

STORNA: River that originates in the Mycean Mountain's, runs southeast through lake Storna then southwest to the Knife point in Navar.

TAAL: Name given to Aridain and his evil counterpart.

TALLUS: Ramca, Animistic and wizard. Follower of Kuelack.

TANCE: Melos, warrior from the ruined land of Turkana, now a member of Pellagrin's elite guard.

TARSUS: Capital of the land of Navar.

TEMPLAR: Town in eastern Durbah.

THE KNIFE POINT: A vast inlet of the Butane Sea.

TIMBER RAT: Large destructive rodent.

TORSK: Former Animistic at Pellagrin's and head teacher, assassinated by Tallus Ramca.

TREERINKS: True name of the dragonlet chosen by Pellagrin to befriend and guide Aridain.

TROVER: Town located in southern wilds of Durbah.

TSANA: Town on Durbah's western border.

TURKANA: Once a powerful land to the east of Durbah.

UMBRA: Umbra Taro, mother to Lascana, Valeria and Neruda, husband is Colonel Shoran Taro.

UNDINE: Joins with the mighty river Storna then runs through the capital Gonda.

URAL: Hamlet in Durbah, on the road between Pellagrin's School and Gonda.

VALLEN: Town to the south of the capital Gonda.

VANHARA: Broken lands far to the south of Aymara devastated in series of atomic wars over millennia, once the centre of the civilised world.

VANHARA: SEA OF: large body of water to the south that encompasses the broken lands of Vanhara.

VANIR: Ulrich, Greysword and weapons teacher at Pellagrin's School, from the town of Trover in the Southern Wilds.

VARA: Scosa, dedicated Witch and grandmother to Aridain, wife of Perak and mother to Magen, Alfic and Kuelack.

VIRION: Large wild cat possessing venomous fangs, sometimes called a Shadow cat.

WIRRAL: Weapon's making town in western Durbah.

WHITLOW: Town on Durbah's North eastern border with Calabash.

WYTCHLEM: Creature inhabiting the Blinks escarpment, a distant ancestor of the Dark Taal.

YARROW: Last settlement of the Dwarves situated to the southeast of Gonda in Durbah.

ZAKAN: Evil wizard who attempted to secretly breach Pellagrin's school, and whose name is used to scare children in bedtime stories.

ZAPATA: Rugged volcanic land to the north of Durbah.

AUTHOR BIOGRAPHY

Born on a farm just outside Oxford, England, in 1961, my families' strong links to the land meant that I grew up with an inbred love of the countryside. I was never happier than when I was helping my father feed the animals, playing in the woods or besides a river defeating imaginary goblins, ghouls and bandits. However, it wasn't to last, and my family found themselves having to move into the city.

Despite having to move to the city my love of fantasy and adventure continued and blossomed when my English tutor over a series of days read to my class, 'The Hobbit,' this inspired me to read more books and to write my own stories.

Whilst at school, I excelled in many sports as well as art, geography, history and story writing in English. It was also where I discovered my love of fantasy fiction and continued, throughout my life, to read many books of this genre. Unlike the majority of my friends, who were really attentive at school and had firm plans for the future, (much to my annoyance), on leaving school I didn't know which direction I was heading, and with a clear lack of direction, nearly joined the Navy.

At the age of fifteen I discovered motorbikes and girls, (in that order), and over the years I extensively explored the British countryside from Lands End to John O' Groats. While travelling, which included time working in Australia, and Germany, I had the opportunity to discover new landscapes, and varied cultures all of which have inspired my writing.

Over the years I worked in a myriad of profession's including furniture removal, scaffolding and the odd gardening job; I even worked at British Leyland for a year, (it was all I could tolerate as it really tested my over active imagination). This meant I could turn my hand to almost anything and was never out of work.

In my early thirties with a young family to support, I together with my then wife, who had just given birth to our daughter, moved to the south coast of Devon.

Rejuvenated I trained in tree surgery, stone walling and hedge laying which greatly enhanced my gardening work. Becoming self employed meant that I could satisfy my love of the outdoors and become my own man, and using all of my new skills I went into business on my own.

But my passion for writing never left me and I began to write short stories in my spare time on bought and borrowed second hand typewriters, I even plucked up the courage to join a martial arts club. However, it wasn't until I was in my forties that I decided, instead of just reading fantasy fiction and adventure, I would fully indulge in my passion and write professionally, proving the old adage that it really is never too late....